PARIS

'Candida,' asked Marcel, 'how does the slave ensure she is always aroused?'

'By exciting herself and using her vibrator.'

'Good. Now, what is the slave's main objective?' he asked.

'To satisfy her masters, to make them climax.'

'What if she fails to achieve her objective?'

'She must be punished.'

'How?'

'She must be chained, caned, whipped, humiliated, exposed, exhibited; anything at all her masters desire. They must have no mercy on her.'

By the same author:

CANDIDA'S SECRET MISSION

CANDIDA IN PARIS

Virginia Lasalle

Nexus

This book is a work of fiction.
In real life, make sure you practise safe sex.

First published in 1997 by
Nexus
332 Ladbroke Grove
London W10 5AH

Typeset by TW Typesetting, Plymouth, Devon

Printed and bound by
Caledonian Books Ltd, Glasgow

ISBN 0 352 33215 8

One

Candie had just settled into her window seat on the early-afternoon flight from Munich to Paris, when a tall, young, good-looking businessman slid into the seat alongside her. 'Hello,' he said, holding out his hand. 'My name is Wolfgang.'

'Candie,' she replied, shaking his hand.

He fumbled for his seat belt and clipped it together. 'Are you visiting Paris or do you live there?' he asked.

'I'm going there to work,' she told him.

'Are you British?'

'Australian. What about you?'

'I'm from Munich: I'm on a business trip.' The doors closed and the engines whined as the aircraft backed away from the terminal. 'What kind of work do you do?' he asked.

She smiled to herself as she imagined telling him that her main job was playing sophisticated sex games, which was in fact the plain unvarnished truth, but he held up his hand before she could frame a suitable lie. 'No, wait,' he said. 'Let me guess,' but then the hostess broke in, telling them about exits and safety regulation as they taxied towards the runway. 'I know it's hackneyed,' he said as they reached the take-off queue, 'but are you a model?'

She shook her head.

'Actress?'

She shook her head again, smiling secretly, wondering how he would react if she told him that she was a secret agent. 'I don't think you're showbiz,' he said. 'There were no paparazzi at the airport.'

'I'm not showbiz,' she confirmed. Before he could ask her any more questions, the engine note rose to a shrill scream, the brakes were released, and the plane leapt forward like a greyhound coming out of the trap. The nose tilted and the airbus bumped twice, then cleared the ground. There was the whine of the undercarriage coming up and then they were up and away, boring holes in the low clouds as the engines applied full thrust. This was the crucial time in any flight, when everything needed to work, and they both fell silent.

They broke through the clouds after fifteen long seconds, into the bright sunshine, and Candie gave a little sigh of relief. The Lufthansa stewardess served them with a glass of champagne apiece and Wolfgang raised his glass.

'*Bon Voyage*,' he proposed. Candie echoed his toast and they sipped their wine appreciatively. 'You must be in the rag trade,' Wolfgang suggested, and Candie decided that she rather liked his wolfish smile and that a small white lie could do no harm.

'You're getting warm,' she told him. 'I design women's clothes.'

'That's a lovely suit,' he told her. 'Did you design it?'

Candie shook her head. 'Suits are very complicated,' she explained. 'I design what goes underneath.'

'Lingerie?' he asked. 'Really? What kind?'

'The wicked kind, what else?' she told him with a laugh.

He glanced down at the tight skirt that clung to her plump thighs, and she realised that he had seen the bumps made by her suspenders. 'The kind that goes with stockings?' he asked.

'The kind that goes with stockings,' she confirmed. 'All those wicked things that women love to feel next to their skin –'

'And men love to feel next to their hands?' he asked.

'Or their mouths,' she replied. 'I always assume that lingerie buttons will be opened by strong male teeth.'

'A very reasonable assumption,' he remarked 'Particularly those fascinating buttons that you find in body-stockings.'

'I make those particularly difficult to unfasten,' she assured him. 'I guarantee that it will take him at least five minutes, even if the girl is totally cooperative.'

'You test the garments, of course, before making such a claim?' he asked.

'Of course,' she assured him. 'I test all my garments personally.'

'Ah, but have you tested that particular claim at thirty thousand feet?' he asked. 'That may make a great deal of difference.'

Candie frowned. 'I hadn't thought of that,' she admitted.

'But you should,' he told her. 'Right now. There isn't a moment to lose.'

'But who could I possibly ask to help me?' she asked innocently.

'Me,' he volunteered at once. 'I have a special watch with a sweep second hand and phases of the moon and everything.'

'I've just remembered,' she told him regretfully. 'I'm not wearing a body-stocking.' She sighed and smiled sadly at him. 'What a pity,' she concluded. 'It was so kind of you to volunteer too,' and she went to pick up her book.

'Don't you have any other buttons?' he asked hopefully.

'Only one,' she told him, 'but it is keeping my panties up, and it is made to open very very easily. Ten seconds at the outside, and then they fall straight off.'

'I'll bet they look absolutely marvellous,' he said enthusiastically.

'On my hips or around my ankles?'

'Do I get a choice?' he asked, looking very wide-eyed and expectant.

'No, you do not,' she replied indignantly, suppressing her smile. The stewardess came along to refill their glasses and Candie quickly spread her napkin to hide her thighs from the eagle eyes of the German blonde. They were at cruising altitude now and the seat belt signs went off. Candie released her belt and wriggled down into a more comfortable position, which made her hem ride up a little more. She picked up her napkin to dab her mouth, and saw his eyes flash to her thighs.

'There are buttons on your suspenders,' he reminded her. 'I'll bet I could unfasten them with my teeth in no time.'

'These stockings cost me the earth,' she informed him, 'and they ladder very easily. You look to me like a man with very sharp teeth.'

'They are very well-trained teeth,' he protested, 'although not, of course, quite as expert as my tongue. My tongue has won several prizes,' he added proudly.

'For boasting about your prowess?' she asked innocently.

'For boldly going where no tongue has gone before,' he corrected her. He casually placed a hand on her knee under cover of his peroration. 'Do you always wear stockings?'

'Almost always,' she told him.

'With suspenders or stay-ups?' he asked.

'Sometimes the one, sometimes the other.'

'It's suspenders today, though, isn't it? That's one of them.' He placed a tentative fingertip on her thigh, over her skirt, and ran it up her leg.

She picked up his roving hand and placed it back on the armrest. 'That's one of them,' she agreed.

'May I peep?' he asked in a whisper.

'Certainly not,' she told him. 'Whatever next?'

'I promised to take back some French lingerie for my sister,' he told her.

She sighed. 'I wish I had a brother like you,' she replied.

He looked at her appealingly. 'If I could see how they look on, I could choose something appropriate for my sister.'

'Try it on the salesgirls at Galeries Lafayette,' she told him. 'They fell out of their cradles laughing at that one.'

He sighed. 'As my sales manager once told me,' he said to her, 'when all else fails, tell the truth.' He took a deep breath. 'I would very much like to make a pass at you,' he confessed.

'I had guessed that,' she replied. 'Subtlety isn't your strong point, Wolfgang.'

'You are right,' he replied sadly. 'My forte is action, not

words.' He moved his hand back on to her knee and she immediately seized it.

'Slow down,' she told him, 'and tell me what you do for a living.'

'I buy and sell things. Pictures, antiques, furniture –'

'Do you always pick up women on planes?'

'I always try.'

'What proportion end up in bed with you?'

'One in eight.'

'I'm not that one,' she told him. 'I'm being met at Paris.'

'Ships that pass in the night?'

'That's right.'

'I'd still like to make a pass,' he said, switching on his sad and lonely wolfhound look.

She sighed. 'I think I'm a little pie-eyed,' she admitted, 'and I know it's very childish, but if you can guess the colour of my lingerie, I might consider giving you a peep.'

He reflected for a moment. 'Yellow, to match your suit?'

'I was sure you'd say black,' she replied. 'Why didn't you say black?'

'Black might show through your suit,' he pointed out.

She sighed. 'You're sneaky, Wolfgang,' she told him, 'very sneaky,' and she looked carefully around. The coast was clear and she lifted her napkin. Her hem was high enough for him to see the suspender clip and just an inch or two of elasticised lace. He licked his lips, then put his hand down and boldly pushed up her hem.

'Wolfgang, what on earth do you think you are doing?' she asked in horrified tones, as if it wasn't clear what he was up to. She watched out anxiously for the stewardess or other passengers but allowed his fingers to caress her bare thighs. She even lifted her hips slightly so that he could pull up her tight skirt and expose the swelling curves of her upper thighs.

'That's far enough,' she hissed in his ear. 'Stop it, please. It's far too exciting,' and she spread her napkin as his hand went higher and higher. Her breathing had become quite uneven. 'This is the last time I drink champagne on an aeroplane,' she told him. 'I must be out of my mind.'

'You're certainly driving me out of mine,' he told her,

and his hand crept up even further, gently but persistently trying to prise her legs apart.

'Stop that,' she told him indignantly, then breathed in deeply and opened the top button of her jacket, as if in need of air. He leant over and saw an intriguing yellow satin shoulder strap and quite a lot of very creamy breast.

'You are wearing a very pretty bra,' he observed. 'Did you design it?'

'Of course,' she lied.

'May I see it please?' he begged.

'No you may not, Wolfgang,' she told him severely, hugging her jacket to her. 'You have seen quite enough already.'

'Please?' he begged, looking at her adoringly.

'No, and stop looking at me like that,' she told him.

'I can't help myself,' he told her. 'You are so beautiful,' and he positively drooled with desire for her.

'I can't show it to you,' she explained in a whisper.

'Why not?'

'It's indecent.'

'How, indecent?'

'If you must know, it leaves me bare, here,' she hissed in his ear, waving a hand over her breast.

'You must look absolutely adorable,' he murmured, and placed his fingertip over the bump made by her nipple in the material of her jacket. She gave a little yelp and breathed in deeply, hoping by so doing to express her outrage at this liberty, but he somehow mistook it for a sign of encouragement. His hand slipped inside the neckline of her suit and caressed the swell of her breast.

'Don't do that,' she hissed. 'Stop it, Wolfgang. It drives me mad to be touched there.'

'Then let me see,' he replied, half beseeching, half threatening.

She hesitated, but he stroked her breast very persuasively and his hand was getting dangerously close to her nipple. 'Oh, very well,' she said at last, 'but no more touching.' She looked around again, then opened the second button, holding her jacket close to her. 'No touching,' she repeated, and opened her jacket.

She blushed furiously as she exposed her bosom to him. He looked down at her bare creamy breasts, lifted up and presented in their yellow satin slings with their edging of black lace that just kissed her areolae and framed her pink, erect nipples. She sat like that for several long seconds, watching the stewardess go to and fro, feeling her nipples tingle, pink in the face and quite amazed at her exhibitionist daring. He kept his hands to himself, but they trembled so much that he spilled champagne on his trousers. She scolded him for his clumsiness, took his hankie and leant over to mop him up.

She felt his erection at once, so hard and big that his lust for her really turned her on. She kept watch, turned towards him, whilst he fondled her breasts and then leant over and kissed her nipples. That really turned her on as well, being kissed so intimately with so many people around. His hand explored her leg, right up to the top, whilst he kissed and licked her nipples, raising them up to a full, glorious erection, but then he discovered her yellow lace panties and she decided to cool things down.

'No, really, I can't stand any more,' she told him, breathlessly. She pushed him away, fastened up her jacket, and, flushed and agitated, she stood up. She turned to face him and started to move past him, but then discovered that the seats behind them were empty and that behind them was the curtain that divided off the first-class cabin. She paused and felt his hand run up the inside of her thigh and fondle the lace ribbon between her parted legs.

'Please,' she murmured imploringly, although what exactly she was imploring was not all that easy to deduce, not even for Candie. He ran his fingertip along the line of her slit and pressed his finger up on to her clit. Her lubrication flooded at once and she gave a little squeal and rushed to the loo, brushing the stewardess aside. She was trembling all over as she took off her panties and washed, powdered and perfumed herself between her legs, but she was determined now to go all the way.

The stewardess was in her cubbyhole when she emerged and she felt the woman's eyes boring into her as she walked unsteadily back to her seat. The German girl would certainly recognise a very randy female when she saw one, and Candie knew only too well how her bottom stuck out when she wore high heels. With that tight skirt, it must have been pretty evident to her that Candie had removed her panties!

She paused again on her way past Wolfgang and he didn't waste any time. His hand went under her skirt and straight to the top of her legs. She heard him catch his breath as he discovered her nudity and availability, then his finger penetrated her. The cabin reeled around and around and she thrust her hand into her mouth to suppress her moans, then became quite abandoned. She pulled her skirt up to her waist and exposed herself to him quite blatantly, biting her lower lip and looking away from him, along the line of luggage lockers, as if not looking at what she was doing would minimise the sin.

His mouth fastened at once on to her sex and his tongue slipped in between her legs. She felt the erotic shock hit her in the pit of her stomach and became so excited that she almost had an orgasm there and then, but just at that moment the seat belt signs came on.

The hostess made her way towards them and Candie hurriedly dropped her hem and made herself decent, then sat down docilely and fastened her seat belt. As soon as the woman had moved on, however, she wriggled her skirt up and spread her legs, seized Wolfgang's hand, placed it over her sex, and covered her thighs with her napkin. His fingers at once penetrated her vagina and probed for her clit.

She began to lubricate like crazy. She grabbed his big, white, starched handkerchief, and pushed it under her bottom as his fingers drove her mad. The stewardess was announcing in three languages that there must now be no smoking, but Candie felt more inclined to burst into flames as his fingers penetrated her. She leant over and bit the lobe of his ear.

'Stop it. You're driving me mad,' she murmured. 'Stop it, Wolfgang, please, or you'll make me have an orgasm.' She knew from experience that this was a request no man ever heeded.

The pilot screwed up his landing and hit the ground about three seconds before he expected to, with such a shock that Wolfgang's finger was driven right up into her. Candie yelped and pushed her knuckle into her mouth to choke back her squeals as his fingertip wiggled inside her and his thumb found her clit. The plane bounced high into the air, but the pilot flew it determinedly on to the ground, got two wheels more or less into contact with Mother Earth, and engaged full reverse thrust before he ran out of runway. The aircraft screamed and shuddered as it careered along, and so did Candie. She was hurled forward against her seat belt and Wolfgang's hand, and was still in the throes of a mini-orgasm as when the plane, leaving big black marks all over the concrete, slewed on to the exit taxi way.

'Her plane's landed.' The girl who spoke was petite, very attractive, dark haired, in her early twenties, with a heart-shaped face, laughing, mischievous eyes and a luscious rosebud mouth. She was slim waisted and wore a navy suit that was tight enough to show off her well-shaped bosom and the swell of her hips. The man she spoke to was a year or two older, tall and slender, with longish blond straight hair, a fine, sensitive face and long musician's fingers. She looked at him secretly as they waited, and thought to herself that he really was incredibly handsome, and just her type. Good looking, witty, fun to be with, and probably very good in bed. He was supposed to be, anyway: her boss had told her that he'd been trained to keep it up all night.

They were standing in the arrivals hall at Charles de Gaulle airport and she leant over the counter of the Hermès shop, pretending to look at the scarves. She felt the hem of her flared skirt rise up provocatively, and purred with satisfaction at his swift sideways glance. Marie-Ange Geneviève was justifiably proud of her long, shapely legs and was wearing sheer black stay-up stockings to set them off. He came to stand beside her, and examined the ties.

'Who's waiting for her?' he asked quietly.

'The man dressed as a chauffeur,' she replied. 'He's Marcel, the second-in-command at the Centre.'

‘What’s it called again, this Centre?’

‘The ‘*Centre Internationale d’Etudes sur la Sexualité Humaine*’, she replied, ‘or ‘The International Centre for the Study of Human Sexuality’, if you prefer it in English. They have a big laboratory out near Compiègne and several other smaller places scattered around Paris.’

‘We’d better follow her, then.’

‘It would be safer. You don’t want to lose sight of her, do you?’

‘I should say not,’ he said in an anguished voice, and she looked sideways at him.

‘She’s your girlfriend, isn’t she?’ she asked. Igor nodded.

‘Are you both Australian?’ she asked. He nodded again.

‘Igor is a funny name for an Australian,’ she remarked.

‘I inherited it from my Russian grandfather,’ he told her.

‘Candida is a funny name too,’ she continued.

‘It’s the code name the Centre gave her. Her real name is Rachel.’

‘How come she’s working for them?’ she asked.

‘She was working in London, as a secretary, and they head-hunted her,’ he explained.

‘In London? She just flew in from Munich,’ she pointed out.

‘She’s been working in Bavaria[1] and has just been transferred to Paris,’ he explained patiently.

‘Where do you come into it?’ she asked.

‘My boss thinks the Centre may be a cover for something illegal,’ he explained.

‘Drugs, vice rings, white-slaving, that kind of thing?’

‘That kind of thing,’ he confirmed with a nod.

‘So you are both working, under cover, for the Australian Secret Service?’

‘That’s right,’ he confirmed. ‘When the Centre recruited her, she told me, I told my boss, and he put her on a retainer.’

‘What is she supposed to do exactly?’ she asked.

‘Try to find out what the Centre does, who funds it, who runs it, whatever she can.’

[1]See ‘Candida’s Secret Mission’.

'Whilst you stay behind the scenes, acting as go-between and seeing that she comes to no harm?'

'That's right,' he confirmed, then slid out of sight. 'That's her now,' he murmured.

She heard the tension in his voice and felt a stab of sympathy for him, then turned to take a good look at the woman who was just leaving the baggage hall. She had been seconded to help Igor, but her boss had also told her to pump him for all she was worth, and her favourite way of pumping information out of a man was to get him into bed. Marie-Ange fully intended to seduce Igor at the earliest opportunity, so she needed to weigh up the opposition.

Her heart sank. The young woman who had just emerged was a real beauty, with clear grey laughing eyes, a full-lipped mouth and shoulder-length blonde curls. Her critical eyes noted that Candida's chin was slightly too determined and that her tip-tilted nose was less than aristocratic, but she had to admit that Candida knew how to shade down her chin and turn her cheeky nose into an asset. She at once identified the acid-yellow suit, with its black ornate buttons, as Yves St. Laurent, and recognised it as this year's Rive Gauche ready-to-wear collection, not *haut couture* but expensive enough to make most working girls sigh and move on. She took in the matching Vuitton handbag and the Jourdain shoes, and her gaze moved to the firm rounded bosom that swelled so provocatively under Candida's tight jacket. Her rival must be a 37C, she decided enviously, and moved on to Candida's wide, generous hips. Her rival would have a weight problem later on, she decided with a stab of satisfaction, but at present Candida was nicely rounded and would look great in a corset. She decided she was up against some pretty stiff opposition.

'Who is that with her?' Igor asked her, noticing that Wolfgang was carrying her case.

'I have no idea. Probably someone she picked up on the plane,' she replied with a slightly catty overtone, but Igor was too distracted to notice.

'We'd better get to your car,' he said. Five minutes later, her Saffrane swung in smoothly behind Marcel's black Mercedes as it accelerated out of Charles de Gaulle airport and on to the north-bound carriageway of the Paris-Lille motorway.

Two

Candie sat in the back of the Mercedes, picked up the envelope the chauffeur had given her, extracted the letter and read the first paragraph:

> *'You will be picked up at the airport and handed this letter. You will then have approximately twenty minutes to decide whether or not you wish to join the Centre.'*

She could still change her mind, then, and ask him to turn around and take her back to the airport, at least in principle, but that option wasn't really open to her. She couldn't chicken out, because she had a job to do; an important, worthwhile job that she had sworn to finish, come what may. She had to solve this mystery of the Centre. Was it what it seemed to be, or was it just a front for all kinds of illegal activity?

She looked down again at her letter of introduction.

> *'As you know, the Centre is involved in top-secret studies into human sexuality. If you accept our invitation, you will be required to play various roles in sexual games. Every effort will be made to make these roles as lifelike as possible, but your partners will all be highly trained men and women, who will themselves be playing roles.'*

That was nice to know, anyway – if it was true. That was the trouble with this job, she thought to herself. You never knew what was true and what was false. She turned back once more to the letter. There was plenty more reassurance, but then the kick in the last few lines:

'If you do decide to join the Centre, you will place yourself completely in the hands of the chauffeur. If he is not satisfied with your performance, he has instructions to return you immediately to the airport, without any explanation or reason being given.'

She felt the excitement grow inside her. She'd changed into fresh undies at the airport, whilst waiting for her luggage to arrive, and was now wearing clinging white satin next to the skin – thin, flimsy and sensual satin. The thought of him looking at her in her erotic underwear made her heart pound, and the familiar tingling sensations started at the tips of her breasts as her nipples erected. He was a big man, with knowing eyes, probably very experienced and very well-endowed, and hopefully very imaginative.

She glanced up and saw him watching her in the mirror. Candie doubted very much that he was a simple chauffeur, and strongly suspected that he was someone important at the Centre. If so, she was already being tested for her new job, and had to prove to him that she was a seductive and cooperative sexual partner. She decided to attack, because she knew that attack is often the best means of defence.

'It says at the bottom of page two,' she pointed out, 'that I am to place myself entirely in your hands. Do you intend to have sex with me?'

'Very possibly, madame,' he replied haughtily. She nodded casually and went back to reading her letter. After a brief pause, his curiosity got the better of him. 'Does madame wish to abort the mission?' he asked.

She looked up from the letter. 'Of course not,' she replied calmly. 'I have had several French lovers and they have all given me an excellent time in bed.' She leant back in her seat and sighed contentedly. 'Wonderful, rapturous, spine-tingling foreplay,' she went on dreamily, 'followed by the sort of devastating orgasm that makes your teeth rattle.' She stretched luxuriously and added, 'I have no doubt you will be just as good as they were,' and then sat back, having lobbed the ball well and truly into his court.

'I do not think you have quite understood your position,' he replied coldly. 'It is not my intention to make love to you. It is my intention to have sex with you, as I wish, with no regard at all for your wishes or desires. It is my intention to humiliate you, exploit you, use you and degrade you.' He paused, and his eyes gleamed wickedly. 'Now do you wish to abort the mission?' he asked.

'Not likely,' she said. 'It's getting better all the time.'

He breathed in deeply, showing his exasperation, and returned to the attack. 'Have you read page three of the letter?' he asked.

'I've skimmed through it,' she replied. 'I see that you want me to make a blue movie that, in your own words, "runs the gamut from mild eroticism to hardcore pornography". Why do you want me to do that?'

'We need sophisticated women who can hold their own with cultured, aristocratic Europeans,' he pointed out with a superior smirk.

She felt her cheeks become pink. 'I suppose you want to find out if my idea of up-market bedroom games is to swing naked from the chandelier, waving a can of beer and singing "Waltzing Matilda",' she said indignantly.

'Something like that,' he agreed.

She took a deep breath and suppressed her anger with some difficulty. 'Perhaps,' she said icily, 'I should propound my "Tin Lizzie" theory of male arousal to you.'

'Please go ahead,' he told her.

'As far as sex is concerned,' she began, 'a man is like a vintage car. You know, the kind where the driver wore huge gauntlets and the women tied their hats on with scarves?'

'I am a vintage car enthusiast, as it happens,' he informed her.

'Well, as you know, they had all kinds of levers and controls that have vanished from modern cars. Levers to advance and retard the ignition, to make the mixture stronger or weaker, to open and close the radiator, and so on.'

'Correct,' he agreed.

'Now, in order to start the car,' she reminded him, 'the driver had to position all these levers most carefully, taking into account the weather, the time of day, and so on. Starting from cold was particularly difficult.'

'It needed a high degree of finesse,' he agreed.

'Eroticism is about starting a man up from cold,' she explained. 'The levers are our clothes, perfume, conversation, comportment and so on. We have to get them all absolutely right before we swing the starting handle, otherwise he floods his carburettor.'

He frowned and nodded thoughtfully. 'A good analogy,' he admitted. 'Could you expand on it a little?'

'Well, for example, our clothes might be compared to warming up the garage,' she explained. 'A clinging dress might be compared to a little gentle background heat to dissipate the morning dew, whilst a vinyl miniskirt and a see-through blouse is more akin to turning a blow lamp on the carburettor.'

'I like it,' he said. 'Do go on.'

'As soon as we have his engine turning,' she went on, 'we have to run around and fiddle with the controls. We lean over and let him see our cleavage, and give him a little flash of our legs, but we must not show too much, of course, or he backfires, or peters out in a cloud of black smoke.' She paused and added, 'At this stage, accidentally showing a suspender may keep the engine ticking over: proving you have no panties on may well stall the engine.'

'Indeed it may!' he agreed.

'Exactly. So we coax him along, and eventually we engage first gear and move off. Now he is warming up: a trickle of steam is emerging from the radiator and we may even fix a wayward shoulder strap in his presence. A little physical contact may not go amiss, so we organise some sexy music and a dance routine. We can begin to concentrate on the steering, avoiding potholes and ditches and pointing him in the direction that only we know leads to the bedroom. We don't want him switching on the television to watch the Test Match, do we?'

'Indeed not, madame,' he confirmed.

'We change up to second gear and increase speed,' she continued. 'This may be the right time for a little strip poker or some "guess what I'm wearing" games, so that we are soon down to our undies. Third gear is engaged when we lose our bra: we are now definitely over the Rubicon and into a sex party, so that almost anything is permissible. He may now be encouraged to browse on our hills, nuzzle into our valleys, and sip our nectar – then, when he is ready, we take a firm hold of his gear lever, lose our panties, and engage top gear.'

'Very good,' he applauded. 'Now, what about pornography?'

'That is about restarting him when he is already hot,' Candie explained. 'If you pause momentarily by the roadside, the engine may splutter a little, but you must not go back to square one: a quick stab on the accelerator is all that is needed to get it roaring away again.'

'A quick stab on the accelerator?' he asked.

'Roughly equivalent to giving him a glimpse of your sex,' she told him. 'Showing a man your pussy is rather like advancing the ignition almost to top-dead-centre. On a white-hot racing engine, it may get you past the finishing line in a blaze of glory, but try starting a Ford from cold like that and you'll probably smash your big ends.'

He unbent a little and smiled at her in the rear-view mirror. 'You are not just a wonderful bosom,' he observed.

'You are not just a wonderful chauffeur,' she replied.

'My name is Marcel. I am second-in-command at the Centre,' he admitted.

'So, what now, Marcel?' she asked him directly. 'I have no objection to winding you up, but you are driving very fast and I would hate to end up in a ditch when I'm expecting such wonderful things to happen in the very near future.'

'We will be turning off in a few minutes,' he told her, 'and then we will see if your actions match your words.' He licked his lips and looked at her in the mirror. 'I intend to begin by testing your ability to play the slave-girl role,' he added with a smirk, 'so that you can demonstrate being obedient, submissive and always on heat.'

'It sounds wonderful,' Candie told him enthusiastically.

'I can't wait to get started,' and she sank back into her seat.

A hundred yards or so behind them, the Saffrane had enough under the bonnet to keep up, but the French girl had to weave in and out of the fast lane to overtake the slower, law-abiding vehicles. Igor ran a hand around his collar as she slipped in cheekily between a BMW and a big Audi, and glanced down. Her skirt had blown up, revealing the reinforced tops of her sheer black stay-up stockings.

'Sorry about the leg show, Igor,' she said, following his gaze, 'but I need both hands on the wheel. Pull my skirt down if it bothers you.'

'My religion forbids me to pull skirts down,' he told her loftily.

'Really? What about panties?'

He turned pale. 'I'm not allowed to consort with girls who wear panties,' he told her in horrified tones, and looked at her thighs. 'I was assured, on very good authority,' he went on, 'that DST[2] girls never wear panties. Was I misinformed?'

'I don't know about the DST,' she replied. 'DGSE[3] girls are allowed to put them on, but we must not protest when a nice man wants to take them off: these unclip at your side.'

He winced as she squeezed past a Peugeot 605 with a centimetre or so to spare. 'I think I'll wait until we slow down,' he told her, then nodded towards the car in front. 'Why does Marcel pretend to be a chauffeur?' he asked.

'He tries out all the new girls en route to the Centre. It's a sort of *Droit de Cuissage*.'

'Not really,' he replied didactically. 'The *Droit de Cuissage*, or *Droit de Seigneur*, was when the squire had to deflower all the new brides on his estate, because breaking

[2] *Direction du Surveillance du Territoire* (approximately equivalent to the British MI5).
[3] *Direction Générale de la Sécurité Exterieure* (approximately equivalent to the British MI6).

maiden heads, as you no doubt know, releases all kinds of powerful magic that only the nobility can handle.'

'I must remember that when I'm deflowered,' she said. 'What about your girlfriend? Shall I get out some holy water, just in case?'

'I don't think that will be necessary,' he told her, with a self-satisfied smirk.

'Was she your first?' she asked.

He nodded. 'It was a double first, actually,' he replied.

'The Big One?' she asked sympathetically. 'Did the earth move?'

'It shuddered a bit,' he admitted.

'Are you still in love with her?' she asked.

'Of course.' He thought for a moment and explained, a little awkwardly, 'We have an agreement. So long as it is sex and not love, and is part of the job, nobody gets hurt.'

'I have a similar agreement with my fiancé,' she replied, 'so I guess we both have carte blanche.'

'I suppose so,' he replied. She drove on for a while in silence.

'We were trained to be very frank and open with our colleagues when we were working in a pair,' she remarked. 'It helps reinforce the bonding process and ensures that sexual hang-ups do not impair the efficiency of the team.'

'Really?' he observed politely.

'Well, it's only natural,' she went on. 'When a man and woman spend a lot of time together, sexual stresses are bound to build up. We were taught to release the stress before it becomes harmful.'

'I see,' he murmured.

'So, if you ever fancy me sexually – nothing to do with love, of course – and you suspect that your feelings are interfering with your efficiency, you will tell me, won't you?' she concluded.

'Well, yes, of course,' he replied, then added politely, 'and the same goes for you, naturally.' There was a longish pause whilst she concentrated on her driving.

'What does your part of the Australian Secret Service actually do, Igor?' she asked casually, fishtailing into a narrow gap and leaving total chaos behind her.

'The same as yours,' he replied evasively. 'We protect the goodies and nobble the baddies. What were your instructions?'

'To help you in every possible way,' she replied. 'We are still trying to make amends for testing hydrogen bombs at Mururoa and for blowing up the *Rainbow Warrior*.'

'You could import some of our Australian Riesling,' he suggested. She at once turned very pale and shuddered as if in a freezing gale.

'We feel sorry,' she explained, 'not suicidal.'

'Australian Riesling goes down wonderfully with chips and HP sauce,' he assured her. 'I really must introduce you to Australian *haute cuisine*. Sharing a bag of chips with a team-mate works wonders for the bonding process, Jenny.'

'My name is Marie-Ange Geneviève,' she corrected him, ignoring his culinary hints. 'In English, that's Mary Angel Genevieve.'

'No angel has thighs like yours,' he told her, and looked at her more closely. 'Would taking your knickers off really count as bonding reinforcement?' he asked innocently, and moved his hand towards her thigh.

'Too late,' she told him hurriedly, and she moved her leg away. 'They're turning off,' she pointed out, and she lifted her foot off the accelerator and pulled down her hem.

Three

Marcel braked hard, moved swiftly across the traffic lanes, then changed down as he left the motorway. They were soon on a Route National, moving towards the forest to the south of Compiègne. 'This is your last chance,' he told Candie. 'Are you sure you do not wish to be returned to the airport?'

'No, thank you,' she replied politely. He touched a switch and she heard solid clicks from each side as the rear doors locked. A moment later, there was a whirring noise, and blinds came down over each of the windows and over the partition that separated her from the front of the car. The back of the car became a dark cell, until several spotlights came on in front of her.

She heard a humming noise. Another blind slid away and she found herself gazing into a TV screen, located between her and the front passenger seat. She could see herself, sitting primly like a schoolgirl with her knees pressed together, and realised that there was a video camera just below the screen, at the level of her knees.

'Welcome to the Centre, Candida,' Marcel said, with a new, authoritative edge to his voice. She swallowed hard but did not reply.

'You will now be given your first set of commands,' his voice went on. 'All such commands must be obeyed at once, without question and without hesitation. Do you understand?'

'I understand,' she said.

'Press the button alongside the screen,' he went on, 'and the video recorder will start. You then have ten minutes to make a blue video for the Centre. It will be passed around and much admired, so do not try to hide those beautiful eyes of yours or any of your more intimate attractions. You will find some accessories in the drawer alongside the screen.'

Candie felt her heart race as she opened the drawer. It contained several vibrators and some lubricating jelly. She picked up the masturbation devices one by one and examined them, trying to think of a way to wriggle out of this trap, but she knew in her heart that she now belonged to the Centre: there was no escape.

'Since you just demonstrated so clearly your expertise in seductive eroticism,' Marcel continued, 'I think we can concentrate on the pornography – but, of course, you will not climax whilst making the video.'

'Of course not,' she promised, 'but you will no doubt wish me to be on the verge of orgasm by the end of it?'

'On the very edge,' he confirmed.

Candie took a deep breath, pressed the start button, and saw a digital timer start to count down. Almost at the same time, she felt the car slow down as they turned on to a minor road.

A hundred yards behind them, Igor saw the Mercedes turn off, and picked up the large-scale Ordnance Survey map he carried on his lap.

'We can't follow them,' Jenny told him. 'It would be too obvious,' and he looked down at the map as they passed the turning, biting his lip as the Merc carried Candie away.

'Turn left at the next junction,' he told her, following their track on his map, but with half his mind elsewhere. His boss had been over the moon when he'd heard that Igor would be working with Jenny. 'She's one of their brightest up-and-coming agents,' he had said, 'as well as being a real sex bomb. Furthermore, she almost certainly works for the Pacific Department, and anything they do interests us. Try to profit from the occasion, Igor: use your famous charm and your other more physical assets, and find out what they are up to.'

Igor sighed inwardly. So he was supposed to seduce Jenny, more or less as a sideline. Still, seducing her in the sacred name of duty wouldn't be much of a hardship. She was different physically from Candie, petite and dark, with long slender legs, but still very womanly where it counted, and she was very like Candie in other ways – vivacious, chirpy, always ready with an answer, and sexy as hell. He glanced at her thighs, remembering how she had looked with her skirt blowing up, but the car was climbing now on to high ground and he picked up his binoculars and searched around until he spotted the Merc.

'They've just turned into that wood,' he told Jenny, and looked at his map again. 'Turn left in a hundred metres or so and we'll go in on a parallel track.'

A hundred yards further on, Jenny paused as they reached the entrance to the wood. There was a big sign saying, '*La Conféderation de La Chasse St Hubert. Chasse guardée. Défense d'entrer*,' and a big, solid-looking gate, but it was open.

'I've heard of it,' she told him. 'It's a very snobby upper-class hunting club for filthy rich Parisians.'

'We'll have to risk going in,' he said. 'There isn't another entrance.'

Jenny turned the car and they bumped along a narrow track for some time, then Igor raised his hand.

'They've stopped in that clearing down there,' he said. 'Pull off into the trees, please.'

Jenny drove the car into the cover of the trees and switched off the engine. 'What if someone comes?' she asked.

'We'll pretend we've come in to make love,' he proposed.

'I'd better try and look the part,' she said, unfastening her jacket, but he was already climbing out of the car.

'I must scout around and make sure that Candie is all right,' he told her, and vanished into the trees.

A hundred yards below, Candie sat forward on the edge of her seat and began her do-it-yourself video. She eased her knees apart and saw her skirt stretch taut. A little more and the camera was able to peer between her legs. The spotlights revealed a touch of white at the apex of her thighs.

She licked her lips and forced her legs further apart. The camera could see a white triangle now, delineated by the stretched hem of her skirt and the plump curves of the thighs. The tops of her stockings were now visible, pulled taut by white satin suspenders edged with lace. She felt her excitement mount, because she was a natural exhibitionist and loved to watch herself pose erotically.

Nine minutes to go. She lifted her bottom and raised her hem, so that she could open her legs further. Her thighs parted and she saw the tight white satin between her legs, hugging her sex. She moved her legs further apart, slid forward, and focussed the camera on the central seam of her satin panties. They fitted snugly over her pussy, and now she could see the faint outline of her slit and the bulge of her plump labia. She slid forward again and opened her thighs as wide as possible: the satin bridge did not completely cover her vaginal lips when she was stretched open like that and the edge of her labia peeped out shyly from behind the lace-trimmed satin.

Eight minutes to go. She felt the car come to a halt, but she was alone in her own erotic world, displaying herself to the insolent camera. She put her hand down and ran her fingertip along her slit, feeling the excitement flash through her body as her body reacted to her stimulation. She kept her legs wide apart and slid back, then used the zoom control to change to a wide-angle shot, so that the camera could see her face and the whole of her body. Marcel had said that the audience would want to see everything.

Seven minutes to go. She smiled at the camera and lifted her hips provocatively, but she saw that she was blushing with humiliation and she had to fight down her desire to cover herself. She raised one leg, placed her foot on the seat, and put her hand through between her legs to ease aside the satin panties and expose her vagina. She was already peeling open and her labia were engorged and pouting, revealing the shiny inner surface of her sex.

Six minutes. She licked her lips and took off her jacket,

then placed her free hand under her bosom and caressed the swell of her breast through the satin cup. Her second finger explored her nipple through the thin satin whilst the second finger of her other hand penetrated her vagina.

She opened her mouth and licked her lips again. She was lubricating vigorously now and took off her skirt before she marked it. It was like casting off her last links with civilisation. Her sensible, civilised clothes would all be taken away from her, she knew that: she would soon be naked and unprotected.

Five minutes. She unclipped her bra, eased it off and presented her bosom to the camera. Now it could see her proud, swelling breasts and her eager, up-standing nipples: the audience would know that she was excited and ready for sex. She unclipped her panties and wriggled free of them. She was naked now except for her stockings, suspenders and high-heeled sandals. She opened her sex with her fingers, focussed the camera to show her inner labia and the pink inner surfaces of her vaginal tunnel, then probed delicately to find her clit, placed her fingertip over the most sensitive part of her body, and rotated it gently. She felt the excitement ripple through her body and her lubrication started to flow more freely.

Four minutes to go. She took out the vibrator she had chosen. It had a main rod shaped like an erect, very big, slightly curved penis and a smaller finger jutting out above the prick.

She squeezed the tube of jelly, anointed the prick, stretched her legs really wide apart and slid the dildo up and into her vagina. She gasped as the huge mock-penis opened her vaginal tunnel, then eased the shaft up and into her until the fake balls pressed against her bottom. She masturbated herself with the penis, rolling on her buttocks to help maximise the erotic sensation, then manipulated the device until she felt the tip of the finger press against her hooded clit. She wiggled it until the finger entered her and pressed against the hard little horn of her clitoris.

Three minutes. She felt down and located the main on-off switch, took a deep breath and pressed a button. At once there was a deep rhythmic hum and Candie suddenly felt the penis writhe and elongate inside her. She cried out, holding the prick deep inside her although all her instincts screamed for her to remove it. The false penis expanded and wriggled, forcing open the tunnel of her vagina and pressing up towards the mouth of her womb. Two minutes. She pressed the second button. A sharper note filled the air and her clitoris was suddenly excited beyond belief. She screamed and rolled over into a ball, clutching the device to her sex, unable to control herself.

One minute left. She forced herself not to switch off. She gritted her teeth and made her anguished body sit up, face the camera and show her tormented sex to the lens. She let it see how her body jerked and undulated as it responded to the writhings of the penis. She let it see how her labia were stretched around this artificial cock that was fucking her so inhumanly but so arousingly. She moved a little to show to the camera the probing fingertip that drove her clitoris wild. She arched her body and thrust her hips forward, holding her vibrator in place with one hand whilst her other hand squeezed her breast.

Candie held on to the vibrator, forcing it into her body, fighting down her arousal, determined not to give way although every fibre of her being screamed to be allowed to climax. Forty seconds. The penis writhed and wriggled inside her like a huge snake and the finger pressed its throbbing tip unrelentingly against her clitoris. Twenty seconds. She was sure she would have to give way, to wrench the vibrator out of her tormented body, but she hung on, willing herself to accept this awful punishment.

Ten, nine, eight. She was moving towards her climax. She could feel the initial waves stream out from her womb to fill every part of her body. Five, four, three, two, one. She switched off the device as the timer reached zero, and wrenched it out of her body, then doubled over, hugging herself, panting, humiliated beyond belief and utterly frustrated.

The door opened, and Marcel appeared in the doorway.

* * *

Whilst Candie was busy making her video, Jenny sat in the Renault, looking down at the parked Merc through her binoculars, but nothing seemed to be happening. She was beginning to feel bored when she was suddenly distracted by a noise coming from outside the car. She put down her binoculars and looked around. A young brown-and-white springer spaniel was sniffing its way along the woodland path, following the lovely, exciting scents. Way off in the distance, she heard a man's voice, calling the dog to heel, but the spaniel was too interested in the wild woodland odours to take any notice. One of the scent trails brought the dog up to the car, and it stopped in surprise as the smell of oil and petrol suddenly overlayed the scents of rabbits and field mice.

Jenny opened the car door cautiously. If the dog went on sniffing and exploring along the narrow woodland path, it may well find Igor, start barking, and give the show away. She called softly to the animal. The puppy circled around her suspiciously, then came closer and smelled her hand. She heard his owner call again. It was a real he-man's voice, deep and virile.

He might be a passer-by, a gamekeeper, or a look-out for Marcel – but a look-out would hardly walk around with an untrained spaniel: he'd be alone, or with an Alsatian or a Doberman. That was good, because she knew how to cope with a casual passer-by or a gamekeeper.

She searched in the glove compartment and found an imported erotic magazine she bought from time to time. She flicked it open and found a picture of a young naked stud, proudly nursing a massive erection. She looked along the path. A big countryman had just come into view, wearing a hunter's jacket with cartridges in his belt and carrying a broken double-barelled shotgun. She left the car door open and sprawled over the back seat. The dog came into the car and lay down quietly beside her, with its chin on its front paws. She picked up the magazine, put her right foot up on to the seat, slipped her left hand down inside her panties, and began to stroke her sex.

The gamekeeper was evidently used to tracking wild

animals, because he came up to the Renault without making any noise. Jenny saw him circle around until he could peep inside, and she hoped he'd enjoy the view. He'd see his disobedient young spaniel next to her, its head against her slim ankle. Above the ankle he'd see a smooth feminine calf clad in sheer black nylon and above that a reinforced stocking top embellishing a bare white thigh. That should turn him on.

She sprawled on the back seat of the car with her legs apart. Her pleated skirt was up around her waist and her jacket was open. She pretended to read the porno magazine, and looked at the picture of the young, virile stud as she gently caressed her sex. He would be able to see her hand, moving gently inside her brief panties, with her pleasure finger penetrating her sex. Her other hand eased down one cup of her brassière and she caressed her breast and aroused the nipple. She saw him move back into the bushes as he enjoyed the show: Jenny breathed in, eased aside the bridge of nylon between her legs and let the peeping Tom see her sex.

At the bottom of the hill, Candie was showing her sex to Marcel. She was panting, fully aroused, wild eyed and eager for sexual relief as she turned to face him, spread her legs and lifted one foot on to the seat

Her vagina was wide open, the outer labia curled outward like a pouting mouth. She had one breast cupped in her hand, and pressed the tip of her finger on to her nipple. Her other hand framed her sex, her fingers slipping on her labia as she opened herself still further. She lifted her hips, imploring him to take her, to fill up this aching void in her body, to heal her wound with his prick. She put out her hand pleadingly towards his crotch, but he pushed it away.

'Not yet,' he sneered. 'You have to work harder than that to earn relief,' and she cried out with frustration.

'Move back,' he told her. Candie slid back and he came in and sat on the seat, facing her. One of her legs was between him and the seat, the other stretched out sideways. She lifted her hips again in a lascivious gesture, inviting him to take possession of her, but he ignored her pleading, felt in the drawer, and produced a leather strap that supported a thin curved rod that terminated in a small button. She sat up to let him place it around her hips, then realised it was a clitoral vibrator, designed to titillate the most sensitive area of her body. He adjusted it carefully, so that the button pressed on to her clit, then sat back and took out a small control box. He looked at her gloatingly and turned the knob that controlled the power. At once a high-pitched buzzing noise filled the air.

Her excitement had just begun to diminish but now at once she was aroused once more to fever pitch. Her eyes opened wide and she almost screamed in agony as the excitation drove her mad. He smiled pitilessly at her as she writhed and squealed before him, and the noise of her cries drowned the sound of a dog barking, high up above them on the hill.

Igor, looking on secretly from the cover of some bushes, heard Candie squeal and began to stand up, ready to run to her rescue, but he realised at once that it was sexual excitation and not pain that caused the scream, and he crouched down again. His orders were to follow Candie, but to intervene only if her life was in danger.

He heard a dog barking in the distance and looked up; the sound had come from where he had left the Renault. Marcel had not heard anything, but the dog might come sniffing around and discover him. In any case, it was drawing attention to the car and to Jenny. He had to leave. With one final, anguished backward glance at Candie, he slipped away and began a long, slow, tortuous journey back towards the car.

The spaniel had smelt his master and had given a welcoming bark. Jenny pretended to be startled, lowered her magazine and sat up. The man emerged from the bushes and approached her as she hurriedly shook down her skirt and buttoned her jacket. The dog wagged its tail and ran up to the man. He patted the dog briefly, then turned his attention to Jenny.

'This is private property,' he told her authoritatively. 'You're trespassing.'

She shrugged. 'So what?' she said insolently. 'I'm not doing any harm.'

'You're trespassing,' he repeated. He took a pencil and notepad from his pocket, licked the end of the pencil, and started to make a note of the number of the car. She climbed out of the car and shook down her hem.

'Do you have to do that?' she asked. 'I borrowed the car from my boss: you'll get me the sack.'

'You should have thought of that before,' he said, and continued to write, looking at the insurance notice attached to the windscreen. She followed him around the car and came closer, until she was almost touching him. His hunter's jacket was rough and coarse, its pockets bulging with cords and snares and traps, and he smelt of the damp earth.

'I don't have a proper driving licence, either,' she confessed.

He sighed and shook his head at her. 'You're really in it, aren't you?' he said.

She came up really close and put her hand on his arm. 'There's no need to be like that,' she said, looking up at him with her big eyes.

'You shouldn't be in here.'

'I didn't see any sign,' she said, becoming angry because he so easily resisted her feminine wiles.

'You should get your eyes tested,' he remarked.

She laughed. 'There's nothing wrong with yours, though, is there?' she sneered.

'What do you mean by that?'

'You were getting a good old eyeful just now, weren't you?' She looked at him challengingly. 'Did it turn you on?' she asked cheekily.

He flushed a deep red. 'You're asking to get your backside spanked,' he told her.

'Who by? You and whose army?'

'Don't push your luck,' he warned her, and picked up her magazine.

'Hey, that's mine,' she said, stretching out her hand. He lifted the magazine out of her reach and flicked through the pages.

'Give it back to me,' she said, grabbing at it. He held it above his head and she let her body press against his as she tried to reach it.

'What's a girl like you doing, wanking off?' he asked.

'I've just broken off with my boyfriend,' she told him. Her body contacted his from her neck to her thighs as she wriggled against him.

'A girl like you doesn't need to go without,' he remarked, and let her take back her magazine.

'Of course I don't,' she replied, moving away. 'I've got a strong left hand and five inches of pink plastic in my handbag.' She turned and threw the magazine on to the seat of the car, then turned back to him. 'Unless you have any better ideas,' she added cheekily.

'Maybe I have; maybe not,' he told her.

'Prefer looking, do you?' she asked. 'Getting past it?'

He grabbed her around her waist and pulled her to him. 'I told you,' he hissed, his voice thick with anger. 'One more crack like that and I'll tan your arse.'

'I'd like to see you try.'

'I'm warning you,' he said to her. His chest rose and fell against her bosom and she could feel his erection against her stomach.

'Promises, promises,' she said tauntingly.

He half turned and grabbed hold of her, passing his arm across her shoulders and bending her over his left knee. She had been trained in judo and it was an easy hold to break, but she let him manhandle her, squealing as he hoisted her skirt and slapped her backside three or four times with the flat of his hand. She wriggled and punched him ineffectually, struggling as if to escape, but arousing him more and more in the process. He let her go and she sprang away from him, then turned to face him, panting now, pink faced and genuinely aroused by the spanking.

'Shove off,' he said, his voice choked with lust.

'That's not the way to get me to shove off,' she told him.

'Shove off,' he repeated, 'before –'

'Before what?' she said, and laughed at him again. 'That's what you want, isn't it?' she said to him, and pulled her skirt up. He looked at her defiant young body, at her long stockings and her skimpy little panties, and he licked his lips. His eyes were bloodshot and he looked like a bull being tormented by a terrier. She laughed again and reached down, unclipped and took off her panties, then waved them in front of his nose.

'Come and get it,' she taunted him, 'if you can.'

He grabbed her panties from her and lunged at her. She skipped nimbly to one side and ran behind the car. He pounded up to the car, and she laughed at him over the bonnet. He pushed her panties into his pocket and opened both car doors on his side, then ran around the front of the car with a surprising turn of speed. She ran around the car, but the open doors and the trees impeded her. She ran away from the car, but now she was at a disadvantage in her high heels. She tripped and almost fell, and then he was on her.

She turned to face him as he locked his arms around her. He was beyond all reason now and yanked her skirt up to her waist, grabbing at her bare buttocks. He pushed her backward and she felt the harsh bark of a tree against her back. Trapped, she pummelled his shoulders with her fists, but his hand forced itself in between her legs and she gave a high-pitched cry as his broad calloused workman's hand caressed her soft pudenda and felt for her sex.

He discovered that she was streaming wet and ripped at his pants. Suddenly savagely aroused, Jenny flung her arms around his neck, and began to kiss his face desperately as his hands excited her. She wrenched her bra catch open and felt her breasts against his rough gaberdine, her nipples hard and sensitive against the coarse material. She lifted one knee and spread her legs. His penis was pressing against her now and she put her hand down, took his shaft, and wriggled her body, standing up on tip-toe to allow him to enter her.

As soon as he was inside her, he put his hands under her

buttocks and lifted her bodily. She grabbed hold of a branch as he began to fuck her. She was extremely aroused now and no longer pretending. Her games and his virility had made her forget, momentarily, what this was all about, and she lost herself in the sheer animal pleasure of being fucked in nature's way, out in the open, with the sun hot on her naked flesh, the rough bark of the tree rasping at her shoulders as his force lifted her bodily into the air.

She felt her orgasm start to build up and then a blind overwhelming flood of rapture overcame her and made her body jerk helplessly against the tree trunk, time and time again. He ejaculated almost immediately afterwards and gasped several times, his eyes fixed and staring, before he began to subside.

The puppy barked suddenly, and he looked around. A large white rabbit had just emerged from its burrow and was standing in the rutted path just a few feet away, twitching its nose. The spaniel leapt into the air, set all four feet going at full revs, for all the world like a comic cartoon animal, then fell back to earth and set off towards the rabbit, yapping furiously, with its long ears flapping. The rabbit bounded away, its tail bobbing as it fled, and the gamekeeper desperately zipped up his pants, grabbed his gun and ran off after the dog, shouting, 'Come back here, you stupid bloody animal.'

Four

Candie was still unsatisfied and pleaded for relief as Marcel took her through her catechism.

'Candida,' asked Marcel, 'how should a slave present herself to her master?'

'With my breasts and nipples and sex all within his sight and within his reach,' she replied.

'What if you are modestly dressed when you meet this man?'

'I must at once expose myself to him.'

'What if you are not aroused?'

'Slaves must always be aroused.'

'How does the slave ensure she is always aroused?'

'By exciting herself and using her vibrator.'

'Good. Now, what is the slave's main objective?' he asked.

'To satisfy her masters, to make them climax, to receive their cream, to feel their semen flood into her.'

'What if she fails to achieve her objective?'

'She must be punished.'

'How?'

'She must be chained, caned, whipped, humiliated, exposed, exhibited; anything at all her masters desire. They must have no mercy on her.'

'What is her greatest joy?'

'To satisfy many men.'

'What should be her reward when she succeeds?'

'More men to serve. Big, strong, powerful men who will drive her mad with lust.'

'Should she be allowed to climax?'

'A slave should be ready for sex at all times. She must control her orgasms to ensure this.'

'Good,' he said, nodding with satisfaction. 'That is well said and you deserve a reward. What kind of reward would be appropriate?'

'To satisfy you, master.'

'Excellent. Come.' He put out his hand and drew her out of the car and into the sunlight. As she stepped out, she saw that he was holding a pair of handcuffs.

Jenny was dressed again and had fixed her make-up by the time Igor arrived back at the car. Her back was a little scratched but otherwise she was fine, and she had decided to say nothing about her adventure to Igor.

'I heard a dog barking,' he said. 'I decided to come back in case it gave the game away.'

'He saw me and then a rabbit,' she told him. 'He preferred the rabbit. What's happening down there?'

'He's putting poor Candie through it, I'm afraid.'

'It certainly looks like it,' she agreed. 'She's just getting out of the car, and she's naked except for her shoes and stockings.' She leant over the bonnet of the Renault and focussed her binoculars. 'Marcel's with her,' she added.

Igor came up behind her and looked over her shoulder as he used his own binoculars. She felt his body make contact with hers and felt a thrill of arousal run through her. The sex with the gamekeeper had not fully satisfied her, and watching Candie getting so much male attention was arousing her again.

'There's a little leather strap around her hips,' he remarked, 'and something dipping down to touch her sex.'

'It's a clitoral vibrator,' she replied. 'It's a French invention. It has a radio control, so that he can excite her whenever he wishes.'

'He's handcuffing her,' he told her. Marcel had pulled Candie's hands behind her back, and she was soon helpless.

'He's arousing her now,' she said, and they saw Candie suddenly gasp, then come up to Marcel and try to rub herself against him. Jenny felt her excitement mount as she imagined what it must feel like for Candie. At the same time, she felt Igor's erection suddenly thrust against her body.

'That device looks very interesting,' he said.

'I have one at home, if you want to see how it works,' she volunteered. 'We were trained to use it: it's quite an amazing invention.'

'I suppose I should know what poor Candie is up against,' said Igor, and leant forward for a better view. His penis pushed into her, and she spread her legs a little wider as she felt his shaft press into the cleavage between her buttocks.

'Does it turn you on, watching her with another man?' she asked.

'Yes, it does,' he admitted breathlessly. 'I feel a bit ashamed.'

'There's no need to be' she said. 'It's perfectly natural.' She paused. 'I'm becoming very aroused as well,' she told him.

'Really?' he asked.

'I think I'm becoming too excited to concentrate,' she told him slyly.

He gulped. 'Really?' he asked again.

'You remember what I said about relieving the tensions?' she asked.

'Yes, of course I do,' he replied.

'It's got nothing to do with love or anything,' she said. 'I mean, if I fell and twisted my ankle, you'd look after me, wouldn't you?'

'Of course,' he replied.

'Well, it's just the same, isn't it?'

'I suppose so,' he admitted, after a short pause.

'Well then,' she said, and spread her legs invitingly.

He gulped, but she felt him put his hand gingerly on her bottom and stroke her buttocks through her thin pleated skirt as he watched his girlfriend fellate Marcel. She focussed the binoculars, watching as Candie knelt on the short grass and Marcel stood over her. She saw him thrust his stomach forward and saw how Candie took Marcel's prick into her mouth, sucking him with her luscious, sensual lips, and how Marcel put his hand into Candie's hair, holding her as her mouth massaged the end of his penis. Through the powerful binoculars, Jenny saw her tongue titillate the rounded knob, run around the sperm hole and flick excitingly at the folds of skin under the tip. Suddenly, he pulled his prick out of her mouth and raised her to her feet. There was a solid flat picnic table close by, with two seats attached. He made her lie on her back on the table, then picked up her legs, lifted her ankles on to his shoulders, lifted her buttocks high in the air and drove his prick into her. Candie squealed aloud and her scream echoed around the woodland as his massive prick thrust hard into her.

Jenny panted as she watched the pair making love. She was genuinely aroused by the scene she was watching, but even more aroused by the feel of Igor's hand on her bottom. Her fingers tightened on her binoculars as she felt his hands raise her hem. Leaning over the bonnet of the car, she had already been showing a lot of leg, but now he must be able to see the tops of her stockings and the inviting curves of her bare thighs. She felt her hem lifted high and her skirt thrown over her hips.

She had spare panties in her handbag but had not put them on, so that she was naked and blatantly available, with her legs spread apart wide enough for him to see her sex, framed by her dark silky hair. She felt his hand explore her buttocks and slide between her parted legs. Her sex was wide open and she was streaming with lubrication. She moaned in delight as she watched Candie being so expertly fucked, whilst her rival's boyfriend slid his finger into her sex. 'I want to be fucked,' she whispered. 'I want what she's getting, and I want it now.'

She felt Igor's hands busy themselves with his zip. A moment later his fingers opened her sex and she was suddenly taken from behind and pushed vigorously forward, sliding bodily over the bonnet of the car from the force of his assault. She choked down her scream of ecstasy as Igor, excited beyond measure by the erotic scene he was witnessing, began to fuck her like a wild animal.

She heard Candie cry out loud, and saw how Candie's body moved now of its own accord, thrusting against Marcel, burying his prick as deep inside her as possible, extracting every last ounce of pleasure from their coupling. Jenny gasped and cried out as Igor pistonned her, almost keeping time with Marcel as his long, hard penis ravished her sex. Jenny saw Candie's body thrash uncontrollably on the table as she came, and a moment later she felt the overwhelming waves of pleasure flooding her body, and could not suppress her scream as she in turn climaxed.

Five

Candie sat in her bedroom and looked at herself in the big mirror that faced her bed. As she had anticipated, all her normal clothes had been confiscated as soon as she arrived at the Centre, and she now wore long, seamed, sheer black stockings with elaborately decorated tops, a scarlet satin suspender belt, scarlet sandals with exaggeratedly high heels, her own personal, made-to-measure clit stimulator, and red leather handcuffs. She also wore a tight scarlet vinyl body-stocking with a sling-bra top and a slit between her legs, designed to ensure she could not remove her stimulator.

A very beautiful raven-haired bisexual girl, who was code-named Sapphi, had explained to her that she would now live in a permanent peepshow, surrounded by see-through mirrors. Later on, she would be allowed to dress up with scarves, gloves, hats and ribbons, but she must never, ever, cover up her breasts and sex.

Candie was waiting for dinner to be served. She had taken a bath and lolled about for some time in the foam, and had then dried herself on a big warm fluffy towel, varnished her toe nails and finger nails, and trimmed her pubic hair. She had made up her face and body and had eventually put on her new outfit, but all this had taken some considerable time, since everything intimate had to be done in front of a big mirror, which was almost certainly half silvered. Candie had to agree that the result made all the effort worthwhile, however; she really looked ravishing. The tight vinyl squeezed her waist and emphasised her hips, whilst the bra lifted and presented her breasts like lovely ripe fruit.

There was a tap on the door and a young, pale-faced manservant came in, pushing a big heated trolley from which arose the most wonderful aromas. Candie hurriedly put one foot up on to the chair and opened her legs wide. He was very dishy: tall, handsome, rather wan but very attractive.

'Are you Candida, the new girl?' he asked

'That's right.'

'I'm Robert. I've brought your dinner. Fresh melon, roast duckling, vegetables, salad, cheese, and a cream gâteau, with a half bottle of Chiroubles and a glass of Sauternes to finish with. Is that satisfactory?'

'I'll say,' said Candie. 'Would you like to have sex with me?' she asked politely, then sniffed the aroma. 'Could you possibly wait until I've had my dinner?' she went on hopefully. 'I feel much randier on a full stomach.'

'That's all right, I'm very busy just at the moment,' he assured her, and went out. Candie tucked in her starched napkin and attacked her dinner.

Several miles to the south, the tourists were enjoying the warm summer evening around the Place de Tertres, by the Sacré Coeur cathedral. They sat at little tables with bright check tablecloths, sipping beer under the trees and listening to accordions as they examined menus and planned their dinners, or bought postcards and watercolours of Montmartre, or sat, blushing with pride and embarrassment, as the pavement artists sketched their portraits.

Jenny sauntered through the crowd with Igor, showing him the sights, playing the tourist, holding his arm and talking about her childhood in Montmartre. They had followed Candie to the Centre and had decided that here was nothing more they could do that day, so Jenny had proposed that they should meet up at the Abbesses funicular, have dinner together, and plan their next move.

They were soon seated in a small intimate restaurant, sipping kirs. The pianist tinkled his way through the ageless Parisian street songs, whilst Jenny hummed 'La Vie en Rose' and talked to Igor about Piaf, Chevalier and Yves

Montand. Some time later, fortified by an excellent dinner and rather a lot of Hautes Côtes de Nuit , she danced close to Igor on the tiny dance floor. A deep tenor sax huffed and puffed its way through Stan Getz arrangements of the classic bossa novas, and Jenny felt Igor's hands explore her body through her thin cocktail dress. The lights went down, a coloured girl sang sad, sexy lyrics in a mock-innocent Astrud Gilberto voice, and Igor's fingers trickled over Jenny's spine as the throbbing guitar helped the sax through 'How Insensitive'. She felt his fingers move down and down until they discovered the thin ribbon of her garter belt and then, much lower, below the line of her coccyx, the elasticised top of her panties. His light, tender touch aroused her at once, and Jenny encouraged him in his explorations by running her arms up around his neck, pressing her breasts against his chest and pushing her tummy against him. They swayed in the centre of the tiny dance floor, locked together, moving gently to the staccato jazz/samba beat, lost to the world.

Jenny was sure that her planned seduction was going well, and, an hour or so later, as they strolled like lovers on the terrace below the Sacré Coeur and looked out over the sleeping city, she moved a stage further. When they passed into the shadows between two street lamps, she 'accidentally' stumbled on the cobbles in her high heels. Igor grabbed her to prevent her from falling and Jenny let her body press against his. A moment later they were kissing like lovers. Jenny surrendered to the magic moment and let herself be carried away, but Igor suddenly pulled back and she realised that he was having an attack of scruples. Sure enough, he moved away from her, thanked her for a wonderful evening, and suggested that they should call it a day.

Jenny at once nodded her agreement. 'Yes, I agree,' she replied, 'it has been a lovely evening, but now we must really get down to work.'

'Work?' he asked, obviously taken aback.

'You asked me to show you the clit stimulator,' she reminded him. 'You said it was absolutely essential that you knew what poor Candie was up against.'

'Ah, yes, so I did,' he admitted.

'I live just along the road and I have taken rather a lot of trouble to get everything ready for the demo,' she pointed out with a little *moue*, and of course he concurred. Five minutes later, she left Igor alone with a big Remy Martin and an Ophélie Winter CD, and vanished into her bedroom. She freshened up, splashed around her favourite perfume, fitted her stimulator around her hips and adjusted the button against her clit. She then put on a very sexy black-and-scarlet bra-and-panties outfit, with black stockings and scarlet suspenders, and slipped into a short, backless, seductive black cocktail dress. She pulled on her high-heeled evening sandals and used much more make-up than usual, so that her eyes were dark mysterious pools and her mouth a big scarlet invitation.

She saw Igor's eyes light up as she went into the room, and she sat down nonchalantly, let her dress ride up, and picked up the Cointreau that he had poured out for her. She produced a small black box with a short aerial attached, sipped her liqueur and started her explanation.

'You probably know that most women achieve orgasm by clitoral stimulation?' she began. Igor nodded.

'Several of our doctors studied what exactly happens when a woman's clit is stimulated,' she explained, 'and they devised a tiny vibrator, which is shaped to fit the clitoris exactly, and applies the sort of movement that seems to be most effective in generating orgasm. Women differ in certain degrees, but this device works well with over ninety-five per cent of all young women. It certainly works with me!'

She sipped her drink and went on. 'Naturally, the device was quickly used for sex games,' she continued. 'In fact, it is almost completely irresistible. No woman, however frigid or shy, can avoid becoming aroused by it, so it also quickly came to be used as a sexual torture. If the girl is prevented from ripping it off, she is completely in the power of the person with that box.'

'It sounds like a really awful macho device,' Igor said hypocritically, looking wide-eyed at the box.

'It is indeed. Do you want to try it out?' Jenny asked casually.

Igor gulped. 'I suppose I should understand what poor Candie must be going through,' he said at last.

'Of course you should,' she agreed, and put down her glass. Her heart was pounding as she produced a pair of handcuffs and placed her hands invitingly behind her back. 'If I'm not handcuffed,' she explained, 'I shall rip the stimulator off as soon as you switch it on,' and she turned so that he could lock the handcuffs. 'Shall we try the lowest power level first?' she proposed.

He nodded, turned the knob to the first notch, and switched the device on. Deliciously sexy sensations immediately flooded over Jenny's body as the device started up. Her body jerked and, gasping, she opened her mouth and closed her eyes as her excitement mounted.

'It's gorgeous,' she told him. 'It feels so wonderful.' She breathed in deeply, her bosom rising and falling. 'I can feel lovely warm waves of arousal running all over my body,' she told him, and writhed lasciviously on the couch, letting her dress rise up to expose her stocking tops and ruched suspenders, and then higher and higher, to reveal her tiny black panties with a scarlet lace trim.

'It makes me feel so wicked and abandoned,' she said, and she stood up, moving to the music. 'Come and dance with me, darling,' she said invitingly, undulating before him.

He stood up and she immediately pressed herself against him, dancing very close, her body contacting his all the way down, so that he would feel the vibration against his penis through her thin dress. He became erect at once and she felt his hard rod thrust up against her pudenda.

'Stroke me the way you did in the restaurant,' she whispered. He put his arms around her, then ran his hand down over her bottom and stroked her garter belt and the top of her panties through her flimsy dress. She sighed and pressed closer, dancing so close that he would feel every contour of her body and would be unable to escape the vibrations.

'There's no need to be so gentlemanly,' she murmured seductively in his ear. 'No one is watching and I'm completely helpless. I couldn't possibly prevent you if you unfastened my dress.'

She knew it was a pretty irresistible invitation and the ribbon tie around her neck featured a big, inviting bow. He pulled it open and the dress immediately rustled to the ground. Jenny thrust herself against him, rubbing her body against his like a very excited, very silky cat, with an unmistakable invitation to take possession of her.

'That's the effect it has on low power?' he asked in amazement.

She nodded. 'Now you can see why the men like it so much,' she murmured, dancing close and sighing contentedly as his hands explored her lovely warm body and her fascinatingly erotic nylon and lace lingerie. 'They called this the background level when we were training,' she told him in a whisper. 'I had to change my panties every hour or so,' she went on, and opened her legs as she danced on the spot.

'I can imagine,' he replied, slipping his hand between her legs. The nylon and lace was very damp indeed, and she felt his fingers on her sex; she was certain that he would take advantage of this opportunity, now that it was so obvious how aroused she was, and was all ready to be carried off into the bedroom, but he held back at the crucial moment.

'Absolutely fascinating,' he told her, pulling away. 'Thank you so much for showing me the device, Jenny.'

'Don't you think you should try it on the next notch?' she asked.

He hesitated. 'Maybe I should,' he admitted.

She laughed coquettishly. 'If you try it, I warn you,' she said, 'I will probably shock you to death.'

'I'm shock-proof,' he said proudly. 'Let's try it.'

'Very well,' she whispered, 'but release me for a moment whilst I go and change. You've ruined my panties,' she added accusingly, but she kissed him as he released her handcuffs, to show she wasn't really cross with him for making her damp.

Six

Candie swallowed the remaining crumbs of her gâteau and washed them down with the last of the Sauternes, then stretched out luxuriously on the bed. There was a knock at the door and she sat up as Sapphi came in. The bisexual girl looked really gorgeous. Her thick black hair, tipped with blonde and auburn streaks, was cropped and stiffened to fan out in a disciplined-punk style, and she wore a wonderfully supple black leather body-stocking. Her big, dark brown, luscious eyes were made up to become deep luminous pools and her generous mouth was enhanced with a vivid scarlet lipstick, with a tiny black line that followed the main contours of her lips. She wore several big circular earrings in each ear, and carried a short black whip which she smacked against her thigh as she sauntered over to the bed on her high heels.

'I have come to initiate you, forcibly if necessary, into the delights of Lesbos,' she told Candie menacingly. 'Offer any resistance, and I will use this whip and your clit tickler to bring you to heel,' she added threateningly.

'Mistress Sapphi,' said Candie seriously, 'you do whatever you have to do, but I can assure you that, having drunk so much wine, and seeing you in that outfit, I'm having the utmost difficulty keeping my hands off you as it is.'

'Well, in that case, restrain yourself a little longer,' her mistress said, and she produced a small key, unlocked a fridge-bar, and took out a half bottle of champagne. The cork popped and Sapphi poured out two big flutes of ice-cold fizz.

'I think I could settle down very easily to this life,' Candie remarked, sipping the delicious wine as Sapphi slid on to the bed.

'You won't be doing this for long,' Sapphi told her. 'You have some important field assignments coming up.'

'Doing what?' Candie asked, as she cuddled close to the dark girl.

'More or less what you are doing now,' Sapphi told her, 'but mostly with men, unfortunately.' She sighed. 'Such a waste,' she murmured, and kissed Candie on the mouth. Candie tasted the champagne and let Sapphi drive her tongue into her mouth, happily playing the submissive role.

Sapphi's agile tongue soon found all the lovely erotic bits that the impatient men bypass, like behind her ears and under her chin. Candie squealed and wriggled with delight as the other girl inexorably raised the temperature.

She lay back and let the dark girl roam over her body with her hands and mouth, but Sapphi carefully avoided all contact with the erogenous zones. After a while, Sapphi lay back and Candie followed her lead. She kissed the other girl's face, neck, arms, then inside her elbow and on down to her wrists. She spread out Sapphi's hands and kissed her palms and between the fingers. Sapphi placed her hands above her head and Candie explored her ribs, kissed up into her armpit, then down again. The dark girl rolled over so that Candie could kiss her shoulders and her spine, and soon became a little impatient. She stood up and unzipped her body-stocking and Candie caught her breath in wonder. Her mistress had beautiful tattoos on the upper swell of each breast, of young girls intertwined in erotic poses, and she wore little gold rings through each nipple.

'You're gorgeous,' Candie breathed, and roamed over the other girl's body, gently flicking at the rings whilst Sapphi moaned with delight. Her mistress removed the body-stocking completely, revealing even more fascinating and intimate rings through her navel and labia. Candie looked at her in wide-eyed admiration, then roamed down the outside of the other girl's long slender legs, kissed her ankles and feet, sucked her toes through her stockings and tickled the soles of her feet with her tongue, until Sapphi took off her stockings and let her new slave play with her bare legs and feet.

They moved away from the active/passive configuration. Now, each kissed and fondled the other, gradually advancing, making slow progress towards the erogenous zones, like the exploratory waves that lap the beach, creeping higher and higher as the tide comes in. Candie breathed in deeply as Sapphi circled around her breast and at last she felt Sapphi's tongue flick against her nipple. 'That's wonderful,' she breathed, and allowed the waves to wash over her for several long seconds before she riposted, licking and sucking Sapphi's big up-standing pink-brown teats with their indented milk-orifices, and tugging gently at her rings.

Sapphi kissed her more forcefully now, between her breasts, then down to her navel, and flicked her tongue into the neat indentation before moving on into her hair. Candie slid down and around until she was lying facing her partner, then she kissed Sapphi's thick dark curls as Sapphi played with her soft blonde hair.

Sapphi used her master key to release Candie's body-stocking and removed her stimulator. Now both girls were free to explore the other's sex, but they did so slowly and gently, as women do. They giggled and whispered to each other, made a game of it, and took their time.

She forced her tongue into Sapphi's slit and separated her labia, then probed inside, tasted her lubrication, and felt her own juices begin to flood. She was very excited now. If she had been with a man, she would have given way to her lust, but she was with a woman. Furthermore, she was on trial, being tested, and so she held back. She forced herself to stay cool, but excited Sapphi deliberately, feeling for her clit with the tip of her tongue, and using her fingers and Sapphi's rings to peel the other girl open and lay bare the mysteries of her sex.

'Ready?' Sapphi whispered.

'I'll say.'

She felt her vagina opened and then the most delicious titillation of her clit she'd ever known. She plunged into Sapphi's sex, tickled her clit and thrust her fingers up into Sapphi's open vagina.

Even now, Sapphi played with her a little. She made three separate attacks, pausing for a moment in between each, but at last neither girl could hold out any longer. Candie felt her orgasm start to explode inside her, like a slow fire that suddenly takes hold.

They had no control over their bodies now. They leapt and bounced on the bed, screamed and panted, licked and kissed and nibbled, bit each other like fighting wild cats and finally, when the waves of utter bliss had totally saturated their bodies, they collapsed in a heap on to the bed, panting and laughing hysterically.

Jenny hummed to herself as she fixed her make-up and slid into nice, wide-leg, easy-access French knickers. The clitoral stimulator was certainly exciting, but the girls had quickly discovered its main attraction. With that thing buzzing away, you had absolute carte blanche. You could be as abandoned and forward and provocative as you liked, and nobody could criticise you.

She had changed into a very daring open-front brassière that really set off her pert, upward-pointing breasts and, with her easy-access panties and sheer stockings, she knew she was irresistible. She had topped up Igor's cognac before she left and, at fifty per cent power, she could really throw herself at him: after all, she had given him fair warning!

She adjusted the feeler of the stimulator to press on to her clit, wondering idly what Candie was up to. She reflected that her big blonde rival was probably having the time of her life, and sprayed around enough perfume to swamp any of Igor's remaining scruples, along with her own.

Candie yawned, settled back on her pillow and looked at her reflection in the ceiling mirror. Her wrists were chained loosely to the head of the bed so that she could not defend herself. The bed was shaped to lift her hips and her ankles were loosely chained to the sides of the bed. She had bathed after her session with Sapphi, and had put on fresh black stockings and suspenders, together with a very pretty black nylon baby-doll nightie, then Sapphi had chained her up and had left her to the mercy of any man who desired her. There were no bedclothes, so that she could see the reflection of herself in the ceiling mirror, and she certainly looked very available. The control box for her clit stimulator was out of sight, attached to the foot of the bed.

There was a tap at the door and Robert entered.

'Hello again, Robert,' she said. 'Have you come to take advantage of me or to take out the trolley?'

'Both,' he replied, and moved the trolley out into the corridor, then came back in and sat on the bed.

'What are you going to do to me?' she asked.

'I'm not allowed to tell you,' he said, 'or it spoils the surprise.' He leant over her and looked at her face. 'You're very pretty,' he said.

'Thank you,' she replied. He put his hand out and pressed down on her chin until her mouth opened, then leant down and pushed his tongue into her mouth, exploring her tongue and all around the palate. She felt the thrill as the tip of his tongue tickled her behind her upper teeth, and then he withdrew. His eyes drifted down her body and she wriggled. 'Don't look at me like that,' she protested.

'Whenever you say, "Don't do something or other",' he told her, 'we have to do it.' He lifted the hem of her nightie and looked at her tie-side matching panties.

'Oh no,' she wailed, and pushed her legs together. He pressed a button and the chains at her ankles tightened and forced her legs apart again. 'That's awful,' she cried. He leant over, placed his head between her thighs, and made little circles in her pubic hair with the tip of his index finger, caressing her through the thin nylon as he looked directly at her sex. Candie wriggled and wailed.

'You're beginning to cream,' he told her, 'there,' and he placed his fingertip on the little damp patch on her panties, and tickled her slit. 'Oh no,' she squealed. She felt his fingers gently pull one of the ties open and her hips bounced on the bed. 'No, please,' she moaned, but he untied the bow and started on the other one.

'I can't stand it,' she said, feeling her lubrication soaking into her panties. The bow gradually released. She looked up into the mirror and gasped: her nipples were standing up so brazenly she felt quite ashamed of herself. He arranged the ribbons of her panties, very prettily, and started to play with the triangle of black nylon, first pulling it down to expose a line of blonde tight curls, then lifting it to one side. She saw her labia peep out and imagined what he could see down there and almost cried out with humiliation and excitement.

He sat up and looked her up and down, then pressed another button. Her wrists were drawn upwards and outwards and the bed lifted to thrust up her bosom and stomach as her head dropped back. She suddenly felt his fingertips, light as thistledown, trickle over her nipples, and she leapt on the bed like a salmon taking a fly. She felt him kiss the exposed curve of her neck and throat whilst his hand tormented her nipples, and her hips jerked with the reflex action. She felt her panties slide away and expose her sex and cried out again as the sticky nylon parted company with her labia. The bed heaved up again, lifting her hips, and her ankles were lifted up and up and out and out. She felt her labia part and sensed that he was now standing by the end of the bed, and wailed again as she realised that she must be totally, exposed. She felt him enter her, sliding into her easily on the lubrication, and then her clit stimulator began to whine and the awful unstoppable orgasm began to build up and up. She wanted to leap on the bed, welcome his thrusts, match them, throw her body on to his penis, but the chains held her rigid as the waves of her orgasm rushed over her and carried her away.

Igor sipped his large Remy and reflected that it really was very kind of Jenny to go to all this trouble to help him understand what Candie must be suffering. He'd try the device out at fifty per cent, he decided, just for a few seconds, and then call it a day. He would certainly not take advantage of Jenny: that would be most ungentlemanly.

He heard a sound and looked up. The creature standing before him certainly resembled the laughing Jenny he had taken out to dinner, but in that sling bra, with her lovely big nipples made up and those daring wide-leg panties, she looked so enticing that his heart leapt. She had her hands behind her back, so was evidently handcuffed, and that of course added to his arousal.

He gulped down the last of his brandy, seized the box, turned the knob to fifty per cent and pressed the switch.

Jenny at once screamed aloud, a high-pitched scream that echoed around the room. He leapt back in alarm and hurriedly reached for the box to turn the device off. The next moment, however, a hurricane flew across the room, landed in his lap and sent the box flying. The hurricane then knocked him on to his back and landed on top of him. A female body wriggled excitedly on top of him, a predatory female mouth opened wide and fastened over his in a kiss that devoured him, whilst two eager lithe hands stripped off his pants. He realised, too late, that he had evidently been mistaken about the handcuffs.

Her arms were now wrapped firmly around him, holding him close whilst she kissed him feverishly and finished ripping his clothes off. He could feel the titillation of the vibrator, very evident now because she had laid bare his penis and the clit stimulator was catching him right next to the tip. Jenny reared up, her eyes wild and abandoned, lifted her body and sank down on to his erection. He felt the enormous shock as his prick slid into her, and now the vibration was all along his shaft. He started to leap about under her and she hung on like a rodeo star, gripping him with her thighs as his body arched and twisted.

To his relief, she retrieved the box, evidently intending to switch off the device and cut short this Jekyll and Hyde transformation, but her fingers seemed to be all thumbs and she inadvertently turned the knob the wrong way.

The hum changed to a high-pitched scream. Jenny

screamed, '*Ah oui, ah oui,*' and her body went crazy. Her vagina grasped his penis firmly and massaged it vigorously, whilst the all-powerful vibrator brought them both up to the no-return point. Igor felt the wild thrill of sexual ecstasy rush through his cock and he was suddenly as wild as she was, banging his prick into her as if his life depended on satisfying her. He heard her scream aloud as her orgasm overwhelmed her and the next moment his prick jerked uncontrollably as he shot his semen into her.

Seven

Gabrielle Lamartine sipped her freshly squeezed orange juice and looked contentedly around the breakfast table. Everyone said that she and her husband, Jean-Luc, made a very good-looking pair and she was inclined to agree with them. She was widely recognised as a beautiful and talented woman, with the face and body of an Italian film star and diplomas in Philosophy and the Fine Arts, who had given her husband a sturdy son and a beautiful daughter and who, at the age of thirty-two, was at the peak of her loveliness. She had furnished their house in the Bois de Boulogne with taste and elegance; she ran it smoothly and efficiently, and she was a perfect hostess – everybody said so. She was, all in all, a pretty bright cookie. Gabrielle finished her morning's self-appraisal, buttered some toast, and told her son to eat more slowly.

'I won't be in to dinner this evening, unfortunately,' Jean-Luc told her. 'I have to attend a meeting of the Management Committee of La Chasse St Hubert.'

'You and your hunting!' she said, smiling indulgently. She knew that La Chasse St Hubert, whilst registered as a hunting association, was in fact a private club where movers and shakers could get together, out of the limelight, to discuss important political events. Jean-Luc was an upwardly mobile politician and going places, a rising star in the new government and destined for a ministerial post in the next cabinet reshuffle, so he had to keep in touch with the powers behind the scenes. The Management Committee of La Chasse met every few weeks, nominally to arrange the programme for the hunting season, but in reality to hammer out deals.

'Will Vivienne be there?' she asked. Vivienne acted as secretary to the Management Committee and general factotum for the Club.

'She'll probably take the minutes,' he replied.

'Remember me to her, will you?'

'Of course. How will you spend the day?' he asked.

'I may do a little shopping,' she told him, 'and maybe have my hair done. As you are going to be late back, I may take in a play or a concert this evening.' There was a noise of a car horn outside, and the children's Scottish nanny came in to collect them. Gabrielle took turns with neighbours to ferry the kids to and from school, and today it wasn't her turn.

There was a flurry of kisses and last-minute parental commands, and a few moments later Jean-Luc and Gabrielle waved goodbye to their children. Jean-Luc went upstairs to collect his briefcase, whilst Gabrielle poured out more coffee, picked up her *Figaro*, read the headlines and the lead story, skimmed though the political pages, then turned to the woman's section to catch up on the fashion news.

The nanny, having disposed of her two charges, returned to her small, neat, tidy bedroom. She was called Janet and she wore a simple grey-and-white striped calf-length shift dress with a white Peter Pan collar, together with clumpy black shoes and grey tights. She wore no make-up, parted her hair in the middle like Jane Austen, and wore steel-rimmed grannie glasses made famous by the late John Lennon.

Janet took off her clumpy shoes, her dress, her tights and her sensible cotton bra and briefs, then looked at herself in the mirror as she unpinned her hair. It cascaded over her shoulders and down her back in an auburn wave, and the erstwhile mouse was suddenly transformed into Scarlett O'Hara. She opened her wardrobe and took out some sheer stockings and a sea-green satin suspender belt that fitted snugly over her hips, then began to dress. She put on a hip-length mini-slip with a bra top, eased her breasts into the cups so that they really overflowed the bra, then pulled up the tight zip. All it needed now were her panties. She drew them on and was just tying the bow at her hips when her bedroom door opened quietly. Her bedroom was conveniently located close to Jean-Luc's study, and he often visited her after breakfast.

She leant over to examine her face in close-up, and to give her lover a good view of her long athletic legs. She saw his eyes take in the bare white curvy thighs above the taut stockings, and knew that her hem just concealed her panties, which of course meant he just had to lift it up. He came up silently behind her and she gave a little shriek of feigned surprise as his hands clasped her waist.

'*Monsieur*,' she said reprovingly. He lifted her hair and kissed the nape of her neck.

'*Chérie*,' he replied, pulling her to him, so that her bottom contacted his groin, and he kissed her under her ear. Janet's eyes misted over and she tilted her head to let him nuzzle into her shoulder. She was a pushover for under-the-ear kisses. His hands slid upward and cupped her breasts and his tongue penetrated her ear. She loved that too: Janet's ears were particularly sensitive and she started to lubricate at once.

She felt her nipples become erect under his fingers. He kept one hand on her breast but used the other to lift her slip. Janet saw her hem come up and expose her provocative panties and her flat tummy, and saw her lover's eyes widen as he took in the view. His lust communicated itself to her and she began to sigh and move her body against his, supporting her weight on her two hands as she leant forward.

'Oh no,' she moaned, as his hands found the tie at her hip, but then she turned her head to kiss him on the lips as her panties dropped away. And then she was facing him, kissing him passionately all around his face as her body moved lasciviously against his. She wrapped her legs around him and gripped him between her thighs, her hands already busy at his zip.

He picked her up and she squealed with delight as he

threw her on to the bed. She ripped open his pants without more ado and he took possession of her. Her legs came up, her ankles wrapped around his neck and she drew him into her, kissing him feverishly as her vagina swallowed up his prick and held him fast, sucking at him, demanding his semen. His penis rubbed against her clit and she started her orgasm. Her eyes flashed fire, her ankles tightened around his neck, her bottom came off the bed and she hurled herself into her climax, sucking his semen from him as his prick throbbed and pulsed, making sure he was bone dry before she fell back on to the bed and released him. She looked up mistily at Jean-Luc, as the warm afterglow of her orgasm enveloped her, and wondered why Gabrielle was so willing to let him stray.

Gabrielle heard her husband run gaily down the stairs and looked up as he came into the breakfast room, waving his briefcase. He looked set up for the day and in fine fettle, but in no condition to service that secretary of his, so that was one in the eye for that bitch! Gaby knew a rival when she saw one and Janet wasn't a rival. Janet didn't see herself as the second Madame Jean-Luc Lamartine, whereas his on-the-make secretary certainly did.

'Have a good day, darling,' she told him, and offered her cheek for a chaste kiss as she escorted him to the door. She heard his car start and waved as he moved away, then silence descended. Five minutes later, she was luxuriating in her bath.

She had heard the muffled sounds of her husband's amorous encounter with Janet and it had turned her on. She allowed her hand to stray between her legs and her lust to build up as she planned her day. She had to make a decision, a serious decision, and one she had thought about for a long time. Ever since the last dinner at La Chasse St Hubert, in fact.

She had met Vivienne there several months previously. Although La Chasse was a man's domain, spouses were invited to a special dinner once or twice a year: she and Vivienne had drunk some wine together and had soon reached the stage of exchanging confidences.

'I want to do the right thing by Jean-Luc and bring our kids up properly', Gaby had told her, 'but I must admit I get bored and frustrated at times.'

Vivienne had given her the address of a very sober-looking house tucked away near the Parc Monceau, where bored housewives could while away the afternoon amid the Louis XV furniture and the rococo decor, examine prospective clients via two-way mirrors, and decide with whom to share a bottle of Veuve Cliquot, but the men were Jean-Luc clones and not much of a change. At the last dinner, having drunk far too much wine, she had confided her really secret fantasy to Vivienne.

'I have always daydreamed about being a street walker,' she had whispered. 'Not a high-class courtesan, you understand, but a lowly hooker, owned body and soul by some hard bastard who beats me up when I fail to deliver and fucks me senseless when I do.'

'That's a pretty common fantasy,' Vivienne had told her. 'It will cost you quite a bit, I'm afraid, but I could fix it for you,' and she had promised to look around for a suitable opportunity.

Gabrielle bit her lip, agonised for a long time, but finally made a decision. She climbed out of the bath, grabbed a towelling peignoir, and rang Vivienne's number.

'Vivienne? It's Gaby.'

'Gaby, how sweet of you to call. How are things?'

'Fine.' They chatted about the children for a moment or two, then Gabrielle got down to brass tacks.

'Vivienne, I'm at a loose end this afternoon, and I was wondering – you know – what we were talking at the dinner –'

'I hadn't forgotten. I talked to Carl about you.'

'Carl?'

'He's an old friend. I showed him your picture. He's dying to meet you.'

'Are you sure?'

'He was over the moon, honestly; really gone on you.'

'I'm not looking for a lover, Vivienne.'

'Gaby, he's a *maquereau*,' Vivienne told her in

exasperation. 'He runs half a dozen girls. He takes on a temp now and again, that's all. No strings, no questions.'

'What if somebody sees me?'

'Come on, Gaby, be reasonable. Which of your friends ever goes to the Rue St Denis? Wear a wig, contact lenses, anything.'

'I don't know,' she said.

'At least go and see him,' Vivienne encouraged her. 'You have nothing to lose. If the vibes aren't right, then split. It's just a business arrangement as far as he's concerned.'

'Oh, very well,' she said at last, and put down the telephone. She'd done it now. She was caught between fear and excitement, and the excitement won. She picked up the telephone again and rang an internal number. A minute later there was a tap at her door.

'Who is it?' she called. She had changed into a heavy satin peignoir and had just clipped a pretty blue suspender belt around her hips.

'Giorgio, madame.'

Gaby sat down on her padded stool, opened her peignoir to expose most of her breasts, offered a long nylon stocking to her foot, and started to ease it on.

'Come in,' she called. A young, very handsome, dark-haired man entered and stood respectfully to attention just nside the door. He wore a chauffeur's uniform, carried a pair of gauntlets, and had his hat squeezed under his elbow.

'Shut the door and come over here,' she told him, pointing with her chin at a spot just in front of her. He did as she instructed, so that he was standing very close to her, looking down at her bosom and legs as she eased up and suspendered her stocking.

'I shall need the car this afternoon to go into Paris,' she told him.

'Certainly, madame.' She fixed the suspender and looked around.

'Give me my other stocking, please,' she told him, 'and be careful not to ladder it.'

'No, madame.' He very gingerly picked up the sheer

nylon sheath and handed it to her. She crossed one leg over the other and inserted her toe into the stocking.

'I may want you to bring me back, or perhaps I will make my own way home,' she added, easing the stocking up to and over her knee.

'As madame wishes,' he replied. She fixed the back suspender, rolling around on her hip.

'The car was filthy yesterday,' she added, looking down at her thigh.

'I am extremely sorry, madame.'

'You don't look very sorry,' she said, and spread her leg sideways to fix the second suspender. He blushed deeply, ran a finger around his collar, and sank down on to his knees between her legs.

She put her leg up and placed her stockinged foot on his shoulder. He put down his gloves, took her foot in his two hands, and kissed her toes. She pushed her foot flat against his face. He pressed his nose against the underside of her toes, turning his head from left to right, then kissed the sole of her foot.

'You're beginning to learn,' she admitted.

'Thank you, madame.'

'You still have a long way to go, though,' she reminded him, and removed her foot from his grasp, then stood up and slipped off her peignoir. She stayed close to him, her legs almost touching his shoulders, and he stayed on his knees and looked up at her as she stood over him. She was naked, except for her stockings and suspenders, and her legs were slightly parted. He could see her voluptuous sex, still almost as virginal as when she was a girl: Gabrielle had an aristocratic face but wide, peasant-girl hips. She picked up a pair of satin French panties, very sheer and feminine, and dropped them on to his upturned face.

'I hope you've cut your fingernails,' she said, and she reached down to put her hand on his shoulder to steady herself as she lifted one foot. He took the panties and eased them over first one foot, then the other, and started to pull the panties up. When the waistband was just about to conceal her sex, he suddenly grasped her hips and pressed his mouth against her pubic hair, his tongue seeking out her slit.

'I didn't give you permission to do that,' she said angrily, but she didn't push him away. His tongue probed between her legs and reached up, searching into her vagina, and then flicking around, seeking her clitoris.

'Stop that, you pig,' she hissed, beating on his shoulders ineffectually. He took no notice. '*Maiale, porco, animale*,' she moaned, switching to Italian. He took no notice, but continued to kiss her sex, thrusting his tongue into her more and more demandingly. '*Basta, basta*,' she hissed at him, pushing at him without any effect. 'Beast, filth,' she cried, then suddenly she stiffened and cried out. Her body pulsated against his face for several seconds, and then she pushed him away for real.

'I've told you before, Giorgio,' she said, trembling with emotion as she fastened her panties and sank back down on to her stool. 'You really go too far.'

'*Scusi, signora*,' he murmured, and stood up.

'I should really tell my husband and have you fired,' she went on.

'Please, *signora*, I will not do it again,' he pleaded.

'Well, don't just stand there,' she told him. 'Go and clean the car.' he hesitated for a second or two and she screamed at him, 'At once, do you hear?'

'*Certamente, signora*,' he murmured hurriedly, and left the room. Gabrielle stretched, wiggled her hips contentedly, and began to dress in earnest.

Eight

It was nearing eleven, and Candie felt rather nervous as she waited to be interviewed by the boss. She looked with interest around the ante-room, but then she saw his photographic souvenirs, and her heart leapt and her legs turned to jelly. The boss was always referred to as the Colonel, but she had never in her wildest dreams imagined that he would turn out to be that ultimate fantasy figure, a Foreign Legion paratrooper colonel. She knew she looked alluring in a very tight, sexy red dress with bootlace shoulder-straps, a bra top and a short flounced skirt, over her black stockings and scarlet suspenders, and was determined to demonstrate her seductive techniques, but, when the clock chimed the hour, she was momentarily so overwhelmed by the military ambience that she marched in, snapped to attention and saluted. 'Private Candida reporting,' she announced, forgetting for a moment what kind of organisation she was in. He looked fantastic close to. His hair was cut *en-brosse*, he was deeply sun-tanned and he had lovely crinkly lines that showed he'd really lived. He was looking down at a document and frowning.

'At ease, Private,' he replied absentmindedly, waving his hand, without looking up. Candie slid her legs apart, frowning, wondering what exactly 'At ease' meant. After a moment's hesitation, she reached down and raised her hem to her waist, draping it carefully to set off her hips. She remembered she had to offer herself to every man she met, which obviously applied even more so to the boss, so, when he looked up and blinked, obviously fascinated by the sight of her lovely black stockings, her scarlet satin suspender belt and her tiny scarlet G-string, she wiggled her hips invitingly.

'I wasn't clear what "At ease" meant,' she explained, and plucked at the top of her panties. 'Would you like to have sex with me, sir?' she continued.

'I'm not sure,' he replied cautiously, which rather surprised her, and he tapped the document in front of him. 'It says here that three of my young men are in hospital, suffering from severe exhaustion, because of you,' he said accusingly. 'I have no wish to join them.'

Candie blushed. This wasn't a good start at all. 'I can explain, sir,' she said confidently. 'Permission to approach, sir?'

'Granted,' he replied. She came around his desk and right up to him, then stood astride his knees. She took his hand. 'They had to do whatever I asked them not to do,' she explained, stroking his palm with the tip of her finger, 'and I kept forgetting and saying things like "Please don't start me off again". I'm very sorry, sir.' To show her contrition, she placed the palm of his hand over her pudenda and tucked his fingers in between her legs

'I see,' he replied, and flexed his fingers to feel the dampness soaking into the thin satin ribbon between her legs. He put out his other hand and squeezed her breast, feeling her erect nipple under his palm. 'How many orgasms have you had since you arrived in France?' he asked. She looked down and frowned, then shook her head.

'I've lost count, sir,' she admitted sadly.

'You are obviously getting ready for another one,' he pointed out.

'Well, you are extremely handsome,' she replied, 'and the Foreign Legion is so romantic, and you must have been to places like Ventiane and Laos and into all those dreamy bordellos, and you must know so much about sex and, well . . .' She sighed and came even closer. 'You must have so much to teach me,' she murmured, and put a hand down.

'Wait a moment,' he said, easing her hand away. 'Now, you are obviously enthusiastic, and, as far as one may judge from this report, very nearly insatiable,' he admitted. Candie blushed deeply, but he waved his hand to reassure her. 'That's good,' he said, 'very good. Keep it up.'

'Thank you, sir. I will do my best,' she promised.

'I am very tempted to cut short your basic training right now,' he told her, 'whilst I still have a few able-bodied men left, but enthusiasm and insatiability are not enough, Candida. You must not only like sex, you must be able to control your sexuality. That is what lies behind all these games, and I must ensure that you can control your sexuality before I allow you to graduate from the Centre.'

'Oh, I'm sure I can, sir,' she told him.

'Really?' he asked her ironically, and he leant back in his chair. 'So you could, for example, easily withstand interrogation whilst being sexually humiliated?'

'Of course, sir,' she told him confidently.

'Very well,' he said. 'Why don't you sit down?' and he indicated a stout wooden chair with a leather seat, close to him and facing him, on his side of the desk. Candie went to sit down, but came to an abrupt halt. There was a stout, penis-shaped shaft protruding from the seat of the chair. She swallowed hard and looked at the Colonel in growing horror. He pushed a jar of lubricating cream over to her.

She felt her face become suffused with a deep blush, then turned away and put her hands down to lift her dress. 'Don't turn away,' he snapped. She turned back and faced him as she reached under her dress and eased off her G-string, then put her hand into the jar and applied the cream to her sex. Still facing him, she hitched up her skirt and put one hand on to the arms of the chair, then lowered herself slowly. She felt the device touch the lips of her vagina and paused for an instant, resisting the intense desire to spring up again. She felt her toes curl inside her shoes and she winced as she allowed her body to slide down on to the vibrating shaft, until her buttocks touched the seat. She released the pressure of her hand and slid down the final centimetre or so, burying the vibrator deep inside her.

'How does that feel?' he asked.

'Awful,' she said. The vibrator was already exciting her, and she could feel her nipples erecting. She put her arms down on to the chair, and discovered two sets of straps. He strapped down her arms, then knelt quickly and strapped her ankles to the stout legs of the heavy chair. He reached down and dropped her shoulder straps, so that her bodice fell down and exposed her breasts, then clipped a strapless bra around her. She felt cones that fitted closely over her nipples, and a moment later these too began to vibrate.

Candie opened her mouth, wriggling helplessly on the chair, held in place by the huge shaft that penetrated her sex.

'Now, how do you come to be here?' the Colonel asked her.

'I was working in London,' she said.

'What as?'

'A secretary.'

'Who for?'

'An Australian publishing company.'

'And?'

'I met a girl at a party. She told me . . .' She broke off, panting. 'Please,' she said desperately, 'turn them off.'

'Turn what off?'

'The vibrators.'

'Why?'

'I shall have an orgasm,' she sobbed.

'Tell me what you are doing here,' he repeated.

'I told you –'

'A pack of lies,' he snapped suddenly, thrusting his face close to hers. 'Now I want to know the truth, Candida. What are you really doing here?'

Candie was quite taken aback, and horrified at this sudden change of mood. What if the Colonel did really suspect her of being a spy?

'I was . . . working in London,' she began again, and repeated her story, but the physical titillation hindered her thought processes. The hum of the vibrators rose in pitch and his interrogation became more and more demanding.

'Let me go,' she cried. 'I can't stand it.'

'You will be released when you have told the truth and

not before,' he snarled, then turned the control up to full power, and she suddenly lost control. 'Oh my God, please . . . no, no,' she screamed aloud as her orgasm swept over her, and her body jerked and twisted helplessly on the seat for what seemed like an eternity, but the hum of the vibrators at last died away and she slumped in the chair.

'Well done,' the Colonel said, and she opened her eyes. 'I think that is enough for one day,' he said. She sat there panting, trying to control her thoughts. What if he did really suspect her? What if this was all part of a plan to make her confess? She was suddenly very scared.

Jenny was hiding in the bushes alongside the road leading to the Centre. After their frantic session the previous evening, Igor had returned, exhausted, to his hotel and Jenny had enjoyed a good night's sleep. He had rung her about nine that morning and had started to apologise for 'what had happened the previous evening,' but she had immediately faked a severe bout of amnesia. 'I remember that I intended to demonstrate the stimulator to you,' she had replied, 'but I don't remember a thing after that. I didn't get carried away or anything, did I?'

'Good Lord, no,' he'd replied, and they had moved on to other things. He had said he had a lead he wanted to follow up and she had agreed to keep an eye on the Centre. She looked up as she heard a car approach, then shrank back again into the bushes: it was not the one she was waiting for.

She had been very impressed by Marcel's performance with Candie the day before, and saw no reason not to combine a little business with pleasure. Marcel normally passed by at around this time and Jenny was all set to intercept him and try to obtain some information from him, but she realised that seducing Marcel was no easy matter. He had access to willing and submissive women twenty-four hours a day, so playing the submissive role would be no novelty, and she had therefore decided to act the brash, bossy role. She heard the big Mercedes coming and stepped out into the narrow road.

The day was hot and that justified shorts and a T-shirt, but Jenny knew that her shorts left a lot of her curvy bottom on show and her shirt was so sheer and transparent that her very sexy and well-filled lace bra showed clearly through it. The car stopped dead in its tracks and Jenny leant in through the passenger window.

'Are you going to Paris?' she asked, offering him a fine view of her cleavage. Her voice had lost its usual rather plummy accent and had taken on the Paris twang, self-assured and cocky, like all big-city accents. She quite naturally used the argot shared by the police, the pimps, the hookers and the small-time criminals.

'Hop in,' he said.

She threw her canvas bag into the car and climbed in, settling down comfortably as he drove off along the narrow country road. She sprawled in the wide seat, allowed her legs to part and saw his eyes flick to her thighs. The shorts were so skimpy that her little nylon panties peeped out and it was obvious that they were nearly transparent.

'Where are you going?' he asked.

'Place Blanche,' she said. 'I suppose you know where it is?'

'I should hope so,' he replied. Of course he knew where it was: that was where all the cabarets were. 'What do you do?' he asked.

'I'm a stripper,' she told him. He looked at her legs again.

'Really?' he asked in apparent surprise. 'When I saw you in that outfit, I had you down as a Sunday-school teacher.'

'I do that too,' she told him and looked at him coolly. 'What about you?' she asked, 'and don't tell me you're a chauffeur.'

'I work back there,' he told her, nodding his head backward, 'in the Centre.'

'What Centre?'

'The International Centre for the Study of Human Sexuality,' he told her. She looked at him, frowned, and burst out laughing.

'The what?' she asked. He repeated his statement.

'You're having me on,' she said. He searched around

and produced a business card. She looked at it and handed it back at him.

'I'll believe you,' she said. 'Thousands wouldn't. What do you do?'

'We study what turns men and women on.'

She laughed out loud again. 'Jesus wept,' she said. 'You mean you don't know?'

'You tell me.'

'I'm no good at explaining things,' she told him. 'I'm better at demonstrations.'

'I can imagine,' he said, and looked again at her thighs.

She looked at where he was looking and eased her shorts between her legs. 'If you can stop somewhere for a couple of minutes,' she said, 'I'd be very much obliged. I need to change into my working outfit.'

'You can change in the back,' he told her.

'With you looking in the mirror and your eyes out on organ stops?' she said. 'Not likely. I don't want to end up in the ditch.'

'I can pull off into the wood,' he suggested. 'There's a place for picknicking up there and there's nobody about.'

'You're sure you can spare the time?' she asked with mock concern.

'If it's in a good cause,' he replied, and they drove on.

'I really am a stripper,' she said after a pause, looking out of the window. 'I'm not on the game.'

'Me neither,' he replied.

'I don't believe in going without, mind you,' she explained, 'but I decide who with and it's never for money.'

'Me too,' he said. 'I never take money either.'

She laughed. 'You don't half fancy yourself,' she said. They drove on in silence for a few more minutes.

'Do you employ women at this Centre of yours?' she asked.

'Uh-huh.'

'To do what, or is that a stupid question?'

'Act as our sex slaves, of course,' he replied.

'I'm sure,' she said sarcastically, and looked at him sideways. 'Where men are concerned,' she told him, 'I give the orders.'

'Maybe you haven't come across a real man yet,' he told her.

She looked him over as if she was examining an animal at an agricultural show. 'Maybe you haven't come across a real woman yet,' she replied.

'Tell me if you see one,' he said dryly, and pulled off on to the winding forest track.

'You're a real old arse and trousers, you are,' she told him.

The car came to a halt in the clearing and they both climbed out. He opened the rear door for her and she emptied the contents of her shoulder-bag on to the seat.

There was a very skimpy black blouse and a vinyl miniskirt, a black satin corset with a sling-bra top, two packets of black fishnet stockings, two garter belts, several G-strings and a couple of bras, one of transparent net, the other open at the front. There was a shiny red plastic mini-raincoat to act as a cover-up.

She turned them over. 'Are you any good with electricity?' she asked.

'I get by.'

'Can you fix this?' she asked, and handed him a vibrator. It was a white plastic egg, with little plastic nodules all over it, and a lead to a control box.

'Is it part of the act?' he asked, 'or are you a DIY addict?'

'Depends on what else is around,' she replied, and took her shirt off over her head, then unfastened her shorts and took them off. Both her bra and panties were semi-transparent, so that her nipples and dark pubic hair were visible. He looked her over.

'I'm around,' he said.

'I can see that,' she said, looking at his erection, and stripped off her bra. She put her hands under her breasts and squeezed them, then picked up the open-front bra and slipped it on, adjusting the straps so that the garment lifted her breasts and made them protrude lasciviously. Her nipples were already erect.

'*Ca t'excite*?' she asked mockingly. 'Does it turn you on?'

'What do you do in your act?' he asked, ignoring her question.

'Get that thing going and I'll show you,' she said, then stripped off her trainers and panties, clipped a suspender belt around her hips, and sat on the picnic table to draw on her fishnet stockings. He was sitting in the car, busy twisting the contacts in the control box, but he looked up at her and caught a glimpse of her sex.

'You like putting it about, don't you?' he said.

'If you don't like it, don't look,' she replied, and fastened her suspenders one by one. He looked down and squeezed the contacts in the control box with a small pair of pliers he'd taken from the glove compartment. The vibrating egg suddenly burst into life.

'You're a genius,' she said. He switched the thing off and handed it to her. 'Do you still want to see what I do in my act?' she asked.

'Sure.'

'You're sure you have the time?' she asked mockingly.

'I have the time.'

She turned her back, licked the tip of one finger and rubbed it between her legs, then placed the egg inside the entrance to her vagina and eased it in, wincing slightly, twisting the device to get the pointed end well up into her sex. The vibrator had ribbons attached and she tied these around her hips, then slipped on a pair of brief scarlet nylon panties that she pulled up very tightly.

'Do you want any help?' he asked.

'I can manage,' she replied dryly, and put on her skirt and blouse. She looked at herself in the wing mirror and tucked the control box into her belt, then turned to face him.

He pushed a CD into the slot and sat down at the picnic table. The deep hard beat of a funky bass guitar burst from the car, with the shrill rippling squeal of a synthesiser bubbling over it like a mountain stream rushing over a rock. Facing him, she moved her hips from side to side in time with the beat, and switched on the vibrator. He heard the hum above the loud music and saw her catch her breath. She looked up and winced again, more expressively, obviously becoming sexually excited, then came nearer.

'Keep your paws to yourself,' she called out above the music as he lifted his hands. He dropped them obediently and slid round on the seat to face her. She came up close and thrust her cleavage against his face, so that he felt her firm up-lifted breasts against his cheeks. She thrust her body against Marcel's, straddled his knees, and sank down.

'Hands off,' she reminded him, and sat down astride him. His body jerked as the vibrating egg contacted his penis through his pants.

She opened her mouth, smiled at his discomfiture and thrust her breasts against him. Marcel was perspiring now. She started to move her hips, forward and backward, so that her vibrator titillated his cock. She used the vibrator to arouse both him and herself, and her own obvious arousal turned him on still more. The raw music throbbed and she felt his prick stiffen under her.

'That's as far as I go in public,' she said at last, 'otherwise the client's pants get ruined.' She pressed her egg down on to him and pushed her hips forward until the vibrations tickled the tip of his penis, then backed away and switched the device off, looking down at his very evident erection.

'What about in private?' he asked, gasping for breath.

'In private,' she said, 'I sort out the men from the boys.'

'Sort me out,' he told her.

Jenny reached down and unzipped Marcel's fly. He put his hands under her skirt but she pushed them away. 'Keep your hands above my waist,' she told him sharply, and took out his prick. She took the shaft in her hand, and raised it until it was vertical, then moved her hips forward, so that her vibrating egg contacted his bare cock. She switched it on and he felt the vibrator contact him just under the tip and force his penis back towards his body.

Marcel fumbled at her breasts through her thin satin blouse and felt for her nipples, his eyes opening wider. He moaned as her vibrator titillated the sensitive underside of his shaft. She eased her hips forward and backward, letting him feel her breasts and her hard erect nipples. She realised that the vibration against his frenum must be devastating, and she knew that if she kept up the pressure he'd come.

'Take that fucking thing out,' he snarled suddenly. She laughed in triumph as he lost control and yanked at her panties, ripping the lace trim as he felt for the catch. His hands wrestled with the tie of her vibrator, but at last it came free and he hurled it away and pulled her down on to his prick.

Jenny gasped as she felt his cock ram up into her. She was wet with lubrication so he entered her easily. She was already stimulated almost to the point of orgasm and he was equally in a desperate condition. She slid up and down, impaled on his prick, and the clearing echoed with her cries.

Jenny closed her eyes as she felt the pre-orgasm tremors start: she was all set to go when his car telephone rang.

Candie had just emerged from the bathroom, close by the Colonel's office, bathed and wearing a peignoir, when he took a telephone call. The Colonel phoned Marcel to recall him, called Sapphi into his office, and hurriedly started an ad hoc council of war.

'What do you know about the Centre?' he asked Candie.

'I know, of course, that the Centre is involved in scientific research into human sexuality,' she replied, 'but I was also given to understand that the Centre is an undercover organisation, and works for various Government agencies.'

'Exactly,' he replied. 'Now, of course, we could not take you into our confidence about the undercover work until you had completed your basic training. However, I think we are now agreed that, in view of your particular attributes and enthusiasm, we may regard your training as complete.'

He looked at Sapphi, who nodded her agreement. 'One of our chief suspects has just arrived in Paris unexpectedly,' explained the Colonel. 'He is prone to certain sexual fantasies, which concern sex in the office environment.'

'You mean, he likes to have an undressed girl in his office, pretending to be his secretary?' Candie asked.

'Rather more than that,' she was told. 'She has to be a fully trained, totally competent and very intelligent executive-level secretary, and his fantasy requires that, each time he comes here, he employs a new temporary secretary, who is subjected to to all kinds of sexual outrage –'

'Without running screaming out of the office, or telling the newspapers, or blackmailing him afterwards?' Candie interjected.

'Just so,' the Colonel replied. 'People with that kind of fantasy need an agency that can provide what they want, with guarantees that the girl will keep quiet afterwards.'

'We own such an agency,' Sapphi told her, picking up the story. 'It provides temporary staff for almost any job that women normally do – secretaries, nurses, models, designers, decorators: you name it, our girls do it. They are all guaranteed expert at their jobs. In addition, however, they are all attractive, personable and sexually available.'

'So you want me to pretend to work for your agency?' Candie asked.

'Exactly,' Sapphi explained. 'You will have to submit to his rather childish fantasies, but at the same time perform your office duties as if everything was normal.'

'Try to worm your way into his confidence,' the Colonel instructed her. 'He usually keeps the girls for just one afternoon, but we know that he usually stays here for a few days. Try to persuade him to keep you on. Find out who his clients are, what he does for them, who else is involved, everything you can. Can you manage that?'

'I can try,' Candie told him. She was secretly pleased to get away and escape further interrogation, but rather appalled at all the layers of deceit that were building up around her.

Nine

Igor was busy with his own investigations, but neither Candie nor Jenny might have been too sympathetic if they had seen what he was doing. He was, in fact, sitting in a darkened theatre in a side street near the Moulin Rouge, and was taking off a young woman's panties.

She was a big, healthy-looking English rosebud with the kind of bottom a girl gets by hacking and showjumping from an early age, so that her panties were very tight and he had problems with the clip. 'Hurry up,' she whispered, 'I'm already five bars behind.' The clip opened and she made a great show of outraged modesty as he stripped off her panties, but then she exposed herself and took her applause, facing the audience, totally naked but quite at ease.

As the applause died away a slim, rather shy-looking, fair-haired man came on to the stage and approached her from behind. He put his arms around her and began to stroke her breasts. She pretended for a moment to be surprised, and then grinned over her shoulder at him.

The girl submitted to her partner's embraces for a few moments, then she turned to face him and they kissed. His hands explored her back and her buttocks and she responded more and more eagerly. After a few more moments, he sat down on a low bed and began to kiss her body. His mouth roamed over her breasts and Igor saw her nipples erect. She was obviously genuinely aroused now, and she panted and wriggled as he kissed and fondled her. Igor sensed that she was shutting out the knowledge of the audience, pretending to be alone with her lover.

She pushed him down on to the bed, knelt over him and parted her legs, offering him her sex. There were mirrors everywhere so that the audience missed nothing, and Igor felt his own arousal grow as he saw her voluptuous sex. Her full, luscious labia were beginning to part and her partner's tongue reached up to lick her slit.

She turned around and began to unfasten his jeans as the young man opened her and licked her sex more positively. She eased them off, and then his underpants. Now it was her turn to arouse him, and she went down on him, taking his penis in her mouth. He was well-built, with a long rod-like prick, initially flaccid, but it soon began to grow and harden.

They now ignored the audience completely and concentrated all their attention on their foreplay. His prick grew longer and longer under her ministrations and her hands and mouth moved more positively. His hand was now between her legs and the mirrors showed his fingers inside her sex, masturbating her, feeling for her clit.

They whispered together and changed position. She lay down, her legs towards the audience, and he knelt between her parted knees. Igor saw his erect prick pointing just above her vagina as she took him in her hands, pressed down the tip and inserted him into her sex. The audience gave a communal sigh as the young man entered her. Igor saw the distortion of her vagina as he penetrated her, and her labia dragged at his shaft. The young man went in and in, pausing occasionally until she nodded and wriggled slightly, until the whole of his long rod was inside her body.

The young couple began their intercourse. The man pistonned her gently but firmly, and after a while they rolled into a new position without missing a stroke. It was an erotic but controlled ballet: both were graceful and moved like trained dancers and always his penis thrust in and pulled out, regularly, smoothly, like a well-oiled engine.

Igor licked his lips and leant forward, absorbed by the show. This was by no means the first time he'd seen a live sex-on-stage show, but it was much more lyrical than most. It was good to be hard at work, he thought to himself, whilst Jenny was holding the fort over at the Centre.

Gabrielle told Giorgio to stop at an intersection in the narrow streets to the north of Les Halles, regardless of the fact that the big car completely blocked the traffic. She climbed out, lifted her overnight case out of the car and walked off, oblivious to the din of car horns all around her. Giorgio threw up his hands, blew his horn, then ran down his window and leant out. He shouted to the man in front of him to get out of the fucking way, which was transparently impossible, then bellowed to the man behind, who was blowing his horn at him, pointing out that any cunt with one eye could see that he was unable to move.

Gaby wore big wrap-around sun glasses and a simple dress, but felt very conspicuous, especially when she passed the indecently dressed girls half hidden in the dark alleyways, or lolling around outside the striptease and video parlours. She felt her heartbeat increase and had to fight down the urge to turn on her heels and run. Her mouth became dry as she paused to look into the window of the dress shop that Vivienne had told her about, and she looked back and made sure that her car had moved away before she went inside.

A tall, straight-backed woman, whose eyes had seen everything, came forward and looked at her inquiringly.

'I have an appointment with Carl,' she told her. 'My name is Gabrielle.'

'Through here.' The woman opened a door at the back of the shop and escorted Gabrielle into a store room, then up a flight of stairs, and knocked on another door. A deep masculine voice called, 'Come in,' and she opened the door and ushered Gabrielle in.

Carl looked to be in his mid-thirties, with a compact hard-muscled body that he no doubt worked out every day of the year. He was extremely handsome and looked as if knew it. His eyes were light blue and piercing; his mouth rather thin and cruel; his hands fastidiously manicured and he was very closely shaved. He was sitting at a table, reading the sports pages of a newspaper, and he looked at her over the top of it.

'I'm Gabrielle. Vivienne sent me,' she said.

'To do what?' he asked. His voice was deep, with a mocking edge to it. She put her bag down on the desk, but he didn't invite her to take a seat.

'She said you might allow me to work for you,' she explained.

'Have you worked out there before?' he asked, nodding towards the window.

She shook her head. 'No,' she told him.

'Do you need the money?' he asked.

'No,' she told him again. He folded the newspaper and put it down.

'Why do you want to do it?' he asked.

She licked her lips and looked down at her hands as she twisted them together, then she shrugged. 'I don't know,' she murmured. 'To see how it feels, I suppose.'

'To see how it feels?' he asked her mockingly.

She blushed and looked down. 'Did you ever see an old Bunuel film called *Belle de Jour*?' she asked him.

'Sure,' he replied. 'Deneuve played a rich, pampered bitch, who went whoring for kicks in the afternoons.'

'That's me,' she explained. 'I'm a rich, pampered bitch, and I want to go whoring for kicks in the afternoons.'

'Turn around,' he said. She turned around slowly and faced him again. 'You're well stacked,' he admitted. 'Show me your legs.'

She caught her breath and felt her blush run down into her cleavage, but reached down and hitched up her skirt to show him her legs: she was wearing black stockings with a gold-thread decoration, and a matching suspender belt.

'I brought an outfit with me,' she told him, holding up her hem to show the tops of her stockings and an inch of her suspenders. 'Would you like to see it?'

'Sure I'd like to see it.'

She shook down her hem and took a flimsy light blue suit out of her bag. 'It has a very deep décollettée and I shortened the skirt,' she explained, holding it up. 'Do you want to see it on?'

'Sure I do,' he said.

She looked around. 'Do you want me to change here?' she asked.

'Why not?' He looked at her and she blushed more deeply. 'Sorry, I seem to have mislaid the screen,' he observed sarcastically.

She put her hand up to her neckline and started to unbutton her dress. Her hands trembled in spite of her efforts and her fingers were so clumsy they fumbled over the buttons. Finally she pulled her dress angrily over her head, then shook and patted her hair into place. Her undies were feminine and very expensive, but she now realised that they were elegant rather than sexy.

He held out his hand and she passed her dress over to him. He turned back the collar and looked at the designer's label.

'You're too high class for down there,' he told her, nodding towards the window. 'You should be in a *maison*.'

She picked up her skirt. 'I tried it,' she told him, stepping into it. 'The clients were just like my husband. They were interested in the same things, told the same jokes and knew the same people. It wasn't what I wanted.'

She pulled the skirt up. It was very tight around her hips and the outline of her suspenders and panties showed through. She blushed and tugged awkwardly at the skirt but her suspender ribbons peeped below the hem. She felt her nipples erect under her bra: she had deliberately shortened the skirt to make it indecent, and now she felt ridiculous.

'I'm over thirty,' she told him.

'So are they,' he reminded her, nodding again towards the window, 'and they haven't got your looks.' Gaby felt a little better as she slipped on the jacket and fastened the button, then produced some matching shoes with very high heels. She sat down and went to take off her shoes, very awkwardly, trying not to show her panties.

'This isn't a convent,' he reminded her. 'Stop covering

yourself up.' She blushed again, but let her legs open momentarily, then turned her body away as her natural modesty overwhelmed her. 'For Christ's sake,' he said in exasperation, 'give the guy something to look at.' She opened her legs wider and hesitated. He would be able to see her panties now. She breathed in deeply, then deliberately opened her legs wide and lifted one leg to pull on her shoe, knowing that her panties would not conceal her sex and he would be able to see her labia glistening against her dark pubic hair. She stood up, teetering slightly, and tugged ineffectually at her hem.

'What do you think?' she asked anxiously, and looked down. The edge of her bra showed above the swooping neckline and she looked erotic with her suspender ribbons on show, but she knew it was pretty low-key stuff for that area.

'Come here,' he said. She came and stood facing him, her bosom rising and falling. He reached out and pulled open her neckline so that her bra spilled out, then hitched her skirt up higher to show the tops of her stockings.

'Like that,' he told her, 'and stand with your legs apart.'

She slid her legs apart and put her hands in her pockets, then pushed her stomach forward, trying to achieve the magic mix of innocence and insolence that makes a man horny.

'I brought a couple of bras with a bit more uplift,' she told him, 'and some G-strings and things,' and she picked up her bag, extracted her underwear and put it on his desk in front of him, then stood there, biting her lip and looking at him from under her long lashes. The lingerie she had brought with her was very erotic and quite indecent, and she was lubricating heavily at the thought of having to strip and change into her sexy undies in front of him.

Carl pushed them to one side and tilted his head sideways. 'Take your pants off,' he told her.

Gaby gave a little gasp: she felt her heart race and her face pucker as if she was about to cry, but she reached under her skirt and pulled her panties down and off, teetering on her high heels. He held out his hand. She gulped in shame and humiliation but handed him the soft, warm, silky garment. He took it from her and looked her in the eyes as he felt the wetness, then raised the garment to his face and smelled her perfume and the musky odour of her sex.

'If he wants to buy your panties, it's another three hundred,' he told her. She nodded and he shifted his eyes down. She looked down too: her flimsy skirt was tight enough for the bulge of her pubic hair to show, and it was obvious she had no panties on.

'Let's see you play with yourself,' he said. She caught her breath at this new challenge, then put her hands over her breasts and squeezed them. She looked down and put her hand under one breast, lifted it out of the cup and titillated her nipple with the tip of her forefinger, feeling the ripples of excitement race from her breast to her womb.

'One man in four will want to watch you play with yourself while he brings himself off,' he told her. 'Make it look good.'

She eased out her other breast, licked her fingers and played with both nipples. She moved her body lasciviously and moaned softly as she explored her nipples. 'Between my legs too?' she asked breathlessly.

'Sure.'

She gulped, stepped back a little and put her hands against the sides of her hips, over her skirt, feeling her face become scarlet. 'Up or off?' she asked him.

'That's up to you,' he told her.

She hesitated. 'It feels worse with it up,' she told him at last.

'Then pull it up,' he told her.

She eased her tight skirt up, wriggling her hips, looking down. When the skirt was just about to uncover her sex, she hesitated, then looked up at him, her face burning with a deep blush, and the tip of her tongue danced over her upper lip. She put her hand down to cover her pudenda as her other hand lifted the skirt.

'It's your cunt he's paying to look at,' he reminded her, and she gasped at his crudeness, knowing it was deliberate and intended to arouse and humiliate her.

She whimpered, but sank down into the chair, then opened her legs. She gulped and blushed furiously, then took her hand away, hesitated for a long time, then hooked one leg over the arm of the chair and exposed herself completely.

'I feel awful,' she whispered. She could feel her sex starting to peel open.

'You look great,' he told her.

Her carmine nails explored her curls and touched the tip of her vagina. She put her first and third fingers on either side of her labia, pressing outward with her fingertips, whilst her second finger hovered. Her vagina peeled open and she moved her second finger into the slippery crevice. Her bosom heaved as she drew in her breath and felt the excitement flash through her body.

'Tell me what to do when I'm with a client,' she said. Her second finger plunged into her sex and explored the inner wall. She gasped and her body arched as her lubrication flooded from her.

'You're selling sex,' he told her. 'Raw sex. Three hundred francs, ten to fifteen minutes; he pays, he fucks you, he goes.'

She winced again at his crudeness but his harsh words excited her still more and her finger plunged deep into her sex. 'Isn't that what you want?' he asked sharply.

She nodded quickly. 'I don't want to know anything about them, and I don't want them to know anything about me,' she told him.

'You've got it,' he told her.

'What do I do for them?' she asked.

'Whatever they want, but if they leave it to you, you give them a blow job.'

She licked her lips. 'Show me how,' she said.

He stood up and came over to stand astride her. She reached up to unzip his fly and extracted his cock. He was stiffly erect and his penis was circumcised and glistened in front of her eyes. Her mouth closed eagerly over the tip. She licked him all around the stiff red knob, then leant forward and took him into her mouth.

'Don't do it like this with a client,' he warned her, 'but if he gets you into this position, place your hand flat against his stomach and hold him away.' She did as he instructed her, feeling the coiled-up muscles under his smooth skin.

'Lick,' he said. 'Use your tongue. Squeeze my balls.'

She licked all around the tip of his cock, and fondled his balls and perineum, stroking him gently and persuasively. He looked down at her, totally in control, able to take her or leave her.

'Stand up,' he said, then stretched out on a bed to one side of the room.

'Make him lie on his back, like this,' he told her. 'Now go down on me.' She leant over him and began to fellate him again.

'This way you're in control,' he told her, reaching out with his hand. 'Move around,' he told her. She wriggled around and felt his hand stroke her thighs, then she opened her legs to show him her sex. He let her fellate him for a few more minutes whilst he caressed her buttocks and sex, then he reared up again, pushed her to one side and leapt off the bed with a single spring of his beautifully muscled body.

'Lie down,' he told her. She lay on her back and opened her legs, drawing up her knees. He knelt over her and she reached out and took his cock, inserted the tip into her vagina, and lifted her hips. He put his hand under her and supported her bottom as he penetrated her. She closed her eyes and opened her mouth as he entered her, gasping as his penis opened her vagina and ravished her body.

'No fancy stuff,' he told her, 'unless he's prepared to pay for extra time.' His penis moved back and then thrust deep into her body. She gasped aloud and moved her hips forward to welcome his thrust. He withdrew and then thrust in again, deeper. She cried out and began to lose control, moaning and undulating as she began her run-up to orgasm. He stopped fucking her and looked down at her.

'You don't ever, ever, come with a client,' he told her

quietly. 'A woman who does that is too disgusting for words. She is an abomination, you understand, an abomination.' She nodded, then panicked as she felt him withdraw. 'I want you,' she moaned, thrusting her body against him. 'I want you, Carl. Please, I want you.'

He withdrew. 'Go get me some money,' he told her with a savage grin, 'and maybe I'll consider fucking you.'

Ten

Jenny had overheard enough of Marcel's conversation to know that Candie was involved in some kind of crisis and was therefore likely to leave the Centre, so that, when Marcel dropped her off, she decided to keep watch. She had no binoculars and so couldn't go too far away, and the only vantage point was up on the hill overlooking the road, which meant entering the private wood where she had met the gamekeeper, which in turn meant negotiating a high wire-mesh fence. She hid her bag in some bushes, found a spot nearby where a tree grew close to the fence, climbed up and used an overhanging branch to scramble over the fence, then made her way up to a point where she could lie down and observe the road.

Her patience was rewarded a few minutes later. She crouched down as she heard a car approach. It was moving very fast but as it swept by she caught a glimpse of Marcel driving, with Candie in the back. It was time to send an urgent message to Igor.

She waited until the car was out of sight, and was just about to get up, when she felt something touch her bare leg. She froze, then looked around. The friendly little spaniel from the day before was licking her leg, pleased to rediscover his sweet-smelling pal.

Jenny rolled over and sat up. The dog gave a little bark of welcome and looked at her with its head on one side. She stood up cautiously and patted the dog, wanting it to remain quiet, then looked back towards the fence she had crossed.

The gamekeeper was there, examining the fence, and

Jenny realised there must have been a tripwire or an electronic beam device or something that had given her away. He picked up a field telephone that was fixed close to the gate and turned the handle. She saw him speak into the telephone and put it down again.

The man was looking around now and she knew that she must have left a trail. The dog barked again and frolicked around her. She made shooing motions towards it but it just stood there with its head on one side.

She cursed her imprudence. If she ran away, the dog would follow her, and she had no idea of the terrain, whereas the gamekeeper was on his home ground. The dog barked again and the man called out to it. It took no notice, and then another dog appeared on the other side of the fence, another spaniel, but bigger; probably the parent of the puppy that danced around her. The gamekeeper opened the gate and let it through.

The bigger dog had found her bag and Jenny realised at once that she had no chance now. The older dog was a trained hunting animal and would be able to follow her scent. The man would be able to follow her trail and the puppy would probably follow her anyway, wherever she went.

She stood up and went to meet the gamekeeper. 'Hi,' she called, and waved her hand as soon as she was within sight and earshot.

He waited for her to come close, and sighed. 'Oh no, not you again,' he said. 'What are you doing here?'

'I was looking for you,' she said. 'May I have my bag, please?'

'Half a minute,' he said. He had the bag already open, and he reached inside and took out her bra. He looked at it, then peered inside the bag, then looked up at her and licked his lips.

'You shouldn't have come over the fence,' he said. 'You set the alarm off. Now I've got to go and reset it.'

'I can wait.'

He looked around, obviously worried. 'They don't like people wandering around in here,' he told her.

'Then don't tell them,' she told him.

'Up there,' he said, and motioned for her to go ahead of him.

She walked ahead of him, knowing his eyes were on her bottom in her scanty shorts. She could sense his unease, his fear of being found with her battling against his desire to have sex with her again.

'What do they call you?' he asked.

'Marie-Ange. What's your name?'

'Gaston.' They were walking now along a narrow path between high hedges, going deeper and deeper into the woods.

'Why aren't you at work?' he asked.

'I'm on holiday,' she told him. They turned a corner and Jenny saw they were approaching a barn. He opened the padlock on the door and ushered her in.

'You liked it yesterday?' he asked, once they were safely inside.

'Why do you think I came back?' she asked.

He grabbed her and pulled her to him. She let her body merge into his, let him feel her breasts and belly, and felt his erection sticking into her. She put her arms up around his neck and pulled his head down to kiss him.

'You'd give a saint a hard-on,' he said, his hands holding her buttocks, pulling her up tight against him.

She pulled her top off with a swift movement and pressed her bare breasts against his rough hunting jacket. He felt rough and smelt of the earth and animals, but he was arousing her again with his virility. 'I didn't know you were a saint,' she told him.

He fondled her breasts and her nipples hardened. His eyes gleamed with satisfaction and he unzipped her shorts and pushed his other hand between her thighs, into the top of her brief panties. She spread her legs and let him in. He stroked her sex for a moment, and she felt his penis become harder and more erect as he did so.

'I have to go fix that alarm,' he said, panting. He wanted to take her now, but he was scared someone might find out what he was doing. Jenny wondered why they were so concerned about trespassers. 'Why don't you go fix it, then?' she suggested. 'I can get dressed for the occasion, and maybe you could bring back a bottle of something.'

He took his hand away reluctantly. 'I won't be gone a minute,' he said, and went to the door. 'I have to put the lock on,' he explained, 'in case somebody comes past and notices it's undone. For Christ's sake keep quiet if anybody comes near.'

The Mercedes stopped beside a taxi rank near La Defense, the big business complex to the north-west of Paris. Marcel opened the door for Candie and wished her, '*Bonne chance*,' as she climbed into a taxi. She gave the driver the address and a few minutes later she arrived at a huge tower block of offices.

She walked into the tower, across to the reception desk, and said, 'VIP Secs for –'

'Ah yes,' the girl said at once. 'Seventeenth floor. Turn right when you leave the lift.'

Candie felt the girl's eyes on her as she walked away. In line with her new role, she was dressed in a smart but decent black suit with a pencil-slim skirt and medium-heeled shoes. Her hair was dressed neatly; she wore dark-rimmed spectacles that made her eyes seem lighter and bigger, and she carried a briefcase, but she suspected that the receptionist knew very well that VIP Secs could be spelt two ways.

She followed the instruction and a few moments later knocked at an unmarked door. A woman's voice called 'Come in,' and she entered.

A tall, slim, elegant, aristocratic young woman looked her up and down from behind an ornate desk. 'VIP Secs,' Candie told her, and handed her the introductory letter. The woman read it carefully.

'Which languages do you speak, read and write?' she asked. She had virtually no accent and her face was a mask, beautifully made up but expressionless.

'English, French and German,' Candie replied.

'What experience have you had with word processing on an IBM PC?'

'WORD 6, WORD for WINDOWS, WORD-PERFECT –'

'They will do.' She handed a small notebook to Candie and sat her down, then dictated a letter to her in English, then another in French. She then asked her to read them back, as dictated, and then translate into the other language. Both texts were spattered with business terminology and jargon, and contained a number of traps for the unwary, but Candie avoided them all. The young woman then bombarded her with questions about French and English business procedures, and again she passed with flying colours.

'Well, you seem to be reasonably proficient,' the woman admitted at last. 'Stand up, please.'

Candie stood up. 'His work is extremely confidential,' the woman explained, 'and he is very security-conscious. I have to search you to make sure you do not have any microphones or anything concealed on you.' She looked Candie in the eyes. 'Have you any objections?' she asked frostily.

'Go ahead,' Candie replied.

'The search has to be carried out in front of him,' the woman told her. 'He likes to see everything for himself.'

Candie drew in her breath as she felt her heart leap, but she faked indifference and shrugged her shoulders. 'It's novel,' she admitted, then went on, 'but hadn't you better make sure I am wearing the right kind of underwear?'

'If you had let me continue,' the woman said, even more icily, 'I would have told you that I have to search you first for weapons.'

'I can't wait,' Candie told her.

'Take off your jacket,' the girl said coldly. Candie unfastened her jacket, took it off, then breathed in. The woman looked at her black satin under-wired brassière and took the jacket from her. She felt it expertly, making sure there was nothing hidden in the lining or the shoulder pads. 'Mind the buttons,' Candie told her. 'They're packed full of Semtex.'

'Do not make jokes like that,' the girl said frostily. 'Take off your skirt and keep quiet.'

Candie took off her skirt and kept quiet. The girl came up close and ran her hands over Candie's bra. Candie's nipples immediately leapt into life, and the girl ran her fingertips over the points, pressing in slightly through the thin satin.

'Are you bisexual?' she asked.

'Yes. Are you?' Candie asked, looking at her appreciatively. The woman wore a wild-silk patterned dress over nothing much, and her breasts were smallish but firm and well-shaped. She put her hand out but the woman pushed her away.

'Not now,' she said. 'We may be required to make love later.'

'In there?' Candie asked, nodding towards the inner sanctum.

The girl nodded. 'If we're going to be that friendly,' said Candie, 'may I perhaps know your name?'

'Vivienne.' She ran her exploratory fingertips over Candie's bottom and investigated her suspender belt.

'What will he want me to do?' Candie asked.

'I am not allowed to tell you.' She ran her hands over Candie's legs, up and down. 'He is quite harmless,' she assured her and eased aside Candie's French panties. The tip of her second finger investigated Candie's sex.

Candie yelped as she touched her clit. 'He may be harmless,' she said, drawing in her breath, 'but what about you, Viv?'

Vivienne looked her in the eyes. 'You call me Viv again,' she said quietly, 'and I'll kick your teeth in.' She came from Beirut: Candie recognised her accent now that she had dropped her pose.

'You don't take anything with you when you leave,' Vivienne told her. 'No papers, no cards, no disks, nothing. Understand?'

'Yes.'

'Once you leave, you forget everything that has happened, and everything you have done, seen and heard,' she went on. 'Everything. Is that clear?'

'Yes.'

'Then don't forget,' Vivienne told her. She unclipped a catch and her silk dress rustled to the ground. Under it, she wore a very slinky, sexy, hip-length mini-slip, also in an expensive patterned wild silk, with brief matching panties and sheer stockings.

'I'd kill for a slip like that,' Candie told her. 'Where did you get it?'

'Alaïa.'

'It must have cost the earth.'

'Much more than you could afford,' Vivienne told her contentedly, and picked up a gold-plated ivory-handled telephone. 'The girl from the agency is here,' she said, listened for a moment, then put down the phone. 'This way,' she said, opening a double door and led the way into the inner sanctum.

A tall man with well-manicured hands, his dark hair just greying at the temples, looked up from an ornate and almost empty desk. He had an aquiline nose, and an aristocratic expression. He looked at Candie disdainfully.

'Is she competent?' he asked his side-kick. He spoke perfect well-modulated French, also with a very slight trace of the Lebanon.

'She seems to be,' Vivienne replied.

'Very well,' he said, and sighed languidly. 'Get on with it.'

Candie faced him across the desk. Vivienne said, 'Hands above your head please: take hold of the rings.'

Candie looked up. Two rings hung from the ceiling, just to her side of his desk. She stepped forward until she almost touched the desk and reached up to hold on to the rings. They descended a little as she slipped her fingertips through them.

'Legs wide apart,' Vivienne instructed her.

Candie looked down. There were two places marked on the floor, very wide apart. She pushed her feet out sideways but her pencil-slim skirt constrained her movements.

She felt herself blush. She would have to hitch it right up to get her legs that far apart.

'Hurry up,' Vivienne said sharply. Candie breathed in,

then reached down and wriggled her skirt up and up, almost to her waist. She felt her blush deepen as she managed to spread her legs sufficiently wide apart, and again reached up to take hold of the rings.

The man looked her up and down. She was still wearing her spectacles and she knew that her conventional suit and rather drab appearance must heighten the erotic impact of her humiliation. He was obviously enjoying himself, and Candie was sure he must be excited by the sight of her, standing before him, spread-eagled, but he was carefully concealing his arousal.

His eyes travelled down to focus directly on her sex, where her plump curvy thighs came together, and she knew that her tiny French panties would not cover her when she was stretched like that. He looked up again into her eyes, and she could sense his excitement under his calm exterior.

'Keep hold of the rings,' Vivienne told her. 'If you release them, you lose the job.'

The man pressed a button under the desk and the cords that held up the rings tightened. Candie felt the rings pulled upward and outward. She hooked her fingers through them, but had to raise herself on to her toes to hang on.

The hum stopped. Candie was now stretched out as taut as a violin string, reaching up on her toes to hang on to the rings. She could feel the pressure in her chest and had some difficulty in breathing. Her heart was pounding and she could hear herself panting.

Vivienne went behind her, reached around, unfastened her jacket, opened it, and showed him Candie's bosom.

'Search her,' her boss said.

Candie felt Vivienne's long cool fingers explore her breasts through the thin satin of her bra. She closed her eyes momentarily.

'Look at me,' he said sharply. She opened her eyes and looked at him through her sensible school-marmish spectacles as her nipples erected. Vivienne's expert fingers played with them, caressing the sensitive pinnacles through the thin satin. She choked back the cry that welled up in her throat, and hung on to the rings with the tips of her fingers as the Lebanese girl aroused her.

Vivienne's hand explored the central catch of her brassière, and Candie gave a little sob as she felt the tension release. The brassière fell open, and Candie's breasts thrust out over his desk, her nipples just above the level of his eyes. Vivienne's fingers kneaded her breasts and caressed her nipples, and Candie opened her mouth and gasped helplessly as her excitement mounted.

She felt Vivienne's hands leave her breasts and reach down, then pull her hem even higher. She felt the woman caress her thighs, high up, above her stockings, where she was most sensitive. She sobbed again and gripped the rings with all her strength, willing herself not to close her legs. The hands crept up and up and moved on to the soft inner surfaces of her thighs. Candie felt the hands hesitate just below the hem of her panties, and knew that Vivienne had felt the lubrication that trickled down her leg, adding to her humiliation.

The hands moved up again and stroked her pudenda over the satin. Candie almost went wild, and had to grit her teeth to hang on to the rings. She felt Vivienne fumble for the button at the waistband of her panties. The button slipped through the buttonhole and her panties fell down to mid-thigh, exposing her sex to his gaze.

Candie was half mad with shame and humiliation. The luxurious office surroundings emphasised her blatant exposure and she knew that she could release herself at any moment. It was worse than being tied up, to know that she could escape; it meant that she was accepting this torture willingly. She imagined the kinky satisfaction he gained by doing this, by taking an intelligent, highly trained, sophisticated woman and turning her into an apparently willing sex object. It was the sheer, raw, revolting power of money in action. Then she remembered that she was cheating him; that she wasn't what he thought she was; that she was here to harm him, to eavesdrop on him, to betray him. The thought gave her new courage.

She looked him in the eyes as Vivienne slid her fingers

up into her vagina, turning the intimate body search into an exercise in sophisticated masturbation. Her body twitched and jerked as the girl explored her sex cavity, then jerked again, much more vigorously, as Vivienne deliberately titillated her clitoris.

What woman could withstand such treatment? Candie knew she could not possibly remain stretched out like that, right in front of him, with her sex just inches from his amused disdainful gaze, and go into orgasm. Her body would shriek and yell at her. She would cry out and double up, push the woman away, yell at the man and beat at him with her fists, then run screaming from this hell hole, out into the sensible world. She was going to fail on her first mission: she couldn't take any more.

The titillation suddenly ceased. 'You may release the rings,' said Vivienne. Candie let them go and eased her feet together. The man stood up and quickly left the office by a side door.

'I suppose you'd like to use the powder room,' Vivienne said, quite sympathetic for once in her life. Candie nodded dumbly, still in shock.

'Is that all?' she asked.

'It is for the moment,' the girl said.

Eleven

Igor sat in the darkened bar at the back of Les Chattes Sauvages, sipping a beer as he watched a new stripper perform. As in most such cabarets, the stripping was just a prelude, and the girl performed most of her act naked. The petite, long-haired blonde had moved around the audience, making whispered invitations, and the men had obediently removed her clothes. Once naked, she had produced a flesh-coloured dildo and now performed with it on stage.

The man who had just finished his act flopped on to a stool beside Igor and ordered a beer.

'Let me get it for you,' Igor offered. 'You've earned it.'

'Thanks.' The man raised his glass and took a deep draught, then looked up as his partner appeared. She sat down alongside him and Igor ordered a *Perrier-menthe* for her.

'She's Suzie; I'm Hans,' the man said, by way of introduction.

'Are you English?' Igor asked her as they shook hands. She nodded. 'I come from Budleigh Salterton,' she confirmed. 'You can't get more English than that. What about you?'

'I'm Australian,' he replied.

'You don't look it.'

'My family originally came from Russia,' he explained, taking out his wallet to pay for the drinks. As he did so, he 'accidentally' dropped a business card and Hans picked it up and handed it back to him. Igor looked at it with a frown, as if it had just triggered his memory. 'I'm supposed to look up an old friend who works for this organisation,' he said, and showed the card to Hans. 'They seem to be ex-directory,' he added. 'You don't happen to know anything about them, do you?'

Suzie leant over to look at the card. 'CIESH?' she asked, and frowned. 'Paul had something to do with them, didn't he?' she asked, and Hans nodded.

'Who's Paul?' Igor asked.

'He's a photographer: he works with a girl called Pascale,' Hans explained. 'A lot of men fancy themselves as blue-film actors – what the French call '*hardeurs*',' he went on. 'Pascale and Paul sort out the no-hopers, especially those who can't maintain an erection with a bunch of cameramen peering up their backsides.'

'It can't be easy,' Igor said, 'but I shouldn't think many men can do what you do: that's a really fantastic act you have there.'

'Had,' Suzie said. 'Hans's father died recently,' she explained. 'He's going back home to run the family business.'

Hans yawned. 'I'm getting too old for this game,' he said.

'You aren't going with him?' Igor asked Suzie.

'Settle down by the *Ijsselmeer*?' she asked, and laughed out loud. 'His home town makes Budleigh Salterton look like the roaring forties,' she told Igor. 'It would drive me mad in a week.'

'You're mad anyway,' the Dutchman told her, and turned to Igor. 'We're going to Paul's studio right now, as it happens,' he told him. 'If you'd like to come along, we'll introduce you.'

'Thank you.' Igor followed his new friends out into the late-afternoon sunshine and they strolled along in a group. 'How did you two get into this business?' he asked them.

'We both started in ballet,' Suzie replied, 'but we moved into modern dance in our teens: we met up in the chorus line at the Lido and decided to try our luck on our own.'

'You certainly made a go of it,' Igor told them, then turned to Hans. 'Won't you miss it?' he asked.

'Very likely,' Hans admitted, 'but it's quite a strain.'

'You're on edge all the time,' Suzie explained. 'There's all the usual problems and tensions that go with any form of dancing; pulled muscles, the grind of the exercises, rehearsing every day, trying out new ideas, and then the performance itself – but then of course there's the sexual tension on top of it all.'

'So, if you want to replace me,' Hans said jokingly, 'you have been warned.'

'How did he guess what I was thinking?' Igor asked Suzie with a smile, but she looked at him quite seriously.

'Did you train as a dancer?' she asked him.

'I was hailed in my teens as a promising nut-cracker,' Igor admitted, 'but when I did my Firebird, they had to call out the *pompiers*.'

'Seriously,' she said, 'were you any good?'

Igor shrugged. 'I knew I'd never be another Helpmann,' he admitted, 'but the Australian Dance Theatre told me I could have made a career out of it.'

'Have you kept in shape?' she asked.

'Don't answer her,' Hans broke it quickly. 'Don't have anything to do with this woman: she is extremely bossy.'

'I am not bossy,' Suzie protested sharply, but at that moment they arrived at a small studio, hidden away down a side street, and went inside. '*Bonjour*, Pascale,' she said.

'Hello, Suzie.' A pretty, rather plump ash-blonde came forward, followed by a tall, pale, bearded man. There was the usual ritual of cheek kissing and hand shaking, then Pascale turned to Igor. 'Have you found a replacement for Hans?' she asked, frankly admiring the newcomer. She had a dimpled baby face and laughing, mischievous eyes, and she seemed to have kept quite a lot of her puppy fat, which was certainly well-distributed.

'Not really,' Suzie replied. 'He's trying to get in touch with an organisation called – what was it?' she asked, turning to Igor.

'Centre Internationale d'Etudes sur la Sexualité Humaine', he replied.

'The Centre? They have a place in the country near

Compiègne,' Paul told him at once. 'We helped them out a few months ago with some studies they were doing.'

'Studies about what?' Suzie asked.

'What kind of clothes turn men on,' Pascale replied.

'You should know,' Hans chipped in. 'You're just about the best *chauffeuse* in Paris.' Igor looked puzzled and Pascale turned to him.

'My job is to turn the men on,' she explained, fluttering her eyelashes at him, 'and Paul films us in action – if they ever get around to any, that is.'

'What did you tell the Centre?' Suzie asked.

'Not much,' Pascale replied. She moved some of her underwear off some chairs and they all sat down. Pascale's hem shot straight up, but she took no notice. She wore a very short, silver-lamé dress with a scooped-out neckline that revealed a lot of her bosom, and white stockings. The stockings had wide lace tops that showed more or less all the time, but were particularly evident when she sat down. 'It was a man called Marcel,' she explained. 'He talked to me and to one or two of the other girls, and we all told him the same thing. Women don't dress up to attract men; they dress up to look pretty.'

'How do you know when you look pretty?' Hans asked.

'We look in the mirror, or ask another woman,' Pascale replied.

'Pascale's right,' Suzie interjected. 'A very sexy dress might well attract the men, but if a woman thinks she looks ridiculous in it, she won't wear it.'

Pascale looked down and plucked at her neckline. 'I always rely on friends like Suzie to tell me if a dress suits me,' she remarked.

'That dress looks great,' Suzie told her, picking up her cue.

'It's not bad,' replied Pascale, purring with satisfaction, and she turned to look at Igor. 'Who do you know at CIESH?' she asked.

'I think my friend may have moved on,' Igor replied evasively. 'I was really hoping they might have a job for me. I could use some money.'

'Couldn't we all?' Paul asked rhetorically. 'What do you do?'

'I'm not fussy.'

There was a pause while they all looked at Igor. 'Have you ever done any acting?' Pascale asked. Igor shook his head.

'What do you think?' Pascale asked Paul. He scratched his chin, and looked at Igor as if he was peering into a viewfinder.

'You'd photograph well,' he replied, then added with a simper, 'You have lovely cheekbones.'

Igor blushed. 'I hadn't thought of anything like that,' he told them.

'All the better,' Pascale assured him. 'Most of the men who come here lie awake for nights thinking about it, getting all excited, wanking away in anticipation, then they have a few beers with the boys to pluck up some courage, and by the time they arrive they can't raise the wind.'

Hans looked at his watch. 'Well,' he announced, cutting short the debate, 'I have to go and see a lawyer.' He looked at his partner. 'Coming, Suzie?' he asked.

Suzie looked at Igor. 'Why don't you try it out?' she asked, with a slight challenge in her voice.

'There's no charge,' Pascale told him persuasively.

Igor shrugged and gave in. 'Well, if you're all sure,' he said, 'I'm game.' Pascale quietly contemplated this small victory, but then Suzie chipped in.

'In that case,' she asked, 'does anyone mind if I stay and watch?'

'Be my guest,' said Paul, and Pascale forced a smile.

'It's fine by me, Suzie,' she said, but without much conviction.

Suzie looked inquiringly at Igor, and he shrugged. 'If you promise not to boo too loudly,' he told her.

Hans shook hands again all round and hung on momentarily to Igor's hand. 'Beware of the Wilis,' he said in a stage whisper, and left. Suzie glared after him and Igor was puzzled. He knew that the 'Wilis' were the spirits of deserted brides, in the ballet *Giselle*, who 'danced men to death', but he had no time to dwell on it. Pascale stood up, patted her hair and shook down her dress.

'Shall we go in, then?' she asked Igor invitingly.

Igor followed Pascale into the studio, leaving the other two outside. It featured a king-size bed and powerful floodlights fixed into the walls and ceiling. 'Take a look at these,' she said, and handed him a big file of photographs, then vanished into a washroom.

It was very warm and the place smelled of her perfume and heavy photographic make-up. He sat down on a low couch and opened the file. The pictures were all of Pascale, beginning with pretty, conventional pin-ups and moving on to soft porn, with hardcore shots towards the end. He felt his erection begin to grow as he flicked through the pictures, but he returned to the beginning as Pascale came in.

She still wore her silver-lamé dress, which was evidently her working costume, but had fixed her make-up – her eyes were much more emphasised. 'What do you think?' she asked, nodding towards her pictures.

'They're good,' he said. 'Did Paul take them?'

'Most of them.' She sat down beside him and looked at her early pictures. 'Just look at me!' she said in horrified tones. 'Don't I look a real piggy porker in that one?'

'Nonsense. You look lovely,' he replied. She snuggled closer and he felt the warmth of her body against his. She turned the pages.

'I was only seventeen when he took those,' she told him, pointing to some pin-ups. 'I was really really innocent in those days,' she said with a sigh, looking at herself bursting out of a black lace body-stocking.

'Weren't we all?' he replied, echoing her sigh. Pascale purred and turned to the first picture where she showed all she had.

'I almost died the first time they asked me to pose like that,' she said, handing him another conversational hot potato.

'Paul certainly knows how to light a picture,' he said, studying it closely. 'Very plastic: beautiful composition.'

'I am showing a lot, though,' she insisted.

'You have a lovely body, Pascale,' he told her solemnly, 'and that's nothing to be ashamed of.'

'That is just what I always say,' she told him. 'If you are happy in your body, then you are happy in the world.'

'How right you are,' he told her. 'There is far too much prudery and hypocrisy around. These pictures are wonderful.'

'I'm better in 3-D,' she said, and jumped up, laughing as she pirouetted before him, then hitched her skirt up to show him her thighs. She skipped around him, making a game of it, swirling her short dress up to her waist. Her panties were almost nonexistent at the back and her buttocks were firm and plump and inviting. She circled again around him, then sat down on his knee, raising her dress so that her near-naked bottom contacted his crotch. She wriggled on his knee deliberately and detected his burgeoning erection, then slipped her arms around his neck.

'Scared?' she asked in a whisper.

'Petrified.'

'There's no need to be. Just pretend I'm your girlfriend.'

'I should be so lucky!'

'I'm going to enjoy doing it with you,' she whispered, and kissed him. It was a passionate kiss, with her mouth open and her tongue probing, but performed in a friendly way, as if they were hidden away in the cupboard under the stairs at a party, kissing and cuddling and expecting at any moment to be discovered.

He kissed her and put his hand on to her thigh, around the rough-textured lace of her stocking top, pulling her towards him. She eased herself nearer to him and crossed her legs at the knee to stabilise her position, which made her upper thigh available. He put his hand up and caressed the swell of her thigh above the lavishly decorated stocking top, then ran his fingertips up the back suspender, across her near-naked buttock. She moved on his lap, rolling her bottom on his crotch, and his erection bore up between her buttocks. She kissed him more passionately, as if they were lovers, deliberately exciting him with her plump womanly hips as she opened her mouth.

He ran his hand up and cupped her breast through her dress. She wore no bra and her nipples were already erect and hard. She opened her mouth wide and went for him like a playful puppy, reaching for him, biting his lip, pushing her tongue into him, giggling and obviously enjoying it.

'Let me help you out of your things,' she whispered. She slipped off his knee and hauled him to his feet by pulling on his tie.

'May I?' he asked, and placed both hands over her breasts.

'Feel free,' she said. He caressed her eager and friendly body through her thin dress, as she unfastened his shirt and opened it, ran her hands over his chest and kissed his throat and breastbone, then reached up and kissed him again on the lips.

'How's it going down there?' she asked, and squeezed his penis. He was almost fully erect now and she kissed him again.

'I can't wait any longer,' she confessed in a whisper. 'OK if Paul comes in?'

He gulped. 'I guess so,' he murmured.

'Paul, we're ready,' she called, and went back to kissing his chest. 'Do you like this?' she asked, kissing his nipple.

'Yes. What about you?'

'I love it.' She dropped one shoulder strap and gave him her breast. Igor nuzzled in, sucking and licking her nipples, then was suddenly aware that the lights were brighter now and that Paul had a big video camera on his shoulder that peered at them. Pascale detected his tremor as he reacted to the presence of others in the room.

'Just ignore him and follow me,' she murmured, and he went back to kissing her breast. Her nipples were fully erect and she started to breathe more deeply. Her hands tugged his shirt right off and she began to open his pants, then sat on the bed to pull them off, followed by his tight underpants. His penis was hard and erect, pointing upward, and she had to pull the elasticised top of his pants right away from his stomach to get it free. Igor sensed that Paul had moved around and crouched down, ready to photograph the ritual fellation, using the zoom so that he could stay away from them and give Pascale room to manoeuvre.

Pascale took his penis into her mouth. Igor winced at the touch and his body stiffened. 'Stop me if it's too exciting,' she warned him. Igor nodded and bit his lips as he felt her mouth sucking away at the end of his penis. He looked up at the ceiling and Paul photographed his face in close-up as he opened his mouth and panted. Pascale's educated fingers played with his balls and scrotum, and her lithe fingers, tickling and scratching at his sensitive skin, almost drove him wild.

Paul backed away for medium-distance shots and murmured, 'Now.'

Pascale pushed Igor back on to the bed and stripped off her dress and panties. There was no attempt at artistry: this was not a striptease film, but a prick-and-pussy epic. She climbed on to the bed and straddled Igor's chest, then sank down. She had perfumed her sex lavishly and her vagina was half open as she crouched down until her could touch her with his tongue. He put his hands up to steady her hips and pushed his tongue into her welcoming slit. She squealed with delight as he tasted her acid perfume and the bitterness of her lubrication, then she began to move her hips backward and forward, so that his tongue reamed out her vagina.

Paul crouched down alongside the bed and filmed the cunnilingus. Pascale was undulating wildly now and Paul filmed her face as she made clear her sexual excitement, then went back to her sex, moving in for an extreme close-up of her vagina as Igor's tongue licked at her labia and probed inside her slit, then sought out her clit. She moaned incoherently from time to time: her hair was becoming unpinned and she was perspiring now under the hot lights.

Paul said, 'Now,' and Pascale rolled over on to the bed

and offered her widely parted legs once more to Igor's mouth. He burrowed in between her thighs and, after a few seconds, she pulled him away from her sex and he lay over her, taking his weight on his elbows and kissing her with his mouth still wet from her lubrication. Her hands played with his spine and roamed over his buttocks.

'Ready?' she whispered, looking up at him. He nodded.

She felt between his legs and opened her own, raising her knees. He put one hand under her and lifted her bottom. She took his shaft in her hand and guided it into her vagina, wriggling her hips and concentrating.

'Now,' said Paul, in position to take the penetration sequence, and Igor pushed forward slowly, feeling his penis enter her. It slid smoothly into a well-lubricated tunnel that gripped his shaft expertly all the way along.

He realised at once that intercourse was her 'thing'. He'd had sex with a lot of women, and he knew that not all of them were really good at intercourse; maybe not even the majority. Pascale was plump enough to provide a soft but firm foundation to support his hips. Her vagina enveloped his penis and sucked him in: there was no chance of it slipping out, she made sure of that. She was very agile, as if she had a universal joint at her waist, so that her hips rose and fell, swung from side to side and rotated under him, caressing his penis but pushing it around inside her body to maximise her own pleasure. He sensed at once that she was deliberately playing it cool and prolonging her enjoyment, but he knew she had lots in reserve.

'OK?' she asked. He nodded and began to take a more active role. He no longer just provided a big erect rod to titillate her vagina, but rammed it into her at his own time, in his own way, catching her off-balance. She looked up at him, one expert recognising another, and their coupling became a contest. He could hear the camera motor and the faint whisper of the music cassette running in the background, but they were alone on the bed and locked in the oldest struggle on earth.

He suspected that he already knew her little secret. The young men who came in here, the skinny young near virgins from the *lycées* who fancied themselves as *hardeurs*, didn't fail to achieve an erection, as she had implied: they came, prematurely, inside her, during the tests. She milked them dry, sighed, kissed them goodbye, and moved on to the next sacrificial victim. She was what the French called a '*croqueuse d'hommes*': she gobbled up men.

Well, that too was part of the test. Blue-film studs have to keep it up all right, but they also have to hold back, then come to order, to shoot their jets of semen on to whatever target the director chooses. No wonder that good hardcore studs, caught between the Scylla of the failed erection and the Charybdis of the premature ejaculation, are always in short supply!

'You're good,' Pascale said to him, in her normal speaking voice. 'Isn't he, Paul?' she asked.

'Yep,' he replied, 'Turn over.'

Igor withdrew and Pascale turned to face the bed, on her hands and knees. He entered her again from behind, what the Brits call 'doggie-fashion' and the French call 'like a greyhound', and began to piston her smoothly and regularly. A half minute later they changed position again, and he fucked her with her legs wrapped around his neck. She lowered her legs and rolled over on to her side without disengaging, and he followed her without missing a beat.

The camera followed their coupled bodies and Suzie sat by the door, with her knees crossed, and watched them perform as if she was in a zoo.

Jenny had changed into her sexy outfit as she waited for Gaston to return. She heard the high-pitched whine of a chainsaw at work, the sound of heavy pieces of wood falling to the ground, and then footsteps approaching. She knew at once it was not Gaston; these were the light, rapid footsteps of a young person trying not to make too much noise. She slipped into a dark corner, crouching down behind a workbench as the door opened and a young man entered. He was carrying a big chainsaw driven by a two-stroke engine and was obviously scared. He looked around and whispered, 'Marie-Ange?'

Jenny emerged. 'Where's Gaston?' she asked.

'Dad can't come,' he stammered. 'One of the boars has got out.'

'How long will he be?'

'I don't know. It could be hours.' He put the chainsaw down on the floor and rubbed his hands.

'Well, I'd better get going then,' she said. He shook his head.

'You can't,' he said. 'A crowd of them have just come down from Paris. They've shut the gates and switched all the alarms on. If you try to get out now they'll catch you, and Dad will be for it and no mistake.'

'So what am I supposed to do?'

'Wait here until it gets dark and they leave.'

'Wait until it gets dark?' she cried. 'It won't be dark for hours.' He shrugged but said nothing.

'Look,' she said, beginning to lose her temper. 'Your father caught me trespassing. That isn't the end of the world. I persuaded him to let me off. So what's so awful about that? Why can't I just own up and your father as well? Who are these people you're all so scared of?'

'I can't tell you that,' he whispered, looking around as if the walls might have ears, 'but please don't let them catch us. Please! They'll be very mad with Dad and he'll lose his job.' He was obviously genuinely scared.

She looked at him, suddenly intrigued by this mysterious establishment that seemed to be so secretive and scared of trespassers.

She sighed. 'Oh, very well,' she said, 'but in that case you must get a message to someone I promised to meet.'

'I can't.'

'I only want you to make a telephone call,' she told him. 'There's a telephone box right by the gate, where I came over the fence. You must be able to get out, surely?'

He shuffled his feet. 'Well, I could tell them I need to go out to lop off another branch,' he admitted.

'Well, do that, please – what's your name?'

'Benoit.'

'Please, Benoit,' she said persuasively, 'go and leave this message for me. It is very important.'

He hesitated. 'Then come back and keep me company afterwards,' she said persuasively. 'I'll be scared here all by myself.' She went up to him and stood close, so that he could feel her bosom touching his chest. 'Please, Benoit, do me this little favour,' she said, and put one hand on his shoulder, pulling him closer, so that their bodies contacted all the way down. He blushed a deep scarlet.

'What's the message?' he asked, his excitement overcoming his fear.

She took a pencil and wrote a telephone number on the palm of his hand. 'It's a hotel,' she told him, 'and this is the room number of my friend. Leave a message for him saying, "Our friend has left: destination unknown".'

'Our friend has left: destination unknown?'

'That's it.'

Twelve

Gabrielle stood inside the entrance to a small hotel, hemmed in by two of Carl's girls, Josy and Line, who blocked the doorway so that she could not be seen unless they liked the look of a prospective client. Carl had explained to her that a new girl was always placed in the care of more experienced women, and she realised that they were protecting her, but she had been there for almost ten minutes, and wished they would move away and let her take her chance with the passers-by.

She didn't look down, knowing that, if she did, the sight of her indecent outfit would cause her to panic. She could feel the hem of her skirt, stretched tight by her parted thighs, well above the tops of her stockings, just below the tiny panties Carl had allowed her to wear. She felt the arrogance of her breasts as they pushed aside the lapels of her jacket. Feelings of guilt, shame and excitement all battled for dominance; but behind them was the ultimate nightmare that she tried to push out of her mind – that nobody would desire her.

A tall, blond, good-looking man, obviously a businessman on the prowl, walked by. Her two minders stood back and Gaby caught his eye. He stopped and looked her up and down.

'How much?' he asked.

'Three hundred.' She held his eyes, fighting down her blush.

'OK.' She felt her mouth become dry and swallowed hard.

'Follow me,' she said, and lead him into the tiny hall. She pushed the button, the gates slammed shut far above, and the rickety old lift wheezed as it descended. 'What is your name?' she asked.

'Wolfgang.'

'*Du bist Deutsch*?' she asked.

'*Ja, naturlich*,' he replied. The lift clanked to a halt, and she stood back to let him go ahead of her into the tiny cubicle, then squeezed in behind him, turned her back to him and pressed the fourth-floor button. She felt her bottom press against him in the confined space, and automatically tried to avoid the intimate body contact, but he put his arms around her hips from behind, pulled her to him and placed his hands over her stomach, feeling for her panties and garter belt through her flimsy skirt. Her body stiffened and her heart raced as his fingers pressed into her pudenda and found the bulge of her pubic hair. She felt his erection between her buttocks and then suddenly, to her amazement, she found herself rolling her hips against his crotch to encourage his assault. He was immediately aroused by her gesture and pulled her skirt up impatiently, but they had reached their destination and the doors opened.

She wriggled her skirt down and walked across the landing to open the door, with her heart racing and her latch-key trembling in her hand; a veneer of ladylike behaviour that had seemed to be an integral part of her had just shattered into small pieces. She went inside and turned to let him enter. The room was over-heated and she felt the small gold cross she wore around her neck, burning against her flesh. She shut out the memory it revived, of her Catholic childhood and of the dark, incense-laden church, and turned to Wolfgang as he took out his wallet and gave her three hundred francs. She folded the money and put it in her handbag, reflecting that it was the first money she had ever earned in her life.

Wolfgang came up close, turned her to face a full-length mirror, then put his arms around her again. She felt her heart race anew as she saw her reflection in the mirror, with this handsome stranger behind her, his hands already raising her hem.

‘*Je peux*?’ he murmured in her ear. ‘May I?’

‘*Bien sûr, cheri,*’ she whispered back, and looked at her reflection as he raised her skirt and revealed the tip of her panties. The sight of her own body excited her as much as the feel of his hands and the pressure of his erection between her buttocks. ‘*J’aime ça,*’ she murmured. ‘I love that.’

It was true. She suddenly realised that providing sex for money was giving her an extra kick. Wolfgang raised her hem to her waist revealing her lace-trimmed garter belt and the tiny black nylon panties that decorated her hips and sex.

She felt his hands seek out her sex. Her lubrication suddenly oozed from her slit and she spread her legs and put her hand over his, thrusting his fingers down over her panties and in between her parted thighs.

‘You’re damp!’ he exclaimed, delighted at making her respond.

‘Of course I am, darling,’ she whispered back, and used his fingers to excite herself. She saw in the mirror how her panties dipped under the slight swell of her belly, how her pubic hair made a bulge in the skimpy nylon triangle that cosseted her sex, how her long suspenders emphasised the firm glory of her thighs. She unfastened her jacket and placed his other hand over her breast, and she gasped and undulated as his hand massaged and titillated her nipple.

‘*J’aime ça,*’ she repeated. Her big blond client slipped his hand into her panties and pressed down and out with his wrist, pushing the elasticised waistband away from her stomach and revealing her thick, dark curls. She allowed him to expose the tip of her glistening vagina, and to slide his finger into her, then put her free hand behind her to squeeze his penis.

‘Undress,’ she whispered urgently. ‘I can’t wait,’ and she turned to help him undress. She unfastened his shirt and pulled it open to admire his broad deep chest. Her hands unzipped his pants and he hopped out of them as she kissed his stomach, then slipped her hand into the top of his boxer shorts.

'These too,' she said, and eased them off, then pushed him gently on to the bed, on his back, the way Carl had shown her. His prick was almost fully erect, standing up away from his stomach, and she stripped off her jacket and skirt, then stretched out on the bed beside him, bent over him, and spread his legs wide apart.

'Lie still,' she whispered, and lifted his balls with one hand, then ran the fingers of her other hand up the inside of his thigh, and stroked the puckered skin between his testicles and his anus. She heard his quick intake of breath as she bent over him, engrossed in her task like a surgeon performing a delicate operation. She made him bend his knees so that his thighs were lifted away from the bed, and caressed his buttocks and upper thighs, flicking her fingertips from his anus to his balls and back again. Every time she touched him intimately his prick jerked. His hands groped blindly for her body and she moved towards him and gave him her legs to fondle.

'*Ca va comme ça*?' she asked him. 'Is it OK like that?'

'I'll say,' he replied, and he lay back and looked at their reflection in the overhead mirror. She bent lower, still tickling him, put out her tongue, and licked the underside of his shaft from his balls to the tip. His prick jerked violently as her tongue contacted the sensitive folds of skin, and he cried out. His second finger pushed her legs apart and searched for her sex, and she wriggled slightly to deny him access.

'It's too exciting,' she said. 'Let me look after you.' He let his hand fall away and she licked his shaft again and again, then placed her mouth over the tip. She took his penis into her and sucked him for several long seconds before letting him go, then licked his tip again and again, like a child with a lollipop.

'Do you want to go down on me?' she asked. He shook his head.

'Stay like that,' he said, and his hand tightened on her thigh. She sucked his knob luxuriously whilst masturbating him, and his hand moved spasmodically on her leg. She allowed him access to her sex, and this time allowed his finger to penetrate her. She was very wet and he opened her vagina easily. His finger slid up into her and she sighed with pleasure as she sucked and stroked and worked at his penis.

'Do you want to come like this?' she asked.

'Please,' he murmured, and his finger found her clit. She gasped and went down again on his penis, scared that he would make her climax, but she knew that the feel of her erect clitoris would help to bring him off. She felt his penis jerk and his balls lift and tighten. He grunted as if in pain and she bobbed her head up and down, then took his prick out of her mouth and licked the sensitive horns under the tip as he exploded. Thick gobs of semen surged out of the hole and ran over her hand in a creamy flood. Gabrielle grabbed some paper towels and mopped them both up, gave him more towels to finish off, and rolled off the bed. He sat up, shaking his head in wonder as she squeezed the last of his semen from his cock. 'You were great,' he said, and went to kiss her. She moved her face quickly, so that he kissed her cheek and not her mouth, and ran to the bathroom.

'Have you been doing this a long time?' he asked through the partition.

'Not very.'

'What's your name?'

'Gabrielle.'

'Are you French?'

'Italian.'

'*Lei parla italiano*?'

'*Naturalmente*.'

The music from the radio swelled into a chorus. 'Do you like Verdi?' he asked.

'Of course I like Verdi,' she replied. 'All Italians love Verdi, and *Traviata* is one of my favourites.' She slipped into fresh panties and went back into the bedroom.

He was dressed again, fastening his shoes whilst he looked at the book she had left open on the shelf. 'I've always found Umberto Eco a bit deep,' he commented.

'Not as difficult as all that,' she replied. She stepped into her tight skirt and zipped it up, slipped on her jacket, pulled on her shoes and prinked her hair, then eased up her skirt to show her suspender ribbons, then higher still to uncover the tops of her stockings.

'I like your outfit,' he said. 'Did you choose it?'

'Of course,' she said. She looked at herself in the big mirror and thought that she looked very exciting like that, with her bra thrusting out of her jacket and her suspenders showing. Carl had told her that a client often gets excited again when the girl is dressed once more, and that, if you don't watch out, he will spin out the visit, so you have to get rid of him quickly, or ask him to pay for a second session. She realised suddenly that she didn't want another session with him. Wolfgang was sucked dry, and she was in a hurry to get back to work and find someone new.

'Shall we go?' she asked, and opened the door impatiently. The lift rattled down and she hummed a little tune as they descended. She smiled and said goodbye to Wolfgang as they reached the road, but her eyes were already searching around nervously as he walked away.

'Take five,' Paul proposed, and he lifted the camera down and rubbed his aching shoulder. 'I'll go and get us some coffee,' he added.

'I'll help.' Suzie followed him out, and left Igor alone with Pascale. He slid off the bed: his penis was wet and sticky with her lubrication, and he went into the washroom nearby. Pascale followed him in and used the bidet without any trace of embarrassment.

'How long have you known Suzie and Hans?' she asked.

'I just met them,' he replied. She stood up and dried her sex on a big towel.

'I couldn't do what she does,' she told him. 'Day after day, night after night, up on stage like that.'

'It must be a tough life,' he agreed.

'You know that she is looking for a new partner?' she asked, bending over to dab perfume behind her knees.

'They told me.'

'She's got her eye on you. I saw the way she was looking

at you just now.' She perfumed her navel and all around her sex.

'So?'

'She's very possessive,' she told him, moving him aside to look in the mirror as she combed her hair. 'Believe me,' she continued, 'poor old Hans isn't allowed to stray far.'

'She hasn't asked me to partner her yet,' Igor pointed out.

'I'm looking forward to the next part,' Pascale whispered, and put her arms around Igor's neck, pressing close to him. He felt her plump breasts squashed against his chest, and her agile pudenda was already massaging his penis. 'I want us both to come with you inside me,' she whispered seductively. 'I'll fix it with Paul.'

Igor put his pants on; Pascale slipped on her dress, and they went out. Suzie was already sipping a cup of hot, strong coffee.

'You have another client,' Paul said to Pascale, nodding towards the door.

'Not today, Paul,' she said angrily. 'We haven't finished with Igor.'

'I want to look through what we have already,' Paul said, and turned to Igor. 'You can come back, can't you?' he asked.

'Sure.' Igor replied, and started to dress. Pascale sulked in the corner like a child, and Paul busied himself with the camera.

'Are you tied up for the next hour or so?' Suzie asked him. 'I'd like to talk to you.'

'Of course,' he said.

They put down their cups and moved towards the door. Pascale hung back and kissed Igor goodbye. As she did so, she slipped a note into his pocket. 'Ring me this evening,' she whispered. 'It's important.'

He nodded, shook hands with Paul, and followed Suzie out into the sunlit road.

'I'm sorry I let you in for that,' she said apologetically, as soon as they were alone.

'You didn't let me in for anything,' he replied. 'I volunteered.'

'You could hardly do otherwise,' she replied, 'but I could see it wasn't your scene,' and she sniffed disapprovingly. 'I don't know how Pascale can do it,' she said, shaking her head.

'Do what?'

'Have sex with all those men,' she said. 'She sometimes has six or seven different men in a day, you know. Paul told me. She might as well be on the streets.'

'It is her job,' he reminded her.

'Her job is what she makes it,' she reminded him, 'but that isn't what I wanted to talk to you about,' and she took his arm as they turned into a tiny alley. They stopped outside an old house that had been converted into several flats, and went in.

Her flat was very prettily furnished, in Laura Ashley and Sanderson fabrics, with *Homes and Gardens* and *The Lady* displayed on a coffee table. Suzie led him into the salon, said, 'I won't be a moment,' and vanished into the bedroom.

Igor looked around. There was a photograph album on the sideboard and he peeped inside. The first half showed a slimmer, younger Suzie, dressed as Odette or Swanilda or Aurora, standing on her points or taking bows with bouquets in her arms. There were also pictures of her in gossamer summer dresses with wide-brimmed hats on English lawns, with croquet hoops in evidence, eating strawberries and cream with the County folk. Suzanne was a brigadier's daughter and obviously from the right side of the tracks.

The second half showed the shift to modern dance, with a more voluptuous Suzie performing in Martha Graham dance plays or to Scott Joplin ragtime, jitterbugging with her skirt round her neck, high-kicking in the chorus line for *Forty-Second Street* and then statuesque, spangled and sequined for the *Lido*, with a towering headdress and bare breasts.

The door opened and Suzie called, 'Come in.'

Her bedroom was much bigger than the salon and one wall was wholly mirrored. There was a *barre* at waist height along it and Igor imagined Suzie religiously working out each morning. She was standing by the *barre*, wearing a standard functional black leotard and leg warmers. 'Shall we see how much you've forgotten?' she asked with a smile.

'Almost everything,' Igor replied, but he slipped off his jacket. She put on a tape and he stood behind her and to one side, facing the mirror. The tape started; just a wire brush against the high hat, a single throb of the foot pedal to mark each bar, and the sharp rattle of the side drum every four bars. She said, 'Eight bars introduction, then follow me.'

He nodded and she started to whisper, 'One and two and three and . . .' On the eighth bar she slid one foot out sideways, turned and closed her feet in a simple step: Igor followed her easily. On the next fourth bar she executed a more complex step, then a rhythmic version of a *fouetté*. Igor followed her, clumsy and hesitant, but getting into the swing of it. After a minute or so he was following her up and down, beginning to anticipate her movements. They went on for ten minutes, warming up, then Suzie changed the tape.

'You could get back into shape pretty quickly,' she told him, and disappeared behind a shoulder-high screen. 'I have several ideas for some new routines,' she went on as she changed. 'Perhaps I could run through one or two, and see what you think?'

'Of course.'

'This routine features a young girl at the *barre*,' she went on, busy with buttons and zips. 'She is daydreaming and fantasising as she exercises.' She started the tape and came out from behind the screen.

Igor blinked. Suzie strutted on her points with her head high, in a classical ballet attitude, and took up her position at the *barre*. She wore a chaplet of white daisies around her head, plus what at first sight appeared to be a standard white leotard and tutu, and standard ballet pumps with reinforced toes. Instead of tights, however, she wore sheer white stockings and suspenders. Her leotard was really a white satin basque with a brief under-wired brassière, and, under her skirt, she wore a very brief pair of white satin panties. The erotic shock was all the more powerful because she had given him absolutely no warning, and because both the environment and the music were classical and refined.

She began to exercise at the *barre*, performing standard warming-up exercises. Many such exercises require the girl to open her legs, so that the exercises turned quickly into an arousing display. 'What do you think?' she asked casually, with one leg out stretched out horizontally, her ankle resting on the *barre* as she looked at her reflection.

'Powerful stuff,' he said. She was obviously a trained and highly professional dancer, but her panties were sexy lingerie items, designed to arouse, and they stretched so tightly between her legs that Igor could see the line of her sex.

The music changed; Khachaturian drifted into 'The Onedin Line', and Suzie began to move again, thrusting out her bosom, changing to an earthier appeal as the music slowed and became more languorous. Now she began to fondle herself, running her hands over her bosom, but with the delicate, formal, bird-like hand movements of classical dance. The music swelled and Suzie began to caress her legs, up and down, facing the *barre* as she aroused her body. Igor watched her, entranced by the show, as her hands danced like mayflies over her thighs and fluttered over her sex.

Borodin was transmuted into 'Kismet' and Hollywood-style strings swept into songs of baubles and beads. 'Now you come in,' Suzie told him, 'to supervise the exercises.'

'Baubles, bangles, bright shiny things . . .' she sang to the violins. He went up behind her as she stood with one foot up on the *barre*, then straightened her knee and ran his hand up her leg until it brushed between her thighs, over her panties. She changed position and he repeated the performance with her other leg.

She mixed instructions into the words of the song. 'Bright eyes, sparkle, right breast, takes wing, ding-a-ling-a . . .' Igor caressed her bosom, under the pretence of correcting her arm and neck positions, then the music swelled and he unclipped her bra. Her breasts spilled out into his hands and she watched herself in the mirror as her arousal took hold. 'Eyes glitter and gleam so,' she sang, her body pressed against his, and he felt his erection become harder as her buttocks pressed against his groin. She spread her legs wide again, and leant back to offer her body to the mirror. 'One day he may buy me a ring . . .' she sang in her clear, high voice. He found the catch at the side of her panties as the music paused, and the next moment her sex was totally exposed to their gaze. The violins went wild and her hand moved down and titillated her vagina and clitoris as his hands kneaded and caressed her breasts. She leant down now to take hold of the *barre* with both hands, pushing her buttocks out, looking at her reflection.

'Baubles, bangles, my heart takes wing, now you fuck me,' she sang, clearly and coolly, in her Budleigh Salterton voice.

Igor ripped at his zip, opened her sex and slid into her from behind. 'I know that's where it leads,' she sang, the strings soared to new heights and he fucked her in time to the music, slowly and luxuriously, whilst she smiled at her reflection. Her lithe body moved to encourage his penetration, to suck in his penis and then, reluctantly, to let him withdraw.

The music changed again, back to 'Prince Igor'. Suzie opened her mouth and the tip of her tongue flicked at her upper lip. She was breathing very heavily now; her face was pink and her eyes glistened as his movements, following the music, built up to a crescendo. The beat was accelerating, and Igor moved in and out of her more rapidly, bringing them up to a climax. The music was going wild now, with cymbals crashing and drums rolling. She watched herself go into orgasm, looked at the way her body jerked and writhed under the shock, and the music stopped dead. It was suddenly very quiet and Igor could hear his heart pounding.

Suzie turned her head to kiss him over her shoulder. 'You didn't come,' she said, her eyes misty with her afterglow.

'You didn't tell me to,' he pointed out.

Thirteen

Candie was sitting at an ornate antique desk in a secretarial annex, next to her boss's office. Vivienne had left immediately after the search, and thirty minutes had passed since her departure, during which time Candie's new boss, Lucien, had dictated three letters. The letters were perfectly normal business communications about shipping instructions, customs regulations and so on, and it was clear that he was in the fine art and antiques import/export business, but she had learnt nothing else. She finished the letters and took them in to him: he checked them and signed the first letter.

'Why did you submit to my rather childish fantasy just now?' he asked quietly.

'I thought I was being searched,' she replied dryly.

The third letter contained two small errors. He corrected them and handed the document back to her, but when she went to return to her office, he motioned for her to stay.

'You know perfectly well that I used the search as an excuse to humiliate you,' he told her. 'Why did you submit to that?'

'I supposed that it excited you,' she replied.

'Is that a good reason?' he asked.

'It excited me too,' she informed him. 'That's a good reason.'

Lucien unbent a little. 'Your predecessors all found my games revolting and disgusting,' he told her with a wry smile. 'They made it abundantly clear that they put up with them only because of the money.'

'That is what they told you, anyway,' she corrected him.

'You mean they lied?'

Candie shook her head. 'Sexual feelings are rather like our sense of smell,' she pointed out. 'We are not born with the idea that some odours are pleasant and others are disgusting: we learn in childhood that flowers smell nice and rotten cabbage smells nasty. In the same way, we are taught that some sexual feelings are nice and that others are nasty. Ladies are not supposed to like being searched intimately in front of a man.' She smiled. 'Merciful heavens,' she went on, in a shocked Victorian voice, 'if women liked such things, it would undermine the very fabric of our society, wouldn't it?'

'They did not teach you the same feelings?' he asked, smiling now quite openly.

'They tried,' Candie replied, 'but I'm an individual. I happen not to like the smell of dandelions, for instance, and I do like the smell of a well-hung pheasant, but nobody gets up-tight about that. God also made me a high-libido exhibitionist, as it happens, but people do get up-tight about that.'

Lucien picked up a solid gold pen and fiddled with it. 'Have you played these kinds of games before?' he asked.

'Some of my bosses liked playing office games,' she admitted. 'One or two of them made it exciting for me as well.'

'Were they the ones who played their roles well, or who read from the script you had written?' he asked with a smile.

She smiled back. 'Both,' she admitted wryly, then added, 'but my scripts have plenty of scope for improvisation.'

'As far as I am concerned,' he told her, 'the rules are that I remain fully dressed and do not touch you. The only other condition I impose is that the game should genuinely arouse you.' He smiled and added, 'Of course, the more embarrassed you are, the better. Have you a script for such a scenario?'

She looked down at the letter she still held. 'You could make me take off a garment for every typo I make,' she told him.

'Who decides which garments come off?'

'Toss a coin.'

He produced a coin from his pocket and tossed it, caught it on his wrist and covered it. He looked up at her.

She felt her heartbeat increase. 'Tails,' she called. He uncovered his wrist and showed her the coin: she had guessed correctly.

'Two garments, please,' he said, holding out his hand.

She looked at him from under her long lashes, felt her blush begin, then unzipped her skirt, stepped out of it and handed it to him. 'I need to look at myself,' she said, and she fled from his probing eyes to look at herself in a full-length mirror. Her severe hairstyle and her spectacles contrasted erotically with her stocking-clad legs, but her clumpy shoes spoiled the effect. 'I really need high heels,' she told him.

'Like these?' He reached into a drawer and produced three pairs of black high-heeled Harel evening shoes, all in her size but in different widths.

'I have a feeling you've played this game before,' she said dryly, and took the shoes. The second pair fitted her beautifully and her legs immediately looked longer and slimmer. She went back to the mirror. The hem of her jacket came down to just below the centre line of her hips. She put her hands into her pockets, pushed down, and saw that her jacket would just about conceal her sex: just about.

'Close your eyes,' she said. He did so and she drew off her black nylon panties, threw them on to the desk and rammed her hands into her pockets.

'I'm ready,' she said. He opened his eyes and she saw them widen, then take in the panties on his desk. With a quick movement, he scooped them and her skirt into the drawer of his desk and locked it.

'Am I decent?' she asked anxiously, holding her jacket down over her pudenda.

He frowned. 'I'm not sure,' he said, peering at her.

'Don't look at me like that,' she said, blushing furiously, and turned to look at herself again in the mirror. 'Oh no,

I'm sure I'm not,' she wailed. 'Give me my panties back, Lucien, please.'

'No.'

'I'll swap for my jacket.'

'No.'

'My jacket and my bra?'

'No.'

'You'll see my bosom,' she reminded him cajolingly.

'You look very fetching like that,' he said. 'Now go and correct that letter.'

'I can't sit down,' she hissed, her face scarlet. The chairs were all covered in antique silk, and her lubrication would mark the seat. He reached into another drawer and produced a towel.

'You really have thought of every eventuality,' she remarked sarcastically, then covered up the seat of her chair and sat down gingerly, pressing her knees together. She corrected the typos, saved the new version, printed it out, and took it across to him. She handed it to him and he signed it, then looked up. She realised that she had forgotten to put her hands back into her pockets, looked down, gave another wail and put her left hand down to take up the classic cover-up position that all women learn to adopt whilst still in the womb.

'I can't go around like this,' she complained. 'It feels awful. Please give me my panties back, Lucien.'

'You have to do something in return,' he said.

'What?'

'Arouse yourself,' he said, looking at her left hand.

'Oh no,' she cried, and blushed a deep scarlet. 'I couldn't,' she protested.

'Please,' he said. 'Do it for me, Candida.'

She gave another little wail, but slid her legs slightly apart, then opened the fingers of her left hand, pressed her first and third fingers against her labia, and crooked her second finger. She touched the tip against the front of her vagina.

'Oh no!' she gasped, and closed her thighs, trapping her hand. 'Lucien, I can't.'

'Please,' he said, his voice hoarse, staring at her. She opened her legs again, penetrated herself with her second finger and pushed her thumb into her pubic hair.

'It feels awful,' she sobbed. She played with herself for several seconds, and started to become excited.

'Do you really want to watch me masturbate?' she asked him, with her hand buried between her legs. He nodded.

'Please,' he said.

She perched on the corner of his desk. 'Ladylike or pornographically?' she asked. He licked his lips.

'Pornographically,' he whispered.

She kicked off one shoe and put her foot on to the seat of his chair, then opened her legs wide, but used her hand to cover her sex. 'Really porno?' she asked. He nodded.

She leant back on his desk on one elbow, then took her hand away.

'There,' she said. 'You see, I really am an exhibitionist.' Her finger plunged into her moist vagina and her thumb felt for her clitoris. 'Look at my sex, please,' she told him, and opened her labia with her first and third fingers. 'Come closer,' she whispered. He leant forward until his face was only inches from her vagina. She let herself fall back on to the broad desk, and her right hand opened her jacket and pulled down her bra-cup to fondle her breast . 'What else will you make me do?' she asked.

'From now on,' he told her, 'you must keep the office sexual temperature at boiling point. Surprise me, shock me, excite me all the time. Will you do that?'

'Of course,' she said. 'What else?'

'Receive my male visitors dressed as you are now.'

'Will they be attractive?' she asked.

'Very, and very horny,' he replied. 'They'll all want to have sex with you.'

'May I have sex with them?' she asked, her hips bouncing and rolling on his desk.

'If you wish.' Her hips pounded his desk and she was beginning to lose control.

'That's far enough,' he said.

'I want to go over,' she cried.

'No, you mustn't.'

'Please, Lucien, let me have an orgasm,' she pleaded.

'Not now. You may have one later.'

'I'm multi-orgasmic, Lucien. I can have three or four in a row.'

'I said no!' he shouted. 'Candida, stop!'

She took her hand away and sat up on his desk, beginning to sulk. 'I want to talk to you,' he said.

'What about?' She looked down and eased her breast back into her bra-cup.

'I'd like you to help Vivienne,' he said.

'To do what?' She stood up, still sulking, and pulled her jacket down.

'Arrange sex games for some personal friends,' he said. 'They are all over the age of consent, by the way; it is all perfectly legal.'

'I thought you imported and exported antiques,' she said moodily.

'I do,' he said. 'This is just a personal favour for some special friends, but it has to be kept secret.'

'Why?'

'The people concerned occupy very responsible positions and dare not risk any media involvement,' he explained. 'You will have to swear not to talk to anyone about it.'

'What will it involve?' she asked.

'Sexual games limited only by your own imagination,' he replied, 'with attractive partners just as imaginative as you are.'

'It sounds interesting,' she admitted.

'You will be paid a substantial bonus, of course, but you will have to keep this an absolute secret between us,' he explained.

'I understand that,' she said.

'So it's agreed then?'

Candie shrugged. 'OK,' she said, feigning indifference, but knowing that this would put her right into the middle of Lucien's secret affairs, and that the Colonel would be over the moon. 'When do I start?' she asked.

'In about five minutes,' he replied. 'One of my friends is coming to see me. I'd like to introduce you to him.'

'In that case, I'd better go and fix my make-up,' she said, and held out her hand. 'May I have my clothes, please?' she asked politely.

He smiled up at her but made no move to unlock his desk, and the awful realisation dawned on her.

'Oh no,' she said. 'You wouldn't.'

'You made me promise,' he reminded her.

'I was mad,' she protested. 'Please, Lucien, at least my panties. You promised to give them back if I –'

'They are extremely damp,' he reminded her. 'You can have this instead,' and he again reached into his desk drawer, and handed her a very minuscule black satin G-string.

'Is that all?' she asked, hanging it over one finger.

'That is all,' he said. 'Now go and get ready.'

'Do I keep my glasses and my Mary Poppins hairdo?'

'Yes, of course,' he replied. 'You are my secretary, after all.'

Gabrielle had serviced three customers by the time Carl arrived. He had a murmured conversation with Line and Josy in the hall, and then told Gaby to follow him upstairs. She did so, and handed him the money she had taken. He counted it quickly.

'Is that all?' he asked, looking at the crumpled notes.

'Well, yes,' she admitted. 'I only had three clients.'

'Did you see how much the other girls took?'

He shook her head. 'I didn't keep count,' she admitted.

'A damned sight more than that,' he told her. 'Do you realise how much it costs me, keeping you out there, standing around, wearing out the pavement?'

'Josy and Line keep a lot of the clients away from me,' she explained.

'It's that outfit,' he said, ignoring her excuses. 'You look like you're going to church.' He opened the wardrobe and threw some clothes on the bed. 'Put those on,' he said.

Gaby picked up a black see-through hip-length blouse and an open-front black under-wired bra. 'I can't go out like that,' she protested.

'What did you say?' he asked, his eyes flashing.

'I can't –' she began, but he leapt forward like a tiger and slapped her face twice, with a left and right blow. He was careful not to mark her, but she stumbled on her high heels, fell sideways, and sprawled on the bed. He seized her chin and thrust his face against hers.

'You do as you're damned well told,' he snarled, and he pushed her backwards again with a fast thrust of his hand.

Gaby cowered on the bed, rubbing her cheek where he had hit her, shocked and amazed by his sudden outburst. 'Put them on,' he shouted, and threw the clothes in her face.

She gulped and stood up, watching him warily, scared he'd slap her again. Tears trickled down her cheeks, and she sniffed and used the back of her hand to wipe them away. She unfastened her jacket, her hands trembling on the buttons, and took it off, then her bra. She put on the sling bra, sniffing and wiping away her tears, but her fingers could not deal with the clips.

'Here, let me,' he said, quite gently, and he fixed the straps. She felt the pressure of the under-wiring as it lifted her bosom, and felt her nipples engorge as his hands, masculine and dominant, squeezed and lifted her breasts. He helped her on with the blouse and she felt the thin, see-through organza kiss her nipples. He tied it tightly around her waist, so that it crossed over between her breasts and further emphasised her bosom. The bottom of it came to just below her hips. He unzipped her skirt and took it off, then picked up a tiny black G-string.

She gulped, but didn't make any protest as he stripped off her panties and pulled the G-string up. He fastened the clip and she felt the lycra pull into her hips. A moment later, he turned her around to face the mirror.

Her up-standing nipples, visible under the see-through blouse, screamed for attention. The bra lifted her bosom and the cross-over blouse separated her breasts and presented each one as a work of erotic art. Further down, her G-string was just a minute triangle that barely covered her carefully trimmed pubic hair, that dipped down low under her navel and drew the eye straight to her sex. Gaby felt the narcissistic excitement start, and then Carl was plucking at her blouse and adjusting her neckline and whispering in her ear.

'Now you look a real woman,' he told her, 'don't you? Don't you look a real woman now?' He waved a hand at her reflection.

She looked at herself, at her long legs with her stockings and suspenders blatantly on show, with her breasts and nipples bare under the black nylon blouse, and agreed with him: now she looked a real woman. He put his arms around her from behind and squeezed her breasts. 'You're my girl,' he whispered. 'I'm proud of you.'

'I must fix my make-up,' she said, and washed away the tears. He continued to caress her breasts as she spread her lipstick thickly over her mouth and emphasised her voluptuous lips. 'I'm sorry I made you angry just now,' she said.

'Forget it,' he said. 'You really are something, Gabrielle,' he whispered. 'You make the rest of them look like rubbish.' She took out her mascara and plastered it on, making her eyelashes thick and luscious, and all the time his fingers made her nipples scream with lust.

'You'll be proud of me,' she whispered, 'I'll work really hard, I promise.'

'Go get 'em,' he said, and patted her bottom, winking at her in the mirror. She took one final look at herself, squared her shoulders, and took the lift down.

Carl went to the window and raised the blind. Josy and Line gathered around Gabrielle as she emerged, congratulating her upon her new outfit as if it was a couture dress. Two other girls crossed the road to join in and this massed praise removed Gaby's remaining inhibitions.

Carl looked across to the opposite side of the road, as a man in a shabby raincoat, hidden in an alleyway, lifted a camera. It was equipped with a long telephoto lens and he photographed Gabrielle several times as she stood on the pavement, surrounded by the crowd of prostitutes.

Fourteen

Jenny realised that the padlock on the barn door was intended to keep people out, not keep them in. All she had to do to escape, was to release the U-shaped clasp, the threaded legs of which passed through the doorpost and were fastened into place by rusty nuts, but she needed a spanner to unfasten the nuts.

She looked around. There was an adjustable spanner on the bench, but it was rusted and unusable. She hunted around and came upon a can of penetrating oil, with a few drops left in it. She squeezed some on to the spanner and the remainder on to the nuts, but realised that it would need time to penetrate.

There was a sink and a tap in one corner, and she washed her hands in cold water and dried them on an old towel, cursing herself for getting into this ridiculous situation. As soon as she could, she decided, she would escape from this barn and scramble to freedom.

She heard new footsteps approaching, and the voices of two men, talking together as they walked though the woods. The voices came nearer and she shrank back into her hiding place as two faces peered though the dusty window.

These were not countrymen: they had the hard, confident faces of big-city gangsters, and Jenny could hear their voices more clearly now. They both spoke with the singing accent of the Midi, and used the argot of the Marseilles underworld.

'I shall be glad to get back home,' one of them told the other. 'Paris really gives me the shits.'

'Me too,' the other one replied. 'How many *putes* this time?'

'Six. Only one of them looks a good fuck.'

They moved away, and Jenny came out of hiding. The men had used one of the many words for 'prostitute', but they probably called all women 'whores', as a matter of routine, except for their mothers and sisters. She sneaked to the window and peered out. The two men were standing some distance away and their discussion was obviously about guns, because one of them suddenly reached under his arm and produced an automatic pistol. He passed the gun to his companion, who hefted it and aimed it, locking one wrist in the other hand, half crouching, the way Jenny had seen in the movies, then nodded and handed it back. They went on their way.

So there were armed men roaming around the place. Jenny could understand now why Benoit and his father were scared, and she felt more than a little scared herself. This was a totally unforeseen complication: she was pretty sure La Chasse St Hubert had no connection with the Centre, but she had stumbled upon something that ought to be reported to her boss. The problem was, how to get out? Even if she could escape from this barn, she had no idea how many men were roaming around. Just at that moment, she saw Benoit turn the corner and come down the path, looking around guiltily as he approached the barn. He unlocked the door and came in, then set down down his chainsaw.

'Did you send my message,' she asked. He nodded.

'Thank you,' she said. 'Come and have a drink. You've earned it.' She had been careful to save most of the red wine, to help loosen his tongue.

He took the glass, eager to show he was a man, and drank deeply. 'Did you have any trouble getting in and out?' she asked. He shook his head, then went over to the sink and washed his hands.

'Come and sit down by me,' she said invitingly, patting the seat next to her. 'I'm sure you can spare a few minutes. Let's have a little chat together.' He sat down cautiously.

‘What shall we talk about?’ he asked.

‘I don’t know,’ Jenny replied, plucking at her hem. ‘You, me, love, life, sex?’

He blushed. ‘I don’t know anything about that,’ he said.

‘Come on, you can’t be that innocent, Benoit. There must be a pretty maid or two up at the house.’

‘We’re not allowed up at the house,’ he said.

‘You must run across them sometimes, in the garden, going shopping, taking a stroll around the estate,’ Jenny insisted. She frowned and raised her hem, examining her fishnet stocking for an imaginary run.

‘The girls aren’t allowed out,’ he said, his eyes on her leg.

‘What are they like, the girls who aren’t allowed out?’ she asked, and adjusted a suspender. He drained his glass.

‘Smashing,’ he admitted. She refilled his glass.

‘I bet you have a little peep at them from time to time, through your father’s binoculars,’ she said. He blushed again.

‘Now and again,’ he admitted.

‘Do you watch them undress?’ she asked.

‘They usually draw the curtains,’ he explained sadly.

‘What do you think about when you watch them?’

He went very red. ‘Nothing much,’ he replied at last.

‘I’ll bet,’ she said sarcastically. ‘You must have seen some blue movies.’

‘One or two.’

‘Tell me about your favourite. What happened?’

His eyes flicked to her legs again, long and slender in their fishnet stockings. ‘It was about a school,’ he told her, ‘where they had sex lessons. Then this new teacher arrived: she looked a lot like you.’

‘What did she do?’

He blushed deeply. ‘She made the boys stay behind, one at a time, after school, for special sex lessons,’ he told her.

‘Individual sex instruction? That sounds a good idea,’ Jenny told him. ‘Then what did she do?’

He turned a deep red. ‘I – I can’t tell you,’ he stuttered.

‘Of course you can. I used to be a schoolmistress.’

‘Were you?’ he asked. ‘Did you teach boys about sex?’

'No, unfortunately, although I'd have liked to. Young men need better sex instruction. They should be taught how to treat a woman properly.'

'How?'

'With respect, for a start,' she said. 'I'd have made them kneel at my feet and look up to me.'

'She did that,' he said excitedly. 'They had to kneel down in front of her.'

'Show me.' She stood up and he knelt at her feet. She looked down at him, then moved towards him until the hem of her skirt was just a few inches from his face, above the level of his forehead.

'Like that?' she asked. He nodded.

'That's good,' she said. 'That mistress obviously had the right idea.'

'The boys weren't allowed to look her in her face,' he told her.

'I should think not,' said Jenny severely. 'That is most disrespectful. You must keep your eyes here.' She drew an imaginary line around her hips and walked around him, so close that her hem brushed his forehead, then stood in front of him, gazing down at him with her hands on her hips. From his kneeling position, he should have a wonderful view up her skirt. She placed her feet apart, so that he could just see the G-string that concealed her sex.

'Did you have any women teachers at your school?' she asked.

He nodded. 'Two or three. One of them was very pretty.'

Jenny sniffed. 'No doubt you used to gape at her like silly idiots, and snigger among yourselves,' she said.

Benoit licked his lips. 'She sat up on a sort of stage, behind a desk,' he said, 'and'

'Go on.'

He gulped. 'Sometimes, when she wasn't thinking, you could see up her skirt,' he admitted.

'What did you see?' she asked.

He gulped again. 'They were white,' he said, and his Adam's apple bobbed up and down.

'What were white?'

He gulped again. 'Her knickers,' he admitted.

'Panties,' she told him. 'Knickers is a silly, old-fashioned word.'

'Panties,' he repeated.

'So you sniggered among yourselves, just because you could see her panties?' she asked him severely.

'Yes,' he admitted, bowing his head.

Jenny hoisted her hem to her waist. 'Well, now you can see mine,' she said, and moved closer, so that her G-string was only a few inches from his face. 'You're not sniggering now, though, are you?' she asked him. He shook his head.

'It's not so funny, is it, when you're on your own?'

'No,' he admitted. Her black lace G-string barely covered her sex, and she knew that it was transparent enough for him to see the slit between her legs.

'Now, tell me exactly what you can see,' she told him.

He gulped. 'Your legs,' he said, 'and your skirt and stockings and suspenders.' He stopped short, his face a brilliant scarlet.

'Stop making such a fuss,' she scolded him. 'They are just clothes, like a shirt or a tie. Nothing to get excited about. What else?'

'Panties,' he said.

'Tell me about them.'

'They're black,' he replied. 'They're made of lace.'

'What are they called?'

'Panties,' he replied.

'What sort of panties, stupid?'

'I don't know.'

'It's a G-string. Haven't you ever seen one before?' she demanded. He shook his head miserably.

'You don't know much, do you?' she said despairingly. 'What else did you snigger about?'

'When she leant over the desk to correct our work,' he admitted, 'you could see down her neck.'

'Her neck? What on earth are you talking about?' she snapped. 'Stand up.' He scrambled to his feet. He was very evidently erect, and stayed doubled over to hide the fact. 'Now what's the matter,' she asked.

'I . . . I, er . . .'

'Out with it,' she snapped. He still hesitated. 'Do you have an erection?' she asked, looking him in the eyes. He nodded. 'Then say so,' she commanded him.

'I have an erection,' he admitted.

'Is it uncomfortable?'

He nodded. 'Yes, very,' he told her.

'Then for heaven's sake make yourself comfortable,' she snapped. 'What did the teacher in the film do?'

'Make the boys take their trousers off.'

'Well, go on then.' He took off his shoes and pulled off his jeans.

'Now, how would you like it if a crowd of silly girls stood here sniggering at you?'

'I wouldn't,' he admitted.

'Well, now you know how it feels,' she told him. 'Maybe you won't be so keen to snigger in future. Sit down.'

She sat him down on a chair, put her hands on his shoulders and leant forward so that her bosom almost fell out of her low-cut blouse.

'Is that what your teacher used to do?'

He looked wide-eyed down her cleavage. 'Not as much as that,' he told her.

'Did she wear a bra?' she asked. He blinked at her in confusion. 'Brassière,' she said. He blinked again, and she opened her blouse to reveal her low-cut bra.

He nodded. 'Hers was white,' he told her.

'Well, why on earth are you making such a fuss about it?' she asked, and took off her blouse and skirt, shaking her head as if in despair at these young men.

'Now, having got all that out of the way, perhaps we can get on with our sex lesson,' she said. 'You'd better take those pants off for a start.'

He slid off the chair, opened his mouth, closed it again, opened it again, then shrugged and slid out of his underpants. He sat down again quickly, his face scarlet, and arranged the tails of his shirt to conceal his erection.

She stood in front of him again. 'Now,' she said bossily, 'what do you do when you are alone with a girl?'

He swallowed hard. 'Put your hand down her front?' he suggested. Jenny suppressed a smile with some difficulty.

'I suppose that is one way of putting it,' she admitted sarcastically, 'but I prefer to use the word caress. Do you know what it means?'

He shook his head.

'Give me your hand,' she told him. He held out his hand, and she separated out his fingers and ran their tips over the satin cup of her bra.

'Very gently and lightly,' she told him, 'as if she was made of eggshell china. Round and round, using just the tips of your fingers.' He started to caress her breast, giving it all his attention, as his fingers drew circles around her nipple.

'My nipples are becoming erect,' she said, 'so it is time to caress them. Remember, very very gently.' His fingertips moved on to the bumps under her bra and she breathed in slowly and moved her hips forward. She felt the tip of his penis touch her pudenda, and felt his body jerk.

She unclipped her bra and let her breasts spill out. 'That is very good,' she said. 'Now you must learn how to kiss a woman's body. Use your tongue and be very gentle.'

She guided his head on to her breast and moved her body against his as his tongue titillated her nipple, then took both his hands and encouraged them to caress the swell of her buttocks.

He was exciting her now. She closed her eyes and let the feelings wash over her. His hands caressed her bottom and she pressed herself against him and spread her legs wide. He moved his mouth to her other nipple and she took his hand and placed it between her legs.

'Women are very sensitive there,' she told him. 'Never press your fingers into her until she is damp.' He fondled her between her legs and carried on kissing her nipple. She unclipped her G-string and eased it away from her damp sex, then pulled it free of the cleavage of her bottom and let it fall. His hand slid between her thighs and he began to stroke her sex. She wriggled her hips, her mouth wide open now. His finger penetrated her and her vagina suddenly peeled open. She felt his finger thrust deeply into her, put her hand down and took hold of his penis. His body reacted violently to her touch and she was frightened that he would ejaculate. He was not circumcised and was obviously extremely sensitive. She moved her hand down to grip the base of his shaft and very carefully worked herself on to his prick, easing it into her, gripping his penis tightly in her hand.

She began to move her body, gently, up and down, fucking herself with his cock, taking care not to over-excite him. He gasped and sobbed, moving his own body as best he could. She started to move more urgently as he kissed her breasts again. She felt his penis swell and squeezed hard to throttle his ejaculation. After a few moments she began again, repeated the process once more, but the third time she was ready too, and used her hand to tickle her clit rather than to prevent ejaculation, and he cried out as he came. She felt her own climax sweep over her, just a few seconds after his first spurt of semen, but his pulsations went on and on, filling her up with his young, virile manhood, even as her own passion subsided.

Candie stood just inside the outer door, waiting for the visitor to arrive. She avoided looking down, knowing that, if she caught a glimpse of her long legs, so erotically set off by her high heels, sheer stockings and taut suspenders, she would be overwhelmed by embarrassment, but she could feel the inadequacy of her G-string every time she moved. It was designed to cover only the tip of her vagina, and left a line of carefully trimmed pubic hair on show above it. It stopped about one-third of the way along her sex, and the two taut thongs that replaced it passed on either side of her labia and then became one to pass between her buttocks.

She heard the lift arrive, stepped back to keep her legs out of sight, and opened the door. She knew the visitor at once from a television newsreel she had seen: Jean-Luc Lamartine, a rising star in the administration, and reputed to be able to navigate successfully in the highly complex minefield of French centre-right politics.

She held the door open, let him in, closed the door behind him and said, 'Follow me, please.' She felt his eyes sweep down as she swayed towards Lucien's office, and rolled her hips from side to side as she walked, flicking her heels in at each step, so that her buttocks moved voluptuously under her jacket. She heard the visitor catch his breath at the sight of her, and felt a little kick of satisfaction.

She stepped to one side at the office door and let the visitor enter, but Lucien called her in and introduced her to the newcomer. Jean-Luc bowed and kissed her hand with a stage-managed, old-world courtesy.

'Where are you from?' he asked, holding her hand in both of his.

'Australia.'

'I have been to Sydney and Melbourne,' he told her. 'They are both very beautiful cities – but the Australian women are even more beautiful.' He squeezed her hand meaningfully.

'Especially when their boss steals their skirt,' she said.

'He stole your skirt?' Jean-Luc asked in a shocked voice. He looked down and then turned to Lucien with his eyebrows raised. 'What does this mean?' he asked indignantly.

'Her legs are far too beautiful to hide,' Lucien argued.

Jean-Luc subjected them to a long and careful scrutiny, whilst Candie blushed furiously, then gave a very Gallic shrug and looked Candie in the eyes again. 'He is quite right,' he told her. 'Such wonderful legs should never be covered up.'

'I can see that I am out-voted,' she sighed, and looked down. 'I suppose I should be grateful I'm not topless,' she remarked, and ran her hands down her lapels and into her cleavage. His eyes moved down to focus on her bosom, and she used her two middle fingers to ease open her neckline and show him her bra. He looked up again, directly into her eyes.

'That may well be a temporary condition,' he told her, but Lucien put a stop to their flirtation. He unlocked a door leading to another annex, rather like hers, and ushered them both in. There was a computer on the ornate desk, and Candie was slightly surprised to notice that it was a powerful Macintosh, not an IBM like hers. Lucien produced a bottle of champagne and three glasses from a refrigerated bar, then uncorked and poured out the wine. Candie clinked glasses with them and wished them, '*Santé*'.

'How did this lucky dog discover you?' Jean-Luc asked Candie.

'She fell like manna from heaven,' Lucien replied.

'The secretarial agency sent me,' explained Candie, more prosaically.

'Candida is very competent,' Lucien added.

'I can imagine,' said Jean-Luc. He dropped the banter for a moment and looked at her seriously. 'What is on your CV?' he asked.

'Commercial English, French, and German,' she said, picking up his serious manner. 'Shorthand. Office procedures. Word processing, spreadsheet and database handling on IBM and Macintosh computers –'

'I didn't know you could use a Macintosh,' Lucien interjected, and Jean-Luc laughed and put his hand on her shoulder. 'Whatever you do,' he said to her, 'don't you dare touch his Mac: no one is allowed to touch his Mac.'

'I don't want any viruses brought in,' Lucien explained.

'What isn't on your CV?' Jean-Luc asked her, changing mood again.

'I can make coffee,' she told him, 'and, as you can see, I have a baccalaureate in stripteasing.'

'Have you thought of trying for a doctorate?' he asked.

'I'd love to,' she told him, looking at him over the rim of her glass, 'but I cannot find a suitable professor to instruct me.'

Jean-Luc laughed. 'When I get the education portfolio,' he promised her, 'your striptease doctorate will be my first priority,' and he sat down opposite Lucien.

Candie caught Lucien's eye and withdrew to her own annex. She was really penetrating Lucien's organisation now, she thought to herself, but had no doubt at all that

Jean-Luc would want to do a little penetrating on his own account before long. Sure enough, only a few minutes passed before Lucien called her on the intercom.

'Jean-Luc would like you to take a letter for him, if you wouldn't mind,' he said.

'Of course not,' she replied, and picked up her notepad. She went into the office, to find Jean-Luc standing by the open door leading to the other annex.

'We are extremely honoured, Candida,' he said. 'Lucien has graciously allowed us to use the conference room,' and he led her into the annex, and through another connecting door.

The conference room boasted a small table and four Louis XV chairs, but it was otherwise furnished like a bachelor pad, with a very large, deep sofa, a large-screen television receiver and a hi-fi unit. Three modern paintings, very explicit nudes, created an erotic atmosphere, and there was a beautiful display of freshly cut flowers. Candie walked over to smell the perfectly shaped roses, wondering whether the display concealed microphones and miniature cameras, whilst Jean-Luc closed the interconnecting door. He had brought in the bottle of champagne and had picked up two new glasses as he passed by the bar.

'Nice place for a conference,' she observed, looking around as he handed her a glass. 'So much more practical without those flip charts and projectors and things making the place look untidy.'

'They are all stowed away,' he told her, and took her arm to escort her to a series of cupboards. Sure enough, the first cupboard contained the flip charts and projectors she had mentioned. She opened the adjacent door, and felt her heart leap. It contained a rather complex framework that was obviously intended for sex games. It featured a leather-clad seat that was cut away to allow access to the victim's sex, with stirrups mounted on long extensible bars that could be arranged to hold the victim's body in any conceivable position.

'What are your qualifications in bondage and SM?' Jean-Luc asked, drawing the love seat out into the office.

She gave a short, rather brittle laugh. 'A levels,' she said.

'Then you will know you are over-dressed,' he murmured.

'I'm dressed for taking dictation,' she pointed out.

'You are over-dressed for that as well,' he told her. She drained her glass and gave it to him, put down her notepad and unfastened her jacket.

'You know who I am?' he asked. She took off her jacket.

'Jean-Luc Lamartine,' she replied, 'but I have an incredibly poor memory. If I saw you again, I probably wouldn't recognise you.'

'Selective loss of memory is a very useful attribute,' he told her, then raised his glass as he looked at her bra. 'You have a wonderful bosom,' he told her.

'I have a wonderful everything,' she assured him. He walked over and refilled her glass.

'Lucien explained to you?' he asked.

'Yes. I have been sworn to secrecy.'

'You know what he does?'

'He imports and exports fine arts and antiques.' He handed her the champagne and she sipped her wine. 'Plus maybe a nubile virgin or two?' she asked.

'It has been known,' he admitted, 'and handsome studs for our bored wives.'

'He didn't tell me that,' she said indignantly, then sighed wistfully. 'I've always wanted to visit a ladies' bordello,' she confided.

'You must ask Lucien to let you join Les Plaisirs d'Anaïs,' he proposed, and she looked perplexed.

'It is a very discreet ladies' club,' he told her. 'My dear wife is a very active member.' He reached out quite casually and placed his fingers in the centre of her bra. 'You are still over-dressed,' he said, and unclipped her bra. She breathed in, and felt her cheeks colour as the cups fell away and exposed her breasts.

'I see you know how bras fasten,' she said coolly.

'French politicians have to know everything,' he told her. 'Everything that is vital to the security and well-being of France, anyway.' He removed her bra and examined it carefully.

'Vivienne checked it for microphones when I arrived,' she pointed out, 'and I can assure you that the security and well-being of France is not threatened by anything concealed under my G-string.'

He looked down at her and shook his head. 'On the contrary, my dear Candida,' he told her, 'the security of France has been menaced more by what lies under your G-string than by all the armies in the world.' He motioned her towards the love seat. 'Why don't you sit down whilst I make sure you are really harmless?' he proposed.

Candie put down her glass and sat down gingerly on the love seat. He at once attached her ankles with the leather cuffs, so that her legs were stretched out straight in front of her as she lay back in the seat. She moved her legs apart experimentally and a ratchet clicked, preventing her from closing them again. He took her right wrist and lifted it over her head, and she felt the leather tighten around her wrist. A moment later, her other wrist was clamped to the machine and she was helpless. He looked down at her, smiled, and pressed a button. Suddenly, a motor hummed, and Candie shrieked as her wrists were pulled up and out and her ankles went up into the air and out until she was on her back with her hips lifted high and her legs forced wide apart. He reached down and released her G-string, and then stepped back and looked at her.

'I must admit that you look quite friendly,' he told her, then leant down and planted a quick kiss on her vagina. Candie wriggled with embarrassment as his tongue probed into her sex

'I hope Lucien isn't peering at us through the keyhole,' she said.

'He can peer all he likes,' he said, 'provided that is all he does.'

'What if he has a camera hidden?' she asked.

'He hasn't,' he told her, stroking her labia. 'If I discovered he was playing games, I would have him killed.' He opened her sex with his first and third fingers, and penetrated her casually with his long second finger.

She yelped as she felt his penetration, then looked up at

him, horrified at his cynicism. 'Could you do that?' she asked.

'His car has been blown up twice already,' he told her. 'All I would need to do is pass the word.' He put his other hand down and caressed her breasts, fondling her erect nipples. 'They might blow off more than his bollocks next time,' he said casually, running his fingers over her body as if she was a statue he had just purchased.

Candie was still digesting the news when she felt warm oil trickled on to her sex and massaged in with his fingers, and then she yelped louder as he penetrated her again, but this time with his prick: obviously, Jean-Luc was not a foreplay enthusiast. She felt him thrust into her experimentally, and then felt her body lifted as he adjusted the machine to maximise his enjoyment. His face became flushed as he began to push his penis deeper into her. He licked his lips and his thrusts became wild and uncontrolled. His body was suddenly an untamed animal that thrashed against her, once, twice, thrice: he groaned aloud and ejaculated with his prick rammed as deeply into her as possible.

Fifteen

By the time Igor returned to his hotel he understood what Hans had meant about being 'danced to death'. Suzie was a very inventive choreographer, but her wild, modern ballets all ended up with full penetration, a well-timed orgasm for her, and an additional bout of frustration for her partner. He felt in need of a long, relaxing bath and a rest before dinner, but there was a message waiting for him, which told him that Candie had left the Centre. He rang Jenny's number but there was no reply, and he realised that he had lost contact with her as well.

He bathed quickly, took a taxi to Jenny's flat and rang the bell, but a neighbour opened a window and told him she had been out all day, so he hired a car and drove out to the camping site which she used as a base. The Renault was there right enough, but there was no sign of Jenny, and she hadn't been seen all day.

He rang the emergency number she had given him, reported her disappearance, then drove back towards Paris, completely at a loss, taking the route that passed by the La Chasse St Hubert. There was a car parked just along the road from the gate and, as he drove by, he noticed a man emerge cautiously from the woods. The man had a furtive air and looked vaguely familiar. Igor slowed down and looked back, wracking his brains, then suddenly remembered: it was the man who had carried Candie's case at the airport. There was a service station just a little further on, and Igor turned into it, parked near the shop until the other car came by, then followed it.

He managed not to lose sight of the other car, even when

they crossed the *periphérique* and merged into the Paris traffic, and tailed him to a quiet area near the Madeleine. The man parked the car and went into a nearby restaurant. Igor drove around the corner and squeezed into a parking spot, then suddenly remembered that he had promised to ring Pascale that evening. He really had more than enough on his plate, but he didn't want to offend her, so he went into the bar of the restaurant, bought a *jeton*, and used the telephone. Pascale recognised his voice at once.

'Where are you?' she asked.

'In the centre of Paris.'

'Listen, can you meet me? I think I may be able to help you get a job.'

'Where shall we meet?' he asked, his mind almost completely taken up with his own problems.

'It's a bar called Le Rendez-Vous d'Anaïs, she told him, and gave him the address. 'Do you think you can find it?' she asked. Igor was looking idly at the notices attached to the wall as she spoke, and suddenly he blinked and almost dropped the telephone. 'Igor, are you there?' Pascale called.

'Yes, I'm here,' he said stupidly.

'Well, I'll see you there in about half an hour. Are you sure you can find it?'

'Oh yes,' he said, and put the phone down. He could find Le Rendez-Vous d'Anaïs' right enough. He was standing in it.

The afternoon was merging into evening and Jenny was still locked in the shed. Benoit had left almost immediately after his sex education lesson, promising that he or his father would escort her off the premises later, but Jenny had no intention of hanging around.

She used some of the petrol/oil mixture from Benoit's chainsaw to free the adjustable spanner, and poured some more of the mixture on to the nuts. She left it to soak in and then attacked the nuts again and again until one of the them moved. Ten minutes later, after a great deal of hard work, she had both nuts off and, after another two more minutes of intense effort, she managed to kick the door open. She took the time to wash her hands thoroughly, and to make sure she had left no trace of her stay in the shed, then slipped out and pushed the staple back into place, so that, to a casual passer-by, the door would seem to be locked.

She moved off into the woods, trying to avoid the thick undergrowth, knowing that wild brambles would tear her to pieces. She soon approached the place where she had looked out on to the road, but she knew now that the high wire fence which ran all around the estate was fitted with electronic devices, and the branch she had used to climb over it had of course been cut away. The place was guarded like Fort Knox when they had visitors, and she could certainly not get over the fence without detection.

She turned and made her way parallel to the fence, looking at the ground and stepping cautiously, wary of unsuspected rabbit holes tripping her up. She caught her breath as what had seemed to be a fallen branch suddenly slithered away. She saw the zig-zag design on the snake's back, the small triangular head, and the darting way it slipped into the bushes, and knew it was a *vipère aspic*, or asp. She waited until it was out of the way, then moved ahead cautiously, but she was only too aware of the pigeons flapping noisily away and of the female blackbirds calling out their shrill warning cries as she approached their nests. Gaston or Benoit would hear her coming a mile away, but the city-bred gangsters would probably notice nothing.

She moved away from the fence, towards the house, thinking that perhaps she could hide in a tradesman's van and escape that way; in any case, she was curious now about the house and what went on there. After a few minutes, she saw the roof and chimneys of an old hunting lodge, hidden in the the trees, and soon came up to the park that surrounded it.

It was at once clear that there was plenty of money around. The lawns were perfectly maintained, with gravel paths and French-style flowerbeds enclosed in tiny box hedges. Several big cars were parked to one side, and there were several uniformed chauffeurs, smoking and talking among themselves. She heard a noise and looked sideways. The two armed men she had already seen were patrolling the perimeter of the park and approaching her. She moved away and circled around the house.

The back of the house was much less ornate than the front. There were big tanks of diesel fuel and liquefied gas, a garage and a workshop, and several outbuildings. She could see into a big kitchen, but most of the windows were shuttered or heavily curtained, and the upstairs windows were all solidly barred. She crept towards an outbuilding that contained a diesel engine and an emergency electricity generator, then used it as cover to move cautiously up to the house; she found a chink in the curtains and peered inside.

There was a big room, luxuriously furnished, with a bar along one wall, and deep leather seats surrounding low tables in discreet, curtained alcoves. The walls were decorated with hunting prints and there were several trophies on the walls, but that was the only evidence that this was a hunting establishment.

There were nine or ten men sitting around in small groups, drinking, smoking and talking, and Jenny recognised some of them at once from the newspapers and television. They were influential, powerful men, and she realised that no-one would thank her for poking her nose into their affairs. If she was discovered now, the best she could hope for would be a new career as a junior filing clerk in some remote and insanitary overseas territory.

As she watched, the lights were lowered and the voices were hushed. A beautiful, aristocratic-looking girl came on to the stage, and the spotlights picked her up as she moved to the centre of the stage. She was tall, slim, dark and elegant, dressed in a long, burgundy-coloured slinky gown that clung to her perfect figure.

'Good evening, gentlemen,' she began. 'I think you all know me by now, but just in case you've forgotten me, my name is Vivienne and I am your mistress of ceremonies for the evening – so may I, on behalf of Lucien, myself, and all the staff, welcome you to the La Chasse St Hubert, for a little pre-season indoor hunting.' There was a laugh from some in the audience, but it didn't last long, and Jenny could detect a growing sense of excitement among the men.

'Now, for anyone among you who does not know our customs,' the girl continued, 'perhaps I can take a moment or two to explain. We have assembled, for your delight and pleasure, some very beautiful and talented young ladies. They will all be blindfolded, and they have strict instructions not to remove their blindfolds. Since they will also be handcuffed, there will in fact be little opportunity for them to do so.' She paused and looked around the audience as she whetted their appetites, then looked up and nodded to a hidden technician. The curtains opened, and there was a communal intake of breath.

A very attractive young woman was standing at the back of the stage, facing the audience, close to a square frame, which was about two metres high and made of steel tubes. Vivienne drew her forward into the spotlights. The girl looked to be in her early twenties, blonde, of medium height, with a soft, delicate face and high cheekbones. She was dressed in a clinging ankle-length black shimmering dress that clung to her body, and wore a thick black silk blindfold that covered her eyes completely. Her hands were held behind her back, and Vivienne made her rotate so that the audience could see the black leather handcuffs that held her wrists fast.

'I would like to introduce you to Erika,' Vivienne continued. 'She hails from the frozen north, but generates more than enough heat to keep herself and those around her at boiling point.' She paused again and the girl wriggled her body as if already aroused. 'Like all our hostesses,' Vivienne continued, 'Erika understands no French, except for one or two phrases, but these contain all the essentials for your communications purposes.' She turned to the girl and said, 'Erika, *ouvre tes jambes*.'

The girl responded immediately, like a clockwork toy, and pushed her feet apart. Her dress was slit in the front up to her navel and the slit opened at once, revealing long slender legs, clad in sheer black stockings, with black satin suspenders leading up to tiny scarlet panties. Her thighs above the stockings were pale and alabaster-like, and contrasted excitingly with the black and scarlet lingerie. There was a communal sigh from the audience, and the girl opened her mouth and pouted.

'Erika,' Vivienne asked 'what is your favourite pastime?'

'*Baiser*,' the girl simpered. '*J'adore baiser.*' 'I love to fuck.' She thrust her stomach forward and moved her hips invitingly. 'I want to be fucked,' she repeated.

Vivienne looked around the audience. 'Well, would any one of you gentlemen like to fuck Erika?' she asked. They looked down like embarrassed schoolboys, still too sober to take up a challenge like that.

Vivienne waited a few seconds. 'Don't be shy,' she said. 'She won't bite,' and she walked over to the girl and slipped her hand between her parted thighs. Erika at once rubbed her body against Vivienne's hand.

'What else do you like?' Vivienne asked her.

'Bondage,' the girl replied. '*J'adore ça.*'

'Well, we can so something about that,' Vivienne remarked, and flicked her fingers. Two men came forward and lashed the girl's ankles to the lower corners of the frame, then released her wrists, but chained them at once to the two upper corners of the frame.

The girl faced the audience, still blindfolded, her body taut and defenceless. Vivienne stepped forward and ran her hands lightly over the thin silk that covered Erika's breasts. The captive breathed in and lifted her bosom, obviously aroused by the other woman's touch. Vivienne fondled her breasts more deliberately, then turned and looked at the audience as she felt Erika's nipples. 'She's really begging for it,' she told the men, then turned back to the girl.

'*Tu aimes ça*?' she asked, still stroking the captive's breasts.

'*Ah oui, ah oui*,' Erika sighed, obviously loving it and wanting more. Vivienne dropped her left hand and ran her hands up the smooth inner surface of the girl's thighs, whilst her right hand continued to caress Erika's bosom. The girl was undulating more and more wildly and the men were perched forward on their seats, their cigars and drinks forgotten as they watched the show.

Vivienne reached up and flicked open a catch. The girl's shimmering dress rustled to the ground and the audience gasped. Her hips and naked breasts were very voluptuous and contrasted with her slim waist to give the impression of a living, breathing sex doll. Vivienne leant across her and kissed her nipples, which were already fully erect, and flicked at her up-standing teats with her cat-like tongue. Erika cried out aloud, and Vivienne, still kissing her breasts, explored Erika's curvy thighs with her fingertips, moving up and up the soft inner surfaces until she reached the lace edge of her panties. Suddenly, she deliberately ran her fingers along the line of the girl's sex, over the sensuous scarlet satin of the tiny bikini panties. The girl gave a squeal of sheer animal pleasure, thrusting her hips out to prolong the contact when Vivienne took her hand away.

'As you know, gentlemen, we have special rooms fitted out for bondage games in the basement,' Vivienne reminded her audience, 'and, as you can see, Erika and her friends would really love to spend time with you down there. *C'est vrai, Erika*?'

'*Ah oui*,' the girl whispered. 'I love bondage.'

'Anything else?' asked Vivienne, pressing her fingers deliberately up into the girl's sex.

'SM,' the captive replied breathlessly. '*J'adore le sado-maso*.'

'Really?' Vivienne replied, pretending surprise. 'Well, Erika, my dear, we can do something about that as well,' and she picked up a short multi-thonged whip, passed the thongs through her other hand, then ran them over the captive's body, up the girl's legs and thighs, and finally along the line of her sex.

'Does that excite you?' she asked.

'*Ah oui*,' the girl whispered. 'I love to be whipped.'

'Where shall I whip you?' asked Vivienne.

'*Partout*,' said the girl. 'Everywhere.'

The frame was supported on a small circular platform and Vivienne rotated the framework until the girl's back was to the audience, her alabaster skin now contrasting even more with her black stockings and scarlet panties.

'How about there?' asked Vivienne, stroking her back with the whip, then she suddenly lifted her arm and lashed the girl quite sharply across the shoulders.

Jenny winced. She could hear the smack of the lash and the girl's cry of pain quite clearly, and several pink stripes appeared almost immediately on the girl's back and shoulders. She saw several of the men flush with excitement as they leant forward, licking their lips at this barbaric ritual. The whip rose and fell again, and the girl screamed and writhed in an agony that was only partly simulated. The frame began to rotate slowly and Vivienne moved around, staying behind the girl as she was rotated to face the audience. Now they could see her face, her eyes still covered by her thick blindfold, and saw her mouth open as the whip fell again and she screamed aloud once more. Vivienne reached out and ripped at the catch of Erika's panties, and they dropped away. The whip smacked again, this time across the girl's buttocks. The frame continued to rotate, carrying the girl with it. Her back was now aflame from her shoulders to her thighs and she was beginning to cry out in a different register as the pain-induced excitement took hold. Vivienne changed target now and lashed with less force at the girl's breasts and sex as she spun around and around, until the girl was straining at her bonds, and obviously on the brink of orgasm.

Vivienne at last stayed her hand. She was panting, her face was pink with her exertions, and Erika's body was a mass of flame. She went to a table and came back with a jar of soothing balm, then turned to the audience.

'I'm sure one of you would like to massage this into Erika's body,' she said, and her eyes alit on a man in the front row. She came forward and handed him the jar of cream, and he stood up, rather bashfully, and went to the bound girl. Jenny just had time to recognise him as Jean-Luc Lamartine before the curtains closed. She stepped back, determined now to escape, but at that very moment a strong arm encircled her from behind, a hand was placed over her mouth, and she was propelled forcefully into the house.

Sixteen

Candie lay in her bath, soaking away her cares. She was now staying in a flat in the north of Paris, which belonged to the Centre but was supposed to be her domicile. Her contact with the Centre was through Sapphi, who played the role of her flatmate. Sapphi had debriefed her immediately she had returned home, and was now reporting to the Colonel, using a scrambled telephone link.

She climbed out of her bath just as Sapphi came in. The dark girl picked up a big towel and proceeded to pat Candie dry as she told her the news. 'The Colonel's over the moon,' she told her. 'He asked me to congratulate you on his behalf, and to put you a little more in the picture.'

'I'm all ears,' said Candie.

'As we suspected, and as you have now confirmed,' Sapphi told her, 'Lucien and that alley-cat Vivienne organise sex parties for the Paris bigwigs. It's all very cozy. Their clients are so powerful they can nip any investigation in the bud, so Lucien feels untouchable, and able to do just as he pleases.'

'Such as?' asked Candie. She picked a lace brassière and leant over to ease her bosom into its fragile cups.

'He is suspected of meddling in all kinds of things,' Sapphi said, 'but the most obvious risk is blackmail.' She clipped a matching garter belt around Candie's hips and seized the opportunity to plant a loving kiss on her coccyx. 'The DST would love to pin something on him,' Sapphi went on. 'They've tried to trap him a number of times, but he always wriggles out of it.'

Candie sat down to roll on her stockings. 'Jean-Luc isn't

scared of Lucien blackmailing him,' she pointed out. 'If Lucien steps out of line, he'll let the Hezbollah or whoever have a go at him.'

'That's typical French macho talk,' Sapphi replied angrily, as Candie carefully clipped her suspenders. 'The fact is, when you have these cozy relationships between politicos like Jean-Luc and smooth operators like Lucien, then almost inevitably, maybe several years later, Lucien will ask Jean-Luc to do him a favour.' Candie slipped into very pretty satin-and-lace French panties, then sat down and began to put on her make up. 'There will be no talk of nasty things like blackmail,' Sapphi went on, 'just a few remarks about the good times they've had together.'

'So where do we come in?' asked Candie, flicking mascara under her eyelashes. There was quite a long pause before Sapphi replied.

'Lucien must keep files on his clients,' she said at last. Candie stopped dead in her tracks, then finished making up her eyes.

'I suppose he must,' she agreed cautiously.

'The Colonel would like a copy of them,' Sapphi told her. Candie whistled softly, then picked up her lipstick.

'He doesn't want much,' she said, applied the lipstick and dabbed off the surplus, then reached for her dress. 'What will he do with them, if he gets them?' she asked, emphasising the 'if' as she slipped into the wraparound dress. She winced slightly as she pulled it tight to fix the clasp.

'I don't know and I don't care,' Sapphi replied cynically. 'They are all stupid men's games, anyway. Why should we care?' she added, and just then Candie's taxi arrived.

Gabrielle Lamartine said goodbye to her last customer and took a few paces up and down the road. She caught sight of her reflection in a shop window, but it didn't shock her any more. She was dressed to do a job, and Carl's working outfit certainly pulled the men. She looked around for another client, but Carl came by and nodded to her. She followed him up to his room and handed over the money she had earned.

'I knew it,' he said, his eyes shining as he counted the stack, then he peeled off a few notes. 'Here,' he told her magnanimously, 'go get yourself something.'

She tucked the notes into her handbag with a ridiculous feeling of satisfaction and pride, although she could have written out a cheque for a hundred times the amount without it even being noticed. The money was hers in a way that her housekeeping and clothes allowance would never be.

'So you made it!' he said, and produced champagne from a small fridge, drew the cork and poured the frothing wine into two glasses. He sat down, raised his glass and toasted her, then pulled her on to his knee. 'You look great,' he told her. 'How do you feel?'

'I feel great,' she replied.

'Do you really have to go?' he asked. 'We're having a party tonight, and I'd like to show you off to the boys.' He made it sound as if she was going back to prison, and Gaby realised that, in his eyes, that wasn't far from the truth. In the old argot, the pimps were the '*affranchis*', the enfranchised ones, the free men, and for them the bourgeois life was intolerable.

'I can't,' she told Carl. 'I'd really like to, but I can't. I have to go home.'

'I should have met you years ago,' he said. 'We'd have burned the town up, you and me.'

'You should have seen me at eighteen,' she told him. 'They said I was Lollobrigida's double – but I didn't know what to do with it.'

'I'd have shown you. You could have had anybody you wanted. Your looks and my brains – we'd have blown the place apart.' He poured out more wine and pulled her to him.

Gaby smiled to herself. She had read quite a few memoires written by French prostitutes. They all said they knew perfectly well what the men were up to, right from the beginning, and now she understood how they felt. The prowling men who picked up the wide-eyed country girls at the railway stations were so handsome it almost hurt, and very fit and tough. They drove big American cars, wore handmade silk shirts and expensive suits, and had money to burn. They called politicians, film stars, and media people by their first names, and had the dirt on them all. They took the girl to discreet restaurants up on the Butte, where the food was first-class and the clientele were all night people, insiders, people who knew how to live. They made her laugh, bought her expensive clothes, and taught her how to relish the very best champagne. They showed her off like a prized jewel and gave her a wonderful time in bed. Men and women have betrayed their country for less, and the girls walked into the trap with their eyes wide open.

'Would I have made a good *pute*?' she asked.

'The best,' he assured her, and cupped her breast in his hand. 'I hope you've been a good girl,' he said.

'Of course I have,' she told him proudly. 'I've been saving it for you.'

He picked her up as if she was a feather, and laid her on the bed. She gave herself to him willingly, sighing and laughing as he browsed over her body. He gave her no respite and she was quickly aroused. She had been on heat all afternoon: excited by the enormity of what she was doing; by the feel of her indecent clothes; by the way the men looked at her with lust written all over their faces; by her brazen behaviour in the street and in the privacy of her studio. Now she could relax. His hands and mouth explored her breasts, lightly pinched and sucked her nipples, then drifted down on to her stomach. He separated her legs and kissed them from ankle to thigh, and then he lavished his attention on her sex, nibbling at her labia and clitoris until she thought she would explode. He murmured to her all the time, mixing loving adoration with hard cynical street talk, and brought her up to a pinnacle of desire. Then he penetrated her, and taught her what fucking was all about.

Gaby was overwhelmed by it all, by his hard body, his delicate hands, his sensitive mouth that kissed and licked every part of her, and his handsome, sardonic face, looking down at her, smiling as he played with her body. She gasped and moaned, wriggled and undulated, called him her one and only lover, and came as she had never come before, in a tidal wave of an orgasm that carried her far, far away from her tame, timid, humdrum world. The afterglow went on and on, and, when she began to wind down, she discovered he was still there, inside her, hard and demanding. He brought her up again, screaming this time and out of her mind, and made her climax again and again, until she was as weak as a kitten, curled up in his arms, and at last the tame, timid, humdrum world intervened once more.

She knew that she could not return home immediately with these memories still racing around in her head. She went to the bathroom, put on one of the sexy G-string-plus-uplift-bra outfits she had brought with her, and pulled her demure dress over it with some considerable reluctance, feeling as encumbered and enveloped as a Muslim woman under her *tchador*. She promised to come back soon, kissed Carl goodbye, then walked out into the evening air and took a taxi to the Les Plaisirs d'Anaïs.

Seventeen

Igor put down the telephone and went back into the bar. He chose a position where he could keep the blond stranger under observation, and noticed that he was talking animatedly to the waiter.

A few minutes later, the waiter, having served the stranger's first course, came in to chat with the bartender. Igor intercepted him, drew him to one side, and took out his wallet; the waiter's eyes took in the wad of notes and he licked his lips.

'What did he want to know?' Igor asked, peeling off a few notes and nodding towards the restaurant.

'Are you another private detective?' the waiter asked. Igor nodded.

'He was asking about Les Plaisirs d'Anaïs.'

'What's that?'

'The club opposite.'

'What did you tell him?'

The man shrugged. 'It's a club for rich bints, isn't it?' he said. 'Bring your own toy boy or pick one up inside.'

'Did he mention the name "Candida"?'

'No,' the waiter told him. 'I must go now,' he added, and he grabbed the money and vanished into the kitchen. Igor thought for a moment, then took his drink into the dining room and went to the stranger's table.

'Do you mind if I join you?' he asked. The big blond man looked up at him. 'I'd like to talk to you,' he added.

'What about?'

'It's about the girl you sat next to on the plane from Munich.'

Wolfgang frowned. 'You mean that lingerie designer?' he asked.

Igor sighed inwardly at Candida's imaginative flights of fancy. 'That's the one,' he replied.

Wolfgang shrugged. 'It was just a pick-up,' he said.

'Then why are you here?'

Wolfgang looked at him. 'That's none of your business,' he said.

'What were you doing this afternoon, at the La Chasse St Hubert, up near Compiègne?' Igor persisted.

'That's my business too,' Wolfgang reminded him again. 'What's the problem with your lingerie designer?' he asked.

'She's gone missing,' Igor told him.

'Has she really?' Wolfgang looked at him sardonically, then nodded out of the window.

Igor looked up, just in time to see Candie pay off a taxi and ring the bell at the club. He emptied his glass and leapt to his feet, but the exit was at the other end of the room and the waiter had no intention of letting him leave without paying for his drink. By the time he was able to get outside, the door to the club was open. He opened his mouth to shout to Candie, but at that moment he was suddenly leapt upon and overwhelmed by Pascale, who flung her arms around his neck and smothered him with kisses.

Jenny was propelled, rapidly and not at all willingly, down a narrow corridor, up a staircase, along another corridor and into a bedroom. The door was slammed to and she turned angrily as soon as she was released, to come face-to-face with Gaston, as furious as she was. He held his hand up to warn her.

'Shut up!' he hissed. She choked back the protest she had been about to make.

'You bloody idiot,' he said, quivering with anger. 'You'll get us all shot. Why the hell didn't you stay where you were?'

'I was frightened,' she said.

'Who are you?' he asked. 'What are you up to?'

'I'm not up to anything,' she said. 'I saw two men

wandering around. They looked like gangsters. They scared me, so I decided to escape.'

He looked around in desperation. 'There's only one way now,' he said. 'Pretend you're one of the girls.'

'What?'

'Look, if they catch you,' he told her, 'you won't get your wrist slapped. You know where you'll end up? In a bloody knocking-shop, or ten feet under a motorway. Now for Christ's sake act sensible for once. Get changed, but smartish, and remember: you don't understand French, not a word, except for one or two bits and pieces.'

'But . . .' she began.

'You waste one more second,' he told her, 'and I'm turning you in, or I'll end up under a fucking motorway as well.'

'OK,' she said, sorry now that she was causing him so much trouble, and was soon naked and under the shower. She had put him and his son in real danger, so she tried to make amends. She dried herself quickly, grabbed a dress from the wardrobe and rummaged in her bag for stockings and panties. She dressed quickly, and made up her mouth and eyes, then transferred her make-up and odds and ends from her carry-all to an evening bag that she found in the wardrobe. She eyed Gaston secretly in the mirror as he opened the door and looked out into the corridor, then felt around for her special vibrator. She crossed her fingers: she would almost certainly get into very hot water for doing this, because she was launching an expensive operation, but she was scared. She pressed the secret switch and put the plastic sex toy in her handbag: it made no noise at all.

Gaston gave her last-minute instructions. 'They've got the lights out down there,' he said, 'so one more or less won't be noticed. When they've finished, sneak back up here and I'll get you out.' They slipped out quietly and crept down the stairs. In the corridor, he hurriedly fastened a silk blindfold around her eyes and manacled her wrists behind her back. She sensed that he had switched off the lights in the corridor, and was opening a door. She felt his hand on her arm, guiding her forward, then felt thick carpet under her feet. She was propelled gently forward, and heard the door close with a dull thud behind her.

Eighteen

The entrance to Les Plaisirs d'Anaïs was decorated with a large picture of Anaïs Nin holding hands with June Miller and gazing soulfully into her eyes, whilst June's husband Henry looked on. Candie was admiring it when the outer door opened and another woman arrived.

'Nice role model,' a new arrival remarked.

Candie smiled at her. 'I remember reading that Anaïs Nin lived every sex session twice,' she remarked, 'one for real and once again when she wrote up her diary. They said she probably enjoyed the second one more.'

'I don't keep a diary, so I have to enjoy the real sex,' the newcomer told her. 'Are you new here?'

'I've just started working for Lucien,' she replied.

'Really? That's wonderful. I'm Gabrielle,' her new friend told her, and held out her hand. 'Let me buy you a drink,' she offered, signed Candie in and took her to the bar. The lighting was subdued and a pale-faced young man tinkled away at a grand piano, whilst very handsome and attentive waiters moved around with drinks and *canapés*. She and Gabrielle sat down on a leather couch in a cosy alcove, and at once a waiter appeared with a list of cocktails and aperitifs. They chose their drinks and he went off.

Candie's eyes were becoming accustomed to the subdued lighting, and she could make out more of the surroundings. In one dark cubicle nearby, a woman wearing a pin-striped suit held hands with a pale, frail, ultra-feminine girl who seemed to have come out in her nightie. Another cubicle was occupied by a woman who was made up in a very brilliant style, with scarlet lips and very heavy dark-green eye make-up, sipping a cocktail and smoking a cigarette in a long holder. Candie registered a shock as she realised that she was wearing only French panties and stockings, plus a very ornate necklace, comprising gold chains and huge artificial gemstones, that half covered her breasts but left her scarlet-painted nipples exposed.

'If you feel like a little exhibitionism,' Gaby told her, 'there are absolutely no rules about dress codes. In fact, most of the women throw off at least their outer clothes as soon as they enter.'

'So the men are dressed and the girls are in their undies, even though this is a ladies' club?' Candida asked.

'The men don't stay dressed for long,' Gabrielle reassured her, just as the waiter reappeared with their drinks. He placed them on the table and looked inquiringly at Gabrielle. She nodded and he drew the curtain that screened off the alcove. He was dark, slim hipped and fierce looking, like a stage pirate, with a sardonic curl to his lip and a carefully managed growth of black designer stubble. Gaby raised her glass to Candie, sipped her drink, and looked appreciatively at the young man.

'Shall we see what he has in his pants?' she asked Candie. Candie coughed as her cocktail went down the wrong way, but the waiter didn't move a muscle.

'Why not?' she replied, feigning nonchalance.

'Why not indeed?' echoed Gabrielle, and nodded again to him. He started to unbutton his shirt and Gaby deliberately pulled up her hem. She was wearing black stockings and a very sexy G-string under her rather demure dress, and Candida was surprised at her streetwalker-style underwear. 'Let's inspire him a little,' Gaby proposed, and opened her legs deliberately.

Candie's hand trembled as she put down her glass. Gabrielle's minute satin G-string barely covered her sex, and she was posing for him like a porno model. He had his shirt off now, and his barrel chest was very heavily suntanned, nicely covered with thick dark hair that made him look really virile. She lifted her hem a little, just enough to show a suspender button, but Gaby took over and opened her dress right up to the tops of her thighs. Candie hurriedly crossed her legs: her satin-and-lace French knickers were more feminine than Gaby's G-string, but there was much more lace than satin, and nothing but lace between her legs. The waiter unzipped his fly and eased off his tight flamenco-dancer-style pants. All he had on underneath was a scarlet satin G-string, shaped like a cod piece to envelop his balls and penis, already stretched taut as he became erect.

Gaby beckoned him to approach. He came a step or two closer until his penis was just inches from them. His erection was now very evident, his huge shaft thrusting upward and outward in front of their eyes. Gaby put out her free hand and delicately stroked the tip of his penis, through the satin. He gasped and looked away for the first time.

'Look at us,' Gaby snapped, and his eyes switched back. 'You know where to look,' she told him severely. His eyes focussed on her opened thighs.

'The servants must look at your sex at all times,' she informed Candie, and tickled his penis-end with her finger-tips, then flicked at the sensitive underside with her long sharp nails. He writhed in agony, and his G-string showed a tiny wet patch where his penis leaked its pre-ejaculation fluid. Candie reached out and ran her fingertips over his huge fat balls, then scratched gently at the skin behind them. He groaned aloud and his mouth opened; he gulped in a huge draught of air and perspiration beaded his forehead.

'Look at my friend,' Gaby told him, and his eyes switched obediently to Candida's thighs. 'Open your legs,' she murmured to Candie.

Candie froze. 'My panties are indecent,' she whispered to her friend. Gaby flicked open the catch at the side of her G-string and the tiny triangle of satin fell away and exposed her vagina.

'He's used to it,' she explained. 'He worships pussies,' she added, 'don't you, Manuel?'

'*Si, senora*,' he said, gazing adoringly at Gaby's plump labia, then turned his gaze back to Candida. Candie felt her blush rush up into the roots of her hair, but slowly opened her thighs. His gaze was fixed on her parting legs, and his prick quivered and grew even longer at this new erotic show. Candie opened her mouth, breathed in deeply, and licked her lips, deliberately easing her legs further and further apart.

Gaby leant forward and pulled away his G-string, and Candie caught her breath. His penis was really huge, glistening in the dim lighting. She breathed in again, then opened her dress to her waist and spread her legs wide.

Gaby pushed one foot out sideways and exposed herself even more blatantly. Candie took a deep breath and followed suit. She spread her other leg out sideways and felt her labia part slightly, whilst her lubrication oozed more and more freely from her slit.

'Would you like to play with him?' Gaby asked, and pushed the waiter gently towards her pal.

'It's too cruel,' Candie said, but she put her hand, palm upward, under his lovely fat balls, and lifted them and squeezed them. She pulled him gently towards her, then opened her mouth and leant forward to suck the tip of his cock, all the time fondling his balls.

'It's a cruel world,' Gabrielle replied, 'and they are extremely well paid.' She turned him back towards her, moistened his prick with her champagne cocktail, and mimicked Candie's treatment of him. 'Would you like him to fuck you?' she asked Candie casually.

Jenny could sense that the lights had been lowered, so that everyone was more or less in the dark. She moved cautiously, holding her evening bag tightly, knowing that, inside the bag, the mock-vibrator was her lifeline – the microchips inside it should be picking up the coded signals from the GPS[1] satellites, processing them, and transmitting her location out into the night. Jenny could hear music, the sound of laughter and muted voices. She took a few cautious paces forward, and her foot touched a partition. Two male voices, deep in a murmured conversation,

[1]GPS = Global Positioning System.

detached themselves from the background hum, and Jenny realised that some of the participants were still wheeling and dealing.

'When is it going to break?' asked one man. Jenny recognised the voice as that of a well-known left-wing anti-racism campaigner.

'The day after tomorrow,' his companion replied. Jenny recognised his voice as well. It belonged to a senior politician connected with the Ministry of the Interior, a right-wing law-and-order enthusiast, and a bitter enemy of the first speaker, at least in public. 'FCR stays in the limelight for another day, and then we blow it apart,' he continued. 'The disclosure will be timed to catch the main television news, and the next day it should make the front page of most of the dailies.'

Jenny cocked her ear. '*Le Front Contre Racism*', or FCR, was a new, far-left, anti-racist movement which was getting a lot of media attention, and their charismatic leader was openly criticising the existing anti-racist groups as being too soft. 'Have you got those fraud details?' the law-and-order man asked.

'It's all here.' Jenny heard the sound of papers rustling. 'He's been stashing away at least half the funds they receive into numbered accounts in Switzerland,' he revealed.

Jenny felt her heart pounding. The existing anti-racist group had evidently decided to get rid of their upstart rival and this man was blowing the whistle on its leader. She started to steal away, but she stumbled over a step, and at once a strong masculine hand seized her.

Several kilometres away, perched high on a tower, a mobile-telephone repeater picked up the signal from Jenny's transmitter, separated it from the telephone calls it was handling, and posted it on to the DST receiving station outside Paris. Their big mainframe computer chewed up this trivial amount of data, flashed a message on to a screen, and the duty office picked up his telephone. 'We've located that DGSE girl,' he told his supervisor.

* * *

Candie looked at Gabrielle in amazement, then at the waiter, then at Gabrielle again.

'You mean I can have sex with him?' she asked. 'Here?' Her voice went up into a squeak.

'Why not? That's what the cubicles are for,' Gaby reminded her, and went back to sucking his cock, whilst her lithe cool fingers stroked his balls. Candie felt her lubrication suddenly flood from her sex, soaking her lace panties, and she stood up, unfastened her dress and stripped it off. She was very close to him now and she threw her arms around his neck and kissed him. His mouth opened at once, his tongue entered her like a rapier, and his hands, powerful and demanding, but infinitely gentle, caressed her breasts through the lace cups of her brassière. Candie made a moaning noise and went for him like a tigress. Her head twisted and turned as she sought out new angles for their kisses, and her fingernails clawed at his back. Throwing all modesty to the winds, she released her panties and seized his penis, taking it away from Gaby like a dog grabbing a bone from a rival. Without more ado, she put one foot up on to the couch and inserted its tip into her sex. She was peeled open already and his penis slid into her well-lubricated tunnel like a sword into its scabbard. She fell back on to the couch, impaled on his enormous shaft, and he began to thrust into her like a powerful machine. She kissed him desperately as her body was split apart by his virility, then felt Gaby's hands release the front-fastening of her bra. The next moment, Gaby's mouth was around her nipple and Gaby's fingers were on her clit.

It was irresistible. She cried out and bounced up and down, pinned to the couch by his huge prick, feeling her breasts being ravished by Gabrielle, and with her friend's expert fingers doing just what was needed to her clit. A moment or two later, she felt her orgasm overwhelm her and she screamed aloud as her passion took control.

'Well I never, we have company,' said the law-and-order enthusiast, and he pulled Jenny forward until she came up against his knee. 'What are you doing here?' he asked sharply. She remembered Erika's catechism, giggled a little drunkenly and swayed forward against him.

'*Je veux baiser*,' she said, in a high-pitched little-girl voice.

'She doesn't understand French,' the other man chipped in. 'They're all from Eastern Europe.' Jenny felt the hand tighten on her wrist.

'She'd better not understand,' the right-winger said threateningly, 'unless she wants to go for a long walk on a short pier.' Jenny giggled some more, and slid her legs apart.

'*Je veux baiser*,' she repeated, pushing her stomach forward so that her dress parted at the waist.

'Old Lucien certainly knows how to pick 'em,' the left-wing activist commented, and Jenny felt his hand on her leg. She fought down her desire to flee and wriggled encouragingly as his fingers followed her suspender up to her panties.

'*Je veux baiser*,' she said once more.

'All in good time. Here, have a drink.' She heard champagne being poured into a glass, and the next moment felt the glass against her lips. She sipped the wine awkwardly, and coughed as the bubbles made her choke. The men laughed, but she felt her handcuffs removed and took the glass gratefully in her left hand as the law-and-order man pulled her on to his knee. Jenny threw her right arm around his neck as her dress opened. His free hand stroked her bare thigh and she crossed her legs to protect her sex, but nuzzled into the side of his neck. He was a big, powerful man, and she could feel his muscles rippling.

'You're sure we can rely on those two Malawi girls?' he asked, picking up the interrupted conversation.

'Sure we can,' his left-wing colleague replied. 'He's not from their tribe, they're being well paid, and they've both been offered a film test.'

'We want all those assault charges to stick,' the law-and-order man reminded him. Jenny giggled again and wriggled on his knee as his hand absentmindedly stroked her thigh.

'They will,' the left-winger replied confidently. 'I've been rehearsing them both day and night, especially at night,' he added. 'The young one fucks like a rattlesnake.'

'So does this one, if I'm any judge.' A predatory hand slid in between Jenny's thighs.

'Not like African women,' his pal assured him. 'They know what it's for and they're genuinely horny. White women are all frigid or dykes.' Jenny felt his hand untie a shoulder strap. She yelped and automatically went to put up her left hand, trying to catch the bodice and cover her breast, but her glass was taken away and her hand was seized. She felt her bodice fall away and expose one breast. A predatory hand squeezed and fondled her bosom.

'Her tits aren't bad,' the left-wing activist said.

'Lucien knows what he's doing, and he trains them well,' his pal replied. He tapped Jenny's thigh and added, '*Ouvre tes jambes, ma belle*,' and made her uncross her legs. He slipped his hand in between her thighs, just above the tops of her stockings and tried to prise them apart. She resisted and he slapped her thigh quite hard. '*Ecarte tes jambes, pute*!' he snapped. Jenny felt the blush burning her cheeks as she let her legs separate. His hand slipped down into the warmth at the top of her legs and his finger pushed down between them, over her satin panties.

'We should ask Lucien to provide us with some African cunt for a change,' he remarked.

'It could be dangerous,' his pal replied.

The right-winger laughed. 'We have the deputy head of the vice squad over there,' he pointed out, 'you, the top union bosses, bankers, financiers, industrialists. Jean-Luc over there. We have our well-placed friend in the DST. Who else do you want ? The Prime Minister? *Monsieur le Président*?'

'Lucien is scared stiff of a leak.'

'Come off it. We all know that there are just three men in this country who control the media, and they are all members of the club.' He forced Jenny's legs wide apart and ran his finger along the damp line of her sex.

* * *

Jenny's boss, a very experienced thirty-eight-year-old named Chantal, looked at an Ordnance Survey map of the region to the south of Compiègne and tried to decide what to do next. La Chasse St Hubert was out of bounds as far as the DGSE was concerned. Any overt search operation would have to be carried out by the police and any covert action would have to be organised by the DST. Neither would move a muscle without copper-bottomed evidence that something was amiss, and she had none. Even if she had, they would need to go very high indeed to obtain authorisation for a search operation: La Chasse was a private rendezvous for top politicos, and one didn't lightly raid premises where one might stumble upon the Prime Minister having a very private conference with an international terrorist, or enjoying an even more private tête-a-tête with a woman. Chantal was pretty sure that, long before they had authorisation to search the place, leaks would occur and Jenny might vanish, perhaps for good.

She had no idea how her subordinate had ended up inside La Chasse, but, if Jenny was caught, it could look like a deliberate attempt by the DGSE to infiltrate a top-secret political meeting place, and the repercussions of such a scandal didn't bear thinking about. She imagined the newspaper headlines, the enforced resignation of the director, and an untimely end to her own career, and decided to take the problem to her boss.

'May I come in?' a voice called.

'Sure, Jean-Luc, come right in,' called the right-wing politico. Jenny smelled fresh perfume and realised that another girl had arrived with Jean-Luc. There was a general squeezing-up to accommodate the newcomers, then Jenny heard the left-winger stand up. He made his excuses and a moment later he left. Jenny felt Jean-Luc slide on to the vacated seat and she felt her knee touch the stockinged leg of another woman.

'How's it going?' Jean-Luc asked.

'The stuff he's given us looks OK,' the right-winger admitted, 'and he needs to get the FCR off his back . . .'

The confidences began again and Jenny continued to register the information, but was genuinely worried now about her safety. She had already overheard far too much, and she could not keep up this masquerade for long. The hostesses probably knew each other, at least slightly, and she was not even sure that the other girl was still blindfolded.

'*Je veux baiser*,' whined the other girl. Jenny recognised her voice as that of Erika, the blonde who had performed the SM show with Vivienne.

'*Moi aussi je veux baiser*,' Jenny repeated.

'We're busy: go fuck each other and keep quiet,' said her partner, and eased her sideways on to the seat. She found her body pressed against that of the new girl and a moment later the girl's hands were all over her and her mouth was being forced open by the other girl's frantic kisses. She felt the thick blindfold over the other woman's eyes and felt a stab of relief, but her body was now being assaulted by new and much more knowing hands. She felt the clip of her dress release and the satin sheath was quickly stripped off her. She put out her own hands. The other girl had lost her dress and panties, and wore just a garter belt and stockings. As soon as Jenny touched her thigh she opened her legs wide, grabbed Jenny's hand and guided it on to her sex, moaning with pleasure. Her kisses doubled in intensity and Jenny felt her hands fumbling at the catch at her hips. The next moment, the girl was ripping off her panties as her mouth sucked at her nipple.

The girl's frenetic assault had raised Jenny's arousal to boiling point, and she had some difficulty in following the men's conversation that went on over her head, but it was clear that double- and triple-dealing was the order of the day, then suddenly silence fell. Jenny realised that the men had been distracted from their business discussions and were watching the erotic show that the two girls provided for them.

'How about changing ends?' Jean-Luc proposed.

'Sure.' Jenny felt the men stand up and change places. The next moment, she felt Jean-Luc's hands come around her from the back and begin to fondle her breasts.

'What's your name?' he asked, whispering in her ear in French.

'Jenny,' she told him, almost without thinking, her mind now totally overwhelmed as she battled with the intellectual and physical stimulation that flooded her brain.

'*Je veux baiser*,' the other girl whimpered.

'Belt up,' said the law-and-order man. 'The cabaret is due to start in ten minutes and I don't want to miss it.'

'*Je veux faire pi-pi*,' Erika whined.

'Off you go then.' Jenny heard the other girl stand up and make her exit. She gave her half a minute and then said she too wanted to go to the powder room. Jean-Luc escorted her to the exit, and she stepped through the door into the corridor. A hand took her wrist.

'Where are you going?' a voice asked. She recognised it as belonging to one of the gangsters she had seen that afternoon.

'Toilette,' she said. He took her blindfold off and she blinked in the sudden exposure to the light. He looked at her appreciatively, and she was acutely conscious of her nudity.

'Don't be long,' he said, tapping his wristwatch, and let her go. She felt his eyes on her as she walked up the stairs.

Nineteen

By the time Pascale released him, the door to the club was firmly closed, and Igor realised that he would do better to take it easy. Candie had been alone and not under duress, and at least he now knew where she was. He allowed Pascale to lead him back into the bar, and they sat down at a table tucked away in the corner.

'I think I may be able to get you a job,' she told him.

'Where?' he asked.

'Over there, at Les Plaisirs d'Anaïs,' she replied. 'It is a very exclusive club for rich, idle women,' she explained, 'especially the wives of the high and the mighty.'

'What sort of job?' he asked.

'What do you think?' she asked impatiently. 'As a stud, of course.'

'You mean, sell by body for money?' he asked in horrified tones.

'Stop playing the fool,' she told him. 'Now, do you want to see Sandrine or not?'

'Who's Sandrine?'

'She looks after the male staff.'

Igor didn't hesitate: it was obviously an ideal way to make contact with Candie. 'Sure I want to see her,' he replied, 'and thank you for taking all this trouble,' he added.

'You haven't got the job yet,' she pointed out, 'and if you want it, you have to keep your mouth shut and have a very short memory.'

He shrugged and finished his drink. 'No problem,' he replied.

'Right. Let's go see Sandrine,' she said, 'but remember, she is as tough as old boots and she doesn't like smarty-pants men, so watch it.'

'I'll watch it,' he promised, and allowed her to pay for the drinks, then left with her. Wolfgang, just finishing his meal, smiled as they passed.

'Try not to lose this one,' he murmured to Igor.

Pascale led him down a small alley and into the employee's entrance to the club, then escorted him along a corridor and knocked on a door. A woman's voice called, 'Come in,' and Igor found himself face to face with Sandrine. She was around thirty-five, very tall and well-built, and very attractive, with long auburn hair, and she was wearing a long emerald-green evening gown with a very deep décolletée.

'Sandrine, this is Igor, the man I was telling you about,' Pascale said. Sandrine stood up, shook hands, and looked him up and down. In her high heels, she looked down on him, which was a novel experience for Igor.

'Pascale tells me you need a job,' she said. Igor nodded.

'She also tells me you have certain talents,' she continued.

Igor shrugged. 'That's not for me to say,' he replied.

'What kind of work have you done?'

'Chauffeur, masseur, tennis coach, ski instructor –'

'Have you ever had any trouble with the police?'

'Just speeding and parking tickets, that sort of thing.'

'Take your clothes off, please. There are some hooks over there.'

He hung up his jacket, took off his tie, peeled off his shirt, then his shoes, socks and pants. He paused for a moment. 'If it makes you feel better,' Sandrine told him, 'I was trained as a nurse.'

Igor took his underpants off and stood facing her. She looked him up and down again. 'You look healthy enough,' she remarked. 'Have you ever had a major illness?'

'No.'

'You don't smoke or take drugs?'

'No.'

'Very well. Let's see how you perform,' she said, then turned to Pascale. 'Warm him up,' she said, and took off her earrings.

Pascal had her dress off already, and immediately pounced on him. He felt Pascale's warm chubby arms link up behind his neck, felt her plump body pressed against his, her breasts against his bare chest, and her mouth open and demanding on his. Her tongue flicked boldly into his mouth, her stomach thrust demandingly against his groin, and his penis obediently erected, pressing up between her parted thighs.

Over her shoulder, he saw Sandrine unzip her dress and step carefully out of it. Underneath, she wore a tight emerald-green corset that was made to fit her slim-waisted figure exactly. He felt his penis jerk vigorously at the sight of her, and the tip pressed upward into Pascale's tight panties. Pascale obviously felt the thrust of his erection, because she at once started to strip off her panties.

'That won't be necessary, Pascale,' said Sandrine warningly.

'No, Sandrine,' said Pascale submissively, and pulled her pants up again.

'Let's give him something to eat, shall we?' the tall redhead suggested.

'Oh, let's,' agreed Pascale, and led Igor over to a narrow padded couch, long enough for a man to lie full length, covered with a thick paper cover. There was a rail along each side and a seat was positioned so that it could run along the rails. The seat was shaped to support the user's hips but the centre was cut away.

Igor lay down on the narrow couch, and Sandrine came and stood astride him. He looked up at her long tapering legs, clad in black stockings held taut by her emerald-green suspenders. She wore tiny green satin panties, and he could see the tight nylon bridging her sex.

He felt Pascale move down and seize his ankles. In a very short while, they were fastened firmly to the couch. A moment later, his wrists were taken and placed in leather handcuffs, so that he was soon immobilised.

Sandrine stood over him during this operation, running her hand gently over her sex, fingering her slit until a line of moisture appeared. Once he was tied down, she unfastened a clip and the panties fell away. She was a genuine redhead and her big, luscious vagina looked as if it won many a hard-fought bedroom battle. She sank down on to the seat, with her legs apart, and moved so that her sex was immediately over Igor's face.

She pressed a button, and the headboard began to lift, so that Igor's face was brought inexorably up towards Sandrine's waiting vagina, and she tilted the seat until she was lying back at almost forty-five degrees. Igor's forehead just passed through the cut-out in the seat and, by the time his mouth contacted her vagina, he was held fast, unable to move his head one way or the other.

'Look after him, Pascale,' said Sandrine, and then to Igor. 'I am told you are an expert in cunnilingus, Igor. Let us see you prove it.'

Igor thrust his tongue up into her sex, and at the same time felt Pascale's soft eager mouth envelop the tip of his penis. Her tongue tickled the skin under the tip of his cock, whilst his own tongue tasted Sandrine's lubrication.

Sandrine's sex was like a live animal as she undulated her body in the chair, moving her hips and legs continuously to vary its position. His tongue darted into the cavity of her vagina and explored its inner recesses, whilst Pascale's fellation aroused him to fever pitch.

He heard Sandrine sigh with satisfaction. 'This one certainly knows what a man's tongue is for,' she told Pascale.

Igor flicked his tongue around her inner labia and licked her vaginal lips, then sought out her clitoris. He heard Sandrine give a sharp high-pitched cry as he found his target, and then she was wriggling much more fiercely.

A moment later, the chair slid away. At the same moment, Pascale's mouth left his penis. She appeared in his line of sight, grinning down at him, then kneeled quickly beside him and started to kiss him passionately. At the same moment, Igor felt Sandrine's pussy descend upon his prick and take possession.

He gave a very muffled sob as his penis was ravished by Sandrine's extremely expert vagina. Pascale lowered a breast on to his face. He sucked her nipple and she moaned with pleasure as her breast enveloped his mouth and nose, whilst Sandrine writhed and undulated with his penis inside her. Igor gritted his teeth and held out, using all the techniques that had been drilled into him. Just feel the pleasure, he told himself; don't think about what you or the others are doing. Orgasm is triggered by the brain; it is not automatic.

Sandrine was really in overdrive now, fucking him more and more furiously until she suddenly jerked three or four times, then gradually became still. Pascale moved away and Sandrine stood up, panting heavily, and licked her lips.

'Release him,' she said. Pascale did so, and Igor sat up, then staggered to his feet like a drunk. Sandrine saw that he was still erect and nodded approvingly.

'You'll do,' she said, and looked at her wristwatch. 'Are you free to start right away?' she asked. Igor nodded dumbly, wondering what he was getting himself into.

'Pascale will take you downstairs and show you the ropes,' Sandrine told him, then turned to Pascale. 'The private cabin,' she told her.

Igor went to pick up his clothes but Sandrine waved him away. 'You won't need those,' she told him.

Chantal's boss was an elegant fifty-year-old called Xavier. He was attending a formal reception when his pager buzzed and he used a nearby telephone to call his office. Like most of the senior DGSE executives, he was a professional military man, and he quickly extracted the salient points from the carefully coded report of his subordinate. He made his excuses to his hosts and went to his car, then called up Chantal again and went into detail on a secure, scrambled radio channel.

He cleared down and thought for a long time, then rang the Colonel, who was an old colleague, but one with whom he now had no formal contact. Even on the scrambled channel, they used a private code that was not part of any standard service protocol. He continued the conversation for two minutes, asked the Colonel to seek out further information, then cleared down the call and lit a cigarette, recalling the past as he waited.

It had all begun just after the Kennedy assassinations. Keeping tabs on President Kennedy's bed companions had been a full-time job for a whole CIA department, and they'd had another section trying to keep pace with Howard Hughes's actresses. The files they had accumulated were explosive enough, but they had decided to anticipate trouble from now on, and to keep files on the sexual appetites of all the top-ranking politicians, industrialists and so on, who were obvious blackmail and corruption targets. That was how the ultra-secret S-Files project had been born.

They needed a clandestine organisation to store their files, that could not be closed down at the whim of a new government or president, and they decided to fund specific research in an international sex-research laboratory and, under cover of these activities, to hide their files among those of the thousands of anonymous volunteers. Under cover of their own research projects, they infiltrated members of their own staff to manage the S-Files and to keep them secure.

Little by little, they had taken chosen friends into their confidence. A group of self-effacing men and women, highly placed executives in the security services, and specialising in sex-related threats, had met together in great secrecy and had set up an organisation to share their data and collaborate in the combat against high-level blackmail and corruption. Xavier was one of the founders, and, like all his colleagues, he kept the existence of the organisation rigorously secret, even from his closest colleagues.

A major problem was acquiring the data. This meant penetrating the very secret organisations that provide sexual partners for the high and mighty, and that required trained agents with unusual sexual skills. They had come up with two cardinal principles: one, the agents should operate well away from their own country, so that they were unknown, and two, they must not know who they were working for, so that they could not reveal the truth even if they were captured and interrogated.

Xavier drew on his cigarette and stubbed it out. The Australian girl, Candida, was a typical example. She believed that she was 'penetrating' the Centre on behalf of the Australian secret service, but she was in fact working for it, and she had certainly infiltrated Lucien's organisation very successfully, but now Jenny was placing the whole operation in jeopardy, and he had to get her out of La Chasse before she was discovered.

His car telephone rang: he switched on the scrambler and listened attentively as the Colonel reported that Igor was at Les Plaisirs d'Anaïs, and was scheduled to perform on stage that night at La Chasse. 'He's partnering an English girl called Suzie,' the Colonel continued, and Xavier suddenly cheered up. He cleared down hurriedly and set up a call to Budleigh Salterton.

Candie was taking a cleansing shower with Gabrielle when her new friend received a message. 'Sandrine's found a new stud for me,' she said excitedly. 'Let's go take a look at him.'

'I don't want to play gooseberry, Gaby.'

'Don't be silly. There's more than enough to go round,' Gaby told her, sorting out a change of underwear from her private locker, and she slipped into a very high-cut body-stocking that set off her voluptuous bottom well. Candie put on new French panties and a camisole top, the girls put on new sheer stockings and garter belts, then slipped on their shoes and set off, arm-in-arm, giggling together like schoolgirls.

'Sandrine knows a girl called Pascale,' Gaby explained to her. 'She runs a small studio and tests out would-be blue-film actors. If they are really good, she brings them to see Sandrine, and if Sandrine takes them on, then I get first bite at the cherry. This one will be ready for us in a few minutes, so I'll show you how it all works in the meantime.'

They took the lift down to the basement, and Candie found herself in a corridor with doors leading off it. Gaby opened a door, let Candie enter, and closed it behind them. There was a big armchair facing a glass screen.

Candie caught her breath. On the other side of the screen was a big X made of black-painted wood, and chained to it was a naked man, facing them. His body was lightly oiled so that his muscles glinted in the spotlights, and it was clear that he was a body-builder. Candie licked her lips like a hungry tigress looking at a tethered, juicy-looking goat.

'We have the choice,' Gaby explained, 'as to how we get the slave ready to pleasure us. One way is to give him a little show,' she said.

'Let's do that,' said Candie eagerly. Gaby pressed another switch and their cubicle was promptly bathed in light, whilst the screen slid away.

The young man had been looking into a full-length mirror, but he was now confronted with two very beautiful women, dressed in sexy lingerie, with their arms around each other, who looked at him appreciatively whilst their hands caressed each other. His penis erected very rapidly, which the girls naturally regarded as a compliment, but just then someone tried the door, and Gaby opened it. Outside was an attractive woman, around forty years old, and a girl of around eighteen, pretty and innocent-looking, dressed in a tiny baby-doll nightie in transparent white nylon.

'I didn't mean to interrupt,' the woman said apologetically.

'We were just leaving,' Gaby told her. 'We have another appointment,' and she and Candie left the cubicle. The young girl peeped in and her eyes almost popped out of her head.

'Well, off you go then,' said the woman. The young girl, blushing furiously, was pushed into the room by the older woman, who closed the door behind her.

'She's my daughter,' she explained in a whisper. 'She's fallen in with a very odd bunch of girls at her college. Very odd. I do believe she may still be a virgin. Imagine, at her age!' But at that moment there was a series of shrieks from inside the room, and Gaby smiled.

'Not for much longer,' she said, and they moved on. 'In the old days,' Gaby explained to Candie, 'French bourgeois men always took their sons to the local prostitute, so that he would learn how to treat women properly. Now, the mothers bring their daughters here, to show them how to treat a man properly.'

'Now, that is what I call progress,' Candie remarked, but Gaby was looking at her watch.

'Pascale should have this new stud ready for us by now,' she said, and she ran eagerly ran along the corridor and used her own key to open a door marked 'Private'. She ushered Candie in – and Candie found herself looking straight at Igor.

'Wow!' said Gaby appreciatively, and Candie could understand why. Igor was naked and chained to another X-shaped cross, oiled, glistening, panting and moving agitatedly in his bonds. Pascale was naked except for her stockings and was licking his shaft luxuriously, with very evident success. As they watched, she stood up and pressed her body against his, rubbing herself against him. The X was tilted slightly backward, so that she could lie against his body, and there were small steps on each side so that the woman could lift herself and impale herself on the man's penis. Pascale gave them a demonstration as they watched, and Candie breathed in indignantly as she saw her boyfriend's penis sink into the soft, eager vagina of this plump little blonde, but Gaby was already rolling away the screen. A moment later Igor, his penis well up inside Pascale, found himself looking into the eyes of his all-time sweetheart.

Candie folded her arms and looked him in the eyes as Pascale bounced up and down on his shaft, but Gaby didn't waste any time.

'Move over, Pascale,' she said bossily. Pascale rolled her eyes but obediently wriggled off his penis and Gabrielle promptly took charge, licking and sucking his rounded knob whilst her hands explored Igor's virile body. 'Come and join in,' she invited Candie.

Candie leant against the bit of Igor that was still available, which wasn't much. Gaby and Pascale were having a little fight over Igor's penis, and Candie managed to get her mouth close to his left ear.

'Wait till I get you home,' she murmured.

'I'm following up a lead,' he replied unconvincingly. 'What are you doing in a girl's bordello in your underwear?'

'Don't change the subject,' Candie hissed, but she realised that she was really in no position to criticise, and then Gabrielle stood up and put an end to the conversation.

'He's gorgeous, isn't he?' she said. 'Where did you find him, Pascale?'

'He's out of work, and he wants to be in blue films,' Pascale explained. Candie tipped her head and raised her eyebrows at Igor. 'He fucks beautifully,' Pascale added helpfully. 'He was in me for simply hours this afternoon, and he didn't come once, no matter what I did.' Igor coughed modestly and rolled his eyes.

'What a wonderful unsolicited testimonial,' cooed Candie, smiling sweetly, and love bit the lobe of his ear, but clamped her teeth secretly until his eyes watered. Gabrielle unfastened the three buttons between her legs, mounted the small steps on either side of the cross, and descended on to Igor's prick. She sighed with pleasure and looked up at Igor with moist hooded eyes, then put her arms around his neck, lay her body against his, and began to move slowly up and down.

Pascale looked up at Candie. 'Hello, I'm Pascale,' she said.

'Sorry, I forgot to introduce you two,' said Gaby, absentmindedly. 'Pascale, Candie,' and she went back to kissing Igor.

'Hi, Pascale,' said Candie. She came up behind Gabrielle, put her hands around Gaby's body, took her breasts in her two hands, and mouthed, 'Sex maniac!' at Igor over Gaby's shoulder.

'Oh, there was a telephone call for you, Candie, when I was with Sandrine,' Pascale told her. 'It was from a man. He wanted to thank you personally: he said you'd given him the most magnificent sexual experience of his life and that he hoped to repeat the experience tomorrow.' Igor looked at Candie over Gaby's shoulder, and raised his eyebrows. 'You must have really wound him up,' added Pascale, with evident admiration.

'It was nothing, really,' Candie protested, as her ears turned pink.

'That's not what he said,' Pascale continued. 'Oh, and Lucien called –'

'He's my boss,' Candie interjected hurriedly, and laughed a little hysterically. 'Probably just some boring old office problem –'

'He called to remind you of your promise to keep the sexual temperature in the office at boiling point,' Pascale continued, 'and to thank you for that wonderful time you gave him this afternoon. Oh, and another man called Marcel called –'

'Don't let's waste any more talking about trivialities,' interrupted Candie hurriedly, and she nuzzled close to Igor and pushed her tongue into his ear. 'I can explain everything,' she murmured hopefully, but at that moment Gaby suddenly started to lose control, so the girls stopped chattering and concentrated all their attention on helping her. Candie squeezed and fondled Gaby's breasts, pinched her nipples very gently, and pressed her pudenda against Gaby's undulating buttocks. The dark-haired woman suddenly began to bounce up and down, crying out in Italian, which obviously expressed her feelings better than French, then she suddenly screamed. Her body jerked violently three or four times, and then she slowed down, and eventually eased herself off Igor's penis.

'You see, what did I tell you?' said Pascale with a self-satisfied smile. 'He's still hard as a rock.' Gaby was blinking dozily and reeling about the place, and evidently decided that she had had enough. 'I'm going home to bed,' she said, and she picked up her clothes, kissed them all goodnight, and went off yawning.

'Would you like to go next?' asked Pascale politely.

'No, no,' replied Candie. 'You found him, after all, didn't you?' she added sweetly.

'Well, that's very kind of you,' Pascale replied, 'but, well, you see, the thing is, he's promised to come inside me.'

'How charming,' said Candie, but Igor intervened.

'I can't,' he explained weakly. 'I have to do an act with Suzie.'

'With Suzie?' Pascale snorted, placing her hands on her hips.

'Who's Suzie?' asked Candie.

'She's a big English man-eater,' said Pascale indignantly. 'I knew she had her eye on you this afternoon,' she said accusingly to Igor, 'when we were in the studio.'

'Doing what?' asked Candie.

'Fucking me, of course,' Pascale replied, 'but that bitch dragged him away before we had a chance to finish things off. Not that you looked all that unwilling,' she said accusingly to Igor, shaking her finger at him. 'Did she have you away in that flat of hers?' she asked him.

'Of course she did,' Candie told her disgustedly. 'Everybody has him away,' she added, and Igor rolled his eyes in despair, but deliverance came in the shape of Sandrine, who tapped on the door, then peeped inside.

'Sorry to break in,' she said, 'but a girl called Suzie is on the phone for you, Igor. She said it is most urgent.'

'Oh, we can't keep Suzie waiting, can we?' said Pascale sarcastically, and she and Candie stalked off with their noses in the air as Sandrine released Igor.

Twenty

Igor arrived at Suzie's flat within a few minutes of receiving her urgent call. He rang the bell and a few moments later he heard the lock buzz and her voice asking him to go up. She did not sound her usual self and, when he arrived, she was obviously on edge. Almost as soon as he entered, she picked up the telephone and keyed in a number, which he recognised as the emergency number he had already rung earlier in the day. She handed him the telephone.

'It's Igor –' he said into the mouthpiece.

'Are you with Suzie?' Chantal asked.

'Yes.'

'Please ask her to explain, then do just as she tells you,' said Chantal, and put down the phone. Igor turned to Suzie.

'I have to ask you to explain, then do as I am told,' he reported.

'I don't have much to explain,' said Suzie, 'except that a girl called Marie-Ange Geneviève appears to be held prisoner at La Chasse St Hubert. Do you know how she comes to be there?'

'I can guess,' he replied. 'She probably went into the grounds to keep someone under observation, and was caught trespassing. I can't see why that should be so serious.'

'La Chasse is a rendezvous for high-ranking politicians and such like,' Suzie explained. 'She has probably seen or heard something she shouldn't. In any case, Chantal's boss wants us to get her out of there.'

'How are you involved?' he asked.

'He knows my father from way back. He asked my father for help, and he rang me.'

'How do we get her out?' he asked.

'I'll tell you on the way there,' she said. 'We don't have much time.'

Jenny was grateful to arrive at the upstairs corridor and dive into the comparative safety of her bedroom. She went to turn on the tap of the washbasin, then suddenly heard the murmur of voices from along the corridor. She opened the door, peeped out, then tiptoed along until she could overhear the whispered conversation through the door of one of the bedrooms. Vivienne was talking with Erika, who was no longer playing the simpering idiot role, but sounded very competent indeed, and both spoke perfect French.

'What did Jean-Luc say, exactly?' asked Vivienne

'They were talking about smearing the FCR . . .' Erica began to explain, then Jenny heard noises on the stairs, hurried back to her bedroom, and locked the door. This was really serious. At least one of the hostesses was perfectly capable of understanding the conversations all around her, and was handing over highly sensitive information to Vivienne. She searched around in her handbag, took out her ornate lipstick holder and pulled back the cover: it contained a custom-built radio pager and it showed the frequency she should use to make contact. She sighed with relief, picked up her perfume spray and unscrewed the bottom. She extracted a minute hearing-aid ear piece and inserted it into her ear, then adjusted a small dial and spoke into the microphone concealed in the spray.

'*Berthe Deux*,' she said softly, listened out for five seconds, and repeated her call-sign. After four attempts her ear piece crackled.

'Hi, Jenny,' said Igor.

'What kept you?' she asked.

* * *

After leaving Les Plaisirs d'Anaïs, Candie and Pascale shared a taxi back towards Pascale's studio, the intention being to drop Candie off en route. 'Have you known Gabrielle long?' Pascale asked.

'I only met her this evening,' Candie replied. 'I work for Lucien.'

'Do you really?' asked Pascale, turning towards her. 'So do I.'

'What do you do?' Candie asked.

'Let him have a copy of some of my videos,' Pascale replied. 'He pays my rent for the privilege.'

'He pays your rent to look at the films you make with the young *hardeurs*?' Candie asked incredulously.

'No, of course not,' said Pascale. 'That's just a sideline. A lot of men like to have a video of themselves on the job, especially the high-ups,' she explained confidentially. 'Lucien has heaps of VIP pals and they all like to see themselves in action. You'd be amazed who comes to my studio. All the bigwigs – politicians, industrialists, everybody – and a right kinky lot they are too, I can tell you.'

'I can imagine,' Candie replied. 'So Lucien sends his high-up friends to make a blue video with you, and then he buys a copy?'

'That's right.' She looked at her watch and leant towards the driver. 'Can you step on it?' she asked. 'I have an appointment in five minutes.'

Candie thought quickly. She wanted to get inside Pascale's studio, because it was clear that Pascale had contacts with Lucien's organisation. 'I don't know why women don't produce more blue films,' she said casually. 'I'm sure they'd be better at it than the men.'

'I agree,' said Pascale, 'but women seem to think their place is in front of the camera.'

'I'd like to have a go at it,' said Candie. 'I've used a cine camera and it isn't difficult.'

'Why don't you come along?' asked Pascale.

'I'd love to, but what about your client?' Candie asked.

'I don't think he'll complain,' Pascale told her, 'provided that you are prepared to join in.'

'Are you sure you don't mind?' Candie asked.

'Not at all. He's a bit heavy going, between you and me, and I'd like to have another girl around.'

'Is he kinky?' Candie asked.

'He'd like to be, but I keep his mind on the straight and narrow,' Pascale told her.

'I'll remember to forget who he is,' she promised.

'Oh, you won't know this one from Adam, or I wouldn't risk it,' said Pascale confidently, then lowered her voice. 'He's right up near the top in the DST,' she murmured, 'so you never hear of him or see his face in the papers, but he's one of Lucien's real old buddies.'

Twenty-one

Suzie stopped her van at the gate to La Chasse, and a guard shone a torch into the car, then recognised her and let them pass. Suzie had already explained to Vivienne that Hans was absent, but that she had a substitute and could vouch for him.

Suzie had explained to Igor en route that a DGSE team was scheduled to blow the fuses at half-past midnight and deprive La Chasse of mains electricity, but Jenny had told them there was a stand-by generator run by a diesel engine, which Igor would have to sabotage. 'It must be that building next to the reservoir of diesel fuel,' Suzie murmured, pointing it out as she pulled into the parking area. A guard came out of the shadows and shone his torch on to Igor's face.

'Who's this?' he asked.

'My new partner,' she said. 'Vivienne knows.'

'Just a moment.' He walked away a few paces and spoke into a portable telephone.

'I'll try to keep him busy,' murmured Suzie.

The man came back and nodded for them to get out. Suzie climbed out and struggled with a big case that she took from the back of the van. 'Can you help me in with this, please?' she asked, panting with her exertions. He picked up her case and she walked ahead of him, through the open door and up the narrow back stairs. She was wearing jeans that were stretched very tightly over her hips, and the seam was pulled right up into her sex and between her buttocks. Igor seized his opportunity and slid away quietly into the darkness as the guard followed her eagerly up the stairs to her dressing room, and put down her case.

'I suppose you want to search my bags?' she asked. He hesitated. 'I don't mind,' she assured him, and she opened the case and turned away to look at herself in the mirror. She had deliberately placed her erotic lingerie on top of the case, and she secretly watched his reflection as he picked up a pair of satin panties and fingered the lace-edged bridge that had clung so intimately to her sex. She saw his hands tremble as he untangled a lace-trimmed suspender belt from a matching lace bra, and she unbuttoned her shirt. He picked up a pair of black nylon panties with a heart-shaped hole in the front.

'The ones I have on are like that,' she told him, 'but red,' and she pulled her shirt out of her jeans. He turned around and saw her standing close to him with her shirt open. She had deliberately worn one of her sexiest bras, one that set off her perfectly formed breasts and hid the nipples only under a thin layer of net. He looked at her cleavage, then down at the panties, then at the tight zip of her jeans.

'Do you want to search me too?' asked Suzie, looking at him with a provocative and mischievous smile. 'I don't mind,' she told him, and spread her legs.

He came close and his hands felt around her shoulders and then moved down to her bosom. He felt the straps of her bra and then the silky material of the cups. 'You have nice hands,' she said, then took his hands in hers and placed them squarely over her breasts. She felt her nipples engorge as his fingers explored her bosom, and lowered her hands to hook her thumbs into the waistband of her tight jeans. He was becoming very excited now as he leant down, his face almost touching her navel, to run his hands over her hips and then up and down each leg in turn. She wore stockings under her jeans, and his fingers followed her lace-edged, ruched suspenders up her thighs. He was panting now and his face was flushed. She looked down at him and deliberately started the zip, easing it down until she exposed the waistband of her panties, and then the hole that allowed her pubic hair to escape.

He seized the zip and pulled it right down. The bottom of the heart-shaped hole dipped far enough to reveal the tip of her vagina. He slid his hand, palm upward, between the seam of her tight jeans and the thin nylon of her panties, with her pubic hair coiled against his palm. Her sex was warm and damp against his fingers, and he pulled her roughly towards him. She felt his erection press against her for a moment, but just then they heard Vivienne calling her name up the stairs. The guard came to his senses and fled down the stairs, then Igor sidled in and nodded secretly to her, just as Vivienne sauntered into the room.

'Is this him?' she asked, pointing to Igor.

'That's him,' Suzie replied. Vivienne took Igor's hand, drew him towards her and looked him in the eyes, holding his hand.

'She's told you the rules?' she asked.

He nodded. 'I know that the men will be wearing masks during the act,' he told her, 'but I have a terrible memory for faces anyway.'

'That's a nice healthy attitude,' she told him. 'Where did Suzie find you?' she asked, still holding him close.

'He fell off the Christmas tree,' Suzie told her.

'What nationality are you?' she asked him.

'Australian,' he told her.

'Australian?' exclaimed Vivienne. 'With those cheek-bones?' She put out her hand and gently stroked his face.

'My grandfather was Russian,' he explained

'I knew it,' purred Vivienne, and smiled at him. 'Do you speak Russian?' she asked. He nodded.

'So do several of the girls,' she warned him. 'No chatting them up, now.'

'He doesn't chat up other women when I'm around,' said Suzie.

'Don't be so possessive, Suzie,' Vivienne scolded her, and gazed into Igor's eyes for a few more seconds. 'We must get together sometime and brush up our Russian,' she murmured.

'Put him down, Vivienne,' said Suzie, and shooed her out.

Aristide Delacroix was a graduate of the Ecole National d'Administration, which trains most of the French administrators, and, as such, he was virtually guaranteed a well-paid job in the upper echelons of the French civil service, and membership of an old boy's network that extended into every nook and cranny of the complex fabric of French political life.

Delacroix was a natural for the DST. He enjoyed intrigue, double-dealing and the shadowy world of espionage. In his youth, he had been a first-rate field operative, and he had quickly developed a natural expertise in the kind of office games where the winners get the top jobs in the country. He also liked sex, in all its infinite variety, but he knew better than to mix business with pleasure. His sexual flings were carried out well away from the office, out of the limelight, and mostly under Lucien's protection. It was a good tit-for-tat arrangement: Lucien protected him and he protected Lucien.

He arrived at Pascale's studio by taxi, looking like a rather nondescript, balding *fonctionnaire*, but his small, furtive eyes missed nothing as Pascale introduced him to Candie. 'She works for Lucien,' she told him, evidently intending to reassure him that his security was intact.

'As what?' he asked her.

'General factotum,' she replied. A champagne cork popped and Pascale filled up three glasses and handed them round. 'We decided we could do without Paul,' Pascale told him. 'We can both handle a camera.'

'So can I,' he told them, and picked up a lightweight video camera. He peered at them through the viewfinder and Pascale immediately reacted to the camera, switched on a big smile and posed next to Candie. He set down his glass and sank down, filming them from a low angle, then switched on a spotlight that was set at floor level, pointing upward at an acute angle, and beckoned to Pascale.

'Come here,' he said. She smiled coquettishly, moved towards him with her hips swaying, and came up close. He leant back as she approached, and she stood astride him with her legs wide apart, letting the camera see right up her skirt.

Candie felt her heart leap. She knew that Pascale was

wearing tight white panties that concealed her sex, whereas she was wearing very flimsy panties that were quite transparent.

'Now you,' he said to her. Pascale moved away and Candie put down her glass and walked slowly forward, feeling her blush spread down into her cleavage.

'I didn't intend to be the model,' she said.

'Oh no?' he sneered, and waited for her to come forward.

'My panties are transparent,' she told him, her blush deepening.

'I'm surprised you have any on,' he told her. 'It must be quite a change for you.'

'I am Lucien's secretary, not a tart,' she reminded him angrily.

'Lucien's secretaries are not usually so shy about showing off their cunts,' he said crudely. 'Are you trying to tell me he hasn't seen yours yet?' Her face became scarlet with embarrassment.

'Yes, he has,' she admitted.

'Now I want to see it,' he told her. He switched on the camera again and Candie looked away. She caught Pascale's eye and the young blonde pointed her finger at her temple, making screwing motions. Her action at once established a woman-to-woman complicity between them and relieved the tension. Candie took a deep breath, stepped forward and forced herself to spread her legs wide, knowing that he could now see all she had. She heard the camera whine and fought down her panic reaction as she imagined him playing the video to his pals.

'I know Lucien didn't fuck you,' he said in a conversational tone. 'What happened?' The camera continued to whine as he used the zoom, and Candie imagined the close-up of her sex, blown up to fill the screen.

'He watched me play with myself,' she admitted.

'How nice for you. Show me what you did.'

Candie felt her cheeks burning with shame and humiliation. She put her hand down and pressed her fingertip against her labia, then began to massage the front of her sex. 'Did Jean-Luc fuck you?' he asked. She breathed in indignantly and took her hand away.

'That is not really any of your business,' she pointed out angrily, and backed away.

'Everything is my business,' he said coldly. 'Come back here.' Candie saw that Pascale was shaking her head and frowning at her, and realised that upsetting him might react back on to her new friend. She moved forward again and straddled the camera.

'You were demonstrating your masturbation technique,' he reminded her. 'I want to see your pleasure finger well up, sweetie.'

Candie realised he was a natural sadist, and would give her hell unless she collaborated. She did as he instructed, feeling her labia part as she thrust her second finger into her sex.

'I know that Jean-Luc visited Lucien this afternoon, and he would hardly be likely to miss such an opportunity,' Delacroix told her.

'He had intercourse with me,' Candie admitted.

'In the conference room?' he asked her. Her finger plunged into her sex, withdrew, then plunged again.

'Yes.'

'How?'

'On the love seat,' she told him.

'You like bondage, do you?'

'Not particularly,' she said.

'Show me your clit,' he said. Candie gulped and felt her anger and humiliation increase to near breaking point. She pulled back the hood and exposed her clitoris.

'Play with it,' he said. She put her finger on to her clit and rotated it.

'You like bondage, do you?' he repeated.

'Yes,' she said, recognising his sadistic game. She had to say 'Yes' to all his insolent questions, or he would humiliate her even more.

'You like SM too, don't you?'

'Yes,' she told him.

'With what?'

'Whips, canes, whatever,' she replied.

'That's better,' he said. 'You might as well answer

straight away, you see. I always get an answer in the end, don't I, Pascale?'

'Oh yes, always,' she said resignedly, secretly rolling her eyes upward, so that Candie had to suppress a smile. He switched off the camera and wriggled upright.

'I learnt how to interrogate female terrorists when you were still in diapers,' he told Candie in a whisper, and he put his hand down the front of her dress and felt her breast. 'I'd have enjoyed having you on the couch,' he said softly, and ripped open her dress to expose her bosom. Candie felt her face become scarlet and she trembled with anger as she fought down the desire to smack his face.

'Oh stop it!' Pascale told him. 'You're giving me the creeps. Come on, drink up.' She handed him his glass and Candie backed away, pulling her dress together. Pascale switched on a CD player and some hot disco music filled the room. She began to dance around the room, twisting and twirling and letting her flared skirt shoot up. Candie joined in, pleased to escape from him, and faced Pascale on their impromptu disco floor as they turned and twisted to the fast techno beat.

Jenny crept back down the stairs and paused by the guard at the door, all ready to put on her blindfold, but he shook his head and let her in.

She could see why she no longer needed the blindfold. All the men were now wearing black silk masks that completely covered their faces. She retraced her steps to the cubicle where she had left Jean-Luc. A hand beckoned her to hurry and she recognised him in spite of the mask, and quickly joined him. Her clothes were still there and she dressed quickly, then sat on Jean-Luc's knee.

Vivienne came on stage and announced that Suzie had a new partner that night, and there was a sigh of expectation as she left the stage. The curtains drew back and showed a back-cloth of a Pigalle-like street scene. The only sound was the sharp, regular snapping of fingers.

Suzie walked on to the stage, swinging her hips, and looked over the audience with a cool, appraising glance.

She wore a very tight, wrap-over, black satin hooker's dress. A double bass started up, and a muted trumpet sketched the opening bars of 'Mack the Knife'. Suzie walked slowly across the stage, as if walking the pavement, following the beat and rolling her hips in an exaggerated manner.

Igor came up behind her on the eighth bar, as the band picked up the melody. The drummer came in, then more muted brass, and Igor followed Suzie across the stage, stepping in her footprints.

The trumpets lost their mutes and she turned to face him as the music swelled, her stomach thrust out. She forced him to retreat step by step, back across the stage, but lured him at the same time. Her dress opened to show her breasts, lifted and offered in a minuscule black bra. She turned and continued her hooker-style walk, back again across the stage, swinging her handbag. Igor, more daring now her back was turned, put his hand out as he followed her again, and dared to touch her bottom. She didn't react, but continued her hip-swinging walk as he came nearer. He lifted her dress to show her black stockings, suspenders, and G-string. She turned at once, like a striking snake, and slapped his face, then mimed that he must pay first.

He took out his wallet and she reached into it, her fingers dipping in time to the music, plucking out the bank notes, one note to each second beat. She folded them and put them into her handbag and, satisfied now, pulled him to her. A high-pitched clarinet joined in, counterpointing the brass, and she rubbed herself lasciviously against him, feeling his penis through his pants as she drew Igor into her lair.

Pascale was kneeling at Delacroix's feet, fellating him, whilst Candie, dressed in her bra, panties, shoes and stockings, filmed the scene. Pascale's intervention had dissipated the oppressive atmosphere in the studio and Delacroix had allowed himself to be jollied along, but Candie felt his eyes upon her all the time, and wondered if he suspected her.

Pascale suddenly drew back, announced that she must fly to the loo, and vanished into the bathroom. Candie at once put down the camera and took her place between his legs. 'How long have you been in France?' he asked.

She leant forward and took his penis into her mouth. 'I only just arrived,' she said, and went down on him.

'From Australia?' She shook her head and pulled back.

'I was working near Munich,' she said, 'and before that in London.' Her mouth sucked again at his cock and she licked the tip, trying to halt the flow of questions.

'Were you sent here especially to work for Lucien?' he asked. She backed away again, wiping her saliva away with her hand.

'I have no idea,' she said. 'I just obey orders.'

'Which are?'

'To keep Lucien happy until he terminates the contract.'

'Does that include sucking me off?'

'He likes me to be nice to his friends,' she pointed out, and sucked his knob luxuriously with her voluptuous lips. 'I'm sorry I was bitchy earlier on,' she said, trying to pacify him and cut short the interrogation.

'You can make amends,' he said, sitting back to watch her blonde head bobbing between his parted thighs. 'Pascale has an SM room down in the basement,' he told her, 'and you said you liked being whipped.'

Igor felt Suzie's arms go up around his neck as the music changed to 'The Deer Hunter' theme. She drew him towards the bed, dancing close to him, exaggerating her erotic movements as she pressed herself against him, and moving her hand boldly against his erection. She undressed him slowly, then sank down on to the bed and took his penis into her mouth. Her fingers lifted his balls and fondled them, tickled him behind the sac, and played with his anus as her mouth and tongue caressed and sucked his prick.

He closed his eyes and breathed in deeply, conscious that this whole rescue operation depended upon him maintaining his erection. She broke off her fellation and lay on the bed. Igor counted the bars, then bent over and buried his head between her strong white thighs, titillating her labia as the guitar picked out the haunting melody. He moved on to her clit and used the tip of his folded tongue to excite the erect horn, and felt the flood of lubrication as the strings joined in. He felt her stiffen suddenly, felt her body jerk as she climaxed dead on cue, and then he was inside her, taking her vigorously as she writhed under him. She lifted her hips under him and pounded against him, becoming frenzied as the music rose to a climax. The trumpeter went mad, her body slammed against Igor's, then gradually slowed down as the music died away. He eased his still-erect penis from her vagina as the applause swelled, then the curtain closed and Vivienne came back on stage.

'Well, gentlemen, I am sure you enjoyed the show as much as I did,' she said, 'and that it has given you and your charming companions some ideas about how to pass the rest of the evening.' She paused for a moment to run her eye over the audience. 'Now for something different,' she continued. 'Suzie and her new partner are seeking a little variety this evening, and if any gentleman in the audience would like some instruction in this fascinating art form, Suzie will be delighted to offer a very private lesson.' She paused as Suzie, dressed once more in her tart's black underwear, sauntered on to the stage and looked over the audience with a challenging, sardonic smile.

'Also, if any of the ladies would care to show us their talents,' Vivienne continued, 'then Suzie's partner is equally ready to provide a free lesson, but this time in public . . .' She paused again as Igor came on to the stage at the other side.

There were giggles from the audience and Igor scanned the audience feverishly. This was the key point in the whole operation. He spotted Jenny in her slinky sheath dress, and secretly waved. She saw his sign and stood up.

'*Allons-y*,' she said, and pulled her partner to his feet. 'Let's go.' The man held back in surprise for a moment, but now everyone was looking at them, and Igor guessed that he would not dare chicken out.

The audience went wild as the two volunteers made their way to the stage. Vivienne moved away and the music began again; there were three minutes and twenty seconds to go before the diversion.

The audience began to clap in time to the music, and Jean-Luc produced his wallet. Igor pulled Jenny into the shadows so that Suzie could hold the audience's attention for a while, because timing was absolutely vital from now on. Suzie took a banknote from Jean-Luc's wallet and crinkled it. 'Half price for students,' she told him. 'We all know how poor you are,' and the men laughed as she slipped it into her cleavage: they all knew he had a considerable private fortune. Three minutes. Suzie began to dance close to Jean-Luc, caressing his body with hers. He was a good dancer and he carefully mimicked the steps he'd seen Igor perform, all with such aplomb that his pals cheered. She drew him to her, and took him away, into the curtained area. He turned and waved goodbye as he vanished from sight.

All eyes switched to Igor and Jenny. 'Two minutes thirty to go,' whispered Igor, picking up the beat. Jenny strutted across the stage as Suzie had done, then imitated her hip-swinging hooker's walk and stance as she unfastened his shirt. He found the catch and her dress came off, revealing her bare breasts, her nipples visibly erect, and the minute lace panties that hugged her mons and set off her hips.

Two minutes. Following Suzie's lead, she eased off his trousers and underpants, and went down on his penis. He let her arouse him, then changed roles, kissing her breasts as he eased down her panties. One minute thirty seconds. She was on her back, on the bed, under the spotlights, and Igor's head was buried between her thighs, his tongue licking delicately at her labia.

One minute. He reared up and knelt over her. Her hand came down and took his penis, offered it to her sex, and he slid smoothly into her.

'The diversion is in forty-five seconds from now,' he told her quietly, thrusting his penis into her. 'As soon as it happens, get downstairs and hide in the back of the Renault van.'

'OK,' she whispered, and spread her legs wide so that the audience could see the sex act as it happened.

Vivienne, off to one side, frowned in puzzlement. She thought she knew all the hostesses by sight, but she didn't recognise the girl on stage. She decided that, when the act was finished, she would go over and draw the girl out on to the stage, so that the audience could give her a well-deserved round of applause – and so that she could see who she was.

Candie lay on her stomach on a narrow bed in Pascale's SM room, her chin on a leather-faced headboard so that her head was forced back. Her wrists were shackled to the legs of the bed and her legs were stretched out wide apart and fastened down at the ankles. Her breasts hung down through circular cut-outs in the couch.

Candie winced as Pascale poured oil all over her buttocks and vagina, then eased in a huge vibrator with two shafts, one thick and shaped for her vagina, the other long and thin, for her anus. The device was not yet switched on, but already she could feel the two shafts rending her body apart. Pascale eased the device out, added more oil, and pushed it in again.

'Are you OK?' she asked Candie solicitously. Candie nodded, but she was perspiring and very scared, not so much because of the SM as the possibility of further interrogation by Delacroix, under duress.

'Switch it on.' Delacroix looked on, licking his thin lips feverishly, and rubbed a hand over his upper lip from time to time. Pascale pressed a button and Candie screamed as the vibrations began, deep inside her vagina and anus.

'Now we'll try this.' Delacroix came to the front of the couch and Candie's eyes opened wide in horror as he forced her to kiss a long, whippy cane. He beckoned to Pascale and handed her the cane, then picked up a whip.

'Make it good,' he hissed, 'or you'll get a taste of this.'

Candie heard her move to the side of the couch, heard the cane sweep up and down and felt the flash of pain across her buttocks. Immediately, she heard another, louder, crack and heard Pascale scream with pain.

'Hit her, you bitch,' Delacroix howled at Pascale. She felt the girl hesitate.

'Do as he says,' she said urgently to Pascale. She felt the cane lifted and then a fiercer flash of pain across her bottom. She screamed and felt another blow, then Pascale screamed again, and then everything dissolved into a Grand Guignol of screams, howls and flashes of pain that swirled and eddied around the girls' bodies. The vibrators hummed and the voices shrieked; the blows rained down and Candie felt the pain begin to merge into pleasure. Suddenly, Delacroix was in front of her, opening her mouth and pushing into it a plastic device to hold it open. He rammed his penis into her mouth and began to belabour the girls indiscriminately with his whip as the tension rose. She felt her all-consuming orgasm begin, deep inside her body, and heard Pascale give a scream as if mortally wounded. She felt the blonde girl collapse on top of her and felt Pascale's body jerk wildly as she climaxed under the flailing whip, and then her own orgasm overwhelmed her. At the peak of her climax, she suddenly felt the hot shock of his ejaculation into her mouth. There was no escape and she gulped desperately, time and time again, as his semen exploded from her mouth and ran down her chin.

Jenny and Igor looked at each other in growing desperation as he rammed his prick into her. The diversion was several seconds late and the music was building to its climax. The show would end when the trumpets screeched out that final top C, and Jenny would then be discovered, more surely than if she had remained in the cubicle. It was a calculated gamble, and they were both terrified it was going to fail.

The music rose to its shattering climax, and suddenly all the lights went out. The taped music died and there was a few seconds of total silence. Igor slid out of Jenny and she immediately leapt off the bed.

'There is no cause for alarm.' Vivienne called, out. The men seized the opportunity presented by the black-out and there were squeals from the girls scattered around the room.

Jenny had committed her escape route to memory, and made for the exit as fast as she could in the pitch dark. Beyond the door, there were tiny emergency lights in the corridor, and she could see the guard half-way along it. He turned towards her.

'Toilette,' she howled, shoving him to one side and holding her hand to her mouth. The last thing he needed just then was an hysterical woman throwing up all over the floor, and he let her go by. She ran up the stairs, along the corridor, grabbed her bag, and made her way down the rear staircase.

Vivienne had an emergency torch in her handbag, and after ten seconds of darkness she set off across the stage to get it, but hardly had she taken a step when someone stumbled against her and she tripped and fell off the stage and into the middle of a group of very drunken men. She struggled furiously, but they now had their hands on her seductive body and they were in no mood to let her go. She lost her dress and found herself on her back, on the couch, with her silk petticoat up around her shoulders.

'*Je veux baiser*,' called out Erika from a position close to Vivienne, and Vivienne felt her panties ripped off. Hands and mouths ravished her breasts and someone kissed her pussy. She realised that fighting only excited her attackers, and stopped struggling. Erika's wish was evidently granted, because the young blonde suddenly squealed like a stuck pig and began to leap about on the crowded couch. Another girl shouted, '*Et moi*,' and the next moment Vivienne found that someone had mistaken his target in the darkness. '*No, no*,' she squealed, '*pas moi*, not me,' but the next moment she was pinned down by a very erect prick.

'It's Vivienne,' she called out, but her attacker drove into her even harder. She suddenly realised that probably the number one fantasy, among her male audience, was to screw that snooty aristocratic bitch who presided over the show but never participated. She'd done it now: they were going to queue up to have her away. Her attacker rammed his prick right into her and Vivienne, a fatalist at heart, stopped fighting and stopped talking and lifted her hips to meet her ravisher's thrusts.

Five minutes later, the lights went on, and Vivienne found herself looking up into the bloodshot eyes of the law-and-order enthusiast. There was a few seconds of embarrassed silence, then she screeched, 'Let me get up, you fat, stupid ox,' and she wriggled free, ran upstairs, locked herself in her bedroom, sprawled on the bed and howled like a baby.

The men decided unanimously that it was time to leave and, a few moments later, a stream of high-powered cars purred silently away from the house. Suzie's van merged into the stream and passed through the main gate without any fuss.

Jenny had climbed into the jogging outfit that Suzie had placed in the van for her, and was dictating her initial recollections into a tape recorder. A few minutes after leaving La Chasse, they pulled up alongside a parked car. Jenny thanked them and climbed into the back of the vehicle, which was driven away at once.

Twenty-two

The next morning, Gabrielle was suffering one of her mysterious attacks, which required her to stay in bed until midday with the blinds drawn, and Jean-Luc had that grey-faced morning-after look that usually followed a meeting at La Chasse. It was Gabrielle's turn to get the children to school, but she was *hors de combat*, so it became Janet's responsibility. Whilst the kids were having breakfast, she went along to ask Giorgio if he would mind driving them to school.

'One good turn deserves another,' Giorgio reminded her, putting his arm around her waist.

'I don't know what you mean,' she said indignantly, and broke free, but not before he had detected her suspender belt through her dress. She had in fact woken up feeling very randy, and had dressed up for Jean-Luc, but she had quickly realised that he was in no condition to satisfy her.

Half an hour later, once she had seen the children into the care of their teacher, Janet climbed up into the front of the car with Giorgio, and waved them goodbye.

'Well, off you go then,' she said to Giorgio, in her usual bossy way.

'I need inspiration,' he said cheekily. 'Show me your legs.'

'The idea! I'll do nothing of the kind.'

'Then I stay here.'

'Not in front of the children.'

'The children have gone into the school.'

Janet blushed a deep red but unfastened several buttons of her dress, which revealed that she was wearing her black stockings. Giorgio promptly pulled her hem up to the top of her legs and revealed her russet-coloured suspenders and tiny satin panties, but she slapped his hand and covered her thighs at once. 'Will you please stop that nonsense and drive away this instant,' she said indignantly, her eyes flashing. He slipped into first gear and the car purred away.

'So, Gabrielle is having one of her turns,' he said slyly.

'You can say that again,' she replied, tossing her head. 'She just managed to scrape into bed before Jean-Luc arrived home,' she added. 'Where was she yesterday?'

'I dropped her off near Les Halles around three.'

'What on earth was she doing there?'

'Hawking her wares around Strasbourg-Saint Denis,' he told her. 'Slumming it and whoring turn her on.'

She gasped in horror. 'I don't believe it,' she said. 'Those poor children.' She shook her head in sorrow.

'Then she went on to her club,' he continued. 'You know, Les Plaisirs d'Anaïs – and you know what goes on there,' he added, jabbing her with his elbow.

'I do not, and I have no wish to know,' she said haughtily. He didn't enlighten her, and after a moment or two her curiosity got the better of her. 'A bunch of no-good men, no doubt,' she said.

'That's right,' he said. 'Handsome young men, virile as fighting cocks, naked as the day they were born, chained down and helpless. Unable to resist, and trained to keep it up all night. How about that, Janet?'

'I don't believe it,' she said, very pink and quite breathless. 'You're making it up.'

'In deep, dark dungeons,' he went on, 'with whips and canes handy, in case they don't obey you instantly.'

'That's quite enough, Giorgio,' she cried, and put her hands to her ears, then took them away again. 'I don't believe you anyway,' she went on, tossing her head disparagingly. 'You're lying, as usual. All Italians are born liars.'

'*Basta*! *Basta*!' he cried. 'That's enough!' He struck his forehead with the heel of his hand, spun the car around with a handbrake turn, and set off back towards Paris with all four tyres squealing.

'Giorgio! What on earth are you doing?' she cried.

'You call me a liar,' he shouted at her. 'Now you throw cold water on my honour. You insult the noble Italian people, who were civilised when you Scottish heathens still walked about with paint on your bodies. I take you. I show you. I prove to you that Giorgio does not tell lies.'

'Giorgio, have you taken leave of your senses?' she cried. 'Turn around at once.'

'No.'

'What if Madame wants you?'

'I say I took the car in to have it fixed.' He swept down the centre of the boulevard, blowing his horn at everyone who got in his way.

'Giorgio, for the love of heaven, slow down and stop making all that din,' she cried, 'or we'll both end up in jail.'

He shrugged moodily, but slowed down and took his hand off the horn.

'I had no wish to insult you,' she said, pouring oil on troubled waters. 'I love Italy, and the Italians. In fact, much of my favourite music is Italian –'

'*Naturalmente*,' he said, and gave a sniggering laugh. 'We gave the world Verdi,' he went on, 'and you gave it the bagpipes,' and he made a noise like a waterlogged drone.

'That remark was uncalled for,' she said stiffly.

'We gave the world Titian, Tintoretto, da Vinci, Michelangelo, Raphael,' he added, warming to his theme. 'Who knows the name of even one Scottish painter?'

'You may have a point, Giorgio, but –'

'We gave the world Armani, Versace, Gucci, Valentino, all those wonderful clothes, and what did you give?' He cackled furiously and laughed so hard his eyes watered. 'The kilt –'

'Now watch it, Giorgio –' she interrupted him.

'We gave you Dante, Petrarch, Giacomo Leopardi –'

'And we gave you Rabbie Burns,' she reminded him.

'Och aye, so you did,' he agreed, 'and haggis –'

'And Scotch,' she added, knowing Giorgio's liking for Glen Morangie.

He nodded a reluctant agreement, and repented. 'And women with red hair and green eyes and fiery tempers and wonderful legs,' he said, and pulled her skirt up again.

'Keep your eyes on the road and your hands to yourself,' she told him, but she did not pull her skirt down. Silence reigned for almost a minute.

'How will you get in?' she asked.

'The night porter, Massimo, is an old fried of mine,' he told her. 'We come from the same village, near *bella Napoli.*' He sang a verse of 'O Sole Mio' to prove he came from Naples.

'Well, I wash my hands of the whole affair,' she said.

'So OK,' he said, shrugging his shoulders, and they drove on again in silence for a while.

'I hope you'll not be thinking of starting any tomfoolery up there in this house of shame,' she told him severely. 'If you have any ideas of profiting from this to have your evil way with me, Giorgio, you can put them right out of your head,' and she pulled her dress down to make her point.

Jenny had no sleep that night, just endless cups of coffee as she poured out all she had learnt into their tape recorders, and made little sketches of what she had seen. Then the professionals started, asking her detailed questions, and making her recover half-forgotten memories before they faded from her mind completely. But at last, in the early hours of the morning, they let her go, and she was driven to her flat and told to lie low: they even left a guard with her, in case of trouble.

Once Jenny had left, Chantal took the whole dossier to Xavier, at his house, and they had a working breakfast whilst he went through Jenny's findings. Jenny had in fact been offered an unprecedented opportunity to infiltrate Lucien's network, and she had seized it with both hands. Names, details of very revealing conversations, and most of all the proof that Lucien and Vivienne were double dealing, and using the opportunity to eavesdrop on their loose-tongued clientèle.

There was only one problem. This was all DST territory,

and Xavier was obliged to hand all this information over to his opposite number, Delacroix. In fact, he had his hand already on the telephone, to call Delacroix, when it rang.

His caller was the Colonel, and what he had to say was an even bigger bundle of dynamite that changed things completely: Candida had discovered that Delacroix was hand-in-glove with Lucien! The working breakfast ended quickly, and Xavier rushed into Paris to see his boss. By nine-thirty, he found himself in a very high-level conference at which both the DST and DGSE were present. The top-echelon DST man, Delacroix's boss, was called Christian, and he started the ball rolling.

'I have suspected for some time that we had a mole inside the DST,' he said quietly, 'and this information appears to confirm my suspicions. However, we obviously need more than the uncorroborated word of two junior operatives before we can act, especially when both of them were, to say the least, operating outside their remit, and very unconventionally – and one of them is not even French.'

Xavier's own boss intervened. 'If, however, this information is correct,' he pointed out, 'no matter how we came to acquire it, we have to act on it.'

'We must remember that Delacroix has powerful friends and so does Lucien,' Christian pointed out. 'You probably know that Jean-Luc Lamartine is almost bound to be in the cabinet after the next reshuffle. I wouldn't be too surprised if he became both your boss and mine within the foreseeable future.'

'If Le Canard Enchainé discovers that security operations and high-level political decisions are being discussed openly, by our lords and masters, in front of a bunch of call-girls laid on by a Lebanese *souteneur*,' retorted Xavier's boss sniffily, 'Jean-Luc and his friends can kiss goodbye to any hopes of high office, in the near or distant future,' and there was a few seconds of silence around the table.

'I have recently launched a strictly personal initiative to harass Lucien,' Christian admitted. 'These recent events could well increase the pressure and force him to crack. Why not wait and see what happens?'

Xavier intervened. 'I am worried about the safety of my operative and the others involved,' he said. 'Jenny's presence yesterday evening may well have been noticed, and if Lucien is threatened, their lives may be in danger.'

'I think that unlikely,' said Christian, waving a nonchalant hand, 'and in any case they are all well able to take care of themselves: they should be, anyway. Furthermore, if he was so foolish as to kill one of them, we might even be lucky enough to catch him with the proverbial smoking gun in his hand. That would tidy things up very nicely, wouldn't it?'

Candie stopped by the reception desk and the duty security officer gave her a spare key to the office door. 'Lucien often listens to classical music,' he told Candie, 'and then he can't hear the door bell.'

Candie opened the office door silently and tiptoed in. Lucien was nowhere to be seen and she crossed the room silently on the thick carpet. He was sitting at his own personal Macintosh computer, looking at the screen, wearing headphones. The screen was hidden from view, and as soon as she approached his inner sanctum, she must have triggered an alarm, because she saw him blank out the screen and look around.

'Good morning,' she said.

'You're early,' he commented.

'Sorry. Am I disturbing you?'

'No, of course not,' he replied. 'Could you make some coffee, please?'

She walked to the small kitchen and switched on the percolator, all the time secretly keeping an eye on him. From there, she could see the screen, which was now blank, and she saw him go through quite a complicated procedure before ejecting the compact disk, which was odd, because it should be basically a very simple one-click operation. The CD ejected at last and she saw him put it into its plastic box, slide the box into the big stack of audio

CDs, lock the bar that prevented them from being taken out, and swing the stack away into a tall wall safe. The telephone rang in his office and he went to answer it, closing the office door behind him.

Candie walked quickly over to the safe and looked at his stack of CDs. Beethoven, Mozart, Vivaldi – they were all boxed and labelled as high-quality audio CDs, but why keep them in an expensive safe? She checked which items of software he had used recently, and the audio CD player was not on the list. She went back into the kitchen as the percolator started to bubble, reflecting that he had not been listening to music, but had been playing with a multimedia CD, which was now hidden among his audio CDs.

She made the coffee and went in. He had finished telephoning, and he looked up at her with a puzzled frown. She was wearing a short light-weight mackintosh with a tie belt.

'Why don't you take your coat off?' he asked.

She went up close. 'Why don't you?' she proposed.

He untied the belt and the coat opened. She had nothing under it but a midnight blue lace bra, panties, suspender belt and stockings. She saw his eyes open wide as the sudden surge of lust hit him, then she slipped off her coat and sat on his desk. 'I didn't have time to play with myself this morning,' she told him casually, and put her feet on to the seat of his chair, one on either side of his thighs. 'I need an orgasm,' she told him brazenly, 'or everything I do will be full of mistakes.'

He looked at her strong plump thighs, spread so invitingly in front of him, at her dark blue stockings that emphasised the whiteness of the bare skin, and a nerve trembled at his temple. 'I can't have sex,' he told her suddenly.

'Why not?' asked Candie sympathetically.

'They blew up my car,' he told her. 'It was in Beirut: I was twenty-two.' He laughed bitterly and shrugged his shoulders. 'I had plenty of money,' he went on, 'and the women thought I was good looking. I slept with a different one every night.' He laughed again. 'I was like President Kennedy,' he told her. 'I couldn't go to sleep without a lay.'

'There's nothing wrong with your hands,' she reminded him. She took his hand in hers and stroked his fingers, then placed his hand on her thigh, just above her stockings.

'I can't,' he said, drawing his hand away. 'I'm not a man any more.'

'Does it hurt when you touch me?' she asked.

'Nothing hurts,' he said bitterly.

'Is it pleasant for you?' she asked, taking his hand again and placing it on her thigh.

'Yes, of course.'

'Look, Lucien,' she told him, squeezing his hand, 'you're a very handsome man. OK, so you can't thrust your penis into me. So what? Women have memorable and wonderful orgasms when they are fondled and kissed intimately, and you can still do that for me.'

'You're feeling sorry for me,' he protested.

'Feel sorry for a man with your kind of money?' she asked with a laugh. 'Not likely.' She seized his other hand and placed it over her breast, and positioned the tip of his second finger so that he felt her nipple. 'That's you doing that to me,' she told him, and moved his other hand between her thighs, opening her legs to let him feel the dampness. 'I'm very excited,' she said, 'and so would any woman be, sitting in her underwear next to a dishy man like you.' She used his hand to caress her breast and sex for a moment, then adopted a mock bossy tone. 'Now, Lucien,' she said severely, 'you either satisfy me here and now – or I leave.'

He leant forward and pressed his face between her breasts. She felt the sobs wrack his body, and held him to her, stroking him and comforting him. After a while, he moved back and opened his mouth to speak.

'Not a word,' she said softly, and unclipped her bra. He took her nipple into his mouth and sucked her eagerly. She smiled as she looked down at him, and let him move at his own speed. When he kissed her cleavage she leant back on the desk and encouraged his mouth to move down, to explore her stomach, her navel, the top of her panties.

He buried his head between her legs and kissed the bare skin of her thighs. She giggled with pleasure and opened her legs to let him browse on the warm tender inner surface of her upper thigh, until he reached the barrier of her panties. She flicked open the catch and ripped the scrap of satin away, taking his head and pressing it down between her legs, so that his mouth contacted her sex.

'Oh no,' she gasped suddenly, and her body jerked. 'It's too lovely.'

He was suddenly a young man again, pleasuring a woman. He laughed and fought to gain access to her secret places, and she laughed too and alternatively welcomed, then repulsed, his advances, with those feminine refusals that are designed to increase the value of what she eventually yields.

He gained access at last to her vagina and then to her clitoris, whilst she held his hands over her breasts. She cried out, again and again, and at last exploded, with a great happy roar of delight, and flung her body against him as she climaxed.

Twenty-three

'There, now do you see that I do not tell lies.' Giorgio opened the door of the cubicle and showed Janet the wooden X-shaped cross. He had persuaded Massimo to let them in and they were in the basement.

'Well, I suppose I owe you an apology,' admitted Janet, not sounding very apologetic.

'What do you mean, suppose?'

'Well, there are some bits and pieces of wood, certainly, but this idea of having naked men chained to them, that's ridiculous. You made it up.'

'Made it up? Why should I do such a thing?'

'To impress me, of course. To make out you're a real he-man. If anyone looked like taking you up on it, you'd run a mile.'

He breathed in deeply. 'Once again you say I tell lies,' he shouted. 'Giorgio never tells lies.'

'Go on, then. Show me.'

'Show you what?'

'What you do when you work here.'

He looked at her. 'You mean, take my clothes off and let you chain me up?' he asked. 'I couldn't do that.'

'Hah!' she said triumphantly. 'You see? You're backing out already. So much for your boasting. I knew it all the time. My boyfriend Willie McGregor would not have hesitated for an instant. He would have been proudly facing me by now, chained up like a hero, his head high, naked and unashamed!' She shrugged and added the final thrust of the dagger. 'But, of course,' she concluded, 'he is a Scot!' and she turned on her heel and flounced away.

'Come back,' he shouted. She made no sign of returning

'Ok,' he shouted after her. 'OK, I do it. I show you. You and your Willie McGregor . . .' He removed his clothes, taking his time, and hanging them carefully on hangers so as not to crease them. He got down to his underpants, and hesitated.

'Willie McGregor never wears such things,' she said, eying his rather sexy pants. 'Scotsmen do not insult their manliness with such effeminate fripperies.' He snorted, ripped off the garment and placed his back against the cross.

'Now you fix my ankles and wrists,' he said, and she strapped him down. He suddenly realised that she knew what she was doing, because the straps were very tight and he was soon stretched out tautly on the cross. She stepped back and admired her handiwork, and he saw the gleam of satisfaction in her eyes.

'There, you see?' he said. 'Now you make me a real apology. Now you admit that I do not boast and tell lies.' Her eyes travelled down. He could feel the hard wood against his legs and arms, and was suddenly aware of his nudity.

'Of course I will,' she said sweetly. 'Giorgio, you do not boast.' She looked deliberately at his penis. 'Except, well, you have implied in the past that you are rather well-hung,' she pointed out.

He wriggled uncomfortably. 'I am,' he said at once, 'but only when I am erect, of course.'

'Willie McGregor is always erect when I am around,' she said proudly. 'He is huge,' and she locked the door and began to unbutton her dress.

Giorgio looked at her in alarm. 'What are you doing?' he asked.

'Taking my dress off.'

'Janet, it is getting late,' he pointed out. 'Madame will surely be wondering where we are.'

'We are getting the car fixed, don't you remember?' She unfastened the last button of her dowdy dress and emerged from it like a butterfly breaking free of its cocoon. Giorgio felt his heart leap and the breath catch in his throat. She wore a brassière in a beautiful autumn-russet colour, that matched her hair, with a complex web of lace over the upper swell of her breasts, and her satin French panties fitted seductively over her hips and enhanced them beautifully . She flicked her shoulder straps into place and and came up close. He felt her body contact his, her breasts thrusting into his chest, her tummy against his, her long legs pressing against him. She reached up and took his head into her hands, kissed him luxuriously, and her tongue thrust into his mouth

His erection grew and his penis thrust up between her parted legs. The tip of his cock touched the satin of her panties, and he felt her lubrication start to flow.

'I was wrong about you, Giorgio,' she confessed. 'You were not boasting.' She looked down. 'I have to admit it,' she went on, quite remorseful, 'you are quite well-hung; almost as big as Willy, in fact.'

'Almost?' he protested. She came close and put her arms around him, then kissed him again. 'I usually coax Willy the last few millimetres,' she murmured, and kissed him again, very passionately, whilst her fingers explored the inner surfaces of his thighs, tickling and stroking his sensitive skin. She sank down and down, kissing his chest and then his flat stomach, and then down and down into his thick dark hair. He panted in anticipation as she licked her lips and then he felt her flick at the underside of his shaft with her tongue. His penis jerked at her touch, and then again and again as her tongue worked him over. She leant down and took his balls into her mouth. He felt her tongue licking his sac, her mouth sucking his balls, then she returned to browse over his penis. When he was very wet with her saliva, she licked the palms of her two hands and stood up, placed them over his prick, then kissed him again, open-mouthed, and pressed her bosom against his chest. Her hands were suddenly alive, writhing and squeezing, performing very complex sensual movements, caressing his penis from the root to the tip. 'I'm beginning to think you outshine Willie McGregor in every department,' she murmured at last, 'except maybe one. Mind you, it is a most important department.'

'I outshine him in every department,' he told her proudly.

'We'll see,' she said, and slipped off her panties, then came up close, laid her warm and seductive body close to his, and kissed him again, very lovingly. Her hand went down and she took hold of his prick, then pressed his erect shaft down until it was between her thighs, almost horizontal.

'When Willie was really hard,' she whispered in his ear, 'he could lift me right off my feet with his wonderful caber.' She put her arms around his neck and hung on, kissing his face, his mouth, cheeks and nose, and his penis pushed up hard between her legs. She was lubricating heavily now and her vagina was opening. He felt the bulbous end of his cock force a passage and she pulled up with her arms and went up on tiptoe. He started to slide into her and she pulled harder. Her feet left the ground and she lifted her knees to grip him around the waist as his penis entered her.

'You are surpassing even my wonderful Willie in every department,' she admitted, letting herself descend luxuriously on to his shaft. 'Just one more thing – but it is of course the most important.'

'What now?' he gasped. He was fully inside her now.

'Willie always made me come first, usually two or three times, before he allowed his iron will to relax,' she told him softly, and began to fuck him in earnest. Giorgio felt his penis suddenly gripped firmly by a very robust vagina and began to respect Willie's forbearance. He hung on desperately a she moved lasciviously up and down, obviously enjoying every minute of it.

'You're a fine man, Giorgio,' she said, and eased herself down so that he entered her completely. 'That's wonderful,' she said. 'Oh Giorgio, it's so marvellous.' Her movements accelerated and her body began to bounce against him, more and more quickly. 'Och, I'm going,' she cried. 'Oh God, it's so wonderful,' and she gave a long wailing sigh as she came in a long luxurious orgasm that reduced him to a quivering wreck, but still erect.

'You angel. You haven't come,' she said, several long seconds later, but before she could start again, there was the sound of footsteps and a clanking noise, a key was turned in the lock, and two cleaning ladies came in with their pails and mops.

Jenny went into the office at ten o'clock, having caught up on her sleep, to find her boss waiting for her. 'Marie-Ange,' Chantal began, 'you will, of course forget that any of this happened, and you realise that you must get right away from here, at once.'

'I understand,' said Jenny, 'but what about Igor and Suzie?'

'What about them?'

'If Vivienne suspects that there was an interloper yesterday evening,' Jenny explained, 'it won't take her long to find out how I got in and to guess how I escaped.'

'Go on.'

'Those guards I saw would stop at nothing, and neither would she,' Jenny pointed out.

'My orders are to get you out of the country as quickly as possible,' Chantal told her, 'and the safety of Igor and Suzie is neither your responsibility nor mine.' She handed a package of documents to Jenny, who opened it and looked at the airline ticket.

'I'm leaving this evening?' she asked in astonishment.

'Yes, and you have a full day ahead of you getting your affairs in order before you leave.'

'I'm off the case?' Jenny asked.

'You are off the case, and you are to stay right away from anyone connected with this affair,' Chantal told her, 'and that is an order.'

'I understand,' she said sadly, and turned to leave. Chantal called her back.

'Do you have a gun?' she asked. Jenny shook her head. Her boss opened a drawer and scribbled out a chit and handed it to her. 'You know how to use a 7.65 Manurhin, of course?' she asked. Jenny nodded.

'One of our cars will take you to the airport,' she said. 'Return the gun to the driver,' she added dryly, 'preferably unused.' She held out her hand, wished Jenny good luck, watched her leave, then rang Suzie.

Vivienne had taken two sleeping pills the night before, and was still asleep when Jean-Luc telephoned her during his coffee break.

'I wanted to thank you for the wonderful evening,' he said to Vivienne, who privately thought it had been anything but a wonderful evening, but who rose to the occasion.

'How did you make out with Suzie?' she asked.

'Fine.'

'That was very daring of you.'

'I wouldn't have done it if that hostess hadn't egged me on.'

'Hostess?' she asked woozily.

'The girl I was with; the one who went up on stage.'

Vivienne frowned again, then suddenly it all came back. She got rid of Jean-Luc as soon as she could, then jumped out of bed and put her head under the cold tap. She asked for a report on the power failure, and learnt that there had been a problem outside the estate and a complete failure of the main electricity supply. The emergency generator had not started up because it had a very subtle fault that had occurred quite out of the blue. She rang another number and a minute or two later Erika appeared, still puffy-eyed with sleep and wearing a rather dilapidated peignoir.

'Did you notice anything odd last night?' she asked.

'Odd?' Erika asked dozily.

'The girl who went up on stage,' Vivienne reminded her.

'Oh yes. She was with Jean-Luc. Who was she?' Erika replied.

'You don't know? I thought you knew all the girls.'

'I didn't know her.' The girl went off and Vivienne lit a cigarette, then rang for the printout from the computerised security system. It showed that an alarm had occurred early in the afternoon of the previous day, but it was logged as being due to a malfunction. The person who had reset the alarm and logged it as a malfunction was Gaston, the gamekeeper, the man who was also responsible for the diesel-electricity generator. She interrogated Gaston and his son, got nowhere, and had both of them worked over by the guards. Gaston held out, stoutly denying any knowledge of anything, but Benoit cracked up completely after five minutes, and Gaston caved in to protect his son, but still denied tampering with the emergency electricity supply. Now she knew that a woman had entered the grounds, had impersonated a hostess during the evening, and had then vanished into thin air. The trail led inevitably to Suzie and her new partner.

Vivienne arranged for Erika and the other hostesses to get out of the country, and then called in the guards.

Twenty-four

The buzzer sounded and Suzie picked up the intercom.

'Interflora,' the voice said.

'For me?'

'Yes, madame.' The caller recited her full name and she told him to come up.

A minute later, the bell rang and she peered through the judas to see a very big bunch of flowers. 'Just a moment,' she called. 'I'm not dressed.' A few seconds later, the visitor heard the bolt click back. He hurled his bunch of flowers to the ground, put his shoulder to the door and charged in with his pistol at the ready.

Suzie was especially proud of her tiled entrance hall, but it was very slippery when wet. It was extremely slippery when awash with liquid soap and the gunman found his charge converted rapidly into a headlong rush on his belly, which came to a halt only when his head hit the far wall. He was almost knocked out by the blow, and his right hand, still holding his pistol, flopped out limply by his side. Suzie stamped on it with her high heel and he howled and let go of the gun. The next moment he had a gag in his mouth, a very pretty cushion cover tied over his head and his hands were handcuffed behind his back. Igor stepped back to admire his handiwork whilst Suzie carefully mopped the floor and replaced the carpet. They unfastened the string that had enabled her to withdraw the bolt from a safe distance, and carefully loaded their victim into the lift. Five minutes later he was stowed away in the back of Suzie's van.

* * *

'Excuse us!' The two cleaning ladies looked admiringly at the tableau for a brief instant, then turned their backs like decent girls as Janet disengaged and stepped back. Her face was scarlet, and she was very conscious of being caught *in flagrente delicto.*

'We won't be long,' said one of them. She took a long feather duster and flicked at Giorgio's testicles.

'You don't need to untie him,' said her pal. 'I can mop the floor around him.' She took off her overall, to reveal a skimpy pair of panties, and the other girl followed suit. They ushered Janet out and locked the door, then switched on their transistor radio.

Janet moved into the next cubicle as the sound of the pop music mixed with swishing and gurgling noises and high-pitched yelps from Giorgio. She was still feeling more than a little randy, and very annoyed at being robbed of Giorgio. He had been good for at least another two orgasms, but he wouldn't be when those two had finished with him, if she was any judge. She decided to try a little experiment to pass the time, so she bent down and fastened her ankles to the cross. It felt very wicked, especially without her panties. She fastened her left wrist as well, and held up her right hand. How awful it felt!

The door opened and Massimo came in. She squealed and placed her right hand protectively over her sex.

'Trying it out?' he asked. 'Here, let me help.' She squealed again as he took her right wrist and strapped it up into place.

'I see how it works, Massimo,' she said hastily. 'Now it is time for me to go and oversee lunch with the kiddies.'

'There's plenty of time,' he said. 'Here, try this as well,' and, to her horror, he locked the door, then produced a big ball-gag, forced it into her mouth and strapped it into place, then stepped back and admired the view.

'What a superb body,' he said, and kissed her nipple. Janet's eyes opened wide, and she squirmed frantically, trying to escape. Then he kissed the other one. Janet wriggled desperately, but she was quite helpless, and the waves of excitement were already racing over her body. He kissed the first nipple again and his hands blatantly fondled her pussy. Her labia were still peeled apart from her recent intercourse, and he had no difficulty finding her clit. He titillated that, very expertly, and Janet was immediately aroused, almost to the point of orgasm, and squealed helplessly and silently, under her gag, with a mix of horror and delight, but then the horror became dominant as he picked up a long cane.

'You like SM, of course?' he asked.

She was totally confused and nodded wildly. He went to one side, and she felt the cane cut across her buttock; just a playful cut, but she squealed again under her gag. He flicked at her again, and again, and now the cane stung her bottom and the pain was real, but was already mixed with a new layer of sexual pleasure.

He came around to the front, bending the cane in both his hands. She shook her head desperately.

'Does that mean yes or no?' he asked, and flicked the cane across her breasts. She felt the pain-pleasure mix hit her hard as her nipple erected. She yelped and shook and nodded her head alternately as he flicked the cane all over her body. It flicked across her belly and made her pudenda smart, then found her sex. She jerked helplessly like a marionette, but the sexual excitement was really beginning to build up now, all-pervasive, like a forest fire that took possession of her body. The cane was a striking snake, tormenting her, but now, at each blow, her lust reached a new peak. He carried on caning her until her body was suffused with a deep pink glow, then he reached up and ripped away the gag. She was completely overcome now, gasping and moaning as soon as the gag was released.

'More,' she said. He struck her again and again, harder now. 'There,' she cried out, as the tip of the cane touched her labia. 'More, more,' she squealed.

The cane flicked across her sex and breasts, then again across her bottom. Her body was alive now, and red hot, like a furnace at full blast. She twisted and turned, not to shield her body from the cane, but so that it would strike her more intimately. It reached the target at last, snapping at her clitoris, and she came again, but this was the big one: the mysterious, wonderful, pain-induced orgasm that makes the others seem like children's games.

He ripped open his zip and took her frantically as she came, ramming his prick up into her without any finesse. She howled and screamed as she felt her tormented sex stretched open by his massive prick, then it all merged together: the pain, the red fire all over her body, her continuous rolling climax, and the hot shock of his semen.

Igor arrived at Les Chattes Sauvages at eleven, for his morning rehearsal. There was no one about and he walked through the darkened theatre and on to the stage. The lights suddenly came on and blinded him. He blinked and put his hand up to shield his eyes, then saw Vivienne seated at a table. There was a gorilla-like man with her, sitting on the table, playing with a gun.

'Hello, Igor,' Vivienne said.

'Hello, Vivienne,' he replied.

'Put your hands up whilst Alfie frisks you,' she said, and produced a small automatic pistol of her own.

'Hey, look out,' said Igor, but he put his hands up. The man put his gun on the table, came around behind Igor, and frisked him quickly but thoroughly.

'He's clean,' he said, and went back to his place.

'Who was that girl?' Vivienne asked.

'What girl?' he asked.

'The one you smuggled out of La Chasse last night,' Vivienne replied.

'I don't know what you mean,' Igor told her.

'Don't play games with me,' said Vivienne. 'There was an extra girl at La Chasse yesterday evening, and you helped her get away. I want to know who she was, what she was doing at my club, and where you come into it.'

Igor hesitated. 'This is all very confidential,' he told her.

'I know how to keep my mouth shut,' she told him. 'Get on with it.'

'What about him?' asked Igor, nodding towards her the henchman at her side.

'What about him?' she repeated. 'Stop wasting time.'

'She was keeping the Centre, the place next door to La Chasse, under observation,' Igor told her. 'She must have strayed into La Chasse by accident.'

'By accident?' she asked, and laughed sarcastically. 'Do you really expect me to believe that?' She laughed again. 'That power failure was no accident,' she went on, 'and that sort of operation needs a lot of clout. Who does she work for?'

'I'm not at liberty to tell you that.'

'We'll see about that,' she said, lifting her gun. 'Alfie,' she said over her shoulder, 'soften him up.'

Alfie smiled, put down his gun, pulled on black tight-fitting gloves, cracked his knuckles, took two steps towards Igor, and vanished. There was a loud crash and a howl of anguish from below the stage. Vivienne swung around, amazed at the sudden disappearance of her henchman, then saw the trapdoor swinging. Before she could turn around again Igor nudged her on to the trapdoor, which opened again, so that she vanished in turn. Igor picked up Alfie's gun and walked into the aisle alongside the stage, where Suzie had manipulated the lever for the trapdoor. They slipped cautiously out of the rear exit and climbed into her van.

Twenty-five

After their sex session, Candie and Lucien had settled down to deal with the mail, and Candie was just finishing off the letters he had dictated when he glanced at his watch. 'I have a visitor due in a few moments,' he told her.

Candie looked up from the keyboard. 'Someone important?' she asked.

Lucien nodded. 'He provides me with girls from eastern Europe,' he explained, then he paused and frowned. 'I've known him for quite a while,' he went on, 'but he has several irons in the fire. To tell the truth, I suspect that one of his irons might burn my fingers one of these days.'

'Which one?' she asked.

'I don't know.' He paused again, and looked at her. 'That is what I would like you to find out, if you don't mind,' he told her.

'I see,' she said, and looked down: she had changed into a black bra-and-panties outfit that left very little to the imagination and, with her long black stockings, she realised that she looked extremely arousing in the office surroundings.

'Dressed like this?' she asked him.

'I am sure he will find you completely irresistible,' he told her.

'I shall be very annoyed if he doesn't,' she said, and went to powder her nose.

After disposing of Vivienne and her two helpers, Igor returned, with Suzie, to her flat, and she went into her kitchen to make them some coffee. 'I'm very sorry,' he told her from the doorway. 'I told you a pack of lies, exposed you to danger, and I have probably ruined your career. You must wish you had never met me.'

'I wouldn't say that,' she replied with a slight smile, and handed him his coffee. He added sugar and cream and sipped his coffee, turning the pages of her photograph album absentmindedly as he did so.

'I don't think I ever explained just how I came to visit Les Chattes Sauvages, did I?' he asked, looking up at her.

'I don't think so,' replied Suzie cautiously.

'When I came down to breakfast,' he explained, 'the waiter showed me to a certain table. A girl had been sitting there, and she was just leaving. She had left behind her a tourist brochure, open at the cabaret advertisements, and she had placed a big red ring around Les Chattes Sauvages.'

'How odd,' said Suzie. 'Who was she?'

'Who knows?' he asked enigmatically. 'I rushed to the door to return her brochure, but she had vanished, so I only ever saw her from the back; but she looked very attractive and she moved beautifully.' He smiled and shrugged. 'I was quite smitten,' he admitted.

'It sounds like it,' Suzie replied.

'She wore a felt hat and big sunglasses,' he told her.

'Really?'

'And a long blonde wig,' he added.

'How very strange,' she commented.

'Just like the one in your bedroom,' he completed.

She smiled ruefully and disappeared into her bedroom, to emerge a few moments later wearing the wig, hat and sunglasses he had described. 'It is my "Woman of a Thousand Faces" outfit,' she explained sadly. 'I always wear it when I rob a bank.'

'When you do,' he advised her, 'walk out backward. You have an unmistakable *derrière*, Suzie.'

She sighed and took off the hat. 'There goes another illusion,' she said, and took off the wig and the sunglasses. 'I was told to take you to see Pascale,' she explained, 'and I was given a run-down on your dancing career to wet my appetite. I was also told you were very handsome and a devil in bed. What girl could resist such an assignment?'

'Who told you all this?' he asked.

'I'm just a tiny pawn in a big game,' she told him, 'and pawns keep quiet about who gives them their orders.'

'Very wise,' said Igor, and showed her a picture he had discovered, in her album, during his first visit. It showed her father standing beside a tall man with a soldierly bearing, but dressed in a polo-necked sweater and jeans. 'I spent a month in Northern Ireland with 14 Intelligence Company, on anti-terrorist training,' he explained, and pointed to the man in the sweater. 'He taught me how to drink Bushmills,' he added. 'Maybe he also taught your father.'

'I think it was the other way around,' Suzie corrected him with a smile, then sighed and opened up a little. 'My father has friends all over the world,' she told him, 'including my honorary Australian Uncle Harry, whom I think you may know.'

'You mean my boss?' Igor gave a soft whistle. 'So my boss and Jenny's boss are both old buddies of your father?' he asked. She nodded.

'Wait a minute,' he went on, 'Candie and Jenny and I were all supposed to be watching the Centre, but we all ended up inside Lucien's organisation . . .'

'Jenny wasn't intended to,' she said quickly, and then stopped short, blushing furiously.

'But Candie and I were?' he asked.

'I've told you too much,' she said, and just then there was a ring at the bell. Suzie was obviously relieved, and rushed off to open the door. A few moments later, Hans appeared, shook hands with Igor, then looked at Suzie and grinned amiably.

'You are tired of him already?' he asked.

'No, I am not,' she said, and patted his cheek warningly. 'You are going to have to work very hard, Lieutenant-Commander, to make me forget him,' she told him.

'I'll do my best, darling,' he replied, and she turned to Igor.

'I guess this is where we part company,' she said quietly, with a hint of tears in her eyes.

'I suppose so,' he replied, knowing he would get no more information out of her. 'I really enjoyed dancing with you,' he told her.

'I enjoyed it too,' she said quietly, and kissed him quickly. 'Look after yourself,' she added.

Igor kissed her and shook hands again with Hans, then started down the stairs. He heard Elton John's 'Sacrifice' begin as he walked away down the road, and smiled at the thought of Hans being sacrificed on Suzie's sexual altar, but then his mind switched to Candie.

Twenty-six

The guard peered into the cell, down in the basement at La Chasse, where Gaston sat nursing two black eyes and assorted bruises. He was alone with his prisoners: two of his pals had gone off in the Renault Espace, with the hostesses, heading for Marseilles, and two more had gone to Paris with Vivienne, to sort out Suzie and her partner. He went to light a cigarette.

'Put your hands up.' He stopped short, his right hand in his jacket pocket, then cautiously turned his head. The muzzle of Jenny's automatic was an inch from his eye, the safety catch was off, there was a round in the chamber, the muzzle was rock-steady and her knuckle was white with the first pressure on the trigger. He put his hands up. It was a pro's automatic and this pint-sized bitch looked like she knew how to use it.

'Take your gun out of your holster with your left hand, drop it and kick it away,' she told him.

'You wouldn't dare,' he said.

'I've already killed two men who thought that,' she told him, 'and I don't mind making it three.' He did just as he was told.

'Unlock the door.' She stood to the side of him as he opened the door, and Gaston stood up.

'I'm sorry about this,' she said to him.

'He's going to be,' said Gaston, rubbing his hands. Jenny stepped away, and the guard put his hands in front of him, palms down, in a classic karate stance, and moved his right foot forward. Gaston ran the outside of his heavy boot down the young man's shin, and stamped hard on the top of his foot, then hit him in the face. Jenny winced and hurriedly opened the door to the next cell to release Benoit.

'I can't stay,' she told him. 'Don't let your dad kill him.'

'I won't,' he said, and kicked the groaning gangster in the ribs. Jenny left them to it, but she did notice as she left that the third cell seemed to be stacked high with videotapes.

Vivienne was not physically hurt by her fall at the theatre, partly because she fell on top of Alfie, but her pride was severely damaged, and it took them half an hour to get out, so she was extremely angry. She picked up her car from the parking lot and was halfway back to La Chasse before she identified the muffled banging noise coming from the boot, and discovered Frankie, her second gorilla, bound and gagged and hooded with a Sanderson cushion cover. By the time she rang Lucien, she was almost incoherent, so that he had to ask her several times to stop and go over it again, and he lost his temper with her in the process, but eventually he got the message. He told her to sit tight and wait for him to ring back, but she was hopping mad, and sent Alfie down to get Gaston and Benoit up for another interrogation. Two minutes later Alfie came back, carrying his colleague, who was covered in blood and in urgent need of a doctor.

'Go and bring back Gaston and Benoit,' she told Alfie and Frankie through her clenched teeth, and rang for an ambulance.

The door bell rang, and Candie emerged from the ladies' room, freshly powdered and perfumed, went to the door, took up a suitable exotic pose, opened the door, and found herself face-to-face with Wolfgang. She felt her face become white and her heart drop into her shoes, but Wolfgang looked her in the eyes without any sign of recognition, and shook his head very slightly.

'Come in, Wolfgang,' Lucien called, and she led him into the office, her mind racing with this new turn of events. This meeting was unexpected, certainly, but not catastrophic, she told herself. Coincidences like this happened all the time, and one ran into chance acquaintances every day, but obviously Wolfgang wished to keep their meeting on the plane a secret. She managed to hide her confusion as Lucien introduced them.

'I like the new office uniform,' said Wolfgang, then turned to Candie. 'Did you design the lingerie yourself?' he asked innocently. Candie blushed a deep red and rushed off to make coffee.

Alfie walked cautiously through the grounds at La Chasse, his gun at the ready, looking for Gaston and his son. The path was narrow and the foliage of the trees made speckled shadows on the ground. He heard a noise, looked around, saw Gaston in the distance, and started to run towards him. The thin wire of the rabbit snare snapped around his ankle and he fell flat on his face, on to the root of a tree, or so he thought, but it wasn't a root; it moved under him, and he realised that it was a viper, tied to a stake. He felt it writhe, saw the pink-and-white mouth open, saw its incisors shoot out, and screamed with horror as the snake slithered towards him. He grabbed it behind the neck and wrenched it away from him, threw it down, scrabbled for his gun and emptied it into the snake, then stood there, gasping with horror.

Frankie heard the gunshots and plunged into the undergrowth, making for the noise. He came out into a clearing and paused, looking around, but he failed to see the wild boar just a few yards away. It had been wounded in escaping from the stockade, hunted all night, and now there was all this noise and people crashing about, disturbing its rest. Benoit crept up quietly behind it and fired his shotgun into the air. The boar put its head down and charged into the bushes like a tank, squealing with rage as it bore down on Frankie. Frankie heard the thundering hoofs, looked around, and started to run, but the boar was moving fast now, and it tossed the burly man to one side like thistledown. Frankie crawled away desperately as the boar stopped short and turned. To his relief, Gaston and Benoit appeared and lured the animal away, then Gaston was towering over him, with his shotgun pointing down at him, the muzzle just an inch from his head. 'If I catch either of you in here again,' he said, 'I'll blow your fucking head off.'

Wolfgang watched Candie leave, sat down, took the cigar that Lucien handed to him, and cut off the end.

'Where did you find that lust box, Lucien?' he asked, leaning over to accept a light.

'The secretarial agency sent her.'

'A secretarial agency? With those boobs?'

'She is an excellent secretary, believe it or not.'

'What about the rest?' Wolfgang asked, drawing contentedly on his cigar.

'The conference room is always at your disposal, if you want to check her out,' Lucien pointed out with an ironic smile.

'I might just do that, Lucien,' he said, then leaned forward and changed the subject. 'Did you know that Jean-Luc's missus is hawking her wares for a pimp called Carl?' he asked. Lucien drew in his breath, his face became pink, and he made Wolfgang repeat his information.

'What the hell does that silly bitch think she's doing?' he asked furiously.

'Getting fucked, of course,' Wolfgang replied. 'Gabrielle is a born whore, Lucien; a straight-up, natural, copper-bottomed whore.'

'How do you know?'

'I tried her out.' Wolfgang sat back and puffed on his cigar, watching with satisfaction as Lucien's eyes opened wide. 'I dropped in to see Carl,' he explained. 'We often do business together, and he told me about this rich woman with streetwalker fantasies he'd acquired from Vivienne.'

'You don't mean to say he actually had her out there in the street?' Lucien cried out in horror. Wolfgang waved his hand.

'Hell, no, he'd fixed it, naturally,' he replied. 'He'd lined up half-a-dozen of his mates to give her the time of her life: I managed to get in there first.'

Lucien sighed with relief. 'Well, that's something,' he admitted.

'That's not all, though,' Wolfgang told him. He sat back and examined the ash on the end of his cigar, then exploded his new bombshell. 'Somebody has been taking pictures of her,' he told Lucien.

'Pictures?' asked Lucien, his voice rising. 'Who?'

'Carl doesn't know,' Wolfgang replied, 'but somebody high enough up to tell the vice squad to stay out of it.'

Lucien breathed in deeply and his cheeks became livid. He picked up the telephone and dialled Vivienne's number.

'Vivienne, did you introduce Gaby Lamartine to a pimp called Carl?' he snapped, little knowing that Vivienne's sitting room was littered with casualties and ambulance men, and that she was in no mood for small-talk.

'What if I did?' she snapped. 'She said she wanted to –'

'Why the hell didn't you ask me?' he shouted, and her temper flared up at once.

'Why the hell should I?' she shouted back. 'You're not my keeper, big brother.'

'Someone has been taking photographs of her,' he told her.

'Who?'

'How the hell do I know?,' he shouted, and put the telephone down, then turned to Wolfgang, trembling with anger. 'Bloody women!' he said.

'Perhaps I should leave you in peace to sort things out,' said Wolfgang, standing up.

'I'm sorry. Would you mind?' Lucien asked him apologetically.

'Of course not. I'll go and help your secretary make the coffee,' Wolfgang told him with a grin, and went into the kitchen.

Giorgio dropped Janet off to do some shopping, and drove home. As he drew up, a shabby-looking man in a raincoat approached him. 'Excuse me, are you Giorgio Manzini?' the man asked. He nodded.

The man held out a press card. 'Press-Dimanche,' he said. 'We'd like to ask you a few questions about Madame Lamartine.'

'Nothing doing.'

'We'd pay you a lot of money for a few simple answers.'

'Nothing doing.'

'We've been following you all morning: you and Miss McAllister.'

'If I talk to you, she'll fire me.'

'If we tell her what you've been doing with Miss McAllister, she'll fire you, so you lose your job anyway,' the reporter pointed out. 'Our way, you get a hundred-thousand francs to tide you over.'

Giorgio bit his lip. 'That's just the start, of course,' the reporter told him confidentially. 'You'll be on the front page, naturally, and we could fix you up with a film test. It could be the start of a new career.'

'I don't know,' he said uncertainly.

'There'll be no shortage of rich women either, from now on, old man,' the reporter pointed out, taking his arm. 'Once this story breaks,' he murmured, 'they'll be queuing up to hit the sack with you.'

'What sort of things would you want to know?'

'Just the details. We'd write the story. You'd just add those little authentic details: you know, how she gets off, what she wears . . .'

'Who says I know?'

'Come on. Women like that don't hire guys with your looks just to drive a car.' He nudged Giorgio with his elbow. 'You've slipped her a length now and again,' he said. 'Her and that Scottish tart, you lucky bastard.'

Giorgio suddenly spotted his mistress at the window out of the corner of his eye. 'She's watching us,' he murmured. 'I'll call you,' and he brushed the reporter aside and made for the house.

'Give her this,' the other man said as he went by, and handed him a large Manila envelope addressed to Gabrielle.

Twenty-seven

'Well, and how is the lingerie business coming along?' Candie looked up as Wolfgang sauntered into the kitchen.

'I'm sorry about that,' she said. 'I thought it sounded more exciting than temping.' She placed two cups of coffee on a tray, but he held up his hand and barred her way when she tried to leave.

'Lucien wants to be left alone for the moment,' he told her. 'He has a few domestic problems to clear up.' He had left the door slightly open and was blatantly eavesdropping; he added sugar to one of the cups and stirred the coffee.

'What is he like to work for?' he asked her, nodding towards Lucien. She picked up her own coffee.

'I feel a little sorry for him,' she said.

'Because he was blown up a couple of times?'

'Yes.'

'You should have seen the other guys,' he told her, and came closer. 'He's a rat,' he added. 'Don't waste any sympathy on him.'

'That's nice to know,' she said. 'What does that make you?'

'Your partner,' he announced proudly. She raised her eyebrows.

'In what kind of business?' she asked coldly.

'Stealing confidential files,' he replied.

Gabrielle had just woken up. She yawned, went to the window in her nightie, looked out into the noonday sunshine, and saw Giorgio standing by her car, talking to a man in a raincoat. She looked down at another car, and straight into a telephoto lens; she rushed to the telephone.

'Lucien?' she asked breathlessly, 'it's Gabrielle. Listen, there are two men outside, talking to Giorgio. They look like reporters.'

'That bloody pimp of yours probably tipped them off,' Lucien hissed.

'Who?'

'Carl,' he said impatiently. 'Your bloody pimp.'

'Vivienne introduced us,' she protested.

'I know. She is a stupid bitch, and so are you.'

'How dare you speak to me like that!' she screamed at him. 'You get me out of this, Lucien, now, do you hear?'

He gritted his teeth. 'Who are they? Which newspaper?' he asked.

'I don't know.'

'Then bloody well find out,' he shouted.

'Wait a moment,' she told him, and ran to intercept Giorgio as he came into the house.

'Who were those men outside?' she asked him breathlessly.

'What men?'

She bit her lip and forced herself to stay calm. 'Whatever they have offered you, I'll double it,' she said quietly, 'provided you tell me exactly what they asked, and what you told them.'

'I don't know what you mean.'

'Giorgio,' she told him, 'those men are threatening my husband's career. He could be prime minister in a few years, and eventually even the president of France. He will not let you or anyone else get in his way, don't you understand?'

He still hesitated and she became desperate. She lifted her nightdress to her shoulders. 'I'll do anything you like,' she said, coming up to him. 'Anything. Please. For me, Giorgio, please . . .'

'*Press-Dimanche*,' he told her, and handed over the business card. She rushed back, grabbed the telephone, and read off the names on the business card. When she had finished, Lucien told her to sit tight, and she put the phone down. Her heart was still pounding, but she felt confident now that Lucien would resolve this problem. She looked up to find Giorgio still there, looking at her in her see-through nightie. She drew herself up and switched to her no-nonsense voice.

'Now, Giorgio, you are not to talk to anyone about this from now on,' she told him.

'They offered me a hundred-thousand francs,' he pointed out. 'You said you would double it.'

'Giorgio,' she reminded him sharply, 'you know perfectly well that your contract expressly forbids you to discuss my affairs with anyone, and I would also remind you that blackmail is a very serious offence. Now, I am prepared to overlook this lapse just this once, and I will talk to Jean-Luc about a small raise, but I wish to hear no more of it. Is that clear?'

'Yes, madame,' he replied humbly.

'Now, what did they want to know?' she asked.

'Whether I had sex with you,' he admitted.

'Sex with me?' she asked. 'They dared to imply that I would have sex with a servant?' and her eyes flashed fire. 'My God, they'll pay for this,' she said, and paced up and down. 'Oh yes, they'll pay right enough,' she repeated, then she looked up. Giorgio was sprawling on her couch.

'What on earth do you think you're doing?' she screamed at him, then saw that he had a big Manila envelope in his hands, addressed to her, which he had obviously ripped open. 'What's that?' she asked. 'Give it to me this instant,' and she held out her hand, but he showed her one of the glossy ten by eight black-and-white photographs it contained, and she felt her knees turn to jelly. 'Oh God,' she said, and immediately started to plead once more. 'Give them to me, Giorgio, please,' she begged, her face scarlet with shame and anger, but he riffled through them, then looked up at her with an insolent gleam in his dark eyes.

'Not so fast,' he said, and switched to Italian, but his accent was that of the Naples back streets, and he no longer used the formal, respectful third person. 'Did you say a small raise?' he asked.

'I was joking,' she assured him hurriedly. 'Of course you can have your two hundred thousand francs.' She held out her hand. 'A quarter of a million', she said. 'In cash. You can drive me to the bank straightaway,' but he didn't hand over the pictures.

'What about sex with a servant?' he asked.

'You're not a servant,' she assured him. 'You can do anything you like with me, Giorgio, you know that. You know how you turn me on.' She leant over and put her arms around his neck. He put his hand up and fondled her breast through her thin nightie. 'Does whoring turn you on?' he asked her.

'It would if I did it for you,' she murmured. He cupped her breast and squeezed it, feeling her nipple harden against his palm.

'OK,' he said, 'so now you work for me,' and he tapped the top photograph. 'Go and get dressed,' he told her, 'then you can show me what you've learnt from this other pimp of yours.'

Lucien waited for his anger with Gabrielle to subside, then dialled another number.

'Delacroix,' the voice said.

'It's Lucien. Listen –'

'I told you never to call me here.'

'This is an emergency,' Lucien hissed. 'Are you alone?'

'Yes.'

'*Press-Dimanche* is harassing Gabrielle Lamartine,' he said. 'I want them stopped.'

'What the hell has she been doing?' Delacroix asked testily, and Lucien told him.

'Is she out of her mind?' Delacroix howled.

'That isn't all,' Lucien added. 'I think we may have been penetrated.'

'Who by?'

'I want you to tell me. The woman's name is Jenny and the man's name is Igor . . .'

* * *

Candie looked at Wolfgang in total amazement, but, before she could react, he put his hand on his lips to make her keep quiet, and indicated the slightly open door. She crept closer, and heard Lucien describing Igor.

'Who is he talking to,' she whispered.

'A man called Delacroix.'

'Delacroix?' she asked in horror.

'Do you know him?'

'I was with him yesterday evening,' she admitted. 'He's way up in the DST.'

Wolfgang whistled. 'Igor is your boyfriend, isn't he?' he asked.

'What makes you think that?' she asked.

'He saw you and me together at the airport,' he told her, 'and has been following me around like a jealous bridegroom ever since,' and he nodded towards the office. 'You and your Igor are in deep, deep trouble,' he told her. 'Now, are you going to cooperate, or shall I spill the beans to Lucien?'

'I don't know anything about any files,' she told him.

'Now listen,' he told her, grabbing her arm, 'everybody knows that Lucien keeps files with enough dynamite in them to blow several governments apart: the question is where? Now, I've been working with him for a long time, and I am quite sure the files are somewhere here in Paris; that means at La Chasse, Les Plaisirs d'Anaïs or here.'

'I still don't know what you are talking about,' she replied.

'Look,' he said, 'we meet accidentally on a plane. I go and take a look at La Chasse, and your boyfriend tails me. I go to sniff around Les Plaisirs d'Anaïs, and he is there, and so are you. I come here, and here you are again. Now, Lucien is on to you, or will be very soon, and it will be a one-way ticket to North Africa for you.' He looked her up and down. 'Do you know how much a blonde like you is worth down there?' he asked. She clenched her fists and her mind raced, but could see no way out.

'The files are on multimedia CDs, hidden among his audio CDs,' she told him resignedly.

* * *

Gabrielle looked at herself in the big mirror in her bedroom. She had done the best she could to reproduce her streetwalker outfit. Her open-front sling bra was under wired and lifted her breasts provocatively under her hip-length see-though organza blouse. She didn't wear a skirt, and her tie-side panties were clearly visible, along with the garter belt that pulled taut her black lace stockings. She found a pair of high-heeled mules and perched up on them as she completed her make-up, then she walked carefully down the stairs and across the courtyard to the old coach house where Giorgio lived. She tapped on his door.

'Come in,' he called. She went in. He was sprawled on the bed, naked, lying back, watching a blue video on the TV receiver as he sipped a whisky. His half-erect penis lay against his belly as he watched the porno star moan with simulated ecstasy. He beckoned to Gaby to join him on the bed. She walked over and sat down on the bed, next to his chest. He held up the whisky bottle but she shook her head.

'Look after me, baby,' he said.

She put out her hand and ran her fingertips over his thigh, up and down, then up on to his stomach, circling around his pubic hair. He finished his whisky, put down the glass, and flopped on to his back with his legs wide apart. She continued to caress his stomach and thighs as he lay with his eyes closed, then he reached up to feel her breast. She half-turned to make the access easier and opened her legs invitingly, so that when he opened his eyes he saw her hips close to him, the bow that tied her panties invitingly near his face. Her hand moved on to his penis and her fingertips explored the tip. He moaned softly and she leant over to take his cock into her mouth. As she eased her lips over his knob, he unfastened the bow and her panties fell away. She took his shaft into her mouth and lifted his balls with her hand to tickle him behind his scrotum.

'How do you want to come?' she asked.

'What's on offer?'

'In my pussy, in my mouth, between my breasts, whatever you like,' she murmured, then went down on him with her voluptuous mouth, licking him all around the red bulbous tip and stroking his shaft with her hands. He was gasping and obviously very excited, and he suddenly reared up.

'Lie down,' he said hoarsely. She changed places with him and lay stretched out on the couch, on her back, whilst he knelt over her. He placed his penis between her breasts and she massaged the shaft with her bosom whilst he reached behind his back and penetrated her sex with his finger. He looked down at her as he fingered her vagina and found her clit. She was suddenly very aroused and her clit was hard and firm under his fingertip. Her arousal increased his excitement to breaking point and he thrust his finger deep into her and then titillated her clit again and again. She started to sob and cry out, and he suddenly ejaculated between her breasts. Gabrielle yelped, in the throes of her orgasm, as his semen jetted up under her chin and covered her neck and cleavage with a sticky whitish cream.

Delacroix called the owner of *Press-Dimanche*, and didn't beat about the bush. 'Two of your reporters are harassing Gabrielle Lamartine,' he told him. 'Get them off her back, now,' and he read out the names on Gaby's card. He rang off, picked up the notes he had made about Jenny and Igor, then suddenly remembered the previous evening, and the Australian girl called Candida, who worked for Lucien. She was probably in his office right now, maybe even listening to his telephone conversations. She almost certainly knew he was in cahoots with Lucien, anyway. He hardly had time to think it all out, however, before the owner of *Press-Dimanche* was back on the line, and very angry indeed. They had no reporters anywhere near Gabrielle Lamartine, he told Delacroix indignantly, and had never heard of the names he'd mentioned.

He called Lucien. 'You have a girl called Candida working for you?' he asked in a whisper.

'Yes,' Lucien replied.

'Could she be overhearing this conversation?'

'No. She is in the conference room.'

'Neutralise her,' Delacroix told him.

'But –'

'No buts,' Lucien. 'Keep her out of the way until I find out what is going on. You will probably have to get rid of her.'

'What's the matter?'

'*Press-Dimanche* is not harassing Gabrielle Lamartine, for a start.'

'What the hell is going on?'

'That is what I intend to find out. No more telephone calls, Lucien. We drop back into the agreed routine.' He sat back and wiped the perspiration from his forehead.

Christian looked at the urgent dispatch from the DST telephone-tapping bureau, and at the transcript of Lucien's conversations, and sent two security guards for Delacroix. Two minutes later, Delacroix was confronted by the evidence of the telephone calls: he tendered his resignation almost immediately and was taken away.

Christian told the telephone-tapping supervisor to put a very obvious tap on all calls to Delacroix, then opened a locked drawer in his desk and took out the pictures of Gabrielle, licking his lips as he flicked through them and feeling his excitement grow. He had been very lucky to learn, from one of his vice squad liaison officers, that Vivienne was catering for Gabrielle Lamartine's street-walker fantasies. It had enabled him to pressurise Lucien indirectly, and very successfully, but that wasn't all. Jean-Luc was an old personal friend, and, if he got to hear of this, he would naturally ask him, Christian, for help. He would of course be able to produce the negatives and clear up the whole messy problem very quickly, and earn the gratitude of a man who could well become his new political boss.

He skimmed again through the pictures. What if Gabrielle herself turned to him for help? He had always envied Jean-Luc his seductive wife, and now he felt his lust for her rise up and stab him in the belly.

* * *

Vivienne slammed down the telephone and terminated the painful conversation she had just had with Gabrielle. So some newspaperman had taken some compromising pictures of her, and now she was having to buy them back the old-fashioned way from that big Italian chauffeur of hers, and, of course, the stupid bitch was blaming her, Vivienne, for all her problems. Well, she had more than enough problems of her own. The ambulance had left some time ago, but the police would soon be round, asking questions about this spate of accidents. That girl last evening had probably blown the whole damned thing to pieces; Igor and Suzie had made her look a real fool, and all Lucien did was swear at her and call her names. She picked up the telephone again.

'Air France, Charles de Gaulle? I want to order a first-class single to Bogota. Today. As soon as possible. Here is my AMEX number.'

A minute later, she put the phone down and cleared out the safe of all its cash and negotiables. She was getting out. She was halfway out of the door when her telephone rang; she ignored it and climbed into her car.

Lucien heard her telephone ringing and guessed at once what had happened. His dear little sister had cleared out the safe and was on her way out of the country! He was really sweating now. He looked at his watch and rang Delacroix again. The phone rang and a new voice answered.

'Mr Delacroix's office.'

'Could I speak to him please?' Lucien asked, then stopped in his tracks. There was an echo on the line, a slight change of resonance that meant that the line was tapped.

'He is not in the office, I'm afraid,' the voice said hollowly. 'Who is it speaking please?'

'It doesn't matter.' Lucien replaced the telephone and decided it was time to go. He picked up his briefcase and unlocked the safe, carefully selected half a dozen CDs, placed them in a black attaché case, and locked it, then suddenly felt the cold muzzle of a gun against his neck, and looked up. 'What the hell are you doing?' he asked.

'Stealing your files,' Wolfgang replied. Lucien looked past him and saw Candie, handcuffed and gagged, standing helplessly by the safe.

'She very kindly told me where you kept your files,' Wolfgang told him, and hit him behind the ear with his gun. Lucien slumped to the ground and Candie screamed helplessly under her gag. Wolfgang turned to her and chained her handcuffs to the steel bar that kept the CDs in place. 'I'm sorry I can't take you with me, sweetheart,' he told Candie, 'but I always believe in travelling light.' He patted her bottom, blew her a kiss, and left.

Candie looked down. She had been taken unawares by Wolfgang, and she knew she had no chance of escaping from the handcuffs, but Lucien was already beginning to recover. He opened his eyes, blinked, and she saw his eyes harden as his memory returned. He sat up, very groggy, but he seemed to be more interested in his computer than in pursuing Wolfgang, and Candie soon saw why. He manipulated the keyboard, and the screen displayed a digital counter that was showing 120 seconds. Lucien quickly stripped his desk and assembled his papers, then turned to her.

'I don't know who you are, you bitch,' he hissed, 'but you will be joining that bastard, in just two minutes, in the next world. This safe is timed to blow up at the same time as the case.' Candie's eyes widened in horror and she tried to speak, but the gag prevented her. He punched a key and the counter began to run down, second by second.

Lucien left the office and locked the door. Candie tried desperately to get to the keyboard, but her handcuffs were shackled firmly to the safe, and the counter was already below 100 seconds.

Igor was just getting out of a taxi when he saw Wolfgang in the distance, carrying a black briefcase. He paid the driver and went into the tower block, just in time to see Lucien step out of the lift, drop his office keys on to the receptionist's desk, and walk quickly towards the door. He walked to the desk, swept up the keys and ran to the lift. The receptionist shouted after him and a security guard lumbered to his feet and blocked Igor's path. Igor hit him viciously in the stomach and he doubled over. He hit him again, this time behind the ear, then stepped into the lift and pressed the seventeenth-floor button as the man rolled on the floor and the receptionist hit the alarm button. The alarm sirens screamed and a second guard started towards the lift, unbuttoning his holster. Igor drew Alfie's gun and held him off until the door closed. The lift stopped at the fourteenth floor as they cut the power, and he raced up the stairs to the seventeenth floor, opened the office door, ran in and shouted for Candie. No reply. He could hear the guards pounding up the stairs as he searched, but at last he saw Candie. He ripped the gag from her mouth and she nodded towards the screen. 'Bomb,' she said. The counter was at ten seconds, and the guards were already pouring in through the doorway. He shouted 'Bomb' to them and used up three precious seconds and five rounds to blow the chains of the handcuff apart, then they raced into the conference room and hurled themselves down behind the big heavy sofa. A moment later, the wall safe was ripped apart and the sofa was lifted into the air by the force of the blast, but it protected them from the metal splinters and debris that showered all around them.

Twenty-eight

The next day, the newspapers disagreed among themselves about the probable cause of the blast that had damaged a tower block at La Defense, but they all gave pride of place on the front page to pictures of Candie, in her bra and panties, being carried to safety by a couple of burly firemen, and fire-brigade offices all over France were inundated with offers from volunteers. The commentators all pointed out that Lucien had many enemies, and no doubt one of them had tried to assassinate him. It was fortunate that he had not been there when the bomb went off, and he had very sensibly vanished from the scene. His half sister, Vivienne, who worked closely with him, had also gone into hiding, whilst his secretary had fortunately been in another room, and had escaped with just the loss of her dress.

There had been another explosion at the same time, which had destroyed a parked car and had, most unfortunately, severely damaged a turn-of-the-century *pissoir* that had just been declared a classified historical monument. The man who had been using it had not been traced.

Jean-Luc and Gabrielle found the lead story so fascinating that the breakfast-table family ritual was abandoned and the children's table manners went unchecked as their parents absorbed the news. The children went off to school and Jean-Luc rushed off to work, in such a hurry that he quite forgot about Janet.

Once her husband was out of the way, Gabrielle was able to concentrate on her own problems. She had no idea whether or not Lucien had been able to deal with *Press-*

Dimanche before leaving so abruptly, and she had no idea how many more copies of the scurrilous photographs were doing the rounds. She thought about it for some time, but eventually took the bull by the horns and rang Christian. He was an old friend, reliable, very influential and old enough to play the big brother role. He had a soft spot for her too, she knew that, although he had always behaved impeccably with her.

Not knowing that Christian had in fact launched the *Press-Dimanche* scam, Gabrielle was pleasantly surprised when he seemed to appreciate her problems almost immediately, and did not ask any awkward questions. He promised to investigate and report back within an hour or so, and she rang off and went to bathe.

When Candie came to, she was lying in a bed in a hospital room, and a very handsome young doctor was bending over her. She had rather confused memories of being rescued from the debris by two burly firemen, of being carried down a ladder, of flashguns popping, and of reporters shouting questions, and then she remembered only the sting of a hypodermic needle in her arm, and then blackness. Her first thought was for Igor, and she tried to sit up, but the doctor pushed her gently down again.

'You have to take it easy,' he told her.

'The man who was with me –' she began.

'He's fine,' the doctor told her, and Candie relaxed. She wasn't supposed to know Igor, of course, so she mustn't ask too many questions about him.

'Where am I?' she asked.

'In a clinic, but don't worry: you will be as right as rain in a day or two.'

She looked down, and blushed with embarrassment when she discovered that she was wearing a baby-doll nightie with tiny matching panties. 'Who undressed me?' she asked.

'I did,' he told her, and grinned at her cheerfully. 'Don't worry,' he told her. 'I am a very experienced gynaecologist. Do you mind if I check your bruises?'

'Of course not,' she replied, although she didn't feel bruised at all.

He drew back the bedclothes, and Candie gave a little shriek and put her hand over her tummy, because her panties were really quite see-through, but then she remembered that he was a gynaecologist and had seen all she had anyway.

'Could you lift your nightie up to your shoulders, please?' he asked. Candie complied, but did it very slowly, feeling more and more embarrassed. He really was very handsome and her nipples were sticking up quite blatantly, so that she hesitated for a long time before letting him see them.

'I don't feel very bruised,' she remarked.

'Not there?' he asked, and pressed a very gentle hand on to the under swell of her right breast. She started to say, 'No,' but changed her mind when she felt his cool fingertips.

'Well, it did hurt a little,' she said hesitatingly, 'but it feels much better now.'

'How about there?' he asked, and his fingers drifted slowly to just above her areola. Her toes curled as his cool fingertips just missed her nipple.

'Oh yes. All around there,' she told him, and twisted her feet together, biting her lip as he gently probed all around her nipple. 'The other one hurts there too,' she whispered, and lay back, blinking, as he explored her other areola, pressing her knees and thighs together as his fingers danced over the summits of her breasts like playful butterflies.

'Are your nipples painful?' he asked, in a calm, detached, professional voice. She gulped and shut her eyes, then nodded and waited for his touch, feeling wicked and abandoned. His fingers pressed on to her nipples; she yelped out loud and ground her hips into the bed.

'Shall I kiss your bruises better?' he asked. Candie thought briefly that this was a rather unorthodox treatment, but quickly decided that it seemed a very good idea, and was probably standard French medical practice anyway.

'Yes please,' she whispered politely, and felt his warm, moist lips close around her nipple and suck it into his mouth, where the tip of his tongue played tag with her milk-orifice. Candie's arms went up around his neck and her hands grabbed hold of the starched collar of his white coat. He lifted his head and she rolled to the right, lined up her other nipple and tightened her grip to pull him down again. As soon as his tongue found its new target, her lubricative machinery went into overdrive and her legs and hips moved uncontrollably as her nipples sent urgent messages flashing all over her reproductive system. He moved down to her tummy, paying particular attention to her navel and exploring the indentation with his tongue.

'Where else?' he asked.

'Here,' she told him at once, and placed a fingertip on her thigh. He kissed her leg at the spot she had indicated, and she moved her hand up and round and on to the soft sensitive plumpness of her upper thighs, with his mouth following her hand. She opened her thighs to let him kiss the appalling bruises she had just discovered at the top of her leg, and led him right up to the lace-edged elastic that held her panties tight around her sex. The elastic of her panties was obviously adding to her pain and he removed her knickers, very carefully, and kissed the whole of her pudenda until it was quite, quite better.

'Anywhere else?' he asked, but Candie was past the conversational phase by now. She pushed his head down firmly between her parted thighs, his mouth fastened over her labia and his healing tongue slipped into the moist welcoming cavity of her sex. Thirty seconds later, with his tongue well inside her peeled-open sex and his fingers massaging her nipples, she felt the tip of his nose press against her clitoris. She wriggled until his tongue touched the hard little bud, then a really beautiful orgasm washed over her, wave after wave, until she fell back on to the bed, quite exhausted, and went to sleep.

Giorgio was determined to make Gabrielle work hard to recover her pictures, and had told her to dress up as a streetwalker when Jean-Luc left for work. Having bathed and powdered and perfumed her body, she put on an open-front uplift bra and a disgraceful G-string with a slit between the legs, pulled on long black sheer stockings with lace tops, fixed a black lace suspender belt around her hips, clipped her stockings tautly, and eased on her high-heeled black satin mules. She looked at herself in the mirror, became excited at once by the sight of herself, and slipped into a very short black silk dress with a flared skirt that skimmed the tops of her stockings. She practised her provocative stance, with her legs wide apart and her stomach thrust forward, then inched up her skirt to show off her thighs.

She was suddenly aware that Giorgio had arrived and was watching her in the mirror. 'Don't stop, Gabrielle,' he said, and she blushed a deep scarlet.

'I'm wearing a slit G-string,' she protested. He picked up a big hand mirror and gave it to her. She gulped and licked her lips, then placed it between her thighs with the mirrored surface upward, lifted it until it was trapped between her thighs, then tilted it slightly. The top of the curved mirror pressed up into her body behind her vagina, and she gasped with horror as she saw the reflection of her sex. Her labia protruded through the lace-edged slit and she was clearly lubricating very heavily.

He came up behind her and looked at her reflection over her shoulder as he put his arms around her and played with her breasts, feeling her nipples harden against his palms as he watched her sex ooze moisture and her labia begin to part. 'That's good,' he said, nodding his appreciation. 'I'll fix a mirror between your legs like that this afternoon, at Les Plaisirs.'

'Oh no, please, Giorgio,' she begged.

'You never say "No" to your pimp,' he reminded her, and slapped her bottom as a warning. 'I have five nice horny clients lined up for you this afternoon,' he whispered, 'and they'll expect a good show. Let me have a preview, Gabrielle.' She sobbed and panted, but dared not refuse. She used one hand to part her labia and to show him the inner surfaces of her sex, the glistening tunnel of her vagina and the hard erect horn of her clitoris, and used the other hand to play with herself and increase her arousal almost to the point of orgasm.

From her own bedroom, along the corridor, Janet peeped through the open door into Gabrielle's bedroom, with one hand clutched to her breast as she watched the erotic foreplay. Giorgio was now fondling Gaby's breast with one hand and running the other hand deliberately up the inside of her thighs, forcing her to keep her legs wide apart even as his probing fingers approached her vagina. Janet felt her lubrication soak the skimpy panties she had put on for Jean-Luc, and her nipples became rock hard and screamed for relief, so that her own hands could no longer resist the temptation. She spread her own legs wide and pulled up her mini-slip, revealing her tiny tie-side panties, and slipped her hand inside them, feeling for her sex, panting with excitement as she watched the tableau.

Giorgio was playing with Gaby's labia now, and forcing her to stand facing him and look him in the eyes as his fingers separated her labia and probed delicately into her sex. Janet's fingers slipped inside her own sex and felt the hard little horn of her clitoris. Now Gabrielle was ripping open Giorgio's zip, and sinking down on her knees before him, fumbling inside his pants. Janet felt her heart turn over as she saw Giorgio's penis, hard and red and menacing, as Gaby submissively knelt before him, took him into her mouth, and sucked his huge bulbous prick.

Giorgio muttered a command and Gabrielle took his penis from her mouth and sprawled obediently on the bed. He came up to her and she swung her legs up and on to his shoulders, then put her hand down and drew his prick deep into her vagina. He rammed his shaft into her five or six times and then both of them screamed aloud as they came. At the same moment, Janet went over the edge, and her hand went mad over her sex as she in turn climaxed.

When the safe blew out, Igor's only concern was for Candie, and he waited until he was quite sure she was safe, although that made it impossible for him to escape, and he was arrested immediately. Twenty minutes later, he was handcuffed and sitting on a hard chair at the local police station when the superintendent came in. There was a whispered conversation and Igor was whisked away, through the back door and into a big Renault. The windows were all blacked out, so he had no idea of his destination. After about an hour, the car came to a halt, the door opened, and Igor found himself facing Chantal, Jenny's boss.

She was of medium height, with thick auburn hair, lightly flecked with blonde at the tips, cut into a short, uncomplicated style. Her face had the clear, fresh, healthy look of someone who enjoyed the open air, and her grey-green eyes were cool and intelligent, but her lips were full and she had a mischievous smile. She wore a knee-length pleated skirt and her white satin shirt was stretched tightly over a full bust: when she leant forward, he caught a glimpse of a deep cleavage and of a well-filled, lace-trimmed, white satin bra.

'I apologise for the secrecy,' she said, leading him inside, 'but we obviously need to keep you out of reach of cameras and reporters for a few days.'

'Where am I?' he asked.

'In is a top-secret training establishment for female agents, like Marie-Ange, who require special bedroom skills,' she explained. 'No one will think of looking for you here.'

'How is Candida?'

'She's fine. We are keeping her hidden as well, just for a few days, but she is quite safe and sound, thanks to you.' She smiled at him. 'You seem to make a habit of rescuing damsels in distress,' she told him. 'You've become quite famous in a very short time, and the girls can't wait to meet you – but no doubt you'd like to bathe and change before I introduce you to them.'

Igor nodded gratefully, because he was still covered in dust, and he followed her along a corridor and into a bedroom, noticing that there was neither lock nor bolt on the door. 'Only the loos have bolts,' Chantal told him, following his glance. 'The lack of privacy is part of the training. Does it bother you?'

Igor shrugged. 'Of course not,' he said, feigning indifference as he looked around. It was a very feminine room and featured a huge bed, fitted with black satin sheets and surrounded by large mirrors. There was a large wardrobe overflowing with feminine lingerie, but there was no sign of any masculine garments, except for a couple of hip-length silk robes and some very abbreviated stretch-satin pants that were little more than pouches.

'There is no outerwear allowed in the school, I'm afraid,' Chantal explained, 'but no doubt you are used to running around half naked.'

'I have a feeling I soon will be,' he told her.

'If you would like to undress,' she went on, 'I will run your bath. Put your clothes in that basket by the door, and they'll be picked up by the maid.'

She went into the adjoining bathroom, and Igor quickly stripped, and piled his clothes neatly in the basket. He was quite naked when the door suddenly opened and a dark-haired, petite maid came in. She wore a white frilly apron over black tie-side panties and long black stockings, with satin suspenders. The bib of her pinafore just covered her bosom, but as soon as she saw him she unclipped a catch and let it drop to expose her breasts, then came up close, blatantly offering herself.

'Not now, Melanie, later,' Chantal called. The maid sighed and made big eyes at Igor, but picked up the basket of clothes and left. Igor went into the bathroom, conscious of his slight erection, and walked over to the bath. Chantal turned as he approached and looked him over.

'Whenever I see a young man like you,' she told him, 'I wish I was a twenty-year-old field operative again.'

'What would you have done?' he asked, sliding into the bath.

'Get us a drink,' she said, and went over to a small fridge. 'Champagne?' she asked.

'Champagne in the bath?' he said appreciatively. 'Very

sybaritic.' He slid down in the foam and stretched luxuriously as she uncorked the bottle and poured wine into two flutes. She brought them over and they toasted each other and sipped the wine. He smacked his lips appreciatively, then picked up a large sponge and went to work.

'You seem to have a dispensation from the no-outerwear rule,' he observed, washing away the dust and the tiredness.

She smiled down at him. 'Igor,' she told him, 'there are a dozen young twenty-year-olds out there who have heard about your ability to maintain your erection, and every one of them is determined to demolish it. If I were you, I would not waste time on a woman with a nineteen-year-old son.' He smiled, but seemed to ignore her remark.

'Did you train Marie-Ange Geneviève?' he asked.

'Yes,' she replied. 'She was one of my star pupils. Why?'

'She made mincemeat of me,' he explained ruefully. 'Her and that damned clit stimulator. She demolished me within ten minutes.' Chantal laughed delightedly.

'So now you are looking for revenge?' she asked, topping up his glass.

'That's right,' he replied, climbing out of the bath. 'Unless you want me to tell the girls you chickened out,' he threatened, slipping into the towelling robe she handed him.

'Ah, so now it's blackmail, is it?' she asked rhetorically, and her eyes sparkled with mischief. 'Ten minutes, did you say?' she asked. He nodded. She hesitated a moment and then faced up to him.

'Very well,' she said. 'If you can make me climax within ten minutes, then we will all become your obedient servants. If I hold out, then you become ours. How about that?'

'What about rules?' he asked.

'Our house rules are pinned up behind the door,' she told him. 'Will they suffice?' He went over, read them through, and whistled.

'I'll say,' he told her. She went into the bathroom and came back with a kitchen timer, which she set to ten minutes. The timer began to tick the seconds away and she came up close, spread her legs, and waited.

'It says here you have to wear call-girl undies,' he pointed out.

'I changed just before you arrived,' she told him, and her voice dropped an octave and became a husky murmur. 'My bra is made of very sensual satin,' she whispered in his ear, 'really sexy to touch, and there is just a thin layer of net over my nipples – which, as you can see, are standing up and giving the game away.'

'So I see,' he said, and he put his hands out quite deliberately and pressed his fingertips on to the bumps. She breathed in, but continued without any pause.

'I'm wearing beige stockings and a white satin suspender belt,' she murmured, 'and white satin French panties with a very indecent lace panel that reveals the tip of my vagina. The panties are cleverly designed so that you can kiss or fondle my sex, or penetrate me, without taking them off.'

'Sounds great,' he replied, and lifted her skirt to her waist. She opened her eyes wider but offered no resistance. 'What do your rules say about lifting your skirt?' he asked, ogling her thighs and the very erotic panties she had just described.

'Nothing,' she said, 'but I just love having my skirt pulled up: so much more humiliating than just taking it off.'

'So you like being humiliated?' he asked, and kissed her on the lips. She at once opened her mouth and thrust her tongue into his, holding on to the kiss as long as possible when he drew back and let her skirt fall.

'Very much,' she said. 'Humiliation is my fast track to orgasm.'

'Is it possible to kiss your clitoris without taking your panties off?' he asked casually, looking her in the eyes.

She blushed for the first time, and hesitated, her blush deepening. 'Of course,' she said at last.

'Access, please,' he said. She blushed more deeply, then reached down and raised her hem, quite slowly, then eased her panties to one side. She swallowed hard, looking into his eyes, and opened her vagina with her fingers, hesitated, and at last eased away the hood that covered her clit.

'My clitoris is at your disposal,' she told him, her face scarlet with embarrassment.

He knelt down, then leant forward and pressed the tip of his tongue against her hard little horn, then deliberately penetrated her vagina with his second finger. He felt her body tense as she fought down the desire to close her legs. The rules stated that she had to stand perfectly still until she climaxed or was let off the hook, and Igor had no intention of letting her off the hook. The clock ticked away and she stood rock steady, but quivering with suppressed energy, holding her skirt high, her panties pulled aside to reveal her sex, and her fingers sliding on the lubrication as she opened her labia to welcome his assault. Two minutes to go.

'Oh no,' she moaned suddenly.

'What's the matter?'

'I'm starting an orgasm,' she said. He bit and nibbled her labia and clitoris, and thrust two fingers deep into her sex. 'You devil,' she said, but remained quite still and let him take her.

'I'm going to make you come and come,' he told her triumphantly, 'until you beg for mercy, on your knees,' and he ravished her sex again with his mouth.

She bit her lip. 'I'm going now,' she cried out, and her body trembled very slightly and gave a series of kicks. She cried out again, a high-pitched, bird-like cry that ended in a sob, then again, and again. He stimulated her until the climax passed, then she breathed out slowly, and began to recover her composure. He scrambled to his feet.

'If it is any satisfaction,' she told him, 'no man ever made me climax that fast before.' He smiled with satisfaction, bowed, refreshed her wine and handed her the glass.

'So,' she murmured, coming close, 'you are going to make me beg for mercy, on my knees, are you?'

'That is my intention,' he told her.

'We'll see about that,' she said, seized a handful of very erotic lingerie, and headed for the bathroom.

* * *

Giorgio had just left Gabrielle's bedroom when the telephone rang. It was Christian, bringing good news. 'About that problem, Gabrielle,' he began. 'Everything is resolved very satisfactorily. *Press-Dimanche* will stop harassing your staff and I have recovered the negatives, so all you have to do is destroy those pictures that the reporter gave you and forget about the whole thing.'

'That's wonderful,' she told him. 'I don't know how I can ever thank you, Christian.'

'Don't mention it,' he replied. 'Shall I destroy the negatives or would you like them?'

'Aren't you going to make me buy them?' she asked, with a mischievous giggle to show it was all a joke.

'It had crossed my mind,' he admitted. 'You look very fetching in the pictures, Gabrielle my dear.'

'I look frightful,' she protested.

'On the contrary, you look ravishing,' he replied, and she detected a strangled note in his voice. She suddenly thought to herself that he had almost certainly made a private copy of the pictures, and that they genuinely turned him on.

'You don't really fancy me like that, do you?' she asked, half serious, half joking.

'I most certainly do,' he replied, and now she was sure of it: he was excited and aroused by the pictures.

'I'm dressed like that now,' she told him.

'How?' he asked, and his voice betrayed his excitement.

She took a deep breath and licked her lips. 'Believe it or not,' she told him, dropping her voice to a husky whisper, 'I'm wearing a see-through black organza blouse over a very provocative sling bra. The blouse crosses over and is very tight around my bust, so that you can see my breasts and nipples and everything through it. Then, stockings and black satin suspenders with a lace trim, and a G-string with a slit in it too. No skirt.' She hesitated. 'It's God's own truth, Christian,' she said, with a slightly hysterical laugh. 'I'm sitting here, in my bedroom, at this very moment, dressed like that.' She paused and went on, 'I'm a whore, Christian, a real whore. I can't help it.'

'What . . . what did you do with the clients?' he asked, and his voice was strained almost to breaking point.

'Whatever they wanted,' she told him. 'I charged three hundred francs, then I let them do whatever they wanted.' She paused. 'Most of them wanted to play with me: you know, fondle my breasts, feel my nipples, stroke my legs, take down my panties, finger my pussy. I loved it: I was always damp, Christian, every time – really damp.'

'Then what?' he asked.

'Mostly fellation. Some wanted to go down on me, but it was mostly fellation. They all liked that. It must be very erotic for a man to have his cock sucked.'

'It must be when you do it,' he murmured breathlessly.

'I loved it,' she said. 'The clothes, the degradation, selling myself, everything, even the semen on my hands and face. I . . . I don't want to stop, Christian. Isn't that awful?' There was a long pause and finally, when he spoke, he was obviously overcome with lust.

'I could protect you,' he whispered. 'We can't discuss it here. Leave it with me.'

In her bedroom, Janet very carefully replaced the extension telephone, then rushed down to Giorgio's room.

'You must be stark-staring mad,' she told him furiously. 'You have to give those pictures back to Gabrielle this instant.'

'What pictures?'

'Giorgio,' she said in exasperation, 'I saw you and Gabrielle just now, in her bedroom.'

'Why don't you mind your own business?' he snarled

'She's asked one of Jean-Luc's high-up friends for help,' she told him, and he turned pale.

'She likes it,' he protested, but he licked his lips anxiously.

'Maybe, but it is still blackmail,' she told him. He tugged at his collar.

'I've got five guys coming to Les Plaisirs this afternoon,' he explained, 'and three tomorrow, and two the day after.'

'That's your problem,' she told him.

'They're nice guys, Janet,' he told her persuasively.

'You'd like them. They're my old college pals. It's a bit of a game, that's all.'

'Not likely,' she said. 'I've had enough of your friends, with Massimo the other day. Talk about taking advantage!'

'He's one of them,' he told her eagerly. 'He'd much prefer you, Jan. So would the others. I mean, you're much younger and prettier and sexier than Gabrielle.' She sniffed.

'You would really be doing it for Gabrielle,' he pointed out. 'Go on, please, for me, Janet.'

Gabrielle hummed to herself as she applied the final touches to her make-up, and admired herself in the mirror. There was a knock on the door, and Giorgio sidled in.

'I'm almost ready,' she told him, and turned to face him. 'What do you think?' she asked.

'Very nice,' he said politely. 'I've, er, decided to let you off,' and he handed her the Manila envelope. She opened it and looked at the pictures disbelievingly.

'Let me off?' she asked. 'What are you talking about?'

'I can't go through with it,' he said, hanging his head. 'I'm sorry, madame. I should never have done such a thing. I feel so ashamed.'

'Why this sudden change of heart?' she asked.

'My conscience,' he explained. 'I could not do such a thing to a lady.'

'What about these men who are waiting at the Plaisirs d'Anaïs?'

He coughed. 'Janet has offered to take your place,' he told her.

'Janet?' He voice rose an octave or two. 'Take my place?' She breathed in deeply. 'That is ridiculous,' she said indignantly. 'Where is she?'

'I'm here, madame,' said Janet as she sidled in. She was wearing a pleated mini-kilt that stopped well short of her stocking tops, and a white silk blouse stretched over an uplift bra that was a masterpiece of civil engineering. 'I am determined to save you from a fate worse than death, madame,' she explained.

'So I see,' said Gabrielle sarcastically, and looked at Giorgio. 'Please leave us alone,' she said. He shot gratefully out of the room and Gabrielle turned to Janet. 'I'm sorry, Janet,' she said firmly. 'I appreciate your concern, but I am, as it were, in loco parentis as far as you are concerned, and furthermore you are responsible for my children. I cannot possibly permit you to lead a life of debauchery.'

'I am twenty-two,' said Janet stoutly. 'I am the master of my fate, and I am the captain of my soul. As for the children, I have successfully hidden from them what I get up to with their father after breakfast: why should they find out what I do in the afternoons?'

'I am beginning to think you are actually looking forward to taking my place,' said Gabrielle accusingly.

'They're only Giorgio's college pals,' Janet pointed out. 'It's just a game, really.'

'I know who they are, Janet,' Gabrielle replied, 'and I promised Giorgio to buy back those pictures, and when I give my word, I stick by it.'

'Maybe we could compromise?' suggested Janet.

Five minutes later, Giorgio crept up and put his ear to the door. Time was running on and he wanted to get away.

'Oh, that's much better than that blouse, Janet,' Gabrielle was saying. 'It really does something for you, but you could do with a new bra. A sling: we simply must go shopping tomorrow.'

'You look really gorgeous, madame,' Janet replied. 'I'm sorry about spoiling things with Giorgio and the pictures.

'You must call me Gaby when we're at the club,' Gabrielle told her, 'and don't worry. I have a feeling that I shall have to pay much, much more for the negatives.' She paused. 'Now, about the men. You take Massimo, and I'll look after Filippo, and then –'

Giorgio tapped on the door. 'We're just coming,' Gabrielle called happily.

Twenty-nine

Three days had gone by, and Candie was chatting to Sapphi as they waited for the Colonel.

'How are you feeling now?' Sapphi asked.

'Fine,' said Candie rather dozily. 'Those three doctors really looked after me superbly.' Sapphi frowned.

'Doctors?' she asked.

'The three nice young gynaecologists,' said Candie with a yawn. 'They were certainly dedicated to their work,' she added ruefully. 'My knees have been so far apart for so long, they don't recognise each other any more.' Sapphi opened her mouth to reply, but just then the Colonel entered.

He enquired politely after Candie's health, then broached the subject of the files. 'We discovered Lucien's copies of Pascale's videos,' he told her. 'Jenny tipped us off: they were hidden in the basement at La Chasse, and very interesting they are too. It is a great pity about his main files, though – but they've all been destroyed, of course.'

'Oh, I'm sorry. I forgot all about them,' said Candie apologetically. 'Actually, they aren't destroyed at all. I know where they are.' The Colonel's eyes almost popped out of his head, and he looked at her as if she had gone mad. 'Is your computer hooked into the Internet?' she asked, pointing to his machine.

'Of course,' he replied.

'May I?' Candie sat down, keyed in an address on the World Wide Web, and a moment later the screen showed a banal welcome message. The Colonel looked over her shoulder as she busied herself at the keyboard and a moment or two later the machine requested a password. She crossed her fingers, typed, 'SEX ORGY' and hit RETURN. A moment later, the screen cleared and the Colonel found himself facing a list of names that went on and on and on, including almost all the well-known public figures in Europe. Candie selected 'Lamartine' and at once there appeared on the screen a complete run-down of Jean-Luc's and Gabrielle's sexual adventures over the past five years.

The Colonel lost no time in setting Sapphi to work, copying the huge database, whilst Candie explained how she had found out the truth. 'Lucien had used the communications package on his machine for no apparent reason,' she told the Colonel, 'and I guessed he kept his real files on an Internet server, and just kept a local copy on CDs. After that, it was just a matter of finding the Internet address, and he kept that hidden on the machine.'

'What about the password?' he asked.

'I pretended to be him, and inserted an alternative,' she explained.

'What made you think of "Sex Orgy"?' he asked.

'She never thinks of anything else,' a new voice interjected dryly. Candie looked up to see a very beautiful, very elegant woman, standing just inside the door.

'Beatrice!' she cried out, leaping to her feet. She threw out her arms and ran across the room to embrace the newcomer, laughing and crying with happiness, and at last Beatrice pulled back, looked at Candie fondly, and then looked across at the Colonel.

'Well?' she asked. 'Was I right about her?'

He nodded. 'You were absolutely right,' he admitted.

'Did she cause much havoc?' Beatrice asked. 'She almost wrecked the Institute.'[1]

'I should say so,' the Colonel replied with a sigh. 'She had most of my young men in hospital within twenty-four hours of arriving.'

'That's not true,' Candie protested, blushing deeply. 'It was only three of them,' she told Beatrice.

[1]See 'Candida's Secret Mission'

'What about your three bodyguards?' he asked. 'They have all asked for a 'rest and recuperation' leave.'

'Bodyguards?' Candie asked, then saw that Sapphi was curled up with laughter. Her eyes opened wide and she breathed in deeply.

'They pretended to be gynaecologists,' she explained indignantly. 'I spent three whole days with my nightie around my neck.'

'Doing what, you poor darling?' asked Beatrice sarcastically. Candie looked down and shuffled her feet, and then peeped up at her from under her long lashes.

'Having a ball,' she confessed, and the Colonel laughed out loud.

'You are quite incorrigible, Candida,' he told her. 'We will all be very sorry to see you go.'

'Oh, do I have to leave?' Candie asked.

'Very shortly, I'm afraid,' said Beatrice, pointing to the front page of the recent newspaper. 'I think we can safely say that your cover has been blown,' she added with a wry smile, and Candie had to agree.

'Now, how is Igor, the young man who rescued you in the nick of time?' the Colonel asked briskly, and Candie felt her heart leap.

'He's fine, as far as I know,' she replied cautiously.

'Let's ask him,' suggested the Colonel, and looked towards the door. 'Come in, Igor,' he called, and Candie almost jumped out of her skin as the door opened and Igor came in.

'Hello,' she said, as if they were perfect strangers, but he came up to her and kissed her.

'How are you?' he asked. 'I've been so worried about you.'

'I'm fine,' she said. 'They hid me away in a nice quiet clinic and I've had a complete rest for three whole days.' Sapphi hiccoughed and Candie glared at her.

'What about you?' she asked Igor. 'You do look awfully pale, darling. Here, sit down.'

'They hid me away too, in a quiet little school out in the country,' he explained with a big yawn. 'Jenny's boss and this kind lady have been looking after me.' He yawned again, and blinked around the room like a punch-drunk boxer.

'What have you been doing to him, Beatrice?' Candie asked indignantly.

'Nothing,' protested Beatrice. 'Let me explain. Now, the powers that be were afraid he might be getting out of practice, so I came over to get him back to concert pitch.' Candie's mouth opened and closed several times as words failed her, then she exploded.

'Out of practice?' she squealed. 'He's been screwing around with Jenny, and Pascale, and Suzie, and Sandrine, and Gabrielle and –'

'Chantal and Melanie and Désirée and Loulou . . .' added Igor, shaking his head and almost falling off his chair.

'As I was saying,' said Beatrice, ignoring the interruption, 'I came over to check him out, but I discovered that my old college rival Chantal had him stashed away in that sex menagerie of hers she calls a training school. I had to smuggle him out when she wasn't looking.'

She looked at Igor. 'He'll be all right,' she assured Candie. 'A nice steak or two and he'll be fighting fit in no time. Oh, and this is for you,' she added, and she handed Candie a fax.

Candie unfolded it. It was from Melbourne, had the usual preamble, was addressed to her, and the plain language decrypt said:

'You are required until further notice to collaborate fully with the Centre. Instructions regarded day-to-day assignments will be given to you by the Colonel, and you will treat those instructions as if they came from this office.'

She looked up at Igor. 'The message is genuine,' he assured her, 'and I have similar instructions. I don't pretend to know what is going on.' He yawned drowsily and she looked at the Colonel.

'I presume that message is from your real boss?' he asked. Candie nodded.

'We all operate on a need-to-know basis,' he told them, 'and I do not need to know who your real boss is, nor does Beatrice, nor anyone else in the Centre, so you will disclose that information to no one. Is that clear?'

Candie nodded. 'I presume you have been instructed by your employer to take orders from me?' he went on. Candie nodded again.

'As far as the outside world is concerned,' he went on, 'from now on you work for the Centre and its associated organisations. From time to time you will be given a special secret assignment, as you were with Lucien, and you will be given a cover story for that assignment.'

Candie reread the fax and then turned to Igor. 'So we are really working together now?' she asked excitedly.

'Not quite,' he told her, and handed her another fax, addressed to him this time. His instructions were the same as hers, with one notable exception: he would receive his instructions from Beatrice!

Candie drew in her breath. 'You're working for Beatrice?' she asked unbelievingly, and reread the fax.

'That's right,' said Beatrice contentedly. 'That is why I came over, to make sure he was really on the ball.'

'He has to take his orders from you?' Candie squealed.

'I'm afraid so,' said Beatrice, 'and in fact I have his new orders right here.'

'What are they?' she asked.

'Igor has a suite reserved at the Hotel Georges Cinq for five days, from this evening,' Beatrice began. 'It is just off the Champs Elysées.'

'I know that,' said Candie testily. 'It is one of the best hotels in Paris.'

'Stop interrupting, Candida,' said the Colonel.

'He will be accompanied by a young woman; one of our best agents, in fact,' Beatrice continued, 'and they have to pretend to be very wealthy honeymooners, and very much in love with each other, so there has to be plenty of bedroom action; that is most important.' Candie breathed in, pink with rage, but the Colonel quelled her with an icy look.

'The girl will of course be provided with a basic trousseau, Beatrice continued. 'Nighties, undies, stockings, all very sexy, of course, but she will be required to do a lot of shopping, and will have accounts at all the best couturiers. Igor will of course escort her everywhere. Seats for them are booked at the opera, the Crazy Horse, the Lapin Agile and so on, and they have table reservations at the very best restaurants.'

'You mean that Igor has to pretend to be on his honeymoon, all expenses paid, for five days, with some woman?' Candie cried, her voice hitting the ceiling.

'It is a special assignment, Candida,' Beatrice told her loftily. 'I don't make the decisions: I just carry them out.'

Candie sniffed and gulped and turned to the Colonel.

'What do I have to do for the next five days?' she asked sulkily, with tears welling up in her eyes. He looked down at his papers and there was a long pause as he shuffled through them. In the meantime, Sapphi crept out and came in again with her arms full of very fascinating-looking bags from the very best Parisian lingerie shops, which she piled around Candie's feet. Candie looked at her in surprise, Sapphi winked broadly, and Candie suddenly felt the tears begin to flow in earnest.

'Now let me see,' the Colonel murmured, then he sighed, leant back, and took his glasses off. 'Candida,' he said regretfully, 'I am very sorry, but I am afraid that you have to play the bride.'

NEW BOOKS

Coming up from Nexus and Black Lace

Nexus

Journey from Innocence by Jean-Philippe Aubourg
November 1997 Price £4.99 ISBN: 0 352 33212 3
When shy young Philippa accepts a houseshare with a young couple, little does she realise the extent of the dark games of bondage and submission they like to play. Investigating their cries of pleasure one night, she begins her own initiation into new realms of perversion, being taken to the limits of her ability to submit – and to the heights of debauchery.

A Chamber of Delights by Katrina Young
November 1997 Price £4.99 ISBN: 0 352 33213 1
Banished from a life of luxury at the opulent Grymwell Hall, the young and beautiful Gael sets out to create a new and even more kinky life in the house of her lesbian lover. Recruiting the naughty housemaid and the raunchy gardener to assist her in acting out the wild sexual fantasies of her guests, Gael finds herself embroiled in increasingly bizarre relationships.

There are three Nexus titles published in December

The Schooling of Stella by Yolanda Celbridge
December 1997 Price £4.99 ISBN: 0 352 33219 0
When English rose Stella Shawn wins a coveted scholarship to Castle Kernece, Scotland's sternest training college, she plans to fulfil her ambition of becoming a schoolmistress. More than a college, Kernece is a way of life, a fierce arena of dominant and submissive females where punishments are frequent and taken 'on the bare'. Only by her own total submission to the rules can Stella learn to dominate.

The Reward of Faith by Elizabeth Bruce
December 1997 Price £4.99 ISBN: 0 352 33225 5
Faith returns from her training to be claimed by her Master and ready to be instructed in the arts of carnal pleasure. Yet her new-found discipline will be severely tested as she enters Alex's decadent world in which Masters and Mistresses have Pleasure Slaves to serve their every sexual need. Faith joins the select ranks of the Chosen, where she has her taste for bondage and submission fully explored as she enjoys bizarre new extremes of humiliation.

The Training of Fallen Angels by Kendal Grahame
December 1997 Price £4.99 ISBN: 0 352 33224 7
Lisa and Janet are two teenagers who are driven by their insatiable libidos to discover new ways to satisfy their depraved desires. They become servants of the enigmatic Mr Gee, who lures them to his rural manor. But there is something sinister happening there. Lisa and Janet are blind to the danger they are in, intent on exploring new realms of debauchery – will they realise the risks before it is too late?

BLACK
lace

The Stranger by Portia Da Costa
November 1997 Price £4.99 ISBN: 0 352 33211 5
When a mysterious young man stumbles into the life of the recently widowed Claudia, he reawakens her sleeping sexuality and introduces her to a new world of perverse pleasures. Claudia's friends become involved in trying to decide whether or not he is to be trusted. As an erotic obsession flowers between Paul and Claudia, and all taboos are obliterated, his true identity no longer seems to matter.

Elena's Destiny by Lisette Allen
November 1997 Price £4.99 ISBN: 0 352 33218 2
The year is 1073. The gentle, convent-bred Elena has been introduced to the joys of forbidden passion by the masterful knight, Aimery le Sabrenn. War breaks out, however, and they are separated. When a chance quirk of fate brings them together again, things have changed. Elena finds that she has to contend with two rivals: the wanton and lascivious Henrietta, and the cunning and sensual Isobel, who enjoys playing dark and dangerous games.

Lake of Lost Love by Mercedes Kelly
December 1997 Price £4.99 ISBN: 0 352 33220 4
Princess Angeline lives on a paradise island in the South Seas. Married to Prince Hari and accepted into the native culture and customs, she has a life of ease and debauched sensual delights. When Prince Hari's young manservant is kidnapped and used as a sex slave by the cruel and depraved female ruler of nearby Monkey island, Angeline sets about planning his rescue.

Contests of Wills by Louisa Francis
December 1997 Price £4.99 ISBN: 0 352 332 239
In Sydney, Australia, in the late 1870s, lascivious young Melanie has married a man old enough to be her grandfather. When their honeymoon is cut short by his sudden death, his will is contested by his grandson, the louche and hedonistic Ric Lidell, and his promiscuous half-sister. Ric's dark satanic looks draw Melanie to him like a magnet – but Melanie's kinky former lover is unwilling to let her walk out of his life.

Nexus

NEXUS BACKLIST

All books are priced £4.99 unless another price is given. If a date is supplied, the book in question will not be available until that month in 1997.

CONTEMPORARY EROTICA

THE ACADEMY	Arabella Knight	Oct
AGONY AUNT	G. C. Scott	Jul
ALLISON'S AWAKENING	John Angus	Jul
BOUND TO SERVE	Amanda Ware	
BOUND TO SUBMIT	Amanda Ware	Sep
CANDIDA'S SECRET MISSION	Virginia LaSalle	
CANDIDA'S IN PARIS	Virginia LaSalle	Oct
CANDY IN CAPTIVITY	Arabella Knight	
CHALICE OF DELIGHTS	Katrina Young	
A CHAMBER OF DELIGHTS	Katrina Young	Nov
THE CHASTE LEGACY	Susanna Hughes	
CHRISTINA WISHED	Gene Craven	
DARK DESIRES	Maria del Rey	
THE DOMINO TATTOO	Cyrian Amberlake	
THE DOMINO ENIGMA	Cyrian Amberlake	
THE DOMINO QUEEN	Cyrian Amberlake	
EDEN UNVEILED	Maria del Rey	
EDUCATING ELLA	Stephen Ferris	Aug
ELAINE	Stephen Ferris	
EMMA'S SECRET WORLD	Hilary James	
EMMA'S SECRET DIARIES	Hilary James	
EMMA'S SUBMISSION	Hilary James	
EMMA'S HUMILIATION	Hilary James	
FALLEN ANGELS	Kendal Grahame	
THE TRAINING OF FALLEN ANGELS	Kendal Grahame	Dec

THE FANTASIES OF JOSEPHINE SCOTT	Josephine Scott	
THE FINISHING SCHOOL	Stephen Ferris	
HEART OF DESIRE	Maria del Rey	
HIS MISTRESS'S VOICE	G. C. Scott	
HOUSE OF INTRIGUE	Yvonne Strickland	
HOUSE OF TEMPTATIONS	Yvonne Strickland	
THE HOUSE OF MALDONA	Yolanda Celbridge	
THE ISLAND OF MALDONA	Yolanda Celbridge	
THE CASTLE OF MALDONA	Yolanda Celbridge	
THE ICE QUEEN	Stephen Ferris	
THE IMAGE AND OTHER STORIES	Jean de Berg	
THE INSTITUTE	Maria del Rey	
SISTERHOOD OF THE INSTITUTE	Maria del Rey	
JENNIFER'S INSTRUCTION	Cyrian Amberlake	
JOURNEY FROM INNOCENCE	G. C. Scott	Nov
JULIE AT THE REFORMATORY	Angela Elgar	
A MATTER OF POSSESSION	G. C. Scott	
MELINDA AND THE MASTER	Susanna Hughes	
MELINDA AND THE COUNTESS	Susanna Hughes	
MELINDA AND SOPHIA	Susanna Hughes	
MELINDA AND ESMERELDA	Susanna Hughes	
THE NEW STORY OF O	Anonymous	
ONE WEEK IN THE PRIVATE HOUSE	Esme Ombreux	
AMANDA IN THE PRIVATE HOUSE	Esme Ombreux	Sep
PARADISE BAY	Maria del Rey	
THE PASSIVE VOICE	G. C. Scott	
RUE MARQUIS DE SADE	Morgana Baron	
THE SCHOOLING OF STELLA	Yolanda Celbridge	Dec
SECRETS OF THE WHIPCORD	Michaela Wallace	Aug
SERVING TIME	Sarah Veitch	
SHERRIE	Evelyn Culber	
SHERRIE AND THE INITIATION OF PENNY	Evelyn Culber	Oct
THE SPANISH SENSUALIST	Josephine Arno	
STEPHANIE'S CASTLE	Susanna Hughes	

STEPHANIE'S REVENGE	Susanna Hughes	
STEPHANIE'S DOMAIN	Susanna Hughes	
STEPHANIE'S TRIAL	Susanna Hughes	
STEPHANIE'S PLEASURE	Susanna Hughes	
SUSIE IN SERVITUDE	Arabella Knight	
THE TEACHING OF FAITH	Elizabeth Bruce	
FAITH IN THE STABLES	Elizabeth Bruce	
THE REWARD OF FAITH	Elizabeth Bruce	Dec
THE TRAINING GROUNDS	Sarah Veitch	
VIRGINIA'S QUEST	Katrina Young	Jun
WEB OF DOMINATION	Yvonne Strickland	

EROTIC SCIENCE FICTION

RETURN TO THE PLEASUREZONE	Delaney Silver	

ANCIENT & FANTASY SETTINGS

CAPTIVES OF ARGAN	Stephen Ferris	
CITADEL OF SERVITUDE	Aran Ashe	Jun
THE CLOAK OF APHRODITE	Kendal Grahame	
DEMONIA	Kendal Grahame	
NYMPHS OF DIONYSUS	Susan Tinoff	
PLEASURE ISLAND	Aran Ashe	
PYRAMID OF DELIGHTS	Kendal Grahame	
THE SLAVE OF LIDIR	Aran Ashe	
THE DUNGEONS OF LIDIR	Aran Ashe	
THE FOREST OF BONDAGE	Aran Ashe	
WARRIOR WOMEN	Stephen Ferris	
WITCH QUEEN OF VIXANIA	Morgana Baron	
SLAVE-MISTRESS OF VIXANIA	Morgana Baron	

EDWARDIAN, VICTORIAN & OLDER EROTICA

ANNIE	Evelyn Culber	
ANNIE AND THE SOCIETY	Evelyn Culber	
ANNIE'S FURTHER EDUCATION	Evelyn Culber	

BEATRICE	Anonymous	
CHOOSING LOVERS FOR JUSTINE	Aran Ashe	
DEAR FANNY	Aran Ashe	
LYDIA IN THE BORDELLO	Philippa Masters	
MADAM LYDIA	Philippa Masters	
LURE OF THE MANOR	Barbra Baron	
MAN WITH A MAID 3	Anonymous	
MEMOIRS OF A CORNISH GOVERNESS	Yolanda Celbridge	
THE GOVERNESS AT ST AGATHA'S	Yolanda Celbridge	
THE GOVERNESS ABROAD	Yolanda Celbridge	
PLEASING THEM	William Doughty	

SAMPLERS & COLLECTIONS

EROTICON 1		
EROTICON 2		Jun
EROTICON 3		Sep
THE FIESTA LETTERS	ed. Chris Lloyd	
MOLTEN SILVER	Delaney Silver	
NEW EROTICA 2	ed. Esme Ombreaux	

NON-FICTION

HOW TO DRIVE YOUR WOMAN WILD IN BED	Graham Masterton	
HOW TO DRIVE YOUR MAN WILD IN BED	Graham Masterton	Jul
LETTERS TO LINZI	Linzi Drew	